THE AMISH QUILTER

MINDY STARNS CLARK
LESLIE GOULD

HARVEST HOUSE PUBLISHERS
EUGENE, OREGON

Cover by Garborg Design Works

Cover photos © LEE SNIDER PHOTO IMAGES, philipimage / Bigstock

The authors are represented by MacGregor Literary, Inc.

THE AMISH QUILTER
Copyright © 2018 Mindy Starns Clark and Leslie Gould
Published by Harvest House Publishers
Eugene, Oregon 97408
www.harvesthousepublishers.com

ISBN 978-0-7369-6294-0 (pbk.)
ISBN 978-0-7369-6295-7 (eBook)

Library of Congress Cataloging-in-Publication Data

Names: Clark, Mindy Starns, author. | Gould, Leslie, author.
Title: The Amish quilter / Mindy Starns Clark and Leslie Gould.
Description: Eugene, Oregon : Harvest House Publishers, [2018] | Series: The
  women of Lancaster County ; 5
Identifiers: LCCN 2017047331 (print) | LCCN 2017052452 (ebook) | ISBN
  9780736962957 (ebook) | ISBN 9780736962940 (paperback)
Subjects: LCSH: Amish--Fiction. | Quilting--Fiction. | Lancaster County
  (Pa.)--Fiction. | BISAC: FICTION / Christian / Romance. | GSAFD: Christian
  fiction. | Love stories.
Classification: LCC PS3603.L366 (ebook) | LCC PS3603.L366 A86 2018 (print) |
  DDC 813/.6--dc23
LC record available at https://lccn.loc.gov/2017047331

Printed in the United States of America

18 19 20 21 22 23 24 25 26 / BP-SK / 10 9 8 7 6 5 4 3 2 1

"The heavens declare the glory of God;
and the firmament sheweth his handywork."
PSALM 19:1

Acknowledgments

Mindy thanks

My husband, John, who is my helpmate, my love, and my best friend. As always, I could not have done this without him.

My daughters Emily and Lauren, who are such an integral part of my writing—and who bring joy to every element of my life.

My wonderful assistant, Tara Kenny, who always goes above and beyond.

My nephew, Andrew Starns, for providing information about painting, design, and the world of art.

The wonderful folks at Country Lane Farm Amish Quilt Shop in Leola, Pennsylvania, for their expertise in quilts and their friendly hospitality.

Leslie, for being the kind of coauthor every writer dreams of having. Working with you has been one of the biggest blessings not just of my career but of my life. I will always be grateful for the artistry you taught me and the grace you showed me, time and time again. Thank you!

Leslie thanks

My husband, Peter, for his ongoing love and support in writing and in life. I'm also grateful for his practical help, including being my driver and sounding board on research trips, and sharing all of the history and beauty along the way! And our children, Kaleb, Taylor, Hana, and Lily Thao, for their encouragement and understanding when another deadline looms.

Marietta Couch, for answering questions about the Amish, sharing her family with me, and reading through the manuscript with an eye toward both Plain living and quilting. (Any mistakes are ours.) Your friendship and sweet spirit are a balm to my soul.

Randolph Harris, consulting historian for Lancaster, Pennsylvania, for his tour of the downtown area and St. James Episcopal Church in particular.

Mindy, for a wonderful run of coauthoring! Writing eight books together has taught me so much about collaborating and storytelling, and also about myself. I'm thankful for each of the novels we've completed, but even more so for your friendship and influence on my life. Thank you!

Mindy and Leslie thank

Chip MacGregor, our agent; Kim Moore, our editor; and the wonderful folks at Harvest House Publishers who have guided us along this writing journey. Thank you for believing in us and our stories and for getting our books into the hands of readers around the world.

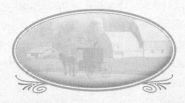

ONE

Driving home from work, I had to pull the buggy onto the shoulder of the road just so I could marvel at the beauty all around me. To my right was an old stone wall lined with purple crocus blossoms. Off to the left, white dots of sheep grazed in a field bordered by clusters of vivid yellow forsythia. Ahead, the afternoon sun streamed through the clouds, illuminating the knoll where my parents' century-old house nestled amid our family farm. Even in mid-April, when some of the trees were still bare, Lancaster County had to be one of the most beautiful places in the world. I'd heard other people, mostly visitors who came into the shop where I worked, say the same thing. I'd never been anywhere else, but I believed them, especially on days like this when the sun had chased away the rain and the long-dormant earth showed so many promises of new life.

I inhaled deeply, wishing I could turn the scene in front of me into a quilt, wondering how I would recreate the light, patterns, and textures with fabric. Because I worked at an *Englisch*-owned fabric and art store, I made fancy quilts to sell to *Englisch* customers, creations that were much more artistic than the ones I made for myself or for my Amish family.

As I urged my gelding, Blue, forward, I thought about the impact *setting* had always had on me—and on my quilting. I'd grown up here and lived in the same house my entire life, the one where my father, grandfather, and great-grandfather had all grown up as well. In fact, our ancestors had worked this land since arriving here from Europe in the early 1700s.

Maybe that's why I felt such a sense of place and why I often wanted to evoke settings in fabric. When I was done, even though it wasn't an exact representation, gazing at that finished quilt always gave me the same feeling of harmony I'd had when I looked at the original scene it was designed to represent.

Ya, that was how I felt, though I'd never try to explain as much to my *mamm* or my sisters. Not being particularly creative themselves, none of them would understand—well, except maybe Izzy, my second-oldest sister, who was an accomplished seamstress and the only other family member with artistic tendencies. But she lived in Indiana now.

There were ten children in our family, five boys and five girls. But it was my sisters who influenced me the most: Sadie, Becky, Izzy, and Tabitha. It wasn't that they didn't have talents of their own. They were strong, gifted women. All of them were smart, witty, and outgoing. Sadie was a great cook and a wonderful mother. Becky was a no-nonsense, take-charge kind of person. Besides being an accomplished seamstress, Izzy was perceptive and wise. Tabitha was socially gifted and the life of every event she attended. *Ya*, I was the youngest girl and felt practically invisible compared to them. They'd dubbed me "Little Sister," and though I knew the term started as an endearment, over time it just became a reminder that I was slight and limited. Diminutive and negligible. Invisible. Other than my quilting, there was nothing special about me at all. I grew to hate the nickname, which always reminded me of the fact that I didn't measure up to Sadie, Becky, Izzy, or Tabitha—and I never would.

I started quilting with my *mamm* when I was eight. I'd learned to do other handiwork too—sewing, knitting, and crocheting—but I was the most interested in making quilts and took to it immediately. From the beginning, I enjoyed working with other women in our district when we'd gather for quilting bees, a long tradition in the Amish community. We would pin the top, the batting, and the back to a frame and then stitch it all into a single piece. The saying "many hands make light work" was especially true when it came to quilting, which we literally did by hand. Now, though, *Mamm* and I often worked together in the evenings at home instead of waiting until we could gather a group of women. And because I produced so many, I did most of the piecing on my own.

I continued on, planning my evening at home as I drove. After helping *Mamm* get supper on the table and then cleaning up, I decided I would spend the rest of my time cutting out squares for a new quilt. A Plain one. I was making it for my sister Tabitha, who had recently been dumped by her childhood sweetheart and needed some tangible form of comfort. She liked yellows, greens, and browns, so those were the colors I was going to use.

I hoped my youngest brother, Thomas, wouldn't have homework tonight, because if he did I would end up being the one to help him. Tabitha, his teacher, refused to do so, and our *mamm* let us both know she'd been assisting with homework for nearly thirty years, ever since our oldest sister, Sadie, started school, and she was tired of the chore. Besides, *Mamm* said it was good practice for when I had children of my own.

The truth was, I doubted I'd ever marry. My parents felt that I was still young and simply hadn't met the right person yet, but my sisters disagreed. They said there were plenty of guys to choose from around here, and the problem was that I was too picky. They said I'd never find anyone good enough.

I understood why it might seem that way. I could be a perfectionist, *ya*, especially when it came to my quilting, but I didn't think my perfectionism extended to choosing a suitor. I had a feeling that sometimes what others took for pickiness was actually a sort of obliviousness on my part. When a young man was interested in me, I usually didn't even notice. And in those rare times when I was interested in a young man, I had no idea how to communicate that to him, especially in the nonverbal ways my sisters had. I'd get stiff and quiet and self-conscious, all of which probably made me come across as disinterested. Hence my sisters' conclusion. Maybe I should ignore their opinions on the matter and stick with what my parents said.

I reminded myself that Tabitha wasn't married yet either, and she was a year and half older than I was. When she was younger, she'd hoped to wed her childhood sweetheart, Mark Wittmer. Then she'd hoped to wed a man who worked construction with *Daed*. Then a farmer who lived in the next county over. Then Mark again, who broke up with her last week and left for Maryland to work with a relative all in the same day.

Tabitha wanted to be married more than anything.

She was the most gregarious of all of us Mueller sisters. She was playful and fun and could tell a good story. She now taught at the one-room school we'd once attended as kids, and all of those traits made her an amazing teacher. She was a little on the wild side but had ended her *rumspringa* the year before and joined the church.

I was the exact opposite of Tabitha, and we'd pretty much had a love-hate relationship our entire lives because of how different we were. I was quiet and shy and couldn't tell a story to save my life. For the most part I'd skipped my *rumspringa* and joined the church when I was eighteen. I also lacked the talents my sister had—my only gift, other than quilting, was my way with a lemon sponge pudding.

As I turned down the lane, I scanned our property. We only had forty acres, and although *Daed*'s parents had been able to survive on such a small farm with only one child, my large family couldn't. *Daed* worked construction to make a living and then farmed on Saturdays and sometimes in the evenings, fitting in his woodworking when he could, while my two younger brothers did the majority of the chores. At the moment my fifteen-year-old brother, Stephen, who was next in line after me, should have been out in the field, but there was no sight of him.

Mamm wasn't in the garden either, even though she was almost guaranteed to be there on sunny spring days like this one. I pulled around to the side of the barn and saw that her buggy was gone. How odd.

I parked mine, unhitched Blue, and led him into the barn. After I brushed, watered, and fed him, I retrieved my bag of fabric—*ya*, even with a good employee discount, too much of my earnings from working at the store went back into the cash register—and hurried into the house. Tabitha would be home from school soon with Thomas, who, at ten, was the youngest in our family. Perhaps I would have a moment of silence to put away my fabric before they arrived.

I'd inherited Izzy's sewing room when she got married four years ago. It was just an old enclosed sunporch in back, but I loved the space as much as she had and always kept it perfectly neat and organized. My quilting supplies were shelved according to color, so I knew exactly where this new fabric would go. Except I didn't make it that far.

I opened the back door to the scent of cinnamon and saw a rack of cookies cooling in the middle of the kitchen table. At the end, by *Mamm*'s place, was a note. I grabbed one of the freshly baked snickerdoodles and began to read.

> *Linda,*
> *I'm at Sadie's. Stephen is with me. Robert took a turn for the worse. Come as soon as you can to get the children. All three have bad colds.*
>
> *Mamm*

Sadie's twin girls were seven, and the baby boy was thirteen months. Sadie's husband, Robert, had been diagnosed with colon cancer the year before, went through treatments, and had beaten it—until last month, when tests showed the cancer had returned, this time in his liver. He'd started treatments again last week.

My stomach lurched at the thought of him taking a "turn for the worse." I hoped it wasn't as bad as it sounded. He'd seemed optimistic about the chemotherapy working again, though Sadie had been awfully quiet when they came to tell *Mamm* and *Daed* three weeks ago.

I left the bag of fabric on the table and went back outside. I was just about to re-harness Blue when Tabitha turned up the highway. I waved, and as the buggy approached, I hurried over to her and told her what was going on and that we needed to head to Sadie's right away. Thomas was slumped on the passenger side, looking exhausted after a long day at school.

"Do we have to?" he asked wearily.

"Yes, we have to. Get in the back!" Tabitha barked and then blew from her face a strand of light hair that had escaped from her bun. It fell across her cheek, and she poked it under her *kapp*. Clearly Thomas was getting on her nerves again.

As I stepped over to the buggy's passenger side, he climbed into the backseat, covered himself with a blanket from the pile on the floor, and closed his eyes. By the time we reached Sadie's house, just a mile away, he was fast asleep.

"It's warm enough for now that he'll be all right in the buggy." Tabitha jumped down and tied the lead rope to the hitching post near the barn.

Leaning into the back, I quickly tucked the blanket more tightly around our little brother. Then I followed my sister, just as I had my entire life. She was nearly a head taller than me and quite slender, and she walked with an air of authority I'd never had—and never would. Her hair was a lighter brown than mine, and in the summer it turned nearly blond. I'd always believed she was the most beautiful of all of us girls, not that such a thought was encouraged in our family. Character was what mattered. The thing was, Tabitha was strong in that regard too. Sure, she could be a little flirty, but she was also kind and compassionate. Except when it came to Thomas, who tried her patience daily.

As we neared the house, a man emerged from the barn, shaded his eyes, and looked toward us. For a moment I thought it was Robert, which was silly considering how ill he was. But this man was so similar in height and build that I had a feeling he must be a relative. Some of Robert's family lived near Pittsburgh, several hours away by car, and even though he and my oldest sister had been married for nine years, I hadn't met all of them—and definitely not this man. As we drew closer, I noticed that he was clean shaven, which meant he wasn't married, despite being in his mid or even late twenties.

Tabitha didn't seem to notice him, which wasn't like her at all. Instead, she charged toward the house, reached the front door, and stepped inside, calling out for Sadie in a loud voice.

I gave the guy an apologetic glance as I hurried after my sister. "*Shh!* Not so loud! Robert might be sleeping."

Tabitha shot me an annoyed look, one I was certainly used to. I doubted anyone in the world loved me as much as Tabitha or could be as irritated with me either.

We traipsed through the house Robert had built before he and Sadie married. It was really nice, not to mention roomy, with a big hutch, bookcases, closets, large cupboards, and a pantry. The floors were an easy-to-clean parquet, and all of the doors and windows were top quality. The place was simple and Plain, like any Amish home, but well made and easy to maintain. Somehow, it was hard to reconcile the strong and capable fellow who had constructed it with the gaunt and sickly person the cancer had turned him into.

When we reached the hallway, *Mamm* appeared holding the baby on her hip. At the sight of us, Bobby began to wail.

"There, there." *Mamm* patted his back and spoke above the roar. "The girls are all packed. I'll spend the night here and help Sadie with Robert."

"What about the morning?" I felt bad for asking, but I didn't want to miss work if I didn't have to. "I'm supposed to be at the shop by ten."

Mamm sighed. "I can't think that far ahead. We'll figure it out later."

Tabitha took Bobby, which seemed to calm him somewhat, turning his wails to sniffles as he settled onto her hip.

"Where's Stephen?" I asked.

"Helping Isaac with the milking."

Tabitha looked up. "Isaac?"

"Robert's nephew. Ruth Mast's grandson. He's living with her."

"Since when?"

Mamm dangled her arms and shook them out, clearly relieved to have a break from the baby. "I'm not sure, Tabitha. A few weeks, maybe?"

"A few weeks? There hasn't been anyone new at church."

"I imagine he's probably spent his past few church Sundays back at home. He's been making the move gradually. Sadie said he came to Lancaster County to open up a house painting business—mostly interior work, I think."

So the man in the driveway was my brother-in-law's nephew, which meant he'd probably been at Robert and Sadie's wedding. I didn't remember him, but I'd only been ten years old at the time. And that had been a very busy day. As the "artistic ones," Izzy and I had been charged with arranging the sweet plates for Izzy's reception, and when we weren't tied up with that and our other chores, I was mostly focusing on my friends.

True to form, Tabitha started asking *Mamm* all sorts of questions about Isaac—was he handsome and how old was he and was he courting anyone? So much for being heartbroken over Mark Wittmer. Straining hard not to roll my eyes, I continued down the hall to the bedroom of my two nieces. Knocking lightly, I opened the door to find Hattie and Hazel sitting on the floor between their beds, playing with paper dolls. They wore matching green dresses, black aprons, and white *kappa*, and as I stepped into the room, the two girls looked up at me with big brown eyes, their lips unsmiling, their noses red from their colds. Identical twins, they would've been nearly impossible to tell apart if not for a small scar on Hattie's face from when she was younger and had tripped on the hose and smacked her chin against the pavement.

"Hi, girls!" I spoke in my cheeriest voice.

"Hi, *Aenti* Linda," they replied softly in unison, without meeting my eyes.

"Time to go over to *Mammi* and *Daadi's* house. We'll have cookies and milk as soon as we get there, and then you can play with your dolls some more."

They shared a glance, looking as if they wanted to protest, but then held their tongues.

At seven, they were the oldest of the grandchildren, so I hadn't realized until the others came along just how odd these two were. They'd play quietly for hours. They seldom spoke. They really didn't interact much with anyone except each other. My twelve other nieces and nephews—even Bobby—adored me and loved coming to the farmhouse. Hattie and Hazel couldn't care less.

When the girls were four, Sadie and Robert had asked the doctor about their behavior. He looked into it and ultimately diagnosed them with ASD or autism spectrum disorder. Apparently they were on the higher-functioning end of that spectrum, with their primary issues being impaired social skills, the need for repetitive patterns, and limited interests and activities.

That diagnosis helped us understand why they seldom made eye contact, only played with each other, and could sit and concentrate on the same thing for days at a time. Thankfully, the doctor said, the Amish lifestyle provided lots of structure, which was helpful with ASD. Otherwise, there was no medication or cure for the condition.

Sadie and Robert both knew God had created Hattie and Hazel to be exactly the way they were, so after the diagnosis they accepted the girls' behavior and didn't let themselves despair about it. The twins were God's gift, and that was that. We all simply loved them for who they were, as did the community. I don't think any of us saw them as disabled so much as just having some obvious differences in the way they socialized and interacted with others.

The truth was, their quiet, self-contained demeanors actually made watching them easy. It was getting to know them that had proven difficult. Now that they were in school, Tabitha was their teacher, and she said they did well as long as they could sit together and weren't forced to endure any extreme changes in routine. For several years I'd been contemplating a quilt of mirror images inspired by the girls. The colors would be cool—all blues and greens and grays—but I couldn't settle on a design. It was as if I was waiting for them to show me some new element of themselves first, something I could use as a focal point.

I stepped to the bedside table, picked up the manila envelope that was sitting there, and handed it to Hattie. With a sigh, she methodically put her paper dolls into it and then gave the envelope to Hazel.

As they did that, I found the bag *Mamm* had packed for them and double-checked it. Hairbrush. Toothbrushes. Nightgowns. A change of clothes. "Okay." I stood up straight. "Let's go get your shoes on." They obeyed, almost mechanically so.

Tabitha stood at the end of the hall, swaying back and forth with the baby.

"Where's *Mamm*?" I asked.

Tabitha nodded toward Sadie and Robert's room.

The girls continued on to the shoe rack by the front door, but I paused at Tabitha's side. "How bad is he?" I whispered.

Her eyes filled with tears. "*Mamm* said it doesn't look good, not at all."

My heart sank. "Should he be in the hospital?"

She shook her head. "The doctor saw him earlier, and he said it wouldn't make any difference at this point."

The bedroom door opened slowly. Our mother stepped out and pulled it shut behind her. As she turned toward us, I saw that her eyes were filled with tears.

My heart lurched. "*Mamm?*"

Her voice shook as she spoke. "He's gone."

I gasped. "Gone?"

She nodded.

"No." How could it be? I glanced over at the twins, who were just out of earshot, now sitting on the floor by the rack and putting on their shoes. "What should we do?"

"Don't say anything yet. The girls should return to their room and play for now. Linda, you tell Isaac the news and ask him to fetch Robert's mother. Also, have him call the undertaker." *Mamm* looked to Tabitha. "You stay with the children. I'll go back in with Sadie."

I stammered, "H-How is she?"

"In shock, I think."

As *Mamm* returned to the bedroom and softly closed the door, I set the girls' suitcase on the floor against the wall. Squaring her shoulders, Tabitha turned toward the twins and called out, "Change of plans, ladies. Back to your room for now. It's not time to go yet."

They barely reacted. They just nodded solemnly, removed their shoes, and did as they were told. Once they'd passed us, Tabitha reached for my hand and squeezed it. Robert had been like a brother to us—not that we needed another one, but we did need Robert. He was good and kind and compassionate. He'd been perfect for Sadie. I fought my tears, squeezed Tabitha's hand in return, and then walked out the front door.

As I moved toward the barn, the world stopped for just a moment. Everything seemed so still yet so vibrant. A robin hopped over the grass, a worm in its mouth. Daffodils bloomed along the fence. A young cat, a black one I'd seen around here a few times before, slinked into the barn.

I swallowed my tears. Just like that, Robert was gone from this world. Thirty-two years old, and his life was over.

We were taught not to make assumptions about a person's salvation. That was between our loved one and God. But I had no doubt where Robert was, and at that thought a feeling of joy surged through me despite the loss. He wasn't suffering. He would never be in pain again. I was certain heaven held him. It was Sadie and the children I mourned for now.

I hurried on to the barn, stepped through the open door, and then paused for a moment as I looked up to the rafters, where the sunbeams filtered through the high window and across the open ceiling. The house may have been relatively new, but the barn was nearly two hundred years old, and it was one of my favorite places in all of Lancaster County. Again, I found myself cherishing that sense of setting. Someday I hoped to design a quilt inspired by this old barn.

It wasn't quite time for milking, but Stephen and Isaac had started anyway, probably so Stephen could get on home to his own chores.

I squinted in the dim light, relieved to see my brother leading a cow out to the pasture. I would tell Isaac first and then share the sad news with Stephen. I began walking down the row of cows and located Robert's nephew near the middle, beside a heifer, adjusting the hydraulic pump that worked to extract the milk with a rhythmic *whoosh*ing sound.

I stepped closer. "*Hallo.*"

He looked up at me. In the dim light I could make out brown eyes and dark hair under the brim of his straw hat.

"I'm Linda," I added. "Sadie's sister."

He stood, towering over me. "Oh, *ya*, sure. *Hallo* to you too."

I nodded. "I have a message from my *mamm*." My voice cracked as I spoke. "It's Robert..."

By the alarmed expression on his face, I could tell he guessed what that message was.

I managed to sputter. "He passed."

"*Nay*," he whispered, reaching for a beam to steady himself.

"*Mamm* wants you to please go get your grandmother. And call the undertaker."

"Of course."

"Stephen and I will finish up with the milking."

"*Danke.*" He took a step toward the door. "I won't be long."

"Take our buggy," I told him, knowing that would be faster. Then I remembered Thomas was asleep in the back. "After I get my little brother out."

Isaac walked beside me, neither of us speaking. When we reached the buggy, I woke Thomas, who was cranky and out of sorts. "Listen." I spoke in my most serious voice. "I need you to cooperate. We have to help with the milking."

"I don't want to," he whined.

Isaac stepped to my side. "It will only be for a short time. Sadie needs your help."

At the mention of Sadie, Thomas squared his shoulders. She was the sort who brought out the best in people, even Thomas, who'd been going through a "difficult" phase for a while now.

"*Danke*," I whispered to Isaac. Why hadn't I thought to appeal to my brother's goodness instead of trying to bully him into obeying?

Isaac nodded, untied the horse, and stepped up into the buggy. I watched as he turned on the highway, and then I took Thomas's hand.

"We need to find Stephen," I said. "I have something to tell both of you. Then we'll get to work."

He gave me a questioning look but didn't say any more. Perhaps he was finally sensing the gravity of the situation.

Stephen had just entered the barn with a cow. We met him inside. I looked at each of my little brothers, inhaled deeply, and spoke. "I have some bad news. It's Robert. He's passed."

"What do you mean?" Thomas scratched the side of his head, tipping his hat forward.

"She means he died." Stephen took a step back and bumped into the cow. He looked up at me. "What will Sadie do?"

"She'll manage. We'll all help. But right now we need to get the milking done. Do you understand?"

Stephen nodded solemnly, but Thomas shook his head, and his big, sad eyes filled with tears. My heart broke anew.

"I don't." He took in a raggedy breath. "Why did Robert die?"

I hesitated, blinking away tears of my own. That was a question best answered by someone older and wiser, so I told him he'd have to ask our parents about it later.

He seemed to accept that, and once he'd gotten control of his crying, I gave him the job of shoveling the grain into the trough for the cows. As he went for the shovel, the black barn cat stopped and stared at him before darting off toward a stack of hay bales.

With a sigh, I took a vinyl apron off the peg by the office door and put it on over my good dress, hoping for the best. I didn't particularly like milking, but I'd helped now and then since the first time Robert fell ill. I'd do whatever I could for Sadie.

She and Robert had been in the process of transitioning their property from a dairy farm to an apple orchard when his cancer returned in February. Once that happened, they put their plans on hold, but by then they'd already whittled down their sixty-head herd by more than half. Certainly that had made things easier during the past two months, but now that Robert was gone, Sadie was left in a strange limbo between not enough cows to justify a dairy and not enough apple trees to produce sufficient fruit. At least Robert's family was in a position to help if need be. I felt sure they would do whatever it would take to tide Sadie over until she could make some decisions about how to proceed from here.

In the meantime, I would be grateful that we had only twenty-five cows to milk rather than sixty.

The boys and I were still at it when Isaac returned. He told me I should go back in the house, but I assured him I could keep working.

He shook his head. "The boys and I can do it, plus neighbors will be arriving soon to help. Your *mamm* will need you in the kitchen."

He was right. As word spread, community members would show up and take over the chores. But in the meantime, there was a meal to prepare and people to soon feed—although Sadie, who was quite efficient, had probably planned out and partially prepared something already, with vegetables cut and meat waiting in the fridge.

Isaac's grandmother, Ruth, was a member of our district and a good friend of the family. I asked him how she was doing.

He shrugged. "She's as stoic as ever. Her first concern was Sadie, of course."

I knew Robert had been one of the youngest children in his large family of fifteen siblings. His mother was nearly eighty, and his father had died the year before. Ruth had to be heartbroken. I'd known her my entire life and had always been drawn to her, perhaps because I had no living grandparents of my own.

When I entered the house, Ruth was helping *Mamm* in the kitchen. I gave the older woman a hug and told her how sorry I was for the loss of her son.

Her eyes filled with tears. "The Lord's will be done."

I nodded. God had allowed this to happen. We all knew, without a doubt, that He would provide for Sadie and the children. Still, it was a trying time.

I worked in the kitchen until the undertaker came, and then I stayed with the twins in their bedroom. Children in our community weren't usually shielded from death, but it seemed telling her girls was more than Sadie could deal with at the moment. The undertaker would be returning the embalmed body the next day, however, so Sadie would have to break the news to them by then.

After he left, I shifted the girls into the living room and returned to my duties in the kitchen, absently gazing out the window at various friends and neighbors who were bustling around outside, handling the chores.

As the afternoon wore on, they relieved Isaac of any further barn duties, but rather than leaving, he joined us inside. He was the one who checked in with *Mamm*, asking about Sadie. He was the one who started the fire in the woodstove as the sun began to lower and the house grew chilly. He was the one who, at the supper table, cut a pork chop—*ya*, as I'd expected, Sadie had them ready to cook—into bites to split between Hattie and Hazel.

He was the one who rumpled Thomas's hair and told him it was good to mourn, especially when we could not comprehend why someone as young as Robert had left us. Isaac was the one who, when all the helpers were gone and supper was done and Sadie came out of her room, stood close by as if protecting her.

She appeared frail. She and I were the smallest of the girls in our family, but she'd always had a fragility to her that I didn't, as if her tiny bones could break like a bird's.

As Hattie and Hazel lingered over their desserts of apple crisp with vanilla ice cream, and Isaac helped himself to seconds of the same, *Mamm* sent Stephen and Thomas home to do our chores and then directed Sadie, Tabitha, and me to the living room. Since Becky and Izzy had moved away, it had been us three girls and *Mamm*. After Robert fell ill, we worked together to care for the children and run the household. There was no one else in the world whom I was as close to as my *mamm* and the two sisters in front of me.

Mamm sat beside Sadie while Tabitha held the baby. "What do you need us to do?" *Mamm* asked. "Take the children home or stay here?"

Sadie looked at me. "I'd like Linda to stay and help with the kids." She turned toward *Mamm*. "And for you to come back in the morning."

"All right." *Mamm* patted Sadie's shoulder. "I'll be here first thing."

It would make more sense for Tabitha to stay—she was better with the children than I was—but I couldn't suggest that, not when Sadie had made her request. My family had this idea that I was good in a crisis, and that I intrinsically knew what to do when a person was hurting. "You're empathetic," Sadie told me once. "You feel things deeply."

I didn't necessarily agree, however. Most of the time I just didn't know what to say, and I think people mistook my silence as an intentional sort of quiet comfort.

Footsteps fell on the porch, and then *Daed* appeared in the doorway. His construction crew was working a job on the other side of Harrisburg, and he seldom arrived home before seven. *Mamm* had left a message earlier with his boss for *Daed* to come as soon as he could, not wanting to relay the bad news via voice mail.

"How is he?" *Daed* asked, fear in his eyes.

Biting her lip, Sadie stood and simply shook her head.

"I'm so sorry." He pulled her in for a hug.

I couldn't stop the tears then. I glanced to the table, where Isaac sat with the girls and his grandmother. Both of the adults appeared moved too. Ruth brushed her hand across her wrinkled cheek as Isaac put his arm around her. It was a sweet moment between the two of them. The girls didn't react at all, however, but instead just kept on picking at their food, watching their mother as they did. Someone needed to tell them what had happened.

"I'm going to call my manager," I whispered to *Mamm*. I wanted to let Kristen know as soon as possible that I'd need the week off.

I grabbed my cape and slipped past *Daed* and Sadie onto the porch. The air had grown chilly, and I hurried toward the barn. When I stepped inside, insulated by the warmth and quiet, I headed to Robert's office. Truth be told, I hated telephones and avoided talking on them as much as possible. Still, sometimes they couldn't be avoided. Like now. Taking a deep breath, I dialed and listened to the ring and was somewhat relieved when I got Kristen's voice mail rather than reaching her in person. I did my best to speak loudly and clearly as I left a message.

I returned to the doorway of the barn and paused there, looking around at the house and yard, the first chance I'd had to do so since all the helpers had come and gone. Diapers no longer hung on the line. The garden was fully weeded, the lawn neatly trimmed, the whole place practically sparkling in the last rays of the sunset.

Glancing toward the shed, I couldn't help but picture Robert there. He'd been up and puttering around just the day before. I shuddered at how quickly death had come for him.

The front door opened, and Tabitha stepped out with Bobby wrapped in a blanket. After her came Isaac. He spoke with Tabitha for a moment and then headed down the stairs. When he saw me, he nodded. As we met, he said, "I'm going to go get the buggy ready and then take my *mammi* home. I'll be back first thing in the morning."

"I'll see you then." We both knew there would be plenty of helpers here to handle the milking and other chores, but I guessed he felt the need to pitch in anyway, as did I.

When I reached the steps, Tabitha nodded toward the little one. "He's almost asleep. I'll put him down and then head home."

"Thanks." I was grateful I'd need to get just the girls ready for bed.

Tabitha nodded toward Isaac. "He's cute, *ya?*"

"I hadn't really noticed."

Tabitha leaned toward me. "Don't you remember him from the wedding? He was so gangly and *doplich* then. He's definitely grown up now." She smiled. "Looking good too."

"No, I don't remember him. But he seems very kind." I stepped to the porch and turned to see him nearing the barn. "And helpful."

Tabitha shook her head. "That's what caught your attention the most? Kind and helpful?" The baby stirred, and she lowered her voice. "Linda, open your eyes."

I pulled my cape tighter. We had more important things to think about right now than Robert's nephew. Even so, I continued to watch until Isaac rounded the corner of the old barn and disappeared from view.

Two

The next morning, first thing, I checked the voice mails in Robert's little phone room. It could hardly be called an office, but it did house his filing cabinets and all of his business records. There were several messages, so I grabbed a pen and paper and began taking notes. A few were from relatives and neighbors. I carefully wrote down names and numbers for Sadie. I'd ask her if she would like me to return the calls for her.

The final message, left last night after eleven, was from my manager, Kristen. She told me to call her back this morning. I groaned, knowing I'd have to remember to do so later. When *Englischers* said "morning," they didn't mean five o'clock.

"What's wrong?"

I spun around.

Isaac stood in the doorway, the black cat a few feet from him.

"Oh, a work issue, that's all. No big deal." I reached out to the cat. He sniffed my hand but then turned and walked the other way, coming to a stop near the cows' watering trough and leaping up onto its rim to lick at the dripping faucet.

Together, Isaac and I started with the milking, moving the first group of cows into through the barn.

"Where do you work?" he asked as we did.

"A little fabric and art supply store called the Arts & Crafts House."

"Oh, sure." He smiled. "In Bird-in-Hand."

"That's right."

"I stopped by there the other day. But all of the clerks were *Englisch*."

"I'm the only Amish employee. I must not have been there. I only work thirty hours a week." Then, teasing, I asked, "What kind of fabric did you buy?"

He grinned. "Calico?" He laughed. "Is that even still a thing?"

I nodded. Not that we Amish used it—except maybe for making handcrafted items for the *Englisch*.

"Actually, I was there for paint," he added.

"We don't sell house paint."

"No." He seemed slightly embarrassed. "Oil paint. Like, for artwork."

"Oh. Really?"

Before he could explain further, *Mamm* appeared in the barn doorway. "*Hallo?*" she called out.

I stepped around one of the machines and into view. "*Mamm?*"

"There you are," she said, more somberly, "*Vee bisht du an du?*"

"I'm okay," I replied. "How are you doing?"

Mamm sighed. "Getting through with the Lord's help." She was quiet for a moment, as if lost in thought, but then she seemed to regain her focus when she noticed Isaac was there too. "Oh, good," she said to him. "Sadie and Ruth need your help. They're trying to figure out who else in your family needs to be contacted. They don't want to leave anyone out."

"Sure," he replied. "I'll be there as soon as I finish the milking."

"*Gut,* thanks." *Mamm* turned to go but then paused, adding, "Though I have a feeling you won't be long."

We figured out what she meant moments later when several men from our district stepped into the barn. They said their hellos and then got right to work. Isaac hesitated, but even more helpers arrived, and soon people were everywhere, shoveling grain into the troughs, securing the cows, hooking up the milking machines, and more.

"Guess your *mamm* was right." Isaac flashed me a smile, and he and I headed for the house together.

Once we'd cleaned up on the mud porch and gone into the kitchen, I was relieved to see that no helpers were inside yet, only family. I deeply appreciated how the community surrounded us with love and prayers, and also with practical help. This early in the morning, however, I preferred the easy quiet of just us.

Mamm was in the midst of making breakfast, so I jumped in to help while Isaac joined Sadie and Ruth in the living room. I could hear Tabitha cooing at Bobby in the back of the house, and I assumed she was getting him and the girls up and dressed for the day.

As *Mamm* and I worked side by side, I kept an eye on the clock. When the hands indicated it was six, I slid my tray of biscuits in the oven, took off my apron, and excused myself, explaining that I needed to make a phone call.

Back in the barn, which now practically gleamed with cleanliness thanks to everyone's hard work, I slipped into the phone room and dialed Kristen's number. Both her husband and baby were early risers, so I hoped she'd be awake. Sure enough, she answered on the second ring.

"Oh, Linda." Her voice was full of concern. "I'm so sorry about your brother-in-law. How is your sister doing? And her kids?"

I teared up at her response. She was truly becoming a good friend. I told her how Sadie was, adding that she hadn't broken the news to the twins yet.

"I can't imagine…" Her voice quivered. "When's the funeral?"

"We usually bury three days after death. So Friday, I guess."

"Well, don't worry about anything. Let's see." I heard the clack of computer keys and realized she must've pulled up the store's scheduling software on her laptop. "Do you think you could work Saturday?"

"*Ya*, sure." That wasn't my usual day, but I didn't mind if that meant I could be off until then.

"Great. I'll cover your shift today, and I'll work things out with the other girls for the rest of the week. Unless I hear from you otherwise, I'll expect you back Saturday morning."

"Thank you." My eyes filled with tears again, and I brushed them away. "I can't tell you how grateful I am for your help."

"Of course. Take care. I'll be praying for your sister and your entire family."

"*Danke.*" I corrected myself quickly. "I mean, thank you."

"I knew what you meant, silly. I'll see you on Saturday."

After we hung up, the tears started to flow. Why had talking to Kristen made me cry? Was it her concern? Her warmth? Or that I was so surprised an *Englisch* woman would pray for my family?

Trying to distract myself and stop the tears, I thought of my earlier exchange with Isaac, about him having bought paint. *Mamm* had said he was a house painter, but now it turned out he did some sort of artwork-type painting as well. I'd never bought any paint myself, but I loved restocking it and reading the names. *Fire red. Rose madder. Cobalt blue. Sap green. Mars orange. Ya*, the names and the colors all thrilled me. Setting and place meant nothing without hues and variations. No doubt, the next time I stocked the paints, I'd think of Isaac.

By the time I got back to the house, my biscuits were done and breakfast was ready. *Daed* was in Robert's chair at the head of the table, and seated around him were Stephen, Thomas, Hattie, Hazel, and Bobby. I washed my hands and then jumped in to help Tabitha and *Mamm* transfer everything from the stove and counter, including steaming stacks of hotcakes, sausage patties, and fried potatoes.

I grabbed a fresh jar of Sadie's homemade jelly from the pantry and then gestured toward the living room.

Mamm shrugged. "They said to start without them. They're still working on the list of relatives."

Lowering my voice, I asked if Sadie had told the girls yet.

Mamm shook her head. We both knew any other seven-year-olds would've figured it out by now or at least demanded to know what was going on. But not Hattie and Hazel.

"She will," *Mamm* replied. "Right after breakfast."

Daed led us in a silent prayer, and then we all dug in hungrily—except for the twins, who only picked at their food as usual. Soon Sadie, Isaac, and his grandmother joined us as well. Isaac's face was solemn, and Ruth looked drained. But the worst was Sadie, who had dark circles under swollen eyes. I jumped up and got her a cup of coffee. Her hands shook as she took it from me.

Tabitha talked with Hattie and Hazel about school, saying she was sorry they had such bad colds and that they'd been missed the day before. They nodded solemnly, in unison.

Then Sadie spoke. "Girls, I need to speak to you for a moment. In the living room."

The twins glanced at each other and then followed their mother to the couch. I could see them from where I sat, and though I kept trying not to look, I couldn't seem to help myself.

Sadie sat between her daughters with an arm around each of them. "You know how ill *Daed* was?"

They both nodded.

"I'm afraid—"

"I told you he was dead." Hattie leaned forward and spoke to Hazel. Then she looked at her mother. "We figured it out."

Hazel nodded in agreement.

Sadie drew them close. "Do you have any questions?"

They both squirmed and shook their heads.

Sadie explained what would happen over the next few days, how the empty pine casket would be delivered to the funeral home, and then their *daed*'s body would be returned in it, ready for the visitation and funeral. Meanwhile, community members would keep showing up to do the chores and start cooking the meals and making all of the arrangements for the viewing and service, including erecting a big tent in the yard and bringing in not just their own district's church benches but ones borrowed from neighboring districts as well. Considering five or six hundred guests might be attending, a lot of preparations would be needed.

"We'll have the viewing here tomorrow. We're going to wait for a couple of your *daed*'s brothers to arrive along with *Aenti* Becky and *Aenti* Izzy and your *onkels*, Matthew, Mark, and Melvin, and then the service will be on Friday, followed by the burial over at the cemetery. You girls don't have to go to the actual burial if you don't want to. Most people won't. They'll just stay here after the service and get started on the meal. It's up to you."

They nodded as if they understood. Perhaps they did. After all, their paternal grandfather had passed away just the year before, so this stuff wasn't exactly new to them.

Hazel wiped her nose on the sleeve of her dress. "I'm tired."

Hattie parroted her sister's gesture. "Me too."

"Go rest in your rooms." Sadie stood. "Linda will help you get settled." I hurried to do as my sister had bid.

The rest of the day passed predictably. We each knew our roles—and as more and more jobs were taken over by community members, we were given time to spend together and comfort Sadie and share memories of Robert.

When Jedediah King, a neighbor, stopped by, I wormed my way into the busy kitchen and retrieved some coffee and a plate of cookies. Sadie had been resting but came out to greet the man, who'd been a good friend to Robert, especially through his illness.

Sadie gave him a detailed account of her husband's last days.

Jedediah shook his head sadly. "You should have called."

"I would have if I'd known how sick Robert was. The doctors didn't give us any indication his body would fail so quickly—not till today anyway, and then it all happened so fast there just wasn't time." Sadie turned toward the man. "He would have liked to have told you goodbye if he'd known."

"*Ach*, that doesn't matter now," Jedediah replied. "But I'm sorry for your loss, and your children's loss too." He said the word *children* with tenderness. Jedediah lived on a farm that bordered this one, and his parents lived on the other side, on more family land. He and his father grew corn and soybeans together, and they'd all been good neighbors.

Jedediah was a couple of years younger than Robert and still unmarried. According to Sadie, he'd had his heart horribly broken a few years ago by a girl from New York, a member of the Swartzentruber Amish, who'd spent a summer here caring for an elderly relative. After that experience he'd seemed leery of courting anyone else. Tabitha had had her eye on him soon after but had given up once it was clear he wasn't ready to court again.

The next day, after the body was returned in the casket, *Mamm* and *Daed* sat with Sadie beside the coffin while Tabitha took charge of Bobby, and I stayed mostly with Hattie and Hazel in their room. We came out for supper but then returned to their room because friends and family, including two of Robert's brothers who lived outside of Lancaster County, were gathering for the official viewing.

The girls had no desire to see their father—some mothers might have forced them to, but not Sadie. Viewing the deceased had never bothered me before, but now that it was Robert, I had no desire to see him either. Though soon I wouldn't have a choice in the matter, I would have preferred to remember him the way he'd been. Strong and young. A devoted husband and father. A kind brother-in-law.

The girls sat on the floor of their room and took their paper dolls out of the manila envelope. They lined up their family from the grandparents to the baby. My eyes filled with tears as Hattie picked up the father in the family and then tore him—not in two, but so that the top half of him flapped as she scooted him along on the floor.

I didn't know how to respond to that, so I didn't. Instead, I concentrated on the hum of the low voices of those who had gathered to pay their respects to Robert and support Sadie. The sound comforted me. It represented love and commitment to my sister and her children. They would never be alone in their grief—nor in their future. That was our way of ministering to one another.

I put the twins to bed as soon as I could, telling them they needed extra rest because of their colds. But I had an ulterior motive. I could tell by the lessened sounds in the house, along with the frequent opening and closing of the front door, that most of the viewers had left, though my other two sisters, Izzy and Becky, would arrive soon.

I couldn't wait to see them. Izzy, who was expecting her first child in just a month or two, was traveling with her husband, Zed, from Indiana. Ordinarily, one might think twice about traveling such a distance that far into a pregnancy, but their midwife out in Goshen had assured them it should be fine. Zed's mother, Marta Bayer—a midwife in this area who'd delivered eight of my parents' ten children, including me—had concurred, albeit via long distance.

On the way, Zed and Izzy had picked up Becky, who lived with her husband and two children in Ohio. Once here, Zed and Izzy would stay over at Marta's while Becky would remain with Sadie.

First, though, the plan was for the three of them to come straight here as soon as they arrived in Lancaster County. Zed would be driving. He'd grown up Mennonite, and Izzy had joined him in his faith rather than becoming Amish.

Becky, on the other hand, had married into a more conservative Amish district. She went from the relative comforts of an Amish home in Lancaster County, Pennsylvania, to a rural Ohio Amish community that didn't have tops on their buggies or running water in their homes. It had to be a tough transition, but she never complained. She and Sadie had always been close, so I knew she'd be a great comfort at this difficult time.

I waited at the kitchen table, listening to the soft murmur of the others in the living room, including my older brothers, Matthew, Mark, and Melvin. Despite the somberness of the gathering, their voices drifted into gentle teasing and joking, a sound that stirred in me an old, familiar feeling of "home." I'd been about fourteen when the last of them married and moved out, and sometimes I forgot how nice it was to have them around.

After a while, Isaac came in and poured a cup of decaf. He returned to the living room and brought the coffee to Sadie, and then he returned to the kitchen empty handed and asked if I would like a cup as well.

I said I would, so he poured two and joined me at the table. I'd just taken a sip when I heard a commotion on the back porch.

The door flew open and Izzy appeared, practically glowing as she stepped into the house. I rushed toward her and we hugged, her round, firm belly filling the space between us. As I embraced Becky and then Zed, the rest of the family joined in, all of us so excited but trying hard to keep our voices down so as not to wake the children. Izzy held Sadie especially close, her brown eyes filling with tears as she released our oldest sister.

Sadie quickly introduced Isaac to the travelers as I began pulling out food, including various salads, a chicken casserole, and one very special dessert a neighbor had brought over. Though *Englisch*, the woman was an amazing cook, and her apple pie was a long-time family favorite.

"Oh, good. I'm starving." Izzy stepped toward the counter to help, but when she spotted the familiar wide-lattice crust in the rectangular pan, she froze. "Is that what I think it is?"

I nodded, grinning. "Miss Freida's fresh-made apple pie. She brought over two, so I set one aside for when you guys got here."

Izzy threw an arm around me and gave my shoulders a squeeze. "Wow, Linda, you're the best."

I waved off her words, but the smile remained on my face as I returned my attention to preparing the food. It had been a long trip for them—something like nine hours in the car, not counting any stops or breaks. And though the rest of us had already eaten, we sat around the dining table with them as they polished off full plates, with double helpings of pie for all.

An hour later, everyone had left except for Becky, Isaac, Tabitha, and me. As Sadie showed Becky to her room, Isaac said he needed to go as well. I thanked him for his help and walked him out, giving a silent prayer of thanks for this man who seemed to know that we needed him around. His very presence was such a comfort, even though he'd been a virtual stranger just two days before.

The kitchen had been so warm that the chilly outside air felt good, and I didn't even grab a wrap before moving onto the porch. A lantern had been left out for visitors, and we stood there for a moment in its glow.

"How's your grandmother holding up?" I asked, pulling the door shut behind me.

"Not too well. She wanted to rest this evening to be strong enough for the funeral tomorrow." That made sense. I couldn't imagine what it was like to be nearly eighty and have your baby die before you. I was about to say as much when the door swung open and Tabitha stepped out.

"Oh, there you are. I was looking for you." She paused to give Isaac a warm smile and then turned back toward me. "*Mamm* and *Daed* are going home. Do you want to go with them or stay?"

Going home was tempting, but I had already promised Sadie I'd spend the night. "I'll stay."

"All right. We'll see you in the morning. I'm going to hitch up the buggy."

"I'll help." Isaac moved down the steps but then turned to me, almost as an afterthought, and gave a quick, "See you tomorrow, Linda."

"Yeah. See you."

Tabitha skipped down the steps to join him, and then the two of them started off toward the barn side by side. Watching them go, I felt a surprising surge of jealousy rise up inside of me, especially when Isaac said something to Tabitha and in response she tossed her head back and laughed. I kept watching until a gust of wind swept through the thin fabric of my dress, chilling me to the bone. With a shiver, I turned and went back into the house, knowing I could never be like her, not even if I wanted to. No doubt, she'd soon be courting Isaac.

The neighbors had taken care of every detail for the funeral day. Cleaning out the shop. Arranging for church wagons to be delivered from other districts so there would be enough benches. Making sure all of the needed food would be ready for the post-funeral meal. By six thirty Friday morning, Sadie's kitchen was full of women. Some fixed breakfast while others prepared for later, making sandwiches, cooking noodles, and wrapping plastic cutlery in napkins. Outside, men finished the chores, directed traffic, unhitched horses, and parked buggies.

The service started at nine. Sadie, her children, and Robert's family all sat up front, with our family behind them. After the singing, the preachers read Scriptures and prayed, and then one gave a long sermon. When Bobby began to fuss, Tabitha took him from Sadie and headed outside.

After the service ended, I stayed with the girls instead of going to the cemetery. By the time everyone returned, the tables and benches had been set up and the food arranged by the helpers. The first group was seated to eat.

As soon as they were finished, the food tables were quickly replenished for the next group. I went through the line behind *Mamm*, and though I thought I'd have no appetite, I found I was suddenly starving. My mother obviously was too because she heaped her plate with pickled beets, two big spoonfuls of noodles, and three mini ham-and-cheese-on-a-bun sandwiches.

I sat between Tabitha and Izzy, and though conversation buzzed all around me, I was mostly quiet, eating my food and taking things in. So many people were here—relatives and friends from all over—including one guy who kept catching my attention. Looking his way now, I finally realized who he was, a fellow named Ezra Gundy.

He had courted Zed's sister, Ella, years ago. After they broke up, she married a nice Plain man, and Ezra ended up going to Florida. And then Louisiana. And then Alaska to work in an oil field.

I'd heard about him through the years. He came from a respected family, but word was that after Ella rejected him, he'd gone hog wild—riding his motorcycle all around the country, living a completely *Englisch* lifestyle, and working with some rough people. He and Zed stayed in touch, and though folks loved to gossip about Ezra, all Zed ever said was that he was a "great guy."

The reason Ezra caught my attention now was because of the way Tabitha was looking at him. Oh, he was definitely worth looking at. Even I could see that. Tall with a solid build, he was clearly a strong guy and a hard worker. He had auburn hair, big brown eyes, and what some might call a sexy smile, though from where I sat, it seemed more mischievous than alluring.

To my surprise, he was dressed Plain, wearing the requisite black pants, white shirt, and suspenders. I hadn't heard he'd joined the church.

Given his past, many Amish girls might steer clear regardless, but not Tabitha. As soon as she finished eating, she managed to make her way over to the dessert table where he was standing and engage him in conversation as she made a big show of trying to choose between raisin pie and applesauce cake.

"Hey, Linda." Isaac slipped into the chair my sister had vacated. "You doing okay?"

I nodded, touched he'd thought to ask. "You?"

He shrugged. "About as well as can be expected."

Before we could say more, a loud giggle erupted from Tabitha, and we both looked her way.

"Who's that?" Isaac nodded toward the handsome young man standing beside my sister.

"Ezra Gundy." I wanted to add, "Lancaster's favorite wayward son," but refrained, not wanting to gossip. Glancing again at Isaac, it struck me that perhaps he thought he had competition.

I sighed. That was the story of my life—watching Tabitha juggle several possible beaus while... I chided myself. It wasn't as if I would ever get married, so why compare myself to my sister?

"What is it?" Isaac asked me.

My face began to grow warm. My expression must have given my frustration away. "Oh, nothing. I'm tired, is all."

"It's been a tough day in a tough week." Isaac gave me a brotherly pat on the shoulder, and then he excused himself and headed toward his grandmother.

If Tabitha had any sense at all, I thought as I watched him go, she'd pursue Isaac over Ezra. It was obvious which one would make the best Amish husband. My heart raced at the thought, but again I chastised myself.

"Linda!"

I turned to see Tabitha waving me over. With a sigh, I stood and went to her.

"You remember Ezra Gundy, don't you?" She grinned as I drew closer.

"Sure." I came to a stop at my sister's side and gave him a nod. "*Hallo*, Ezra. I'm surprised to see you here."

"I wouldn't have missed it. Robert was a good man."

"Ezra and Robert both used to work for the Gundys way back when," Tabitha added.

He nodded. "Robert was a couple years older than me, but he was really nice. Took me under his wing and sort of showed me the ropes, even though it was my own family's business." He grinned. "Which shows how much help I needed back then."

The Gundy family had a nursery that included several large greenhouses. Through the years, lots of young men had worked for them—and still did. One of the Gundy sons, Will, now ran the place with the help of his wife, Ada. She was a cousin of Zed's, and I'd met them both at Izzy's wedding.

"Well," I said, "it was nice of you to come. I hope you didn't have to travel too far."

Again, Tabitha answered for him. "No. Ezra joined the church last year while he was in Ohio and then moved home a few months ago."

I was surprised I hadn't heard that from anyone. He was in a different district, so it wasn't as if I would've run into him at services, but somebody should've mentioned something about it by now. Maybe it had come up and I'd simply missed it in my general avoidance of gossip. "Well, welcome back."

"It's good to be back," he replied and smiled again. *Ya*, I could see how he attracted the ladies.

"He's working with his brother," Tabitha said. "At the greenhouses."

I'd always thought that sounded like a lovely job. Actually, a greenhouse design would make a great quilt…

It took me a moment to realize Isaac was motioning toward me, a look of concern on his face. I excused myself from Tabitha and Ezra and hurried over to him.

He whispered, "My *mammi* isn't feeling well. Is there some place she can rest?"

He and I helped Ruth to stand, and then I suggested she lie down in the twins' room. Their colds were waning, and I'd changed their bedding that morning. Once we reached it, I was surprised to find the girls playing with their paper dolls on the floor. I started to shoo them away, but Ruth said, "No, let them stay. They won't disturb me."

The twins scooted over toward the wall but otherwise ignored us. The torn father was still part of the family.

Isaac hovered nervously in the doorway as I helped Ruth settle on the bed, so I asked him to get her a glass of water.

"Is this better now that you're lying down?" I asked her once he was gone.

Ruth nodded. "My blood pressure has been low…" Her voice trailed off. "Anyway, I was feeling light-headed just now." She sighed and closed her eyes. "I'm sorry to be a bother."

"Don't be silly." I pulled over a chair and sat next to the bed. "To be honest, I think you've held up remarkably well, considering. This must be so difficult for you."

Her eyes fluttered open, and she gave me a grateful look before closing them again.

Leaning forward, I took Ruth's cool, papery hand in mine and gave it a squeeze. Ever-so-slightly, she squeezed back.

Looking down at her, I thought again of the role this dear woman had played in my life. She hadn't just been a surrogate grandmother to me. She'd also been my best source of information about my actual grandmother.

For me, being one of the younger children in such a large family had its drawbacks, including the fact that by the time I was born all but one of my grandparents had passed away. The one who was still living at the time of my birth, my father's mother, died when I was still little, so I didn't even remember her.

But Ruth did. She'd grown up in the same district as *Mammi* Nettie, and though Ruth had been a good ten years younger than my grandmother, she had plenty of memories of the woman, which she'd always freely shared with me. Sadly, not everyone spoke all that well of the late Nettie Mueller, saying she'd been "odd" or "unfriendly" or an "isolationist." But Ruth seemed to judge her more kindly, and I'd always enjoyed hearing her version of this enigmatic woman from my family's past. What some saw as odd, Ruth called creative. Unfriendly, Ruth said, was really just shy. Isolationist was more like introverted, not to mention overwhelmed— by life, by dealing with others, by the deprivations of the Depression. In short, Ruth's version of my forebear was reassuring in the face of less charitable opinions from others.

The only person I knew besides Ruth who spoke fondly of *Mammi* Nettie was Izzy, who had been especially close to her. *Mammi* Nettie, whose given name was Annette, lived with us for the last few years of her life. Reportedly, her death affected Izzy the most, as if she hadn't just lost her grandmother but also one of her best buddies.

"Here we are." Isaac bustled into the room with a glass of water, interrupting my thoughts. He still seemed a bit flustered, so I calmly took charge, helping Ruth to sit up and then taking the glass from his hand and holding it out to her. She drank a few sips before giving it back and leaning against the pillows.

"I'm fine," she reassured her grandson. "Really. It's warm today. The water will help." When Isaac seemed unconvinced, she added, "I'll call my doctor tomorrow. I promise."

He seemed to calm down after that, especially because it was easy to see the color returning to Ruth's cheeks. She was a hearty woman. She would be okay.

I could tell Isaac wanted to sit with her, so I offered him my chair and told him I'd be nearby if they needed anything else.

"Thanks." His eyes were on his grandmother as he grabbed the chair, moved it even closer, and sat.

Smiling to myself at the sweetness of his concern, I stepped into the hallway and then busied myself with neatening the bookshelf there. The two of them quietly conversed, and I was glad to hear Ruth's voice growing stronger as they spoke. I was only half listening until Ruth asked Isaac if he'd started "that painting you've been talking about, the one of Robert's barn."

"Not yet," he replied. "But I will."

My mind went to the quilt I wanted to make of the very same barn, and I was pleased to think we'd both been inspired by it. But my smile faded as I considered the implications of an Amish man who dabbled in painting.

It wasn't that art wasn't allowed in our district, but it certainly wasn't encouraged. I knew a few women who used painting in the creation of various craft items, which they then sold to *Englisch* tourists for some pocket cash. But I didn't know any men who did that. They were to concentrate on real sources of income, on making a living and supporting a family.

As I listened to him go on about the size of the canvas he was planning and a special technique he intended to use, however, I realized Isaac was serious about his art. I found myself wondering just how serious. Was this a passing hobby—or was it something he truly cared about?

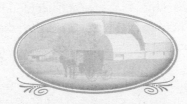

THREE

The Arts & Crafts House was in a historical building located on Highway 340. Originally a private home, the structure featured hardwood floors, high ceilings, and antique moldings. Kristen's aunt had bought and renovated the place about ten years ago, and over time it had become one of the most popular stores in Bird-in-Hand.

Throughout the building, the walls were lined with quilts for sale, including a few done by me. The checkout counter sat in the center of the two largest rooms, which were for sewing supplies. They held bolts of material, racks of thread, ribbons, and more, with a big cutting table off to one side. The next two rooms were for the art section and offered numerous supplies, such as canvases, oil and acrylic paints, brushes, and sketchpads. A small kitchen and an office, for employees only, was in the back.

Outside, the parking lot was big, with enough room for cars plus one tour bus. For customers who came via buggy, a couple of hitching posts sat along the side. Behind that was an old stable, where I was allowed to keep Blue when it was cold, and a small pasture, where he went when it wasn't.

When I showed up on Saturday, I was relieved to find that Kristen was working, which would help me ease back into my tasks. I hadn't anticipated how tired I would feel from all of the doings of the week, not to mention the grief.

Kristen did her best to get me back into the swing of things, first by encouraging me to talk about Sadie and her children and the funeral, and then by trying to distract me. As she twisted her blond hair into a knot and secured it on top of her head with a hair tie, she asked, "Did you notice one of your quilts sold?"

"Which one?"

"The sunshine-and-shadow pattern. A woman from Virginia bought it the other day. She loved the jewel tones against the navy background. She was so impressed with your work—the tiny stitches, the hundreds of squares."

Four hundred and fifty squares to be exact. It was a lap quilt, or the perfect size to hang.

"She really seemed to know her stuff," Kristen added. "Didn't even blink at the price."

I nodded, pleased. Not a lot of people wanted to pay four hundred dollars for a mere 4' x 5' quilt, though considering how long it had taken me to make it, that wasn't unreasonable. I'd sold quilts before, at other shops in Lancaster County, but this was my first at the Arts & Crafts House, even though I'd had several on display for a while.

"Here's the check for your share." Kristen's blue eyes sparkled as she handed me an envelope. Her aunt kept a percentage of the proceeds, but I was fine with that. I slipped it in my apron pocket, knowing I'd put the money in the bank as soon as possible.

Kristen nodded over to where the quilt had hung. "We have high hopes this one will sell too."

I turned to see that they had already filled that space with another of my quilts, one I'd just finished the month before. It was traditional appliqué—not the artistic or modern appliqué Kristen had shown me examples of online, which were quite complicated. Mine was simple, a sampler with nine different images, including a heart, two birds facing each other, four flowers in a square, that sort of thing. I'd used burgundy, pink, and green fabric against a cream background.

"Do you have any more quilts for us to sell?" Kristen asked.

"*Ya*," I replied. "A shadow quilt, a queen-sized one." *Mamm* had helped me do the hand quilting during the winter.

Kristen clapped her hands together. "Perfect. If it's a queen, we can charge a thousand."

A thousand dollars. It was hard for me to imagine. On the other hand, quilting took so much time that even at that price, my hourly wage was merely sufficient.

I asked Kristen how her week had been, and she told me she and her husband had celebrated their fifth wedding anniversary the night before. "I was pretty young when I got married," she said. "Only twenty-one."

I laughed. "That's practically an old maid in the Plain community." That wasn't quite true, but we did tend to marry younger than the *Englisch* did.

"Guess you only have two more years left, then," she teased. "You'd better get busy."

I'd watched my older sisters court, and they all did it with such ease and confidence, two qualities I definitely lacked.

I felt Kristen's gaze on me. "What is it?" she asked.

I shook my head. "I doubt I'll ever marry."

Kristen's eyes sparkled as she turned to flip the sign to *Open*. "Just wait. The right guy will come around when you least expect him."

In no time the place was crowded with shoppers, and it stayed that way all day. Near closing time, a busload of women from New Jersey showed up. They were thrilled to see a genuine Amish girl working in the shop, and several of them cornered me, asking me questions. Some of those questions were perfectly fine—such as why did we dress the way we did or why could we ride in cars but not drive them—and I was happy to answer. Other questions weren't so fine, and it was all I could do not to groan.

"Do you have arranged marriages?" one asked, a short stout woman with heavily rouged cheeks.

"Oh, no. We—"

"I heard the Amish don't go to doctors," said another. "You've never even been vaccinated."

"Of course we go to doctors when we need to. And, *ya*, I've been vaccinated."

"Do you feel guilty not paying taxes?" asked the first.

"We *do* pay taxes, though not all of us pay into Social Security."

A third woman spoke up to ask about Amish quilts, and I wanted to give her a hug. Seizing the moment, I launched into an enthusiastic explanation of various patterns, starting with the Nine Patch, and showed them an example on the wall that Kristen's aunt had made. Then I shared about a few of our more complicated patterns, some of which they were familiar with, such as the Log Cabin and Broken Star.

One of the women was so thrilled with me that when I was finished, she asked for my address "so we can be pen pals." Thankfully, Kristen called me to the cash register before I could answer, and by the time I'd finished helping check out the long line of women, the question had been forgotten. When the last one made it out the door, I told Kristen I would turn the sign.

"Wait a second. Looks like we have another customer."

I expected it to be one of the women coming back in, but as I walked toward the front of the store, I saw through the window that it was an Amish man instead. His head was down, but when he stepped inside I realized it was Isaac.

"*Guder nochmidaag,*" I said.

He took his hat off and smiled. "I hoped you'd be working."

I smiled back and then quickly introduced him to Kristen. After she told Isaac she was pleased to meet him, she turned and gave me a knowing grin. Except she didn't know anything. There wasn't anything to know.

Before I could ask Isaac how I could help him, he gestured toward the quilts on display. "Are any of these yours?"

I nodded. "One of them is."

"Don't tell me," he said quickly. "I'll guess."

He didn't speak as he stood and stared at one quilt and then another. Finally he said, "I think it's this one, the appliqué." He pointed at mine.

My face grew warm.

He grinned. "I'm right, aren't I?"

I nodded. "How did you know?"

"Rumor has it you're a gifted quilter, and it's the best one here."

I shook my head. "That's not true." It wasn't even the best of mine.

"No, it is," he said. "You clearly have an eye for composition and color. And your technique appears to be nearly flawless."

Embarrassed, I quickly changed the subject. "You didn't come here to look at my quilting. What can I help you find?"

He smiled at me kindly, as if he understood that it was hard for me to hear praise about my work. Then he pointed toward the art section. "I just need a few tubes of paint to finish a project I've been working on and some new canvas for what I'll be doing next."

He followed me, and then I watched as he chose burnt red and Naples yellow. Next he stepped to the canvases and grabbed an entire roll.

"That must be some painting," I said.

He smiled. "I stretch my own, so I'll get more than a few out of this. Though you're right. This particular project will be on the larger side. It's going to be of a barn, painted on canvas and then framed with barn boards.

"Oh, right. Robert's barn," I said. When he looked at me, surprised, I added, "I wasn't trying to eavesdrop, but when Ruth was resting in the twins' bedroom, I heard her say something to you about it."

When he didn't reply, I kept talking. "I've always loved that barn. It's one of my favorite places."

He still didn't say anything.

So of course I kept talking. "I'd like to pattern a quilt after it."

He glanced at the quilts on display. "A traditional Amish quilt?"

I considered that for a moment. "I'm not sure. I'll have to put more thought into it."

He eyed me curiously. "I see." He started toward the checkout, and I stepped ahead to take my place behind the register.

"What do you do with your paintings?" I asked as I scanned his items.

He glanced around as if someone might be spying on him, not realizing Kristen was the only other person in the shop. In a low voice he said, "I sell them."

My eyes widened. "Do you sell many?"

"I used to." He handed me his credit card. "It's a little harder now. Most people around here don't know about my art."

"Plain or *Englisch* people?" I slid his card through the scanner and waited for it to process.

"Well, I'd love for the *Englisch* to know. They're much more likely to buy my paintings." That was true. We Amish wouldn't buy artwork—and we certainly wouldn't display it in our houses. Calendars were okay. And homey decorations, such as plaques with the word *Family* or *Love* or *Faith*. Dried flowers. Those sorts of things, but not paintings.

His card went through, and I handed it back to him. "Do you plan to keep doing your art now that you have a house painting business?"

"I'd like to," he said. "That's the plan anyway."

I knew of a few Plain women who shopped in our store and sold their work at tourist locations. Only one of them painted on canvas, but the others used painting in their handicrafts—creating decorative scenes on birdhouses or depicting primitive-but-charming farm animals on old slate roof shingles. Apparently the *Englisch* loved that sort of thing, especially when they could say it had been "handcrafted by the Amish."

Those ladies lived in different districts than mine, but their bishops didn't seem to have any problem with what they were doing. Then again, these were women supplementing their families' incomes, not men with jobs to do or businesses to run.

I slipped the tubes of paint into a bag. "Where do you sell your stuff?"

He hesitated for a split second. "At a couple of different galleries in Philadelphia mostly. And online," he added, sounding almost embarrassed.

"Like from a website?"

He nodded, picking up his bag and the roll of canvas.

"Whose website?"

"Mine," he answered. "A friend administers it for me."

"Interesting." It wasn't unheard of for Amish people to sell their products through the web, but I was still surprised.

"I'd love to see your artwork sometime," I blurted, startling myself. "That is, if you'd be willing to show me."

"I'd like that." He smiled kindly. "Come by on a Sunday or early evening, whatever works for you."

I nodded. It wasn't that I entirely approved of what Isaac was doing, but I was curious. I walked him to the front door, told him goodbye, and then locked it behind him.

As I turned around, Kristen grinned like a schoolgirl. "Linda? What have you been keeping from me?"

"Nothing," I replied.

"Are you sure?" she teased. "Because the two of you are adorable together."

"Positive," I answered, although I did look forward to seeing his paintings. Maybe they'd give me inspiration for the quilt of the barn I wanted to make.

Instead of going home, I drove my buggy to Sadie's house. All of us girls were spending the night there, while Becky and Izzy were still in town. *Englischers* would have called it a slumber party perhaps. Plain folk might have dubbed it a bee or a frolic, a time when Amish women got together to tackle a project, such as painting someone's kitchen, tying a quilt, or planting a garden. But we weren't tackling a project—except for Sadie's grief.

When I arrived, Tabitha called out, "Little Sister's here!"

I wrinkled my nose but didn't reply.

She and Izzy were in the kitchen, putting out leftovers, with five places set at the table.

"What about the kids?" I asked. "Aren't they going to eat?"

"They already did." Tabitha pointed to the dishes in the sink. "The twins have been a handful all day. Becky decided to put them to bed early."

"What were they doing?"

"Complaining."

"But they hardly talk."

"Well, they were crying."

"Their *daed* just died."

Tabitha shrugged. "Becky said they were awful."

I couldn't help but think maybe Becky's ideas about children had grown as strict as her Ohio district.

"What did Sadie say?" I asked.

"Not much. She's mostly been in her room, resting."

"I tell you what," Becky blurted when she came into the kitchen a few minutes later, "Sadie had better train these girls now, or they're going to be a handful when they're older."

Her harsh words made us all uncomfortable. I was about to respond, but then Sadie emerged from her room, oblivious, so I held my tongue. We all turned our attention to finishing up with the food, and then we sat down together. Sadie led us in a silent prayer.

When that was done, Izzy brought things around to a lighter tone by teasing Tabitha about Ezra. "He's a bad boy, you know."

"Not anymore," Tabitha shot back.

"How can you be sure?" Becky began scooping ham and cheese casserole onto everyone's plate. It seemed she'd taken charge of the children and the food.

"He's already joined the church. He's home for good."

"But what about his past?" Becky handed me my plate. "How can you live with that?"

Tabitha wrinkled her brow. "What exactly do you mean?"

"He's been all over the country, living as an *Englisch* man. Don't you think he has a history you might not want to…join yourself to?"

Tabitha shook her head. "Who said I was going to marry him?"

Becky laughed. "Don't tell me that's not what you're thinking. Why else would you court a man?" Becky sized up Tabitha. "Except maybe not you. You seem to play with boys—men." She shrugged. "Whatever you call the guys you chase after."

"Becky!" Izzy said. "Don't be mean."

"It's true."

Tabitha's face grew red. "I am not chasing after Ezra," she said evenly. "And I doubt very much if he'll be the person I marry, but some girl will fall for him. And I hope whoever does shows him more forgiveness than you."

Becky just shrugged and coolly said, "Forgiving a man is one thing— marrying him is another."

"That's really harsh," Izzy said. "What about the grace God shows us? Don't you think a woman who loved Ezra would be able to show grace to him? Besides, I have to point out that none of us actually knows what sins Ezra might have committed. And it's not really our business. Our job is to forgive *and* forget."

"Not when it comes to a potential spouse." Becky dished up Sadie's plate. "And don't be naive. We can certainly guess the sorts of things Ezra was up to."

"But why would we?" Izzy asked.

Becky smiled at Tabitha. "To protect our sister."

A crying sound came from down the hall, from the girls' room. I pushed back my chair.

"Don't." Becky held up her hand. "Give it a few minutes. They'll stop eventually."

I glanced at Sadie, who seemed more amused than irritated. She tilted her head toward the hall. I kept going, glad to hear Izzy scold Becky with a hushed, "Their father passed away four days ago. Give them a break."

The truth was, the twins had always been bad sleepers, and Hazel was the worst of the two. She was the youngest, by an hour, and the smallest at birth. She'd barely slept as a baby.

When I opened the door, I realized the girls' battery-operated night-light wasn't on. They were both afraid of the dark and wouldn't sleep without it. No wonder they were crying. "Where's your light?" I asked.

Hattie was curled up against the wall, but Hazel sat on the edge of the bed. "*A-Aenti* Becky took it away," Hazel sputtered. "She said only b-babies use night-lights."

Annoyed with my sister, I felt along the top of the dresser in the dark. Sure enough, the night-light was there. I flipped the switch and put it back on the bedside table.

Hazel let go of a raggedy breath. "*Danke.*"

I put my arm around her, but she scooted away, under the covers.

Taking her place on the side of the bed, I asked, "Do you want me to stay for a few minutes?"

She nodded. I glanced over at Hattie, who had stretched out and was no longer sniffling. Leaning forward, I patted her arm, and then I lay down next to Hazel.

There in the quiet, my mind went back to the topic of Ezra. I didn't agree with Becky's harshness, but I doubted I would want to marry him either. I'd never been interested in the bad-boy type—or anyone who'd lived so extensively among the *Englisch*. I wanted to marry someone who shared my values, who lived the way I did—and always had and always would. Someone as inexperienced with that sort of thing as I was.

Of course, I'd never say that to my sisters, lest it set them off into another round of "Linda's too picky." But I wasn't being picky; I was being realistic. Was it too much to ask for a husband who, like me, was relatively innocent in the ways of the world?

I stayed until both Hattie's and Hazel's breathing changed. If I hadn't been so hungry, I would have remained there and fallen asleep too. I was that tired.

"I didn't realize that's who he was, honestly," Tabitha was saying when I returned to the kitchen. Everyone laughed.

I couldn't believe they were still talking about Ezra.

"What's so funny?" I asked.

"Tabitha," Becky said with a roll of her eyes. "And how many men she can be interested in during the same week."

Ah, then perhaps their gossiping had landed on Isaac now. To be honest, I was curious what they were talking about but didn't want to let on. Time would tell whether Tabitha's interests would be with Ezra or Isaac.

Everyone else was finished so I ate my supper alone while they cleaned up. After that we played Rook, but soon we were all yawning and ready for bed. Becky slept with Sadie in her room, Izzy got the single bed in Bobby's room, and Tabitha and I shared the hide-a-bed in the living room.

Tabitha wanted to talk, most likely about Ezra, but I couldn't keep my eyes open. I drifted off to her saying, "What do you think…"

The next day was a Sunday, and Zed picked up Izzy first thing so they could go with his mother to her Mennonite church. As for the rest of us, it was our off week when we had no service but instead were free to spend time in quiet contemplation or connecting with family and friends. Becky went over to *Mamm* and *Daed*'s to visit, and I asked Sadie if I could take the twins to see their grandmother. Bobby was down for a nap, and that would give Sadie a chance to rest, not to mention it would be the first time all week she'd had her house to herself—or mostly so.

"*Danke*." She put one hand on the small of her back. "I think that would be good for the girls—and you can let me know how Ruth is doing too."

I hoped Sadie couldn't see through me and know that my main motivation in visiting her mother-in-law was to see Isaac. But judging by the bags under her eyes, I decided she was too tired to think of anything other than a nice long rest.

The twins came with me without protest. They seemed to be doing better today, perhaps because Becky wasn't around. They sat in the back, each staring out the window on her side.

The problem with April in Lancaster County was that on any given day the weather could be sunny or rainy or hot or cold or somewhere in the middle. Today was sunny but chilly. At least there wasn't much wind, and we were warm enough inside the buggy with our blankets.

It only took a few minutes to reach Ruth's place. I hitched Blue to the post as the girls climbed down. After I helped fasten their coats, they walked behind me as I headed toward the front door.

I knocked and then knocked again. When no one answered, I wasn't sure what to do. Perhaps Ruth was napping. And Isaac could be painting, though I doubted he did that in the house. Chances were he used one of the outbuildings.

Then again, this was a Sunday, so he probably wasn't painting right now—or at least he shouldn't have been. For a moment I hesitated, unsure of whether to go looking for him or not. If he was painting, I didn't want to embarrass him by catching him in the act. I thought about that for a moment and finally decided that perhaps he was simply on a walk on the property.

"Let's look for your cousin," I said to the girls. Like many Amish families, Ruth had close to a hundred grandchildren and probably twenty or so great-grandchildren by now too. Isaac was one of the oldest, and Bobby was the youngest.

Pulling my wrap more tightly against the chill, I led the way to the large shed. Hattie didn't seem happy, but Hazel took her hand and off we went. No one was inside, so we traipsed to the barn. Before we reached it, however, Isaac stepped out of the side door.

"Linda," he said. "What a surprise."

I smiled and glanced back at the twins. "Hi, Isaac. I brought the girls over to visit Ruth, but she didn't answer the door. I'm afraid we may have come during her nap."

"She'll be up soon," he said.

"How's she feeling?"

"Better. She hasn't been light headed again, though we'll still call the doctor tomorrow just to be safe.

"Good." I hesitated. "Maybe I could see your paintings? While we wait for Ruth?"

"Sure." He nodded toward the barn. "I made a studio in here. Come on in."

I motioned to the girls to follow Isaac, and then I traipsed behind, closing the barn door after me. Ruth's barn was much newer than Robert's, but it didn't have nearly as much character. It also wasn't used as much. There was no longer a dairy herd on the property, so all that was left were two horses, a flock of chickens, and assorted barn cats. Ruth rented out the pasture and fields to a nearby farmer. I wondered if Isaac would inherit this place one day, or if it would go to one of his many uncles or cousins instead.

Isaac opened a door at the far end of the barn. On one side of the room were gallon-sized cans of paint, ladders, and drop cloths—the supplies for his house painting business. The wall on the other side was lined with oil paintings in varying stages of work. Several were completely done. Most were landscapes, many of them not on canvas but instead on old weathered barn boards.

I stepped closer to a painting of a field of sunflowers. Why hadn't I ever thought to base a quilt design on sunflowers? *Englischers* often commented on their beauty when they were in bloom.

I wasn't sure how to tell Isaac how good his work was. His art showed passion and emotion. It conveyed how I felt about my quilting, though I doubted those things came through in my work the way they did in his art. This stuff was incredible.

The next painting was of a rolling emerald field with a large white house and barn, and a clothesline strung with Plain clothes, all painted on barn boards that somehow had been fixed together. It was a typical Lancaster County scene, the kind tourists loved.

"How did you do this?" I asked.

"I glued the barn boards together and then prepared them with gesso, just like I do with the canvases. It keeps acids and oils from the wood out of the paint."

I moved on to the next one as he continued talking. "There's a long history of working with panels of wood, way back to the masters. Not that I'm comparing my work to theirs, and obviously the barn boards are much more rustic in comparison to, say, oak. I actually use hardboard some too." He pointed toward a painting of a covered bridge on a smooth wood panel. "So many things can be done—gluing canvas to the wood, painting directly on the wood, using the hardwood or barn boards as frames. I'm always trying something new."

I moved on to the next painting. It was of a red cardinal perched on a bare branch and framed by barn boards. The bird appeared so vivid that I realized I was holding my breath. "You taught yourself to do all of this?" I asked in wonder.

"No." He hesitated for a moment as his face reddened. "I attended art school."

"Really?"

He nodded.

"Where?"

"Philadelphia."

"Oh…" That explained why shops in Philadelphia sold his work.

He shifted his weight from one foot to the other. "I didn't join the church until last year."

"Oh," I said again. "I guess that makes sense." He certainly couldn't have gone to art school if he'd joined the church at a younger age.

Hattie and Hazel seemed to have no interest in the paintings. Instead, they had each perched on a gallon of paint on the other side of the room, but Hattie was beginning to grow restless. She stood and bumped against one of the ladders.

"We should go for a walk or something," I said.

"It's too chilly for that," Isaac replied. "Let's go back to the house. *Mammi* is probably awake. Maybe the girls would like some tea and a snack."

As we stepped out of his studio, I thanked Isaac for showing me his paintings. He was much more gifted than I'd thought possible, and I wondered if that had made it harder for him to join the church. It would be difficult not to be prideful with talent like that, and he'd have so many more opportunities as an *Englischer* to pursue his artwork than as a Plain man.

Perhaps he hadn't been able to make a living as an artist, though, and that had been part of what had led him to come back, join the church, and paint houses instead.

"*Aenti* Linda?" Hattie had stepped to my side as we left the barn.

"What is it?" I asked.

"Can we go home now?"

"Not yet," I answered. "We're going to see your *mammi* Ruth."

She yawned, and Hazel sighed.

"We'll make it a short visit," I added. I was embarrassed and wanted to explain to Isaac that their attitude had nothing to do with Ruth. They disliked social encounters of any kind, even ones with their sweet grandmother, whom I knew they both loved.

I glanced at him, but he didn't seem bothered. Instead, he put a hand on top of his hat and cried, "Race you to the house!" Then he took off running. The girls hesitated only a moment before taking off as well, the ties of their *kappa* flying over their backs. They wore identical black coats, brown dresses, and black shoes. Isaac slowed and let them get ahead of him.

When they reached the back door, he opened it and the girls rushed in. By the time I caught up with them, they were sitting at the kitchen table and Isaac was checking on Ruth. A few minutes later, she appeared.

Thrilled to see us, she sat down by the children. Isaac started the kettle for tea and then dished up sticky buns for all of us. His ease with the food and drink reminded me that he'd spent time as an *Englischer* while in art school. Roles in that world weren't nearly as defined as they were in ours, which was probably why he seemed to think nothing of doing so despite the fact that there were four capable females sitting right here.

As he worked, the conversation turned to his art, and I told Ruth how much I enjoyed it.

"*Ya*," she said. "This boy has a gift. That's for sure."

Isaac shook his head. "I love to paint, is all."

"I'm thankful things have changed," Ruth said. "In the old days, such talents were discouraged." She turned toward me. "Like your poor grandmother."

"My grandmother?"

"Nettie used to paint. She was quite gifted, actually, but all it brought her was trouble."

I looked at her, startled. "You always said *Mammi* Nettie was creative, but I didn't realize you meant she was an artist."

"Oh, yes. But she had to hide her skills under a bushel. I always felt so sorry for her. I remember discussing the matter with others more than once. I'd say, 'Would the good Lord give a bird wings and tell it not to fly? Of course not. So why would He give Nettie such a gift and then tell her not to use it? Couldn't she paint for His glory?'"

She glanced at Isaac when she said that, and I had a feeling this was ground they'd covered before. Her position on the matter was probably one more reason he'd wanted to live here, because he knew she would support his art rather than try to stifle it.

"But others didn't see it that way," Ruth continued. "To them, art was wasteful and prideful and self-indulgent. So she lived out her life denying that part of herself, that part that yearned to fly."

The twins again seemed restless, so I excused myself and ushered them into the living room, where Ruth kept some toys. I got them started on a game and then mulled over this new information as I made my way back to the kitchen.

Becky's words from last night kept coming to mind, how if Sadie didn't do something about the girls, they would end up being a handful. I'm sure Becky thought *Mammi* Nettie had been a handful too. Once back at the table, I lowered my voice and told Ruth about that, curious what she'd have to say.

"Oh, I wouldn't worry," she told me, patting my hand. "It's our duty to train up children in the way they should go, to shape them. Sadie is a good *mamm*—she'll shape these girls. Our bodies form inside our mothers' wombs, but then our parents shape us to serve God and others." She nodded toward the twins. "The community will make sure those two turn out to be productive adults. Just because they're different doesn't mean they don't have purpose—or that we shouldn't love them. We just have adjust our expectations."

I certainly had high expectations for myself. And, if I was honest enough to admit it, for others too.

"Each child has to know they are needed and that they are capable of helping," Ruth added, nodding toward the twins again. "That's what we all should concentrate on when it comes to these girls."

For a moment I felt a wave of jealousy. Isaac was so fortunate to have a grandmother like Ruth. But who was I to covet his *mammi*? She was my friend. I could be thankful for that without being jealous.

"As for your grandmother," Ruth said, "there could have been something wrong biologically, and what she really needed was some good medical help. I can't say that for sure. No one in our community back then knew much about mental illness. And to be honest, even if they had, I don't believe there were many treatments and medications and such like there are now to help with that sort of thing. But regardless, Nettie was a special woman with a lot to offer. She wasn't perfect by any means, but she was just fine."

That was more information than I'd expected, but I did appreciate it. *Not perfect but fine.* That was a lesson I needed to learn and apply to myself—and others.

Isaac placed the teapot on the table along with the cups, and Ruth poured the tea. As I took mine, I was filled with gratitude to be here. "How wonderful for the two of you to have this time together."

Ruth nodded. "It's been such a delight getting to know Isaac better." She smiled at her grandson. "It worked out well that he needed a place to stay and that I had the room."

I turned toward Isaac. "Remind me again where you're from. Out near Pittsburgh, right?"

"Well, sort of. About eighty miles this side of Pittsburgh, in Somerset County."

"Oh, Somerset County. Isn't that where they have meeting houses instead of holding services in homes?"

He smiled. "*Ya,* that's right."

"And from there you went to college in Philadelphia?"

"*Ya*, in a roundabout way."

"So why didn't you go back to Somerset when you joined the church?"

"I did," he said. "In fact, it was there that I joined the church. And where I started my house painting business." He shrugged. "But it didn't work out as I'd hoped it would. Then a few months ago I went to Philadelphia, and on the way back stopped to visit my *mammi*. I was telling her about my troubles, and she's the one who suggested I move here." He patted her wrinkled hand. "It turned out to be a great idea."

Isaac seemed to be full of all sorts of surprises—though with each revelation he grew more mysterious, not less.

Four

When I arrived home from work the next day, Becky and Sadie were sitting at our kitchen table with *Mamm*. Sadie's eyes were rimmed with red, and *Mamm* held Bobby. Hattie and Hazel played with their paper dolls on the floor in the living room while Thomas was sprawled out across the couch, asleep.

A pot simmered on the back burner, and several loaves of bread were baking in the oven. *Mamm* motioned toward the stove and asked me to stir the stew.

It was a huge batch, filling up our biggest stockpot. It looked as if we were expecting a crowd. I breathed in the savory smell as I washed my hands.

"Where's Tabitha?" I stepped to the stove and stirred the simmering meat, potatoes, carrots, onions, and celery.

"With Stephen, over at Sadie's doing the milking," *Mamm* said.

"Why isn't Thomas helping them?"

Mamm dropped her voice. "Tabitha didn't want him to."

"Oh." She must've been tired of him after a full day of school—either that or she'd set her sights on Isaac and didn't want him to witness how gruff she could be with our little brother.

When Thomas was younger, he'd been so sweet and eager, always ready to jump in and help out with whatever was going on, like other boys his age. But in the past few years, that readiness had changed. These days, more often than not, he avoided work when he could, preferring to bury himself in a book or simply nap. It was almost as if he'd turned into an *Englisch* child, expecting everyone to serve him rather than the other way around.

For a while *Mamm* thought maybe he had a medical problem, that perhaps he was anemic or had some other disorder that was sapping his strength. But our doctor had given him a full workup and proclaimed him to be "a healthy, normal youngster who just happens to prefer mental exertion over physical."

The doctor may not have seen that as much of an issue, but in our culture, we placed a high value on physical exertion—regardless of preference. Thomas would need to change if he ever wanted to join the Amish church.

We went on with our lives after that, each of us reacting to the doctor's conclusion in a different way. *Mamm* mostly ignored Thomas's behavior, waiting for him to grow out of it. *Daed* got frustrated sometimes, though he never spoke sharply. Tabitha, on the other hand, found Thomas so irritating that she never stopped being sharp. She was always prodding him, especially once she'd become his teacher and saw that, despite what the doctor had said about mental exertion, Thomas wasn't exactly a go-getter in that department either. "He's just *lazy* all around," she would say, usually within his hearing. And, again, lazy was not something any Amish person could afford to be.

Some in our district agreed with Tabitha and even called him *ferdarva*. Spoiled. Maybe they were partly right—after a dozen proddings and scoldings and reminders, sometimes it was easier just to give up and do a thing yourself instead—but I didn't see it that way. His laziness didn't seem intentional to me. Watching him, I could tell it truly was an effort for him to get off the couch and go do a task. He went through periods where he'd rally and start acting more like the happy, helpful little boy we used to know, but eventually he'd fall back into these newer habits, and before long he was *that* Thomas again, the one who wanted nothing more than to be left alone.

"The girls told me you saw Isaac's paintings yesterday," Sadie said, interrupting my thoughts.

"*Ya.*" I turned back toward the table. "He's really good. And he actually sells his art in shops in Philadelphia—" I almost added, "And on the Internet," but stopped myself, not sure whether he'd shared that part with me in confidence or not.

"I doubt he will for long," *Mamm* said. "It sounds like his house painting business is picking up." For a moment I found myself hoping *Mamm* was right, but then that was followed by a twinge of guilt for even thinking such a thing. He was good at what he did, and he really enjoyed it. How would I feel if someone, Isaac in particular, wished I would stop quilting? I'd be hurt and doubted I'd even want to be his friend anymore.

"I heard they got a contract to paint the interiors of a new group of houses near Lancaster," Sadie said. "Big ones."

"They?" I put the lid back on the stew. "I thought he was a one-man operation."

"No," Sadie replied. "He has three workers."

"How do they get back and forth?"

"He hires a van at the beginning of the project to get all of the equipment there. Then he hires a car to take them back and forth each day. From what I've heard, he's building a lucrative business."

I sat down at the table. "He probably *will* stop doing his art, then."

"I doubt he makes much money from it anyway," Becky said. "He'll see that it's a waste of his efforts soon enough."

I nodded. Becky was being too critical, but it was true that artistic painting did seem more suitable for a Plain woman than a Plain man.

I looked to my mother, reminded of the question I'd been wanting to ask. "So, yesterday Ruth mentioned that *Mammi* Nettie used to paint."

Mamm nodded. "She did when she was younger. She'd given it up by the time I met her, though, like most responsible Plain folk do."

I nodded, thinking that if Isaac didn't stop painting soon, he would with time. It sure sounded as if *Mammi* Nettie had outgrown it.

"I remember one painting of *Mammi's* from when I was little," Sadie said. "It was of two girls, from the back, out in a field or something."

Mamm thought for a minute. "You're right. I forgot about that."

My eyes widened. "What happened to it?"

Mamm shrugged, but Sadie said, "Last time I saw it, it was stuffed away in the back of a closet."

"Here?"

"*Ya.* I don't remember which one, though."

"*Mamm?*"

"Sorry, Linda. I'm not sure. Ask Izzy when she arrives. She did some organizing for me before she left home."

I nodded, remembering. Part of Izzy's organizing had included clearing out the little sunroom so I could use it for my quilting.

"She and Zed are coming for supper," *Mamm* added.

I felt a rush of sadness when I realized this must be our farewell dinner. Izzy, Zed, and Becky were all going home tomorrow morning, and I would miss them.

As Becky and I set the table, I heard Tabitha and Stephen out on the mud porch, back from milking at Sadie's with Isaac. When they finished getting cleaned up and came inside, Tabitha saw me, and her eyes lit up.

"Linda," she said in a teasing voice, "Isaac asked about you."

"Ooooh," Becky and Sadie cooed in unison.

I could feel my face grow warm.

"He thought you'd be helping this morning."

"Why?" I muttered. "He knows I have a job in town."

"Not sure." Tabitha grinned. "Wishful thinking, I guess. He seemed disappointed until I cheered him up with stories from school."

I could only imagine what a good job she did entertaining Isaac. Thankfully, Izzy and Zed came through the door at that moment, so the subject was dropped. They were followed by Ezra, and from the look on Tabitha's face, it was clear she hadn't been expecting him to show up. I ducked my head to keep from laughing. Now she was the one who was blushing.

"Hey," Izzy said. "We kidnapped Ezra and brought him with us. Hope that's okay." She bent down and gave *Mamm* a hug. "I figured you probably had an extra bowl of stew."

"Of course." *Mamm* patted Izzy's hand. "*Wilkom,*" she said to Ezra. "We're happy to have you join us."

"Yes, we are. Aren't we, *Tabitha*?" I teased. Two could play at this game.

I thought she would smile, but instead her face grew an even brighter shade of red. Perhaps she only had eyes for Ezra—and not for Isaac too—after all.

Feeling guilty, I quickly changed the subject. "Hey, Izzy. I have a question for you. We were just talking about *Mammi* Nettie. About a painting she made of two girls? *Mamm* thought you might remember where you stashed it."

My sister had a confused look on her face.

"Before you moved out, you did some organizing for me," *Mamm* added. "You came across it."

"I remember a painting, but I didn't know it was *Mammi* Nettie's."

"Who did you think did it?" *Mamm* asked.

Izzy shrugged. "I never thought about it. But I can tell you what I did with it. It's in the closet in the sewing room, top shelf, in the box on the far right."

I started down the hall, but *Mamm* called out, "Wait until after supper, Linda. Go tell your *daed* it's time to eat. He's out in the shop."

My disappointment at being derailed was tempered by the news that *Daed* was here. "He didn't go to work?"

Mamm shook her head. "No, he took the day off."

Daed never took time off. It felt almost festive to have all of us together for supper at a decent hour. But this wasn't a celebration.

It was another gathering in the days after Robert's death.

I hurried out to get *Daed* from his workroom in the barn where he did carpentry. The scent of sawdust mixed with linseed oil met me as I stepped through the door. *Daed* didn't see or hear me at first. With a serious look on his face, he concentrated on sanding a table he'd recently made. As I watched, his expression went from serious to sad, and it became obvious that his mind was no longer on the piece of furniture in front of him. He, too, was grieving. Not only would he miss Robert for his own sake, but he had to be hurting for Sadie as well. She was still his little girl, even though she was grown. It must have pained him horribly to have her suffer such a loss.

After a minute he must have sensed my presence because he glanced my way.

"Time to eat," I said.

He cleared his throat and stood up straighter. "Are Sadie and the children here?"

"*Ya*. And Izzy and Zed and Ezra too."

"Sounds like a crowd." *Daed* put his sanding tool on his workbench. Then he grabbed a rag and rubbed down the top of the table. When he was finished, he met my gaze again. "How is Sadie doing?"

"All right," I answered. "Well, sad of course. It looked as if she'd been crying when I first got home."

Daed sighed heavily, and then we walked toward the house in silence.

Fourteen of us gathered around the table. In the old days, before Sadie married and then Becky and the three older boys left home, we often had that many to feed with the usual couple of extras around our table. But it wasn't the norm anymore and hadn't been for a good while.

After *Daed* led us in a silent prayer, *Mamm* dished up the stew and passed the bowls around the table. Just-baked bread, applesauce, and broccoli salad completed the meal. It was all very simple but delicious.

Daed asked Ezra how he liked being back in Lancaster County.

"It's *gut* to be back. I missed my family and friends here." He seemed self-conscious, which surprised me. He'd always been portrayed as such a rebel. I expected him to be talkative and...well, even cocky. But he seemed a little shy. He gave Tabitha a quick glance. She must have sensed his reticence as well because she smiled back at him encouragingly.

The conversation changed to Indiana, where Zed and Izzy now lived. Zed had gone to college out there and afterward came back to Pennsylvania to marry my sister and attend grad school, and then they'd returned to Indiana, where he was a professor at his alma mater.

"How does that region compare to Lancaster County?" Tabitha asked.

"There's not nearly as much tourism, at least not in our area," Izzy said. "There's some, but not the crowds of people we get here. And the communities aren't as wealthy."

Mamm laughed. "Wealthy? *Ya*, more like land rich but cash poor."

"True," Izzy said, "but the influx of tourists here puts more cash into the overall economy."

Mamm responded, "If one caters to the tourists."

"But it gets spread around. Like Linda's work at the fabric store. Tourism brings in more customers, which allows the owner to hire more people, which provides a job for Linda."

That was correct, even if it meant sometimes having to deal with the sorts of tourists who asked silly questions or wanted to be my pen pal.

Mamm conceded that Izzy was right. She often complained about how much worse the traffic had become in Lancaster County. Every year it seemed as if more and more tourists came. I didn't mind. I was thankful for my job at the Arts & Crafts House and hoped it would last the rest of my working life. It would be nice to have an Amish coworker or two, but at least I had Kristen, my first and only *Englischer* friend.

As our meal continued, the conversation jumped from topic to topic, though no one brought up Izzy's pregnancy or inquired when exactly the *boppli* was due. If I'd been alone with her, I might've asked, but it wasn't a proper discussion for the group as a whole.

When Bobby grew fussy, Tabitha stood, pulled him from his highchair, and walked him around the kitchen. I couldn't help but notice Ezra glancing her way a few times.

Thomas was even more quiet and subdued than usual, and I had a feeling part of that had to do with Becky's presence. Throughout our supper she seemed to be on the lookout for any aberration, giving Hattie a glare when she dropped her spoon and clicking her tongue at Stephen when a little gravy dribbled on his shirt.

Toward the end of the meal, Izzy brought up to *Daed* the topic of *Mammi* Nettie's painting. "We're going to look for it after we clean up," she said. "But what can you tell us about her artwork?"

Daed held a piece of bread in his hand, but he returned it to his plate. "She was talented, I know that, and I also got the idea that she sold her paintings, or at least she did when I was young. That helped with the family finances."

"What happened to all of her works?" I asked.

"Well, like I said, she sold most of them. Plus, there did come a point when she stopped painting all together."

"Maybe the one we have is the only one left," Sadie said.

Daed shrugged. "Maybe. She kept it a secret for a long time—although

I'm not sure exactly how. But gradually others figured out what she was doing and eventually she stopped."

"Did the bishop make her?" I asked.

Daed shrugged. "I don't know if it was the bishop or if she decided to stop on her own." *Daed* picked up the piece of bread again. "One thing I do know is that my father wouldn't have forced her to quit. He loved her work. Later in life, in fact, I overheard him several times suggesting she paint again. He seemed to think it might make her happy. But she never did, as far as I know."

For the first time in my life, I felt a pang of sadness for my grandmother. What a loss that I had never known her. Ruth's and Izzy's stories about her were interesting, but they hadn't caused me to feel empathy toward her the way *Daed*'s brief account had. It sounded as if she was a troubled woman—yet one who'd been dearly loved by her husband.

"My grandmother and great-grandmother were artists too." Zed glanced at Izzy, and she nodded in agreement. "Especially my great-grandmother Sarah. My sister did some research into her work a few years ago."

That was interesting to hear, but, again, we were talking about women. I still hadn't heard of an example of a Plain man painting.

"In our Mennonite community," Izzy said, "art is encouraged as a way of worshipping God."

We knew how Izzy's life had changed after marrying Zed. After all, he was a college professor. But Zed never acted as if he were smarter than the rest of us, and he always deferred to *Mamm* and *Daed* and their wisdom. The truth was, he and Izzy often did have insights into topics that we didn't. Izzy had the typical eighth-grade Amish education, but she'd continued her learning through travel, reading, and occasional classes with the school's adult education program. She also loved to do research, including with a computer. When she first joined the Mennonites, she didn't use one, at least not often, but gradually that had changed, and these days much of her information came from sources she found online.

"More traditional and utilitarian forms of art have always been accepted and encouraged in all Plain communities," Zed added. "Carpentry, quilting…"

At the very mention of the word, I felt a sudden strong urge to go do some quilting of my own, no doubt inspired by all this talk of art, not to mention thoughts of my grandmother's creative endeavors. I often found myself filled with the urge to *make* something, to work on a quilt, to hold a needle in my fingers and draw it through layers of fabric, my stiches tiny and even and perfect. Tourists were always asking me if quilting was a tedious process, and I never knew how to reply. *Ya*, on the one hand, it could be incredibly tedious, not to mention time consuming. On the other hand, it brought me such a deep sense of peace and relaxation and excitement and satisfaction all rolled into one. Usually, I just said, "*Ya*, it's tedious, but it's fun too," and left it at that. But fun didn't begin to describe the gratification I found in the very act of quilting.

My thoughts were interrupted by *Mamm*, who'd begun clearing the bowls and plates, and I jumped to my feet to help as Zed continued talking. After I'd picked up the last bowl, *Mamm* brought two cobblers, made from canned peaches we'd put up last August, to the table.

It seemed the meal would never end. The conversation tilted back to Ezra. *Daed* asked him about his favorite place he'd been while on his travels.

"Definitely Alaska," he said. "Not so much out in the oilfields, but when I had the chance to go exploring. On one of my days off, I went fishing on a charter boat."

"Did you catch anything?" Zed asked.

He nodded. "*Ya*, a fifty-pound halibut."

That caught Thomas's attention. "A fifty-pound fish?"

"*Ya*, and that's not that big for a halibut. The record is four hundred."

I couldn't imagine that, not at all. It would be the size of a half-grown calf.

Ezra went on to describe hiking in the summer months and the long, long days of sunlight. "Twenty-two hours," he said. "There's actually no night. It goes from twilight to dawn."

"No way!" Stephen said.

"Yep. And in the winter, it's the opposite. The sun never rises at all, from like mid-November to mid-January. It's dark all night *and* all day."

"I bet you don't miss that," *Daed* said.

Ezra laughed. "You're right. I sure don't."

"But otherwise do you miss it?" Tabitha asked. "Alaska, I mean."

"No." Ezra smiled at her. "I saw it. Lived it. I don't need to ever go there again. There's no place I'd rather be than Lancaster County."

Tabitha smiled back. I took the last bite of my cobbler, wishing everyone would finish quickly so *Daed* could lead us in a closing prayer, and then I could search for the painting.

The conversation dragged on. Ezra gave a few details about Wyoming, such as how it took acres and acres and acres there to raise beef.

I yawned.

"It's the least populous state in the nation," Ezra said. "The ranches are hundreds of acres, and the mountains are absolutely beautiful."

I yawned again. Tabitha told him they'd been studying the states at school.

"Those were my favorite lessons when I was a scholar." Ezra's eyes shone.

I started to yawn a third time, but a knock on the back door caught my attention. Stephen hurried to answer it, revealing Isaac with his hat in his hand.

"*Gut'n owed*," he said. "I'm looking for Sadie. She has a heifer in labor who's struggling."

Sadie stood. "Come on in, Isaac."

Daed asked Isaac if he'd eaten.

He shook his head. "I wanted to check with Sadie before I called the vet."

Daed stood too. "You get some supper. I'll go take a look." He motioned to Stephen. "Why don't you come with me?"

"I'll come too," Ezra said.

Izzy elbowed Zed, who cleared his throat and said, "Me as well."

Tabitha looked as if she wanted to tag along, but that would be pretty obvious, even for her.

As the men left, *Mamm* dished up some stew for Isaac and then began clearing the dessert dishes with Becky's help. Sadie took Bobby into the bathroom to clean him up, and Hattie and Hazel drifted back toward the living room to play.

Tabitha, Izzy, and I stayed at the table with Isaac, even though I was itching to head down the hall to the sewing room. Thankfully, he ate quickly, and *Mamm* put a bowl of cobbler in front of him as soon as she picked up his stew bowl.

"Delicious," he said after he'd finished it too.

Izzy must have been as anxious as I was to find the painting because she told Isaac all about it as he ate.

He took the last bite of cobbler and then said, "What are we waiting for?"

"The closing prayer," *Mamm* replied. She bowed her head, and we all prayed silently with her.

After she finished, I piped in with, "*Now* what are we waiting for?"

Mamm nodded toward the sink. "Helping with the dishes." Then she grinned. "Tabitha and Becky and I can do them. Izzy, you and Linda and Isaac go along."

Izzy grabbed my hand and pulled. "Come on."

I glanced back at Isaac, and he smiled and followed us down the hall.

I kept the sewing room neat and tidy, probably even more so than Izzy had back when it was hers. I liked things in order. Some might say I was obsessive about it, but I didn't apologize for that. To be fully productive, I had to have my workspace just so. It was my domain, after all—well, except for the boxes Izzy had stored in the closet, which I had ignored entirely until now.

Izzy went straight for the door on the far right. "Like I said, I think it's in here."

"I'll get it." Isaac stepped forward and wrestled the box off the shelf and out of the closet.

He put it down, and we began pulling things out of it. Several old recipe books. A couple of woodworking books. An old book about painting. I handed them to Isaac and kept rummaging. At the very bottom was a thin wooden box, about one foot long by one foot wide by four inches high. I pulled it out.

"The painting is in there," Izzy said. "*Daed* made that box to protect it. It's kind of like a wooden envelope."

She was right—an envelope with one end missing. I tipped the box and a painting slipped out, canvas stretched over a wooden frame.

"It's done in oils." Isaac held up the painting.

As Sadie and *Mamm* had described, the image was of two Amish girls walking toward a sunset. They wore black bonnets and brown homespun dresses. One of the girls, her head held high, was a step ahead of the other, whose posture was a bit slouched.

Off to one side was a field of bright-orange pumpkins and cornstalks, bordered by a rustic rail fence. On the other side, laundry flapped on a clothesline, all vivid colors of burgundy and emerald green and sapphire blue against a darkening sky, in contrast to the girls' plain dresses. In the far background was a white barn. A flock of geese flew overhead.

But the sunset was the most striking element. Oranges, reds, and pinks all blended together in an abstract swirl of light. The most vivid of the reds swooped down into the horizon and became the path upon which the girls were walking. Between that and the shadows the girls cast, the painting seemed foreboding somehow and a bit forlorn, despite its beauty.

Its "look" was absolutely original. The local Amish women I knew who painted as part of their craftmaking all had a primitive style, so that's what I'd been expecting here. But this wasn't like that at all. It was as good as a photograph, but even better because the colors popped and the forms of the girls showed even more emotion than a photograph could.

"What kind of training did your grandmother have?" Isaac asked.

"None," Izzy said.

I added, "That we know of." I'd been surprised by Isaac going to art school. Perhaps *Mammi* Nettie had too.

Izzy chuckled at me. "Oh, come on. When did she grow up? The thirties? Do you think any Amish family would have sent their daughter off to art school back then? Even if they could have afforded it, which hers definitely could not."

Isaac rubbed his hand through his hair. "*Ya*, that seems highly unlikely. She must have had individual lessons."

That was nearly as difficult to imagine. Izzy was right. Who would have had money for any kind of art lessons during the Depression? We eyed him skeptically.

"Both her execution and interpretation are highly developed," Isaac explained. "That's unusual for someone with no training." He shrugged.

"But probably not impossible, especially given that she seems to have a real gift with composition. Are there more?"

Izzy and I both said no at the same time. "At least not any more that we have," I explained. "*Daed* seems to think most were sold, so there's a chance they might still exist, but we have no idea where they would be."

"Interesting." He returned his attention to the art book. "I supposed she could've been self-taught with the help of some good resources."

I placed the painting on my sewing table, setting it up so we could keep looking at it.

Isaac opened the book and leafed through it. "This one isn't bad. It's probably a typical art book for that time period. The copyright says 1935." He turned to the front.

"Who's Natasha?" he asked.

"What?"

"The book was a gift from a Natasha to Nettie."

Izzy and I leaned forward and Isaac held the page up. Sure enough, the writing read: *To Nettie, With love, Natasha.*

"Nettie was our grandmother," I said.

"But I have no idea who Natasha was," Izzy added.

"Maybe Nettie and Natasha are the two girls in the painting," Isaac offered.

"I doubt it." I took the book from him. "The girls in the painting are Amish, but Natasha is definitely *not* an Amish name."

FIVE

We brought the painting out to the kitchen to show everyone, but Sadie and Becky had already taken the kids home, and *Mamm* and Tabitha didn't seem all that interested.

Isaac left after that, and I returned to my sewing room, finally able to indulge the creative urge I'd been feeling all evening. About an hour later, I was carefully piecing together Tabitha's quilt when she poked her head into the room to say everyone was back from Sadie's except *Daed*, who'd wanted to stick with the heifer and the new calf until he was certain they were both out of the woods. "Anyway," Tabitha added, "I'm going to take Ezra home so Izzy and Zed don't have to."

"How thoughtful of you."

She ignored my sarcasm. "I'll try not to wake you when I get back. Oh, and they're about to leave too."

I rose, saddened at the news, and followed her down the hall. Izzy and Zed would be heading home to Indiana tomorrow morning, so this was our goodbye. Out in the kitchen, as I hugged my sister tightly, I tried not to think about how much I would miss her.

"Keep me posted on the *boppli*," I whispered, giving her stomach a gentle pat as we pulled apart. She nodded in return, flashing me a shy but excited smile. Turning to Zed, I hugged him as well. After a round of goodbyes from everyone else, they were gone.

Back in my sewing room, time flew, and I was still piecing by lamp light when Tabitha got home two hours later.

She appeared in my doorway, surprised I wasn't in bed already.

"I got a little distracted." I turned toward her, catching the sparkle in her eyes. "How was your evening?"

"Great!" She grinned and pivoted around into the room, lifting her other foot as she pivoted out again. I thought she might elaborate, but instead she simply told me not to work too late and then headed for the stairs.

With a sigh, I picked up the section of the quilt topper I'd pieced together. Once again, Tabitha had already moved on to the next guy. I folded the fabric in my hands. She didn't deserve a quilt. The truth was, she didn't need comfort. Mark Wittmer was already a distant memory.

As for her infatuation with Ezra, who knew how long that would last? She could easily still change her mind. As far as I knew, even Isaac wasn't out of her sights just yet.

I held the quilt I'd started to my chest, wondering what do with it. I would figure out something eventually, but for now I stashed it and the remaining squares I'd already cut in a plastic storage box, which I slid into the closet. As I picked up the lamp to light my way to bed, I wondered how Tabitha could be so fickle. Would I ever understand my sister?

The next morning, I stopped at Sadie's to tell Becky goodbye. Izzy and Zed would be picking her up soon for their long drive west, but not until after I had to be at work.

Daed had left home before I was up, so I didn't see him until evening. He was extra late, so we'd gone ahead and eaten without him. Once he was finally home and at the table, I brought him the painting, and he studied it as he ate his supper.

"*Ya*," he said. "That's the one I remember. I made that box for it to keep it safe."

"That's what Izzy told us."

He took his last bite of chicken as *Mamm* dished him up some blueberry pie.

I held out the book. "Someone named Natasha gave this to your *mamm*, to Nettie."

"Really? I remember seeing it before, but I guess I never thought to open it." *Daed* said he had no idea who Natasha was either. He pushed his plate forward a little, and *Mamm* swooped in with the dessert.

"I wonder if any of my older cousins would know." *Daed* sighed. "My *mamm* came from a really big family. They mostly live in the northern part of Lancaster County."

Typically, Amish families were huge. Izzy and Zed had traced *Mamm*'s side all the way back to the 1700s, before the Revolutionary War. So at least we felt that we knew about them. But *Daed* had been an only child, so we didn't have any aunts and uncles or cousins on his side at all. And I'd never heard of cousins on his mother's extended side of the family or seen any sort of genealogy records.

"Why don't I know about any of these relatives?" I asked.

He shrugged. "It's not like it's a secret. *Mamm* was the youngest and didn't have much of a relationship with any of her siblings. But believe me, there are lots of cousins. More than a hundred and twenty at one time. Of course many are dead now—the oldest would probably be at least a century by this point."

I shook my head in disbelief. "Are you sure? I never heard this before."

He nodded. "I'm certain of it. Some of my *mamm*'s oldest nieces and nephews were close to her age and probably even older than she was."

"I'm not questioning their ages." I crossed my arms. Overlapping generations were quite common in Amish families. "I just had no idea you had so many first cousins. Do you know any of their names?"

"We have a directory around here somewhere." Plain folk were into genealogy and frequently put together directories of thousands of family members, but I'd had no idea there was one in the house for *Daed*'s family. "Bender was her last name. Look in the bookshelf in the living room. You'll find it there."

"After we clean," *Mamm* said.

Tabitha had helped with the milking again over at Sadie's and then stayed to feed the kids, so it was my turn to do the housework at home. That was fair. Tomorrow we'd switch jobs.

After we finished, *Mamm* asked me to make sure Thomas brushed his teeth and was on his way to bed. I walked with him up the stairs to the bathroom all of us kids shared. He stepped inside and closed the door. I could hear water running but had no idea if he was brushing his teeth or not.

I didn't remember Stephen as an infant, but I remembered Thomas. I'd been absolutely in love with him. I was eight when he was born, and I'd held him as much as I could. I'd changed him and rocked him and was the best helper I could be to *Mamm*. She claimed he was her easiest baby of all, though whether that had to do with his sweet temperament or the fact that she had plenty of others around to share the load, I wasn't sure.

He turned off the water.

"Did you brush your teeth?" I called through the door.

He didn't answer but instead simply opened it and started down the hall. I checked his toothbrush. It was dry.

"Get back in there," I scolded, following him into the room he shared with Stephen.

With a heavy sigh he turned toward me. "What does it matter?" he said softly, almost more to himself than to me.

For a moment I felt like Tabitha, irritation surging within my chest. But then I met his eyes and saw such apathy and exhaustion there that the feeling immediately passed. Something was wrong with my little brother, no matter what the doctors said.

I reached out and tousled his hair, my heart swelling with fondness for this mess of a boy who couldn't seem to care about much of anything sometimes.

"What does it matter?" I replied lightly. "Well, let's see. For starters, if you don't brush your teeth, by the time you reach courting age, the girls will all be calling you 'Toothless Thomas.' Do you really want to be that guy? Old and toothless and alone?"

He cracked a small smile despite himself. Then with a sigh he headed back up the hall to the bathroom and brushed his teeth.

Back downstairs once Thomas was in bed, I found the Bender family directory between our volume of the *Martyrs Mirror* and an *Ausbund* hymnal.

It was thicker than I'd expected. I opened it to the first page and saw that it had been compiled in 1979—*Daed* would have been twenty-one then—by a woman named Ina Mae Bender.

I leafed through it until I found Nettie Bender Mueller. My grandmother. She was listed as marrying Joshua Mueller in 1940 and having one son, Eli, born in 1957. That was *Daed*. I didn't realize his parents had been married for seventeen years before he was born. I knew they'd wanted more than one child, but for some reason I'd always assumed *Daed* was born and then no others came after. Instead, it looked as if they'd gone through seventeen years of childlessness first and then their prayers had been answered with the birth of my father. How shocked—and thrilled—they must have been after wanting a baby for so very long. Just like Elizabeth and Zechariah in the Bible.

I worked my way backward. Nettie's parents were Mary and Albert Bender. And, *ya*, she was the youngest of thirteen children. I looked for her birth date, but one wasn't listed. That seemed odd until I looked up her siblings and saw that a few of them were also missing birth dates beside their names.

I found Ina Mae Bender's name and information. She would be eighty-eight now. Perhaps she was no longer living. Or if she was, her memory might not be intact. But I was curious about my grandmother and why she wouldn't have a birth date included in her own family's directory.

There was an address and a phone number beside Ina Mae's name, and I decided to give it a try the next day. It wasn't that I expected Ina Mae to still be alive—but it wouldn't hurt to call the number just in case.

Stephen and I arrived at Sadie's before Isaac the next morning. We parked our scooters, stripped off our orange safety vests, and hung them on coat pegs just inside the barn. While Stephen saw to the vat in the milk room, I stepped into the phone room.

I took a deep breath, worked up my courage, and then dialed the number I'd gotten from the directory. It rang seven times and went to an answering machine. "Hello, this is Ina Mae," a woman's voice said. "Leave a message, and I'll call you back."

Grinning to myself, I relayed my name and how I was related to her, and then I said I was looking for someone who remembered my grandmother, Nettie Bender Mueller. I left my number and asked if she would call me back.

A knock fell on the door as I hung up. I opened it to find Isaac.

"I thought I heard someone in there." He smiled down at me.

"*Ya*," I answered. "I'm trying to locate one of my *daed*'s first cousins who might remember my grandmother."

His eyes lit up. "Good for you. You've got to be so curious about the stuff we saw."

I nodded. "I am. I want more information about her—for example, I'd love to know why she chose painting rather than quilting."

The black cat I'd seen before came around the corner of the stalls. This time he rubbed against Isaac's leg and then mine. I reached down, and he let me pet him for just a second, but then he darted off again.

"He's like a whisper," Isaac said.

"Whisper." I liked the way the word slipped between my lips. "That's a good name for a cat."

As we put on our vinyl aprons, he said, "Tell me more about the quilt you want to make using this barn as inspiration."

I pointed to the ceiling. All the things that made me love the barn were to its detriment. The light wafting through the roof was where the shingles needed to be repaired, and the swallows who'd nested in the rafters were contributing to the wear and tear too.

"I love how the light comes down onto the hay bales and the cows during the milking."

"You'd do a patchwork quilt of it?"

"*Ya*," I answered. I had given it some thought, but I couldn't imagine making an appliqué quilt of the barn. Such an undertaking would be far too complex and...unpredictable. Too many things could go wrong. Patches would work best, though I had to admit they couldn't do justice to the structure.

"So lots of brown squares?"

I laughed out of nervousness but then answered, "Exactly. Different shades of brown, though." I hoped I sounded as if I had a plan. "Maybe some blue for the sky. A little yellow for the sunbeams." It didn't sound very creative. I'd have to do some more brainstorming.

Stephen came out of the milk room, and we all got started on our chores. As we worked I asked Isaac what his idea was as far as painting the barn.

"I'd do it on canvas and probably take an abstract approach."

We grew quiet after that. A few minutes later, I asked him how work had gone that day, and he said well.

"Do you get all of your hours in if you do the milking in the mornings *and* the afternoons?"

"*Ya*," he said, but he didn't sound all that convincing.

I wondered if trying to handle both milkings was making his days too difficult.

We were about halfway done when a strange voice reverberated through the barn, calling Sadie's name.

I stepped out from by the troughs. It was Jedediah King. "She's in the house," I told him.

"Oh, I was hoping she'd be out here." He hooked his thumbs through his suspenders.

I shook my head. "Stephen and Isaac and I have been doing the milking. Well, Tabitha too. She and I are taking turns."

"Do you have a schedule set up?"

I nodded. "The small size of the herd really helps."

"Still, it's a lot of work. Could you use another pair of hands?"

"Actually," I said, "if someone else could help with the afternoon milking, Isaac could work later in the day."

"I can do that," Jedediah said just as Isaac approached.

The two shook hands, and then we talked things through. In the end we decided that Tabitha, Stephen, and I would take turns in the mornings with Isaac, and then Stephen would help in the afternoons with Jedediah.

Later, as I left for the day, I stopped by the corral and turned on the water in the trough for the horses. Almost immediately, the black cat jumped up on the metal rim and walked around it as if he were on a balance beam. "Whisper..." I said the name quietly.

He turned and blinked his beautiful green eyes at me but kept going around the trough, all the way to the faucet. There he leaned out and started lapping at the stream of running water. He was so intent on what he was doing that he didn't even seem to realize that the two horses were trotting toward us. When they reached the trough, one of them nickered loudly, at which point the cat finally took notice. He jumped down and slipped back into the barn. After watching him go, I looked up at the structure as the morning sun spread across the roof. Maybe I'd add a green-eyed cat to my quilt.

When I reached home, I washed up and then went and found Tabitha, who was in the bedroom she and I shared. I explained to her the new milking schedule.

"That sounds great," she said. "I'll take tomorrow morning since you helped today. Just remember, though, I'm done with school in two weeks. After that I'll probably go to Indiana for a while, to help Izzy with her baby."

"What?" I blurted. Why did Tabitha get to have all the fun?

"I'll only stay a few weeks," she said. "Don't be jealous."

My face must have shown how hurt I felt.

"She said she wanted one of us to come." Tabitha crossed her arms. "But you have a job during the summer, and I don't. We all figured it would only work for me."

We could mean all sorts of combinations of people. Tabitha and Izzy. *Mamm* and Tabitha. Sadie and Tabitha. All of them. What *we* didn't mean was *me*.

I tried not to stomp as I left the room, but I'm not sure how successful I was. The truth was I wouldn't want to give up my position at the shop, even if it did mean going to Indiana. It was the best I'd ever had. And I couldn't take a month off work and expect to have a job when I got back, especially not with tourist season starting. But I still should have been involved in the decision.

Two mornings later, when it was my turn to help with the milking, I noticed a message on Sadie's machine. It was left the day before. I pushed the button and heard a shaky old person's voice say she was calling for Linda. I turned up the volume.

"This is Ina Mae Bender," the woman said. She sounded much older than the voice on her message machine, but at least she was still alive and functioning. "I don't know if I can help you much, but I do remember your grandmother, and I'd be happy to try and answer any questions you have. Why don't you come for a visit so we can talk in person?" She left her address and said mornings were best for her, any time after eight.

The nice thing about calling a Plain woman was knowing her phone wasn't in her house and I could leave a message instead of speaking directly to her, considering how much I hated talking with anyone over the phone. I dialed her back, waited for the beep of her machine, then spoke, thanking her for responding and telling her that Friday was my day off this week. "I'll plan to come around ten if that's all right with you," I said. "Call me if it's not." I'd have to hire a driver to take me to the north part of the county.

I hung up the phone and stepped out of the little office. As I traded my safety vest for a vinyl apron, I heard whistling and then Isaac stepped into the barn.

"*Guder mariye.*" He beamed at me.

Ya, every morning was good when Isaac was around. Did he flash that particular smile at everyone or just at me?

Later that day, during my break at work, I told Kristen about my plans to make a quilt with a barn-inspired pattern. Ever since my conversation with Isaac, my mind had been playing with the idea, shapes, and colors, forming the image I wanted to quilt. Now that I was ready to begin, I could describe it to her without lessening my own creative anticipation.

"Have you thought of doing an artistic appliqué?" she asked.

I shook my head. "No, I'll make a traditional quilt with smaller patches—both squares and triangles." That would help with the sky and the light coming through the barn.

"Want to look at some examples online?" Kristen stepped toward the computer.

I thanked her and joined her there. I didn't go on the Internet unless I absolutely had to—sometimes to order fabric or to find a certain pattern a customer was looking for. It wasn't as if the bishop would be upset or anything. It was part of my job. I was expected to do it well even if that included computer time.

But I still didn't feel comfortable using it.

Kristen hopped around various quilting sites. I didn't see anything that struck my fancy. Then she skipped over to Pinterest, a site I'd become familiar with in the course of my job. We viewed several different pages. On the last one was what looked like a quilt square, but it had been created with wood, not fabric. It was called "rustic wall art" and was literally made out of rough-hewn boards cut like quilt pieces. It made me think of Isaac. It looked like something he might create.

I pointed toward the screen. "I really like that."

"I'll bookmark the page so you can find it again later."

"Thanks. As long as we're online..."

"What do you want me to look up?"

I felt heat creep into my cheeks. "Isaac has a website." I spoke as casually as I could.

"The Amish man who was in here a few days ago?"

I nodded. "For his artwork."

"Cool." Kristen jumped back to Google. "What's the address?"

"I'm not sure. His last name is Mast, though."

"Isaac Mast." She typed the letters in and hit the "search" button. A couple of options popped up, but none looked promising.

"Try adding 'art,'" I said.

She did and hit "search" again. Immediately a site appeared and Kristen clicked on it.

There wasn't a photograph of Isaac, but the paintings were absolutely his. An image of the sunflowers was posted, and one of the bird. There were other paintings I hadn't seen, including the back of a woman sitting on a hay bale. A woman who wasn't dressed Amish.

I couldn't help but be reminded that Isaac had lived in the *Englisch* world. It hadn't dawned on me that he might have had a girlfriend during that time. I couldn't imagine. True, Isaac was no Ezra Gundy, but perhaps he wasn't as innocent as I'd thought.

"Wow," Kristen said. "He's really good."

"*Ya*," I answered. "Isn't he? And the paintings are even more beautiful in person." I told her that he sold his artwork in a couple of shops in Philadelphia too, which led to me explaining that he'd been to art school, to college in fact.

"Fascinating." Kristen enlarged the photo of the sunflowers. "I didn't think Amish kids went to college."

"He hadn't joined the church yet," I explained. "So he was able to."

I could have done with a little more of a boring story when it came to Isaac, but the important thing was that he'd come back to the Amish in the end. I chastised myself. Why was I so easy on Isaac when I'd been so critical of Ezra? Was it because I wanted to somehow justify Isaac's behavior—whatever it might have been?

Kristen continued from page to page on Isaac's site, landing on the "about" page last. A brief biography stated Isaac had grown up in Somerset County, Pennsylvania, attended art school in Philadelphia, and was now residing in the Lancaster County area, where he was a member of an Old Order community.

"I wonder who runs his website." Kristen continued to scroll down the page.

"He said a friend does."

"I assume it's a non-Amish friend," she teased, "considering how comfortable *you* are with the Internet."

I laughed, but the truth was Isaac probably had it all figured out—he'd only committed to abstaining since he joined the church. It was one thing to use the Internet at work the way I did sometimes. It was another to run a business that was almost entirely based on a website and not an actual store.

"Can you buy his art on the site?" I asked, wincing in anticipation. "Or is it more of a showcase for his work?"

"Let's see... Yep, he has a shopping cart. You can buy any of these, or you can commission him to paint a specific scene. Like send him a photograph or something, and he'll take it from there."

"That's cool."

"We should start a quilting business like that." Kristen pointed toward the screen. "Take custom orders online. Baby quilts. Wedding quilts. Graduation quilts."

I wrinkled my nose. I knew how long a good quilt could take to make, and it was hard to charge enough for the time to be worth it. That was why Amish quilts were so expensive—and why, for me, quilting for loved ones was so much more rewarding. *Ya*, I quilted for money too—my quilts sold through several different shops in the area, and now at the Arts & Crafts House too—but my heart was never in those the way it was for the ones I quilted for family.

Three customers stepped into the shop, and we went back to work. A little later I thought about Isaac's website as I cut fabric for a middle-aged *Englisch* woman with spiked hair. She was sewing a quilt for herself. "I've made quilts for everyone else," she said. "My sisters. My kids. My grand-kids. I decided it's time that I make one to keep." She was planning to use a Log Cabin pattern with browns and blues and yellows.

"It's my favorite pattern," she said. "I've loved it since I was a little girl and first saw one at the county fair."

"It's going to be beautiful," I answered. "The colors you chose are perfect."

"My grandparents had a cabin." She put her hand on the counter. "Up in the Poconos. We'd go up there in the summer. The brown is for their place, the yellow is for the sun coming through the trees, and the blue is for the sky."

I smiled at her. "That sounds really beautiful." It made me think of my idea to add golden light to my quilt that would represent both the sun-beams and dust beams.

Later, when my shift ended, I mapped out the idea for my quilt of the barn on graph paper. I used browns, from light to chocolate, and yellows and golds and blues. And a black cat at the bottom. Ordinarily, this part of the process could take a while, but I was so excited that I managed to hammer out the entire plan in record time.

Once I was done with the sketch, I began collecting the bolts of fab-ric. Kristen cut what I needed while I chose the thread.

"This is going to be really cool." Kristen slipped it all into a bag for me.

I went straight home after work, shut myself away in my sewing room, and got started. The beginning of a quilting project was so important that ordinarily I wouldn't dive into one this complex in the evening when I was tired from a long day on the job. But this time I just couldn't wait. Tired or not, the excitement of what I yearned to create compelled me to action.

I carefully measured and then cut out the squares and triangles. Except for a break for dinner and dishes, I stuck with it, working late into the night, imagining how perfectly the pieces would all fit together. That was what I loved about quilting. Everything fit. The result would be just what I'd planned for. If I measured, cut, and sewed just right, there would be no surprises.

And the completed product would be a lasting reminder of Robert's beautiful barn. This was definitely a quilt I wouldn't be selling.

All of us continued to do what we could to support Sadie. Other than at milking time and at church, I didn't see Isaac at all. A couple of times Tabitha went out in the evenings without saying what her plans were. I guessed she was courting Ezra, but she played dumb when I asked where she'd been, just saying, "Out with a friend."

The truth was, for as much as I believed I'd never court or marry anyone, I found Isaac appealing, and I was relieved that Tabitha seemed taken with Ezra instead. I felt comfortable around Isaac in a way I never had with anyone else. I wasn't my usual awkward self. And I enjoyed talking about art with him. Oddly, even though I doubted he'd ever truly be interested in me, I thought he might be. By the way he looked at me. By the questions he asked about my quilting. By his kindness. Over and over, I had to remind myself that he was kind to everyone, though. I had no proof I was special to him in any way.

The night before school was out for the summer, Tabitha came in extra late. It was a Thursday evening, and the May weather had turned warm and dry.

"Where've you been?" I asked.

"Over at Sadie's." She changed into her nightgown. "You're going to have to do the milking every morning starting next week because it's definite. I really am going to Indiana to help Izzy. I'm leaving on Monday and staying for a month or so."

"Oh." I battled a wave of jealousy even though I'd known she'd most likely be going.

Tabitha crawled into bed, and within moments her breathing changed—she was already asleep. I chided myself. I couldn't be the one to go to Indiana, so why was I jealous that she could? I should be grateful Izzy would have the help.

I knew that. But still I felt overlooked. Discounted. My entire childhood, my sisters had made decisions for me without consulting me. I was the youngest girl. The baby for four years until Stephen came along. I don't think they intended to keep secrets, but they did. And I don't think they realized what little control I had when they made decisions for me.

Perhaps that lack of control was one reason I liked quilting so much. I could choose the pattern, fabric, and thread. My quilt, my choices.

But was it wrong to need that much control?

I stared at the ceiling. I had to admit, it wouldn't hurt for me to lighten up at least a little bit. I knew I took everything and everyone too seriously. Including Tabitha. And myself. And, I feared, Isaac's feelings toward me. Sure, he smiled at me and asked me questions and talked and laughed, but I had no indication that he cared for me more than he did for anyone else.

An odd sort of emptiness clenched at me from somewhere deep within. Shifting onto my side, I bent my knees, arms clasped at my stomach. I felt almost...lonely. With such a big family and a close-knit community, that wasn't a familiar emotion for me. Then again, this seemed like a particular kind of loneliness, a longing for more than just family and friends. It wasn't even necessarily about Isaac. It was bigger than that. It was about me and my expectations of going through life as a single woman, alone. I'd always said I would never marry, but was that truly what I wanted? Or was that a lie I told myself because deep inside I knew that no one would ever want to marry me?

I sat up, my heart pounding. For the first time in my life, it was as if I could see my whole future opening up before me, the future God had in mind and not the one I'd cut and stitched for myself. In His version, I wasn't alone. I was with a helpmate. A soulmate. A partner.

A husband.

And whether that husband ended up being Isaac or someone else, I realized I *did* want to be married. Suddenly I wanted it more than I'd ever wanted anything in my life. Overwhelmed by a piercing need, it was as if years of yearning that had been tamped down out of sight were finally being set free. Swallowing back a sob, I slipped from the bed, got to my knees, closed my eyes, and brought all of it to the Lord. The pain. The loneliness. The insecurity. The self-deception. The lack of trust. I prayed for an hour, maybe more. He took it all, in His wide-open arms and nail-scarred hands, leaving me, in the end, unburdened, comforted, and at peace.

I ended my prayer and got back in bed. I knew I wouldn't change overnight. And I knew that by admitting to myself that I wanted a marriage, I was setting myself up for potential heartbreak. But at least I knew now what I truly wanted. Most important of all, I knew what God wanted for me.

Six

The next morning I yawned several times while helping with the milking. Isaac must have been tired too because he didn't say much. Stephen, on the other hand, chattered away about the singing he planned to go to on Sunday. At fifteen, he'd recently started participating in youth activities, which he loved.

I remembered that phase as well, how I felt so very grown up when I was allowed to join in with these fun events that my older sisters had been enjoying for years. The first few singings I attended, I just looked around in awe, amazed at how the group was made up primarily of other teenagers, with just a few adults hovering in the background. Something about that felt so dangerous and exciting and new, at least for a while. Over time, it had grown safe and boring and old.

"How about you?" Isaac asked. "Will you go?"

I shrugged. "I doubt it." I'd stopped attending the singings after the thrill had worn off. Tabitha thought it was foolish of me not to go—she still went and she was older than I was—but I had no interest. There was no one who attended that I wanted to marry, and I felt uncomfortable hanging around as if I expected one of the boys I'd known my entire life to suddenly transform into my ideal mate or for someone new to show up.

"How about you?" I asked Isaac. "Will you go?"

He smiled wryly. "No," he said. "I think I'm too old for all of that."

"No," I said. "You aren't. Tabitha goes."

"I think I'm a bit older than Tabitha."

I shook my head. "How about Ezra? Do you think he'll go?"

Isaac was quiet for a moment. "Are you asking for your own sake? Or Tabitha's?"

I felt my cheeks burn. "Neither," I muttered. "I'm just making conversation."

The air grew odd between us, and it struck me that my question had rubbed Isaac the wrong way. Was it possible he was jealous? That Isaac didn't want me wondering about Ezra because he was interested in me for himself?

I let out a breath. No, that was silly. Maybe he didn't want *Tabitha* interested in Ezra, which was why he'd asked. Not knowing how to ease the awkwardness of the moment, I dropped the subject and turned my attention back to the milking.

Later that morning the driver I'd hired picked me up to take me to Ina Mae Bender's in the northern part of the county. It was a forty-five-mile ride to the hamlet of Hopeland.

Ginny Richards was a middle-aged woman who regularly "hauled Amish," which was what *Englischers* called transporting us for pay. She was my favorite driver, one of several my family used when we needed rides to the doctor, to a store far from home, or for some other kind of errand or trip where going by buggy wasn't feasible. We'd hired a van to visit Becky and her family in Ohio a few years ago. So far, we hadn't had to do the same for Izzy because she and Zed visited us regularly. And Tabitha would be taking the bus when she went out in a few days because that was the cheaper option with only one person going.

As we traveled I kept my gaze on the landscape whizzing past. Farmers, both *Englisch* and Amish, worked on their land. A Plain man dragged his field with a team of mules. An *Englisch* fellow drove his tractor along the side of the highway. A herd of Holstein cows grazed in a green pasture.

An Amish farmer drove a mower, pulled by workhorses, between his field and the road.

As we approached the city of Lancaster, the farmland gave way to old brick houses with large, expansive yards. Then those homes gave way to brownstones, crowded together, one after the other. We slowly passed through the heart of the city and then turned onto a highway and were soon zipping through farmland again. Perhaps helping with the milking so early was getting the best of me because I dozed after that and didn't awake until Ginny turned onto an unpaved lane.

I rubbed the side of my face that had been pressed against the window. "Are we here already?"

Ginny chuckled. "You've been out like a light. And, yep, we're here, or nearly."

It was a bit of a ways up the lane, but eventually we reached a big white house. Ina Mae had said that she lived in the *daadi haus*, which came into view as the lane curved.

"How long do you want to stay?" Ginny asked.

"Two hours?" I wondered if that might be more than I'd actually need. But if Ina Mae turned out to be talkative, I'd hate to have to leave in the middle of a really good story or ask the driver to wait.

Ginny stopped as close to the *daadi haus* as she could get, next to a garden that was brimming with young plants—what looked like lettuce, spinach, chard, tomatoes, corn, beets, potatoes, peppers, cucumbers. Really, everything imaginable. Someone was industrious, but I doubted it was Ina Mae. I couldn't imagine anyone at age eighty-eight keeping up with the cultivating, watering, and weeding such a big garden would require.

"Thank you," I said to Ginny as I grabbed my bag and climbed out of the car. "See you soon."

"No problem. I'm going to zip back down to Lititz and do some shopping." Ginny waved and off she drove, back toward the road.

I paused for a moment and took in the setting of the farm. The main house was old and huge. It had definitely been added onto over the years, which was pretty common with older Amish farmhouses. A play structure with a slide and swings was on the other side of the garden, and clothes of all sizes—from a man's big shirt to a baby's T-shirt—were pinned to the line that angled up to the pulley system connected to the house. Woods bordered the far side of the lawn, where the leaves of spring intermingled in all colors of green, from emerald to chartreuse.

I stepped onto the porch of the *daadi haus* and knocked. Then I knocked again.

"Come in!" a shaky voice called out.

I tried the knob, which was unlocked, and eased the door open to reveal a woman using a walker heading toward me. Her hair was snow white and thin from what I could see, though most of it was covered by her *kapp*. She was tiny—both in height and weight—as if she were wasting away.

"Ina Mae?"

The woman smiled. "You must be Linda."

"*Ya.*"

"Come on in." She let go of the walker with one hand and gestured toward the inside of the house. "I already have the kettle on. We'll have tea and key-lime sugar cookies."

I set my bag beside the door and followed her into the kitchen as she rolled ahead. She reached for a hot pad and then the kettle, filling the tea-pot that sat on the counter with the bags already in it. The kitchen was so small that everything was in ready reach.

"Would you bring over the plate of cookies, dear?"

I did as instructed, carrying them from the counter to a table for two. I also brought the teapot to the table, along with a hot pad to set it on and two mugs.

Glancing around, I saw a living room with a couch and one chair. There was also a bookcase and a china cabinet. A hall led, I assumed, to a bedroom and a bathroom. Ina Mae's house was tiny and efficient.

"I take a little milk in my tea," the woman said. "Would you get it?"

Her refrigerator was the smallest I'd ever seen. All that it had in it was a quart of milk, a stick of butter, and a few condiments. Obviously she took her meals over in the big house.

Once the tea had steeped, she asked me to pour, which I did. There was nothing physically familiar about Ina Mae, but her kindness and relaxed demeanor immediately made me feel like family.

"Who lives in the main house?" I asked.

"My great-nephew and his brood." Ina Mae nudged the cookies toward me, and I selected one. "They take good care of me and always have. Would you believe I've lived on this property my entire life? Since the day I was born."

"Wow." I held up my half-eaten cookie. "This is delicious, by the way."

"*Danke.* I got the recipe in Florida."

I smiled. I knew of Plain folk who vacationed in Florida, but it surprised me that Ina Mae was one of them. I told her we had a family friend who had lived down there for a while.

"What's his name?"

"Ezra Gundy."

"Oh, I know the Gundy family. And I remember Ezra from Florida. Flirty gaze? Killer smile?"

I chuckled even as I nodded.

"He worked in a restaurant I used to go to," Ina Mae said. "He was always so friendly and kind. Such a sweet young man."

I found her comments about Ezra interesting. Maybe he wasn't as wild as I'd thought.

Ina Mae sighed. "I really miss it. I used to go to Florida every winter from the time I retired."

"What did you retire from?"

"Teaching," she said. "I started in my forties, believe it or not, and kept at it until I was seventy."

My eyes widened. "That was allowed?" In our area, teachers were always young, in their early twenties, and only taught for a few years.

"*Ya*, that was back when we first had our own schools. Things were different then. Before that, I did whatever I could to get by. Helping families with their children. Selling quilts and other handwork. I was always a saver."

Despite years of believing I'd always be single, I never once thought about how much money I'd need to support myself, especially if I wanted to go on vacations and that sort of thing. I took the last bite of the cookie. "Well, these certainly taste like something from a sunny location."

She smiled, eyes sparkling. "I don't bake anymore. My great-niece makes them now from my recipe. She also sends plates over for my meals, or I eat with the family."

I smiled in return. Like most of the elderly among the Amish, she was well cared for. I brushed my hands together and sat up straight, ready to move from small talk into the conversation I'd come here for.

"So how can I help you, Linda?" she asked as if reading my mind. "You said in your phone message that you had some questions about your grandmother? Nettie Bender?"

"Well, she eventually became Nettie Bender Mueller. And yes. I'm just so curious about her. I was thrilled when you agreed to meet with me."

"Happy to do it. So fire away. What do you want to know?"

Needing to gather my thoughts, I stalled for a moment by retrieving my bag and pulling out pen and paper. Family trees were complicated, and I knew I'd never be able to keep things straight if I didn't write them down.

"Before we get rolling," I told her, "just to keep things straight, can you tell me exactly how you and I are related?"

"We're first cousins once removed. My father and your grandmother were siblings."

"That's right. What were their parents' names?"

"Albert and Mary Bender."

After turning the page sideways, I drew a box at the top and filled it in with *Albert and Mary Bender*. Then I drew a line down from that box to the next generation, their children. *Daed* had told me there were thirteen kids all together, and that his mother had been the youngest, so as I went across that row, I wrote numbers rather than names, except for Ina Mae's father, whom she said was Uria, and my grandmother, Nettie. I gave them each a spouse and then drew lines down from there to the next generation. Below Uria and his wife, I put *Ina Mae*, and below Nettie and her husband, Joshua, I wrote in my father's name, Eli. As a final touch, I couldn't help but add in my own mother, brothers and sisters, and myself. When I was finished, my little family tree looked like this:

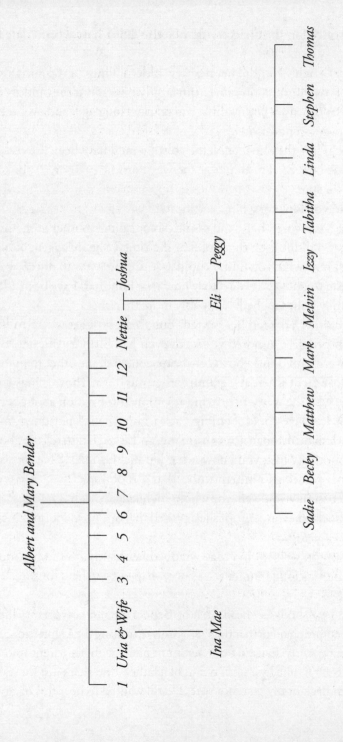

Albert and Mary Bender

1 Uria & Wife 3 4 5 6 7 8 9 10 11 12 Nettie — Joshua

Ina Mae

Eli — Peggy

Sadie Becky Matthew Mark Melvin Izzy Tabitha Linda Stephen Thomas

"I noticed in the directory that Nettie didn't have a birth date listed," I said.

"That's right. Nor did her next few older siblings. It was such a shame. A lot of my information came from family Bibles. But the binding on my father's old Bender family Bible had cracked long ago, and over the years some pages went missing."

"Including the one that Nettie's birth would have been listed on?"

She nodded. "I'm thinking she was born in 1920 or '21, but I can't know for sure."

"Did you look for a birth certificate?"

Ina Mae waved her hand at me. "No, I didn't bother with anything like that. I didn't even think of it at the time." She shrugged. "If you do, let me know what you find. I could at least pencil it into my copy. I keep meaning to update the directory now that hundreds have been added to the family." She laughed. "Probably more than that."

I told her I'd keep her posted, but I had no idea where to look or if Plain people a hundred years ago even had birth certificates. Besides, there wasn't anything a birth certificate could tell me other than the date and location of where my grandmother was born. Those things couldn't change who she was—or give me any more information about her art.

But Ina Mae could. Settling back in my chair, I put down my pen, focused on the woman across from me, and asked her to tell me about my grandmother. "Just, you know, what her life was like. What *she* was like. How her painting fit into the mix. That sort of thing."

"So basically you want the whole enchilada."

I chuckled, wondering if she'd picked that one up in Florida. "As much as you can, anyway."

"All right, well…" Ina Mae wrapped her hands around her mug and thought for a long moment. "It's not a happy tale, that's for sure."

"No?"

Ina Mae shook her head. "Nettie Bender did not have an easy life." She began counting off on her fingers. "Grew up during the Depression. Raised in abject poverty. Evicted from her home along with her parents more than once. Kept in line by a stern tyrant of a father. And that's just for starters."

I sat back in my seat, not sure if I still wanted to hear this or not.

"Her childhood was tough, but her life was even worse as a teenager. Her mother took ill, and since Nettie was the only one still living at home, the burden of care fell to her. By that point, her siblings were spread out all over and too wrapped up in their own lives to pay much attention. Eventually her mother died, followed not long after by her father. Nettie was only eighteen at the time, so the family had no choice but to step in and do something. My father barely knew his baby sister—he was grown and married and out of the house by the time she was even born. But none of the other siblings were willing to take her in, so—"

"Wait. I'm sorry to interrupt," I said, "but this sure doesn't sound like any Amish family I know. Who wouldn't care for one of their siblings this way? Didn't they love her? Didn't they understand they had a responsibility, one that went beyond mere food and shelter?"

Ina Mae sighed. "It's more complicated than that. Frankly, I lay the blame here with Nettie's father." Looking down at my chart, she pointed a wrinkled finger at his name, *Albert.* "As I said, he was not a nice man. He wasn't abusive, I don't believe, at least not physically. But he was mean and bitter and angry all the time. It made for a very…what's the word they use these days? Dysfunctional?"

"I guess."

"A very dysfunctional home. When kids grow up like that, they learn to fend for themselves—and to get as far from the misery as they can, as soon as they can. Things like love and responsibility end up taking a backseat to personal survival."

"I see." I thought about that for a moment. "So maybe we should backtrack a little. When all the kids were young and still at home, where did the family live?"

"They had a farm in Caernarvon Township. That's about twenty miles east of here, just this side of the county line."

"Do you know where in the township, exactly? Maybe you have an address?"

She shook her head. "Sorry. That's as specific as I've ever heard."

"Okay." I grabbed the pen and below my little family tree I wrote *Farm in Caernarvon Township.* "You said something earlier about them being evicted? Did you mean from that farm?"

"*Ya.* I don't know the whole story, but my understanding is that they had a run of misfortune, starting with a blight that ruined an entire year's corn crop. Then came the Depression, so things were tough all around."

I thought about that. "I always heard that the Plain community had an easier time during the Depression than the *Englisch* did, for the most part. I mean, they already grew much of their own food, already lived simply and frugally, rarely carried any debt, things like that."

"I imagine that was true for some. But not for everyone. In the case of Nettie's parents, they did have debt, a very big debt, one that her father couldn't pay. He'd taken out a loan against the farm, I think shortly before Nettie was born, and by the time the payment came due ten years later, between the blight and everything else that had happened in the meantime, he just couldn't cover it. So the bank foreclosed, and they lost the farm."

"How sad. What did they do?"

Ina Mae's brow furrowed. "From what I recall, they found a little house to rent south of Lancaster somewhere. But after a couple of months, they couldn't even afford that. So they ended up moving in with one of their sons and then later one of their daughters. I can't remember the specifics. Bottom line, they were living hand to mouth, even when they did have somewhere to stay. Then, like I said before, Nettie's mother fell ill, and things got even worse. Four years later, she died, and then soon after that, Nettie's father died too."

"And now we've caught back up to where we were when I interrupted you."

We shared a smile.

"That's right. Well, as I was saying before, Nettie was just eighteen then, and she needed somewhere to live. So that's how she ended up here."

"Here? As in, this very farm?"

"*Ya.* I was just a girl then myself, maybe eight or nine, when she first came. She ended up staying with us for about two years, until she married your grandfather and moved away."

I sat forward, eager to hear more. "What was she like?"

Ina Mae smiled, her eyes twinkling. "Oh, Linda, your grandmother was the most fascinating person I'd ever met. Smart, talented, and full of ideas and creativity. She could be moody, but she was never unkind. And she was especially sweet with me. Mostly I felt sorry for her. She'd been through so much in her young life, and it showed. She hardly ever smiled or laughed, rarely even talked much, now that I think about it, except when we were alone. And really, what was there to say? She knew she wasn't wanted here, so I suppose she spent most of her time just trying to be as unobtrusive as possible."

"How sad," I murmured, unable even to imagine it. Parentless at just eighteen, unwanted by her brothers and sisters. No wonder there was so much depth and emotion in her painting. She'd been through a great deal.

"She was very unhappy," Ina Mae said, "and she cried a lot when she thought no one was looking. Thinking back, I realize now that she was grieving. She had a lot to mourn. But no one talked about their feelings back then, and I think the expectation was no one should have any, not even a young woman who had just lost both of her parents."

I nodded. I knew a lot had changed over the years. We were still expected not to wallow in those sorts of emotions for long, but at least now it was okay to acknowledge them—for a time.

"How about her art?" I asked, hoping to move to a happier topic.

"Oh, yes. That was one of the things that made your grandmother so unique. It also got her into a lot of trouble—with her parents, with the bishop, with my father. It was a real bone of contention between them. She wasn't supposed to paint. Period. But no matter who tried to stop her, or how, she always eventually went back to it anyway, whatever the cost."

I leaned forward, my hands flat on the table. "How would a young, poor Amish girl even get started with painting?"

Ina Mae shrugged. "I don't know." She took a sip of tea and then said, "She sure had a natural gift for it, though. She could draw anything and would collect scraps of paper and stubs of pencils. She'd use charcoal from the fire. I even saw her make paints from egg yolks, not that we had any to spare then—but she would skip meals so she could justify using them to make paint. She would find wild berries in the woods to make color. And then she would use old scraps of plywood and such to paint on."

My mind swirled at the thought. I could just picture it, this sad young woman finding solace in her artwork, despite the fact that it was forbidden.

"Did she ever have any official training in art?"

"Not that I know of."

"How about any access to real paints, real canvas, things like that?"

Ina Mae was quiet for a moment, considering my question, and then her face lit up. "Oh my goodness, I just thought of something. Excuse me for a second."

With that, she reached for her walker, rose, and shuffled out of the room.

"Do you need any help?" I asked.

"I don't think so. I might. I'll holler for you if I do."

She disappeared into what I assumed was her bedroom, and then I could hear sounds of her rummaging around. As I waited at the table, I reached for my pen and jotted down notes on all I'd learned thus far. I had just finished when Ina Mae reappeared, her hands gripping the walker, a big smile on her face.

"What is it?" I asked, intrigued.

"Our little secret. Mine and Nettie's." Eyes twinkling, she sat back down and caught her breath for a moment before she went on. "You have to understand, I was so fascinated with my mysterious *Aenti* Nettie. I was always poking around, trying to learn more about her, trying to understand who she really was. She would disappear sometimes, for hours on end, and I never knew where she went. I had a feeling she was off painting, and eventually I decided to find out where. I wasn't going to tell on her. I just wanted to be a part of it somehow, you know?"

I nodded, totally getting it. As the youngest of five sisters, I remembered all too well how it felt as a child to be excluded from their private teenage worlds.

"So I did a little snooping," Ina Mae continued, "and one day I caught her, way out back behind an old, unused shed. She was sitting on a blanket on the grass, painting on a canvas, deeply immersed in her work. When she realized she wasn't alone, she just about jumped out of her skin. She was angry with me, and I felt so bad. I knew I should've minded my own business. I apologized and promised not to say anything, but then I noticed something. She wasn't using her usual homemade work-arounds, her pieces of old cardboard and cups of homemade paints and such. She had real art supplies—and lots of them too. Tubes of paint. All kinds of brushes. She even had one of those pallet things, those oblong boards that you mix paints on, with a hole for your thumb?"

I nodded, smiling at the thought.

"Best of all, she was painting on an actual canvas, like a real artist. And the picture she was making was absolutely beautiful. I was so shocked, I couldn't imagine where she'd gotten all of that stuff—and she wouldn't tell me, other than to say it had been a gift, and that she'd brought it with her when she first moved in. Early on, she said, she'd hidden the whole pile of supplies out in the shed so that my father would never find them and take them from her. She told me she used the paints and the canvases very sparingly, knowing that eventually they would run out and then there wouldn't be any more."

"Wow. Did you ever find out where the gift came from? Who gave it to her?"

Ina Mae shook her head. "No. But I did get a little gift of my own. From her."

Smiling mysteriously, Ina Mae reached into the pocket of her apron and pulled out a small canvas square, no bigger than a man's wallet, and set it on the table in front of me. Taking in a breath, I carefully picked it up and studied it.

It was a tiny painting—either oils or acrylics, I wasn't sure—of a goat nibbling on some purple pansies. It was adorable and very well done, and very similar in feeling, somehow, to the painting of Nettie's we had at home. The artistry wasn't as developed, but the talent was clearly there.

Turning it over, I saw written on the back, *Jonijumbub, 1938*. That was the Pennsylvania Dutch word for pansies, but I didn't understand why it had been written there. I flipped the painting back over and then looked at Ina Mae in wonder. "What is this?"

"That day out behind the shed, Nettie said if I promised never to tell a soul about her art supplies—and I never did, not until now—that in return she would make a special little painting just for me."

"Jonijumbub?"

She nodded. "My pet goat. He loved to eat pansies despite the fact that they upset his stomach, so that's where he got his name. I called him Johnny for short."

I grinned. "So Nettie made this little painting of your pet goat and gave it to you in exchange for your silence?"

She nodded. "I'd never been so thrilled. I had to keep it hidden too, but it's so small it wasn't hard. No one ever found it, and I never got rid of it." Gesturing toward the bedroom, she added, "It was in an old box of childhood treasures I keep in my cedar chest."

"It's precious," I said, leaning forward to set it down in front of her, blinking away tears that for some reason had come to my eyes. "Thank you for showing it to me."

"Of course. Thank you for bringing it to mind. As I said, I hadn't thought about that in years."

"I wonder who gave *Mammi* Nettie the art supplies," I mused, the wheels turning in my mind. Who could it have been? I thought of the art book we'd found in my grandmother's things, the one signed by a Natasha. Whoever she was, she'd given Nettie that book on painting—maybe she'd given her art supplies too. "Do you know of anyone named Natasha?" I asked.

Ina Mae seemed to consider for a moment. "Certainly not anyone Amish."

"That's what I thought too."

"Perhaps a Russian Mennonite? Though I don't know of any named Natasha."

I hadn't considered it might be a Mennonite name.

"Are you sure *Mammi* Nettie didn't have any formal training?"

"Oh, goodness no. No one had money for that sort of thing back then. Even if they did, it wouldn't have been allowed."

I nodded.

Ina Mae continued with her story. "About a year after Nettie moved in with us, she started being courted by a man she'd met at a cousin's wedding. Joshua Mueller. Believe it or not, after that he started calling on her all the way up here, from his family's farm down in…what? Lampeter Township?"

I realized she was talking about my farm, my own grandfather. "West Lampeter, *ya*, south of Lancaster."

"I thought so." A faraway look clouded Ina Mae's eyes. "Nettie didn't exactly encourage Joshua's attentions, but he kept coming around anyway. He was always asking about her drawings and paintings, and not like others did. He wasn't condemning, just curious. I think that's one reason she softened toward him and eventually agreed to marry him."

"Maybe he's the one who gave her the supplies."

Ina Mae shook her head. "No. She told me she'd had that stuff when she first moved in. She didn't meet Joshua until two years later."

"What was he like?"

"Oh, he was one of a kind. The strong but quiet type, exactly the sort of husband she needed. He seemed in awe of her creativity, just like I was, and ready to support her. It wasn't that his family was wealthy, but they owned their farm and always had enough to eat."

She smiled. "Joshua was so handsome. Dark hair and dark eyes. Strong as an ox. A sweet smile that said more than any small amount of words he ever strung together. I supposed I developed a bit of a crush on him myself."

We chuckled.

"He just seemed so capable, as if he could move a mountain. My parents, and probably the whole extended family, were relieved when Nettie married him. It seemed her problems had all been taken care of."

"Weren't they?" I asked.

She shrugged. "They were as far as all her siblings were concerned. None of them had an obligation to care for her anymore. Nettie moved down to Joshua's farm, and I don't know much after that. They didn't have a child for years and years, and then they only had one."

"Did you ever see her again?"

"Just a few times. At a cousin's wedding. At my *daed*'s funeral—though I got the feeling the reason Nettie was there that day was because Joshua had insisted. She had such resentment toward all of her siblings that even a brother's death hadn't softened her heart. Neither had motherhood, surprisingly, though I knew it was something she'd yearned after for years. I realize now, back when she lived with us, she hadn't just been grieving or sad. I believe she'd also been struggling with depression. That's why, even once she was married and living a much better life than before, she still struggled. Motherhood couldn't change that."

"What happened with her art? Do you know?"

Ina Mae shrugged. "We heard rumors. Some were true, I think."

"Like?"

"Like, her artwork was for sale in a shop in Lancaster. All she was doing was painting. God hadn't blessed her with children because of that painting. Then later, she was neglecting the one child God had blessed her with so she could do more painting." Ina Mae frowned. "Some of the rumors were pretty convincing, I'm sad to say. People talked about her mental state too."

Ina Mae glanced at me, looking almost embarrassed. "Not much was known about mental illness or depression or any of that back then. People said depression was caused by sin or by not trusting God." She leaned back in her chair. "But over the years I've come to learn that it can also primarily be a physical issue—and that it runs in our family. I can name five or six cousins off the top of my head who I know are struggling with the disorder. Of course, it can look different in different people. In some it comes out as anger; in others, it just makes them withdraw. One of my nieces becomes sluggish and quiet, like she doesn't have the energy to do anything more than sleep, and she just wants everyone around her to go away."

I nearly gasped aloud. She was describing Thomas. Was that what was wrong with him? That maybe he really wasn't lazy, as Tabitha thought, or spoiled, like so many outside our family believed, but instead clinically depressed, just as our grandmother had been? A chill of recognition crept down my spine, followed by a deep sense of hope. If we knew what was wrong, we could get him some help.

This wasn't the time to think about that, but I knew I would revisit it later. For now, I tucked such thoughts away and turned my attention back to Ina Mae.

"I have to tell you too," she was saying, "that many believed Nettie's artwork was what made her depressed." Ina Mae took a sip of her tea, which had to be nearly cold by now. "I never did, though. Personally, I thought that was the one thing that kept her sane."

By the time I heard Ginny's car turn onto the gravel by the garden, I could tell Ina Mae was growing tired. I thanked her for her help and told her I'd let her know if I found out anything more about my grandmother. She took my hand in hers and squeezed it with surprising force. "I haven't thought of Nettie in years. You remind me of her."

"Really?"

She nodded. "Any chance that you paint?"

"No," I answered. "But I do take my quilting very seriously."

"Oh, good," she said. "That makes life much less complicated, doesn't it?"

I nodded. How many times had I thought that myself?

I told her goodbye and walked out to Ginny's car, taking another look at the house and barn as I went. My grandmother had lived here, painted here. She'd left when she was about my age, most likely feeling all alone in the world except for the man she was marrying.

I soaked in the view, sensing a deep connection to her. It dawned on me that besides finding her birth certificate, I should try and find the farm she grew up on. Perhaps it would offer some clues about the girl, and then the woman, she'd become.

SEVEN

I didn't sleep on the way home. Instead, I stared out the window at the dark clouds growing on the horizon. I'd learned a lot about my grandmother, but there was still so much I didn't know. And although I wanted to track down her birth certificate and find out about where she grew up, that information wouldn't answer the two questions that puzzled me the most. Why did she start painting, especially considering it was forbidden? And why did she stop?

When I arrived home, *Daed* was just being dropped off by one of his *Englisch* workmates, even though it was only one o'clock. Sometimes his crew was released earlier on Fridays to make up for the extra-long hours during the week. When he spotted me, his face lit up in a warm smile.

"Hey, where have you been?" he asked, giving a wave to Ginny as she turned around in the driveway.

"Visiting Ina Mae Bender."

"Who?"

I smiled. "Your first cousin. She's the woman who put together the family directory you told me about. Remember, a few weeks ago? After we dug out that painting of *Mammi* Nettie's?"

"*Ya.*" He tugged on his beard. "I remember. You went to see her in person? Why?"

Ginny pulled out onto the highway and sped off. Turning back toward *Daed*, I shrugged, feeling a little silly but hoping he might understand. "The whole thing with finding that painting made me wonder about *Mammi* Nettie. The directory didn't offer much information, but it did include the name and number of the woman who'd compiled it, so on a whim I called to see if she could answer some questions for me. She responded by inviting me up, so I went."

He glanced at me, one eyebrow raised. "Don't Ina Mae's people live north somewhere, up past Lititz?"

"*Ya*, in Hopeland. That's why I used Ginny." Again feeling a little embarrassed, I added, "It took less than an hour to get there." We started toward the house as I continued. "And it wasn't just about getting my questions answered. I kept thinking there was this whole other side of the family we've lost touch with over the years, you know? All those cousins you mentioned? Seems like such a shame *Mammi* Nettie didn't keep in contact with them."

I expected *Daed* to be pleased that I'd seen Ina Mae, but instead he said, "Sometimes a person has a reason for not keeping up with relatives."

"What do you mean?"

"My *mamm* was never close to her siblings. I got the idea she wasn't treated very well."

I thought of all I'd learned from Ina Mae. "You're right. She wasn't."

I glanced at *Daed*, who seemed surprised.

"This woman admitted as much to you?"

I nodded. "She told me all sorts of things. I promise, once you hear it all, you won't be sorry I went."

Daed was quiet for a moment. "I'm not sorry you went," he said. "It's just… There's a reason my mother lost touch."

I nodded. "But everyone who hurt her is gone now. They've been gone for years. Don't you think it might be a good thing to reconnect? At least with Ina Mae? She loved your mother."

He shot me a glance, and I could see he was at least considering my perspective. "*Ya*, you may be right. I suppose it can't hurt." He smiled. "Why don't you tell me what you found out."

I stepped into the kitchen, and *Daed* followed.

"Well," I said, "before *Mammi* Nettie was married, she lived with various siblings, including the brother in Hopeland, who was Ina Mae's father. Ina Mae was still a kid then, so that's how she got to know her. Nettie lived there with them for about two years before marrying your *daed* and moving away."

"I see." He set his lunchbox on the table and then lowered himself onto a kitchen stool. I took that as a sign that he wanted more information.

I filled a glass of water and handed it to him. "Did you know that when your mother was young, she would make her own paints out of berries and egg whites and stuff? I think that's amazing."

Daed smiled at the thought. "Really?"

I nodded. "Ina Mae said Nettie was the most fascinating person she ever met. Said she was inquisitive and smart. A real deep thinker."

"That she was."

I leaned against the counter and took a sip of my water. "She had to struggle for her art her whole life. No one in the family was happy about her painting, not her parents when they were alive, and not her siblings once the parents were gone. They all tried to stop her. But she persisted." I paused for a moment and then spoke. "One thing Ina Mae couldn't tell me was when your mother was born. Do you know?"

He blinked. "That wasn't in the directory?"

"No. That's one reason I called her, to find out why the date was missing. She said she got a lot of info from the old Bender family Bible her father ended up with, but the binding had cracked and some of the pages were gone, including the one that would've had that information on it."

"What a shame," *Daed* said, and then he drained his glass of water. "Family Bibles always have the final say on that stuff." He thought for a moment. "Wasn't she seventy-seven when she died?"

"*Daed*, how would I know? I was a baby."

He smiled at me, handing me his glass, and said, "Sometimes I forget you were ever a baby."

"What's that supposed to mean?"

"That you're an old soul."

I put both glasses in the sink. "Well, I'm not an old enough soul to remember *Mammi* Nettie."

"I'm pretty sure she was seventy-seven when she died, which would mean she was born in 1921."

"That's what Ina Mae said too, that she was probably born in 1920 or 21." I pulled the notebook from my bag and flipped through the pages of notes I'd taken earlier. "Any chance there's a birth certificate around here?"

"No, sorry. I'm not even sure Amish babies got birth certificates back then."

I'd wondered that too. I leaned forward and penciled in *Born Approx. 1921*, next to Nettie's name.

"So how about the art book you found?" *Daed* asked. "Was Ina Mae able to tell you who— What was the name in there?"

"Natasha. No. She didn't know of any Natashas, Amish or not. But she did say it might be a Russian Mennonite name."

"Huh. That's a thought. I wish I could tell you more, but my mother never mentioned any old friends. She didn't talk much about her family either, except to say that her relationship with her siblings was strained. Sadly, I never really asked."

I thought of my sister Izzy, who used to love listening to our grandmother's stories when she was young. That meant she probably had more information than anyone. I decided I'd give her a call once *Daed* and I were done.

"I do know that the Depression had a big impact on my mother," *Daed* offered. "Even late into her life, she still saved tin foil, butter wrappers, plastic containers—all sorts of things she could use again. 'Waste not, want not' was her favorite saying."

I smiled at *Daed*. I'd heard him use that one a few times myself.

He gestured toward my notebook. "So, anything else important you learned from this cousin of mine?"

I flipped back through the pages, showed him the family tree and the map, and then I quickly skimmed my notes. "Just how *Mammi* Nettie was often sad. But I already knew that."

Daed's expression grew pained.

"Ina Mae wonders now, looking back, if your mother suffered from depression."

"I've wondered that myself," *Daed* said. "Back then people didn't think about things like that, but now some might."

"It can run in families." I cleared my throat and tried to keep my voice light. "In fact, that made me wonder if maybe Thomas has depression too."

Daed looked taken aback. "He's just ten years old."

I shrugged. "Maybe it can happen to kids as well. It might be worth looking into."

He stepped to the cookie jar and took out a snickerdoodle. When he turned back toward me, he still had an uncomfortable expression on his face. He took a bite and then said, "I think Thomas is just going through a stage, but I'll talk with your *mamm* about it."

I didn't want to push the issue anymore, so I changed the topic back to *Mammi* Nettie and her painting, asking *Daed* if anything came to mind when he thought of his mother and her art.

"She was definitely happier when she was painting, more content." He finished off the cookie. "She told me once that it gave her a sense of harmony."

I understood that. I felt that way when I quilted. "Why do you think she stopped painting?"

"I have no idea why, but after my conversation with you the other night, I started thinking about *when*." His eyes took on a distant expression. "It happened in a single afternoon. I was probably nine or ten. It was a couple days after we had a small fire. An old wash house on our property was struck by lightning and burned to the ground. My *daed* had been using the little building for storage, just some old farm tools, so the loss was disappointing but not exactly a tragedy. With the help of a few neighbors we managed to get the fire out before it spread to any other structures. That's what was important."

I nodded, listening.

"Anyway, once all was said and done, I expected my parents' primary emotion to be relief, just like everyone else's, because at least the fire hadn't spread. But instead they were both upset. Really upset. No one knew what to make of it, especially not me. I just knew something big was going on, and I had a feeling it was somehow tied in with my mother's painting."

"Huh."

"Then, a few days after that fire, I got home from school to find my *mamm* sitting at the kitchen table with her head in her hands. Whenever she was feeling especially depressed, she would just sit there and sigh, over and over and over, and that's what she was doing that day. Concerned, I was heading out to the barn in search of my *daed* when a car pulled into the driveway and an *Englisch* woman climbed out."

"Who was it?"

"I don't know. She wore fancy clothes and had curly, reddish-brown hair and a friendly face. I'd never seen her before that I could recall, though something about her seemed familiar to me. She was younger than my *mamm* but resembled her, so I assumed she was a cousin or something." *Daed* exhaled and then continued. "Whoever she was, she clearly knew me. Her face lit up in a big smile, and she called out my name."

"What did you do?"

"Nothing. Before I could even respond, my father stepped out of the buggy shed with something wrapped in brown paper and thrust it into my hands. He told me, 'Take this into the house, Eli, all the way upstairs. Now. Wait in your room until I come to you. But go in through the front door.' I did as I was told."

Daed went on to explain that as he came in the front, he heard his mother storming out the back, and he realized that's why his father had sent him that way, so that she wouldn't accidentally run into him and see what he was carrying. He ran upstairs to his room, dropped the package on his bed, and then ran to the window to watch what was happening down below. It looked as if his father had given the *Englisch* woman a couple of other packages, which she was putting in the trunk of her car. "Then all of a sudden I realized my mother was yelling at the woman, telling her to leave and never come back."

"So your mother did know her?"

"It sure sounded like it, though I'm not sure how. Like I said, I'd never seen her before—or since, for that matter."

"What happened then?"

He sighed heavily. "My father rushed to my mother and wrapped his arms around her. The woman stepped toward them, but my father waved her away. She got back in her car and drove off. I watched him hold my mother as she sobbed against his shoulder for what seemed liked the longest time. Then they turned toward the house, and he helped her inside."

He nodded toward our back door. "It was probably an hour later that *Daed* came up and got me. When I went back down the stairs, my mother was in bed. She stayed there, pretty much, for a week or so while my father did what he could to keep us fed and clothed. Eventually she emerged and started doing some things around the house. She'd been moody before. Sad. Despondent. Then she'd paint and she'd seem better. But after that whole incident, things were different. It's like she just couldn't snap out of it. She never went back to painting again. I remember a few times my father suggesting it, but she would just frown and walk out of the room."

"What had been in the package your father gave you?"

He shrugged. "I was so worried about what was going on outside and then in the kitchen that I never even peeked. And when I went up to bed that night, it was gone. Looking back now, I'm pretty sure it was the painting we have of my *mamm's*."

"Because it was the same shape and size?"

"Yeah, but it was more than that. The next morning when I went out to do my chores, I stepped into her workroom in the barn to find that all of her paintings were gone and her art supplies were everywhere. Brushes. Paints. It was a mess. Obviously my mother had thrown some sort of fit, probably because she found out my father had decided to send all the pictures away with that woman—well, except for the one he sent upstairs with me, which I assume he wanted to hang on to for himself."

"That makes sense. What did your father tell you about all that?" I looked at my *daed*, and for a moment I could see in his eyes the scared and confused little boy he must have been then.

"Nothing really. He and I cleaned up the mess together later, and when I asked him what happened, all he said was, 'Sometimes a person has to make a choice between what they want for themselves and what they think the Lord wants for them.' That didn't tell me much, but my *daed* seemed so upset by the whole matter that I didn't have the heart to press him for more."

I thought about that for a moment. "Maybe your mother was feeling convicted about her art and decided that the church was right. It was a sin, and she needed to give it up."

Daed shrugged. "Maybe so. She certainly never painted again."

"And you never found out who that woman was?"

"No. My guess was that she had a little shop or something where she could sell the artwork, and maybe my *daed* had called and asked her to come get it."

"How embarrassing, though, for a total stranger—an *Englischer* no less—to witness such a scene."

He grew quiet for a moment. "Somehow the woman didn't feel like a stranger. I don't remember the things my mother was yelling at her, but at the time I remember thinking that not only did this woman know my name, but my mother knew things about her too. It was all very confusing. And sad." A woeful expression passed over his face. "For a while after that, my *mamm* threw herself into gardening, growing lots of flowers and arranging them beautifully in all sorts of creative ways. But eventually she stopped doing that too."

"No wonder she was so unhappy," I mused, resting my chin in my hands. "Depression or not, that must've been terrible to have to give up the one thing that brought her peace."

After *Daed* and I finished talking, I headed to the barn and called my sister in Indiana.

"I wish you could come out and help me," Izzy said when she answered the phone. "I wish both you and Tabitha could."

"*Danke,*" I replied. "I wish I could too."

We talked about how she was feeling—big. And how Zed was doing—nervous. And how the weather in Indiana had been—warm.

Finally she said, "What's up?"

I started by telling her about my visit with our elderly cousin in Hopeland, and she became curious right away. Izzy had always been drawn to the elderly and had worked for a time as a caregiver. She'd also always been interested in family history, and I had no doubt she'd be doing all of this stuff with me if she were around. I said as much now.

"*Ya*, I would love that. Sometimes it's hard to be so far away." Izzy sounded as if she might cry.

I wished she was closer too. "Tabitha will be with you soon. That will help."

"I know," she said, pulling herself together. "But that's enough about me. Keep going."

I did as told, sharing the things I'd learned from Ina Mae and then about my conversation with *Daed*. "I know you loved spending time with *Mammi* Nettie when you were little," I added, "and she was always telling you stories. So I'm hoping maybe you can fill in some blanks for me about her and her life."

She thought for a moment. "I don't know, Linda. I was young then. I don't remember much. Plus, I'm not sure if everything she said was even all that accurate. She was really old."

"Whatever you can tell me is more than I have now. I doubt Sadie or Becky could help."

Izzy chuckled. "No, they stayed away from her as much as possible. But not me. I found her fascinating."

There was that word again. "Ina Mae did too. Can you tell me what you do remember?"

"*Ya*, I'll try…" Her voice trailed off. "Mostly she talked about the Depression and what she and her family had gone through. I remember that."

"*Ya*, *Daed* said the Depression had a big impact on her."

"She was always going on about what it had been like to be constantly hungry," Izzy continued, "and how her family did whatever they had to do to get by. They never wasted a thing. They made their own soap, turned flour sacks into dresses, stuff like that."

That did indeed sound difficult, though not necessarily all that unusual for the time. There were probably a lot of families, *Englisch* and Amish, who lived with the same hardships.

Izzy continued. "I remember her telling me once, after *Mamm* had taken me to the doctor for something, that they didn't have any medical care at all back then. She said her own mother died before her time just because they couldn't afford to take her to a doctor."

"Oh, that's so sad."

"It is. There was a phrase she used a lot…" She was quiet for a moment. "'Just trying to survive,' that was it. She said things were so hard and money was so tight that they were 'just trying to survive' almost all the time. There was no room for leisure or laughter or any sort of frivolity. They were so poor, plus I got the impression that her father was really harsh."

That matched what Ina Mae had told me.

"Her stories often included things he'd said and done that sounded cruel to me. And her siblings hated the man. Would you believe not one of them ever came back for a visit? Once they moved out, they were gone for good—except for poor *Mammi* Nettie, who as the youngest ended up getting stuck caring for both parents in the end. Even when their mother took ill, they left their baby sister to serve as nursemaid until the woman died. I shouldn't say this, but it's probably a good thing her father's death was sudden—I think it was a stroke or something—because otherwise Nettie would have had to do the same for him too."

The next morning Stephen and I rode our scooters over to Sadie's as the first rays of light revealed a strip of fog over the fields. Fog always felt so mysterious to me. What was behind it? How long would it last? I knew it was a low cloud made up of water droplets. But it was more than that somehow, and I wondered if it could ever be sufficiently incorporated into a quilt.

A cow mooed in the distance. We were a few minutes late, and I increased my pace, doing my best to keep up with my little brother. The cows didn't care what day it was. We were obliged to keep to their schedule. We zipped up Sadie's drive, leaned our scooters against the barn, and raced inside to find Isaac already at work.

As Stephen, Isaac, and I did the milking, the topic fell to my grandmother and if I'd discovered anything. I told Isaac about all my conversations—with Ina Mae, with *Daed*, and with Izzy.

"What a story," he said. "She was traumatized as a teen, she didn't have any formal training, she suffered from depression, and she destroyed as much of her artwork as she could."

I nodded, bending down to pet Whisper, who day by day warmed to me more and more.

"So she was pretty much your typical tormented artist." He grinned.

I chuckled as I rubbed the cat's neck.

"What else would you like to learn about your grandmother?"

"I want to find the farm where she lived until her father lost it. And her birth certificate if there is one. No one seems to know for sure when she was born."

"Both should be available. You could look online for a birth certificate, although that would cost something to access programs that would have it on file. You could go to the state office to look for the birth certificate—and look for the deed to the farm at the county records office." He shrugged. "But you might want to start online with both."

"*Danke*," I said. I'd get Kristen to help me.

"Or I can go to the library with you if you want."

"All right." I smiled up at him. My sudden motion was too much for the cat, and he darted off, a streak of black against the white wall.

"The library opens at ten. Want to go then? I'm not working today."

I replied, "Neither am I. But wouldn't we have to hire a driver?" The closest branch was all the way over by Mountville.

He nodded. "It's probably ten miles or so."

"We could go to the Arts & Crafts House instead and use the computer there," I suggested. "The one back in the office, not the one out front. Kristen is working. She won't mind. Neither will the owners."

"Great," Isaac answered. "How about if I come by and pick you up at nine thirty?"

I was ready at 9:20 and waiting on the front porch, where I could see Isaac approaching. Then I'd hurry out to the driveway before anyone saw me leaving with him. It wasn't that I was embarrassed or anything. I just didn't want to answer a bunch of questions. Besides, I didn't want to feel foolish if it didn't work out. And, as much as I hoped otherwise, I knew it most likely wouldn't work out.

Tabitha, of course, ruined my plan. She stepped out the front door with a dust rag in her hand. "Where are you off to?"

"An errand," I said.

"What about the housework?"

"I already finished my part."

She twirled the rag around in her hand and stepped closer. "What kind of errand?"

I wanted to tell her it was none of her business, but that would only make her more curious. "I'm stopping by the shop for some…thread." I'd buy a roll while I was there to save me from my own lie.

"How are you getting there?"

"A friend is picking me up."

She shielded her eyes. "Amish or *Englisch*?"

I heard Isaac's buggy before I actually saw it. A moment later, as he rounded the bend of our drive, it was evident to Tabitha who was inside.

She shook her head. "Why are you so deceptive with me?"

"Deceptive?"

"Aren't sisters supposed to tell each other their secrets? All these years I've told you everything. And you won't tell me a thing."

"You haven't told me everything. How about those nights when you said you were 'out with a friend' but wouldn't say who?"

She shrugged and then gave me a sassy smile.

"Besides, there's nothing to tell. Isaac is giving me a ride into the shop, is all."

She crossed her arms. "When will you be back?"

"I won't be long. Why?"

"Ezra is coming over for supper tonight."

I wanted to roll my eyes but didn't.

"You could ask Isaac to join us."

"I don't think so." I didn't want anyone to think Isaac and I were courting, which we weren't.

"Would you make your lemon sponge pudding?"

I wrinkled my nose. "That would take away from my quilting time. You know I always quilt on Saturdays."

"Please," she begged. "I'm leaving for Indiana on Monday. I'd like tonight to be nice. That dessert is Ezra's favorite."

"All right," I said.

Isaac's buggy reached the end of our drive. I waved and then started down the front steps. "Bye!" I called out to Tabitha in the cheeriest voice I could muster.

"Bye," she echoed back.

Isaac had jumped down from the buggy and was waiting for me.

"Thank you," I said as he helped me up.

The day had grown warm, and as we rode along, I realized that the fog had burned off. I stared out over the landscape.

"What do you see?" Isaac asked.

"A thousand shades of green," I replied. "How did we ever come up with so few words to describe so many colors?"

"I've wondered the same thing many times," Isaac said. "How can the blue of a winter lake be anywhere close to the blue of a summer sky?"

"Exactly." We shared a smile.

He urged the horse to go faster. A white silo was framed against a green hill. A dozen sheep grazed alongside a pond. A string of pink dresses hanging on a clothesline blew in the breeze.

"It's such a beautiful world," I said.

"Indeed."

I glanced toward Isaac, and he smiled at me again, causing my heart to skip a beat. I settled back against the seat, ready to enjoy the ride—and the time with this man sitting next to me.

Kristen was happy to see us. "Of course you can use the office computer," she said. "Let me know if you need any help." She nudged me when Isaac's back was turned, a big smile on her face, and mouthed, "He's hot."

I clapped a hand over my mouth to stifle a giggle, waited till it passed, and then calmly told Isaac to follow me back to the office.

He sat down in the chair, and I stood behind him. "Let's start with the farm," he said. He Googled the records department, clicked a few more buttons, and then asked me for the name of my great-grandfather.

"Albert Bender," I replied.

He typed it in, but nothing came up. He clicked around a few more places and then said, "It looks like deeds that old haven't been digitized. We'll have to go to the Archives Division, downtown."

We'll. I smiled. "All right."

"Or I could go for you one afternoon after work."

That didn't appeal to me as much, but I tried to keep the disappointment from my voice as I said, "Sure. If that's more convenient for you."

As it turned out, birth certificates couldn't just be viewed online, not even ones that old. Instead, I'd have to submit a request and it would be sent to me in the mail in return. The problem was that the process could take up to three months and cost as much as ninety dollars. No thanks. The only way to get it faster and cheaper than that was to request it in person in Philadelphia, but because that wasn't exactly a viable option either, I decided I'd just have to do without.

Isaac turned toward me. "I'm sorry."

"It's all right," I said. "You've been a big help. It would have taken me a lot longer to figure it out on my own."

I was about to add that it didn't really matter, and I already had a lot of answers to my questions, when he said, "Here's a thought. I need to go into Philadelphia next week. I've already arranged to be off. Would you like to go with me? We could make a day of it. I have a few quick errands to run there, but otherwise we could have lunch, do the tourist thing, maybe enjoy dinner at a good restaurant. And while we're in town, we can visit the office that archives birth certificates."

A whole day. In Philadelphia. Just Isaac and me?

"When?" I tried to sound nonchalant even as my heart was pounding in my chest.

"Next Friday."

I was always off on Fridays, so that would work great. I probably should've said something coy and hard to get, like "I'll think about it and get back to you," but instead I just blurted, "*Ya!* I'd love that!"

My cheeks flushed with heat, but fortunately he'd turned back to the computer to log off and didn't notice. "Great," he said. "It'll be fun."

As we came out of the office, Kristen said, "That was fast."

I nodded. "We didn't find what we were looking for."

Isaac excused himself and wandered off to the art section while I stood there with Kristen, trying not to grin. I couldn't believe I had just been asked out on my very first date—a whole day! With Isaac! In Philadelphia!—maybe. I wasn't really sure if it was a date or not. Had his invitation been about romance or just friendly companionship and the pursuit of information about my enigmatic forebear?

"You two are so cute together," Kristen whispered.

I mouthed, "We're not together."

"Well, you should be." She grinned, showing her dimples.

Isaac must have known exactly what he was looking for because he returned quickly with tubes of Indian yellow paint and burnt umber.

"More sunflowers?" I asked.

He nodded. "Something like that."

"Sunflowers in a quilt would be cool too," Kristen said.

I nodded, remembering that I'd had the same thought before, the day I took the twins to visit Ruth and first saw Isaac's paintings. "They would be."

"We should make coordinated quilts and pictures, like complementary sets," Isaac said. "You know, the same subject matter, the same color scheme, same basic approach, but do one in paint and the other in fabric? *Englischers* would really go for that sort of thing."

I couldn't tell if he was teasing or not. "What exactly do you mean?"

"Well, I could paint a sunflower, and you could quilt a sunflower. There are people who'd like both. Can't you just see the two in an *Englisch* bedroom?"

Actually, I'd never been in an *Englisch* bedroom, but I tried to imagine it anyway.

"Ooh, good idea." Kristen stepped to the register. "Sunflowers would be great, but Amish scenes would be a big hit too. We could sell the sets here."

I was actually thrilled by the idea, and even more so that Isaac would want to work with me to see it to fruition. I tried to sound low key about it, though, not wanting to come across as too eager. "So many ideas, so little time," I said gamely.

"One by one," Isaac replied. "That's always been my motto. Just concentrate on what's next. Right now that's your *mammi*'s story, right?"

I nodded. A deed. A birth certificate. Any remaining paintings. Although that wasn't all I wanted to focus on.

Isaac smiled at me.

For once in my life I was thinking about more than my quilting—quite a bit more, in fact.

Back outside, as he gallantly helped me into the buggy, I realized I was falling for Isaac Mast in a big way. *Ya*, it bothered me that he'd lived as an *Englischer*, in a city no less, but I couldn't seem to help the way I felt toward him. My heart raced as I shot him a quick glance.

No question about it. I was falling in love.

Eight

I asked Isaac to drop me off at Sadie's house on the way home. I planned to invite her and the kids over for supper tonight—I knew *Mamm* wouldn't mind. When we arrived, however, there was a buggy I didn't recognize.

Isaac did, though. "Looks like Jedediah's here."

"Oh," I said. "Do you mind waiting a minute?"

"Of course not."

The day had grown even warmer, and if I could avoid walking the mile home, I would. If Jedediah had just dropped by, perhaps I would stay. But if he seemed to be making a formal visit, I didn't want to stick around.

My heart lurched a little. Robert had been gone less than month. I knew Sadie wasn't courting or anything like that, but still the thought of another man hanging around made me uncomfortable. Then again, Jedediah was younger than Sadie by a good two years or so. Perhaps she saw him as a younger brother.

We stopped in front of the house, and in the shade of the porch I could see Jedediah sitting with Sadie.

Isaac set the brake and then jumped down to come around to help me.

"*Danke.*" I reached for his hand.

We both called out hellos to Sadie and Jedediah. Isaac followed me up to the porch. The front door was open, and I could see the girls playing in the living room. Perhaps Bobby was down for a nap.

After talking about what a beautiful day it was, I asked Sadie if she and the children wanted to come over for supper that evening.

She thanked me but declined, saying they already had plans. She gave Jedediah a sideways look but didn't elaborate.

"Do you want me to come over in the morning before church to help with the kids?"

"That would be great, Linda. I'll see you then."

And with that, apparently I had been dismissed. How awkward.

"See you folks tomorrow," Isaac said, obviously picking up on it too.

At the buggy, once I was settled back on the bench, I just happened to glance Sadie's way. She gave me a sly smile, one that had nothing to do with Jedediah and her and everything to do with Isaac and me. I just nodded in return, hoping we would be able to talk in the morning.

For a moment I considered inviting Isaac and Ruth for supper. But for some reason I held my tongue, maybe because I didn't want him to think I was chasing him. Or my family to think I liked him. Because what if I was wrong about his intentions, and he saw me only as a friend?

I'd felt so invisible my whole life, and then Isaac had come along, the first person to ever really *see* me. What if I was mistaking that connection, that deep level of understanding and friendship, for affection? Just because I'd fallen for him didn't mean he was in love with me too.

Please, Lord, show me how he truly feels about me.

"Linda?"

I turned toward Isaac. Had he been speaking to me for some time?

"I asked if you wanted to go for a drive tomorrow after church. I'm a little old for the singing, but I'd like to spend more time with you. I hope you feel the same."

I was utterly speechless, but somehow I managed to squeak out a few words. "*Ya*, that sounds nice."

Then to my surprise, as we sat there side by side, he leaned my way, pressing his shoulder against mine for a long moment. Heart pounding, I pressed back, feeling utterly connected, as if electricity pulsed between us. When he finally sat up straight, he was still only an inch or two away, but my shoulder felt suddenly cold and empty, and I wished he would lean into me again.

In our community, there was only one reason a man asked a woman to go for a drive after church, and that was because he wanted to court her. But did Isaac know that? Was that how it worked back in the community where he was from? His people worshipped inside church buildings, not in homes as we did here, so who knew what other customs were different as well?

I settled back against the seat, telling myself to put it in God's hands for now. We rode in pleasant silence, and as we clip-clopped our way home, I decided two things. One, only time would tell what his intentions for me really were.

And two, if he truly meant it as a date, then that was the fastest answer to prayer I'd ever received in my whole life!

I started two batches of the lemon sponge pudding as soon I got home, meticulously measuring each ingredient. I doubled the recipe but baked the batches in separate soufflé pans that were placed in boiling water and then in the oven. It was more complicated than most of the desserts I baked. It took me quite a while, and I doubted that Tabitha would truly appreciate the time I'd put into the process. As it turned out, I had no chance to quilt because *Mamm* wanted me to help fix the main meal as well.

"Can't Tabitha do it?" I asked.

She shook her head. "She's getting ready to go to Indiana. She leaves Monday morning."

Mamm hummed while she worked, but I scowled as I concentrated on mixing breadcrumbs into the ground beef for meatballs. Saturdays were for quilting, not for going to all this trouble to help my sister land a guy she didn't even know for sure she wanted.

Thomas came in from working with *Daed* and Stephen, saying he was hungry.

"You're just *gluschdich*," *Mamm* replied, using the term for when a person wasn't really hungry but wanted to eat anyway.

"No, I am," he insisted. "My stomach's even growling."

"Sorry. You'll have to wait."

With an obedient nod, Thomas headed for the living room, no doubt to crash on the couch.

"*Schtop*," *Mamm* snapped. "Where are you going? Get back outside. Now."

Wearily, Thomas obeyed, shuffling across the room and out the door as if it was the most difficult thing anyone had ever asked of him.

"That child."

"Maybe he really is hungry," I said.

"He needs to learn self-discipline. We'll eat in just over an hour."

That seemed like a long time for a growing ten-year-old. "*Mamm*," I said. "Maybe his blood sugar is low." Kristen had used that term at work about her little one when he woke up from his nap. Of course her boy was still just a tot, but this could be something similar. "Maybe he needs a snack. What if I take a couple of slices of cheese out to him and an apple?"

"It will only make him expect that all the time."

I shrugged. Others thought *Mamm* was too lenient with Thomas, but occasionally I thought she was too harsh. Tabitha also.

For a moment I considered sharing my thoughts with my mother about how his malaise might actually be a sign of depression. But I held my tongue for now. She was different from *Daed* that way. Her sharp, no-nonsense demeanor made her far less approachable for certain things. Besides, *Daed* had said he'd talk to her about it, and I knew that was probably the best way to go about it—as long as he got around to it sooner rather than later.

"An apple and some cheese might be worth a try." *Mamm* interrupted my thoughts.

Stifling a smile, I set aside the bowl, washed the meat mixture from my hands, and pulled together a snack to take out to my baby brother.

The evening started out well enough. While *Mamm* and I finished things up inside, Thomas and Stephen threw a baseball back and forth out on the lawn, and Tabitha and Ezra sat on the porch, watching them.

The meal was good, and when it came time for dessert, Ezra raved about the lemon sponge pudding, going on and on about how delicious it was. Obviously, he thought Tabitha had made it—and when I realized she wasn't going to disabuse him of that notion, I did it myself. Ordinarily I would've let it go, but I was still irritated about having lost my afternoon to everything except quilting.

"I'm glad you like it, Ezra," I said. "I'll have to teach Tabitha how to make it for next time."

He looked over at me, his eyes wide. "You made this, Linda?"

I nodded smugly, not daring to glance at my sister, who was undoubtedly shooting me daggers at the moment.

"Well, it's incredible. That's all I can say. I've had lemon sponge pudding before, but never as delicious as this."

I smiled and met his handsome gaze. "It's nothing special."

Ezra grinned. "*Ya*, and the aurora borealis is just a couple of kids playing around with flashlights."

We all laughed, even Tabitha, though I knew she would've preferred I'd kept my mouth shut and let her take credit for my efforts.

After dessert was done and *Daed* led us in a closing prayer, *Mamm* told Thomas it was time for a bath.

"No, please," he said softly, as if he didn't have the energy to even consider such a thing.

Daed stood and excused himself. "*Kumm*," he said to his youngest son. "Now."

Thomas did as he was told.

Tabitha stood as well. "On that note, Ezra and I are going to go for a drive."

After they left, *Mamm* excused herself to check on *Daed* and Thomas while Stephen headed outside and I started in on the dishes. After I finished, I sat out on the porch and thought about Isaac. My night really would have gone better if I'd asked him to supper. Next time I'd try not to be so timid.

Without him here, I'd spent the evening feeling again like the invisible sister—except for when Ezra complimented me on my dessert. Maybe he wasn't so bad after all.

The next morning when I arrived at Sadie's, she had Bobby in the bathtub and the girls were still in their pajamas. "Could you get them dressed?" she asked. "And then go harness the horse?"

She had bags under her eyes again—something I hadn't noticed the day before when she was on the porch with Jedediah.

"Rough night?" I asked.

"*Ya*. The girls had nightmares. Bobby woke up and wouldn't go back to sleep." She yawned.

"Do you want me to take the kids to church? You can stay home and rest."

She shook her head. "I'll nap this afternoon when Bobby goes down."

In the buggy on the way to church, I asked Sadie how her visit with Jedediah had gone the day before.

"*Gut*," she said. "We went over to his parents' house for supper."

I wanted to ask more but wasn't sure how to phrase my question. I knew she wasn't courting Jedediah. *Ya*, Amish people tended to remarry earlier than *Englisch* people did after a death. I'd grown up seeing widows and widowers remarry within a year or so. But no one started courting *this* soon after a spouse died. Most people waited at least six months. True, before Robert died, he had made my sister promise more than once that she would remarry, but I felt certain he hadn't meant for her to get started on that so soon!

We were a few minutes late getting to church. I kept Bobby with me and slipped in next to Tabitha. On the men's side, next to Jedediah, sat Ezra. It wasn't surprising he'd decided to visit our district, and I wondered if it was the off Sunday in his.

After the service, Sadie approached me and said she didn't feel like staying for the meal. "But you don't have to come with us," she added. "I'll take the kids home."

She looked terrible, pale and tired and weak. And as much as I had been looking forward to my afternoon drive with Isaac, there was no way I was going to send Sadie off without me.

"No," I told her. "I'll come along and help."

I found Isaac in the crowd and explained the situation, and he looked as disappointed as I felt. But then he glanced over at my sister and seemed to understand.

"Do you want me to drive all of you to Sadie's?" he asked.

I shook my head. "No, we're fine. Thank you, though."

"I'll get her buggy," he said.

Jedediah approached Sadie, and they talked quietly. He took Bobby from her and held him as if he weighed nothing. Bobby reached for Jedediah's hat, and the man smiled as the baby pulled it from his head.

Isaac returned with the buggy, jumped down, and opened the door for me. As I climbed up and took the reins, he said, "I'll see you tomorrow morning."

I nodded, flashing him a grateful smile. Jedediah helped Sadie and the children into the other side and then we drove off. As we left, Tabitha and Ezra joined Isaac, and he walked off with them. However, Jedediah stayed to watch us leave.

When we reached the house, Sadie rested for a while, and I fed the children. Later, it sounded if she were ill, and I went to check on her. She stepped out of the bathroom, a glass of water in her hand.

"What can I do to help?" I asked.

"Could you get me some crackers?" She grasped the doorframe of her room.

"I'll be right back."

When I returned, she was sitting on the edge of her bed with her head in her hands. I sat down beside her and rubbed her back, the crackers in my other hand.

"I'd thought about starting some sort of business," she said. "Of wrapping up the dairy herd and skipping the apples and figuring out another way to make money altogether. Maybe opening a stand and selling baked goods. Or even a small café."

I could see Sadie doing something like that. She'd always been smart and capable and outgoing. Even as a widow with children, I knew she would succeed at whatever she set her mind to. "That's a great idea."

"Yeah, it was. But not anymore."

"It's just stomach upset, Sadie. It will pass."

She shook her head. "No. It's not that."

"What is it then?"

"I'm pregnant."

The next morning, before I went over to Sadie's to help with the milking, I told Tabitha goodbye because her bus for Indiana would be leaving before I'd get back.

My sister gave me a big hug. "I'm guessing you'll be courting by the time I return."

"I'm sure one of us will, but I doubt it'll be me."

"I wouldn't be so sure about that, Linda." She pulled back and met my gaze. "To be honest, I'm actually proud of you. I really didn't think Isaac was your type. Too much backstory, you know?"

I responded by quoting the scripture *Daed* had read to us that morning. "'If any man be in Christ, he is a new creature: old things are passed away.'"

Tabitha's eyes narrowed. "Seriously? You?"

"Okay, so I'm still working on it," I admitted, "but that's the mind-set I'm going for."

We both laughed. And I really meant it. I was going to try and get past the issues I had with Isaac's backstory, as my sister had called it. He'd lived in a city, *ya*, and he'd gotten a higher education. But the important thing was that in the end he'd come back to the faith of his youth and committed himself to the church. If God could forgive whatever wild things he'd done while he was living as an *Englischer*, then surely I could too, eventually. The real question was whether I'd ever be able to forget as well.

"So did Ezra promise to wait for you?" I teased, expecting my sister to blush.

Instead, she just got an odd, faraway look in her eyes and said, "Nah. I'm hoping to find someone in Goshen, actually."

I thought she was joking, but she appeared serious.

"What about Ezra?"

She shrugged. "I just don't see that working out."

I stared at her for a moment. "So you're not interested in him after all?"

She eased up a little and smiled. "Let's just say I'm looking forward to seeing what's available in Indiana."

I shook my head. That was my sister, to a T—for Tabitha. We couldn't have been more different.

"Give Izzy a hug, and kiss the baby for me when it comes." I forced a smile.

"I will." Her eyes grew serious, and she hugged me again.

"I have to get going." I pulled away, blinking back tears. Tabitha and I had never been apart for more than a couple of days. I'd thought having her go to Indiana would be a nice break, but a month was a long time. I hurried out of our room and down the stairs.

Stephen had already left, so I rode my scooter by myself.

Sadie had made me promise not to tell anyone her news, not even *Mamm*. "Robert knew before he passed," she had said. "He'd already made it clear he wanted me to remarry, as you know, but when we realized a baby was on the way, he grew even more insistent, saying I needed to do so sooner rather than later. I agreed to try, and that brought him much comfort. He knew I'd need help."

She had us there, though I didn't see what a new husband could do that we couldn't. Besides, it was one thing to take on another man's children—but another man's unborn baby? It all sounded so bizarre to me. A newborn would be a reminder of the fact that it hadn't been that long ago since Sadie was...I searched for the right word. *Intimate*. With someone else.

I was surprised when she'd told me the baby would be born in September. That was only four months away. She said she hadn't been sick recently but that she must have gotten overtired the last couple of days. She'd had a rough time with both of her earlier pregnancies too.

I asked her if Robert had anyone in mind as far as whom she should marry *soon*.

She'd answered, "Not really."

I asked if Jedediah was a possibility, and all she said was that Robert thought very highly of him.

I slowed on the narrow shoulder as a truck sped by and then picked up my speed on the scooter again.

I just wished Sadie would get around to telling *Mamm* and *Daed* about the baby. It was too much for her to bear alone, and I wasn't much help. Today I had to work, otherwise I would just stay.

Yesterday I'd wanted to tell her how excited I was about the baby but sensed it wasn't what was needed. Not yet anyway. And I could see how it was a bit much for her at the moment. But it was great news in the long run. I hoped a time would come when we could celebrate.

When I reached the barn, Stephen was working alone. It wasn't like Isaac to be late. I asked after him, but Stephen just shrugged his shoulders.

I got busy hooking up the cows, but after a half hour, when Isaac still hadn't shown up, I went and checked the answering machine. Sure enough it was blinking. I pushed the button.

"Hey, it's Isaac. It's four on Monday morning. My *mammi* isn't doing well again. I'm going to take her into the doctor as soon as I can and don't think she should be alone. Sorry to leave you in the lurch. I'll let you know what the doctor says as soon as I can."

Ruth had been to the doctor right after Robert's funeral, but they'd told her the dizziness had been caused by the stress of such a difficult day and not to worry. Now, however, it appeared it might be something more than that.

I called Ruth's number and imagined her answering machine picking up in her phone shed. Instead of her usual message, however, Isaac's voice came on, saying that the caller had reached the home of Ruth Mast and the business of Isaac Mast. "Leave a detailed account of what you need."

I simply told him I'd received his message, that Stephen and I were doing fine, and that I'd really appreciate it if he'd let us know how Ruth was doing as soon as possible.

Stephen and I muddled through, but it was almost eight by the time we finished. I rushed home, cleaned up, and started for work. When I arrived, Kristen was just unlocking the door.

When we entered the store, she pulled a book from her bag. "I thought you and Isaac might enjoy looking at this together." It was on old barns in Pennsylvania.

I took it from her and leafed through it, fascinated by the setting of each photo. Several, not surprisingly, were in Lancaster County.

We were busy for a Monday, and Kristen and I barely had a chance to talk all day. The time passed quickly, and as we were closing she asked me if I would be willing to change my work schedule, permanently. She blushed a little. "What if you have Mondays off instead of Fridays, plus you start working Saturdays? That would give you more hours."

"Beginning when?"

"As soon as possible."

"I have plans for this Friday," I said, realizing that Isaac and I might have to cancel our day in the city anyway, depending on Ruth and what was wrong and how she was feeling. "Or I may have, I'm not positive yet."

"That's fine. We can start the new schedule next week." After a beat, Kristen added, "It wasn't my idea. My aunt came up with this."

"It's okay. You don't have to explain it." As long as no one expected me to work on Sundays, I could be flexible. And if I had to change my quilting time from Saturdays to Mondays, at least I'd be less likely to get pulled away in order to whip up fancy desserts for my sister's boyfriends.

"She's heard really good things about you," she said. "And not just from me."

"Oh?"

"She wants you to work Tuesdays through Saturdays because they're our busiest days." She blushed again, and I realized there was something she wasn't saying.

Then I began to catch on. Kristen's aunt liked my *kapp* and apron. She liked that I was Plain. I added to the tourist experience. To the Lancaster County Amish Country setting. To the bottom line.

"Don't worry about it," I said, but the truth was Kristen's embarrassment made me feel better. She appreciated me for who I was, not for my value as a marketing tool.

Kristen appeared so uncomfortable that I reached out and gave her a hug. "The only downside is that we'll have fewer days that we work together."

"Actually not." She hugged me back. "I'm going to work the same schedule as you. My aunt will cover Sundays and Mondays."

As soon as I reached home, *Mamm* approached with a box in her hand. I stopped the buggy in the driveway, and she opened the passenger door.

"I need you to take this over to Ruth," she said, setting the box on the seat beside me. "They dropped by on their way back from the doctor."

"How is she?"

"Her blood pressure is low, and they ran some tests." *Mamm* pointed to the box. "That's why I need you to take them their supper. They've had a long day."

"Gladly," I answered. "What about the milking in the morning? Without Isaac there to help, I was almost late for work today."

"Thomas can help Stephen tomorrow instead."

I wrinkled my brow.

"I'll have *Daed* talk to him. Now get this over to them before it turns cold."

I drove Blue back to the highway and on to Ruth's. Once there, I tied my horse to the hitching post and retrieved the box. By the time I reached the back door, Isaac met me, dishtowel in one hand and an oven mitt in the other.

His eyes lit up. "Linda, hey. What are you doing here?"

"*Mamm* sent supper for you and Ruth."

He glanced back toward the kitchen.

"She's not in there trying to cook, is she?"

He shook his head, a smile on his face. "No. I am. Spaghetti. My specialty."

I tried not to act surprised. Most men I knew could barely boil an egg, much less whip up a meal. But if it tasted as good as it smelled, I thought Isaac might actually know what he was doing.

"Oh, well. I'm guessing this is only a casserole." I gestured to the box in my hands. "It will keep for a day."

"That would be great." He motioned me into the kitchen, so I stepped inside and followed him to the counter.

"How is Ruth?"

"Better. She fell during the night, but she didn't break anything, thank the Lord."

"You don't seem very worried." I studied his face.

He shrugged. "Low blood pressure isn't that big of a deal as long as she doesn't fall again. If that's all it is, she should be fine. I picked up a cane for her to use when she needs it. Anyway, she's resting now, but I'll tell her you stopped by."

I thanked him, adding that Stephen and Thomas would handle the milking tomorrow so he wouldn't have to worry about it.

"That's good," Isaac said. "Thanks."

I put the box on the table and peeked under the lid. "There's a lemon pudding in here too." The leftover one that I had made Saturday. "You should eat it tonight." I shot him a teasing glance. "Unless, of course, you have a chocolate soufflé in the oven."

"Nope. That would be a stretch even for me."

We shared a smile and then he turned to stir his sauce. I stepped toward the door.

"Wait," he said. "I have an update for you."

"About?"

"Your great-grandparents' farm. I found an address."

"When?"

"Today. On the way home from the doctor. Once I told *Mammi* Ruth the story, she said we had to stop at the Lancaster County Archives Division."

"She went into the office with you?"

"*Ya*. They had comfortable chairs. She just sat and rested."

"Oh." I felt guilty at the thought, but it didn't seem to bother Isaac—and apparently Ruth hadn't minded either.

"Anyway, I have an address, where Ina Mae said, in Caernarvon Township. I thought we could go by there and check it out on our way to Philadelphia."

My eyes widened. So our trip to Philly was still on, I thought, excitement coursing through my veins. I could kid myself that my reaction had to do with seeing the city or tracking down more information about my grandmother, but I knew it was mostly about spending a whole day with this man.

Oblivious to my thoughts, Isaac began digging in a pile of papers on the table, looking for the one he wanted. As he did, I noticed a letter-sized envelope addressed to him, written out in a feminine hand.

"Isaac?" Ruth called from her room.

"I'll be right back," he said, and as he walked away, I couldn't help but take another look at that envelope.

Keeping my hands at my sides, I leaned slightly forward and studied it for a long moment. There was no return address—at least not on the front—but it had been postmarked in Philadelphia. I was tempted to flip it over and see if there was an address on the back flap, but I resisted the urge.

Good thing too, because at that moment Isaac returned with Ruth holding on to his arm. She smiled at me as he helped her sit down.

"You shouldn't have gotten out of bed," I said.

She shook her head. "I've never been so bored in my life. I had to get up." She began leafing through the mail and then started opening the top envelope, the very one I'd been looking at.

Isaac cleared his throat.

She glanced up, the envelope in her hand. "What?"

His eyes twinkled. "That one's mine."

"Oh my," she said, dropping it on the table. "I wasn't thinking."

He took it from her and placed it on the other end of the table. "The rest are yours—except for the piece of paper with information about Linda's great-grandparents' farm on it." He went back to rummaging through the pile and retrieved the page he'd been searching for.

I took it and grasped it in my hand, but my mind was still on his letter. Who was it from? What was it about? My guess was that it had to do with his business. Or at least that was my hope.

What was the term Tabitha had used? Backstory. She'd said he had too much backstory. I didn't know many of the details, but what if that backstory included an old girlfriend in Philadelphia, one he still kept in touch with? Surely not.

"Because I had to take today off," he said, interrupting my thoughts, "going into Philly won't work this Friday. But the next Friday's fine if that's good for you."

I'd have to talk with Kristen, but I assumed she'd be okay with it. I nodded.

"And, like I told you before, we can swing by the old Bender farm too."

I held up the paper with the address. "Isn't it out of the way?"

He shrugged. "Actually, it's not as long as we take the Turnpike and not Route 30. I've already hired a driver. Your *mamm* recommended her a while ago. Ginny?"

"She's great," I said. "And I can pay my half."

"I've got it," he answered.

I thanked him, but I'd still try to help pay. I remembered the book in my buggy that Kristen had loaned me, and I told him about it. "I'll bring it along so we can look at it. The pictures are gorgeous."

The pot of water began to boil, and Isaac turned back to the stove. "Sounds great."

I told Ruth goodbye and that I hoped she'd feel better soon.

"Oh, I will," she said. "I refuse to be an invalid."

"I'll see you Wednesday morning, at Sadie's," I said to Isaac.

"See you then," he replied, glancing over his shoulder. "Tell your *mamm* thank you for the food. We really appreciate it."

I waved and let myself out the door.

On the way back to the house I decided to check on Sadie and offer Stephen a ride home if he was finished with the milking. When I pulled into her driveway, I could see movement in the garden, and I assumed it was *Mamm*. Robert had passed away in April, so not only had she and *Daed* done most of Sadie's planting, but she'd been helping to keep things weeded ever since.

As I drew closer, however, I realized she wasn't here. It was just Sadie and the girls, with Bobby playing on a blanket nearby. Sadie was pulling the hoe down the far edge of the garden, probably to make a mini ditch for a second planting of radishes or greens, and the twins were weeding— though it seemed that wasn't all they were doing. I watched as they each pulled up fistfuls of weeds, carried them over to the side of the garden, and then laid them down very precisely on the grass to form the outline of a square. Oddly enough, inside that square was the black cat, Whisper, who was sprawled on the grass, looking perfectly content as the pile of weeds took shape around him. For being so skittish before, he seemed awfully comfortable now.

"What on earth are you two doing?" I called out with a smile as I set the brake on my buggy, tied the lead rope to the hitching post, and went to join them.

"Making a house for Whisper." Hazel glanced my way for just a moment before returning her attention to the job at hand.

"He likes it," Hattie added. "And watch what else he likes."

Smiling, she retrieved the hose and carried it over to the cat, knelt down, and held it out so that a small stream of water dribbled onto the ground. To my surprise, Whisper stood and began lapping eagerly at that stream.

"He likes to drink from running water, not still water," Hazel explained as she pulled up more weeds.

Several thoughts hit me at once. First, that she was right. Without even really thinking about it, I'd been leaving the faucet on, just slightly, in the barn whenever Whisper was around, because he always came and drank from it.

My second thought was that this was the most engaged I had seen the girls in a long time—maybe ever. I looked to Sadie, and she gave me a nod and a bemused smile, as if to say, *I know. I don't get it either, but isn't it great?*

Seizing the opportunity, I stepped closer, hoping the girls would let me join in on their game. But Whisper stiffened, and so I stopped, not wanting to scare him away. Instead, I sat down with Bobby and began entertaining him as I chatted with Sadie. I told her where I'd been and why I'd come by.

I stayed there for a while, just enjoying being with my sister and her children. Bobby had a basket of plastic blocks from inside the house, and I stacked up a few in front of him and then let him knock them down. He laughed, so I did it again, using more blocks this time.

A short while later, I was just finishing a veritable tower for him to knock over when I spotted Jedediah coming toward us from the barn, Stephen walking behind him.

"Okay, buddy, your turn," I said to my nephew, who squealed with laughter as he promptly swung out an arm and knocked down the whole thing.

"Better get inside folks," Jedediah said.

I glanced over at him, and he gestured toward the sky. Looking up, I was surprised to see a bank of dark clouds spreading out across the horizon. A storm was rolling in.

"We need to get going anyway." I began gathering Bobby's toys and putting them into the basket as Jedediah stepped to the garden and took the hoe from Sadie. She relinquished it eagerly and then her hand fell to the small of her back.

"Are you working too hard?" he asked her, his voice low.

She shook her head.

His tone sounded protective. I'd never understand what went on between two people, not for the life of me. Robert had probably asked Jedediah to look after Sadie and the children, but still, I found his closeness alarming.

I felt a drop of rain on my forehead. Hurrying now, I finished with the toys, and then I stood and scooped up Bobby, resting him on my hip.

"Girls, get the blanket and the toys," Sadie directed, giving her hands a quick rinse with the hose before turning it off and putting it away.

I told Stephen to throw his scooter in the buggy. Jedediah stepped toward me, taking Bobby with his free hand. He probably could hoe and carry the baby at the same time. It seemed as if the man could do anything.

I saw Whisper dart away, a black blur against the green grass. I looked to the twins, fearing they'd be upset by this abrupt termination of their little game, but they were calmly folding up the blanket.

"He'll be back," Hazel said to her sister.

Hattie nodded, intent on the folding.

"But for now," Hazel added, "he can go around and drink from all the rain gutters."

Hattie gave a small chuckle—a chuckle!—and then the two of them put the folded blanket atop the basket, took a handle each, and set off toward the house together.

It was raining in earnest by the time Stephen and I pulled onto the road. As we rattled toward home, I asked my little brother what he thought of the twins' unusual-for-them behavior. But he replied that he hadn't been out there long enough to notice anything.

So I asked him what he thought of Jedediah.

"He's great," Stephen answered. "He's like Superman when it comes to getting work done. He's been really helpful in lots of ways."

"Do you think he's interested in Sadie?" I shot Stephen a glance.

His face grew red. "What do you mean?"

I just gave him a look. At fifteen, he knew exactly what I meant.

"Linda. What are you trying to say?"

"Nothing." Stephen probably didn't know about Robert making Sadie promise she'd marry soon. I shouldn't have brought it up. Thankfully, my little brother wasn't the type to talk. Otherwise I'd be afraid I'd passed on gossip, which certainly hadn't been my intent.

NINE

R uth's tests showed that her potassium levels were low, and the doctor guessed she'd probably been dehydrated the night she nearly passed out. She was on the mend, much to the relief of us all.

Each time I saw Isaac, I felt closer to him. We joked and talked as we did the milking, and it seemed his smile grew warmer and his eyes brighter each day. Kristen was happy to give me the next Friday off for our trip into the city, and that morning, after the milking, I hurried home and got ready. Ginny would pick him up first and then me. All I'd said to *Mamm* was that I'd be running errands, that Ginny was driving, and that I'd probably be gone for most of the day. I never mentioned Isaac would be with me because I didn't want to have to explain anything. *Mamm* would think it was a date, but I still wasn't sure. And the last thing I wanted to do was to get her all excited about something that might never be.

Ginny had a smile on her face when she pulled into the driveway. Thankfully, *Mamm* didn't come out to say hello, and Stephen was still over at Sadie's, cleaning out the milk vat.

Isaac sat in the front passenger seat, and I was in the back, so we didn't say much to each other at first beyond our initial greeting. I passed the book up to him, and he seemed to find it interesting. He thumbed through it for the first ten minutes or so, putting it aside once we reached Lancaster and our route began taking some twists and turns.

Ginny and Isaac chatted about all sorts of things. Her garden. His painting business. The quarter horse we passed. Farming. Ruth, who was over at her youngest daughter's for the day.

I slunk back against the seat, aware of how bored Ginny must have gotten when she took me to visit Ina Mae. I'd barely said a word on that entire trip. This time, however, Isaac's gift for conversation kept her entertained the whole way.

I expected a rundown house when we reached the old Bender farm, but instead there was absolutely nothing. Just fields with no buildings. Not even a barn. Obviously, at some point, all of the structures had been torn down. There weren't even any foundations left. Isaac turned toward me and shrugged.

"*Loss uns geh*," I said. *Let's go.* I hoped we'd have better luck in Philadelphia.

Ginny and Isaac continued chatting as we drove, but I drifted off to sleep and ended up dozing for a while. Awakened by the sounds of heavier traffic—honking cars, rumbling engines, thumping radios—I sat up and looked around. I'd never been to Philly before, but now it seemed we were almost there. Filled with a surge of excitement, I tried to wake up and soak in every sight I could.

Through the front window, I spotted skyscrapers ahead in the distance. To our left ran a majestic, sparkling river, its far bank hilly and lush with trees.

"What river is that?" I asked, the first words I'd spoken since we'd left the old farm.

Isaac flashed me a surprised look over his shoulder, followed by a warm smile. He seemed so pleased I'd finally woken up and was taking an interest in our surroundings that I felt guilty. I shouldn't have slept at all.

"That's the Schuylkill," he replied.

I'd heard of it but had never seen it before. "It's so pretty. Does it keep running alongside us the whole way?"

He chuckled. "Actually, considering that the river was here first, I guess you could say we're running alongside it."

"That's why they call this the 'Schuylkill Expressway,'" Ginny added.

"Ah," I replied, feeling rather stupid, though that wasn't their intention.

"To answer your question," Isaac continued, "we'll stay with the river for a couple more miles, but then we veer off to the Vine Expressway."

Nodding, I settled back against my seat and looked again to my left. The scene really was beautiful, especially when we passed a charming cluster of houses that Isaac said was called "Boathouse row." The name fit because there were plenty of boats in the water nearby, though the vessels were odd. They looked kind of like canoes, but they were longer and skinnier, with multiple passengers, each sitting in a line, one behind the other, rowing in unison—well, almost. In every single boat, there seemed to be one passenger who wasn't rowing at all. That guy got to be up front, though I didn't know what good it did him because he always seemed to be sitting backwards.

After that, the ground rose up to form a knoll, atop of which sat a huge, elaborate building with stately pillars and multiple rows of long, rectangular windows.

"What's that?" I asked.

"The Philadelphia Art Museum," Isaac replied, his voice almost reverent. He gazed at it in silence for a moment. "I'll have to take you there some time. It's amazing."

The traffic grew thicker until we were almost at a standstill.

"Do you mind driving in cities?" I asked Ginny.

"Well, you won't catch me behind the wheel in New York or DC, but Philly's not so bad. I have a sister up by Pennypack Park, so I'm used to it. I'll visit her while I wait for the two of you."

She talked more about the city, and then Isaac told her we'd be done by six. "Will that be all right?"

Ginny glanced in her rearview mirror. "Is your mom okay with that?"

I nodded, although I hadn't thought we'd be so late. I did tell *Mamm* I'd be gone all day. She usually didn't worry, and I hoped she wouldn't this time either.

Ginny slowed and took an exit that put us on a two-lane, one-way street flanked by a giant parking lot on one side and a big fancy building on the other. I thought we'd be making our way toward the skyscrapers

I'd glimpsed earlier, but after just two blocks she began to slow down and crane her neck, as if looking for somewhere to pull over.

"What's wrong?" I asked.

"We're here," she replied, gesturing toward a nondescript building on our right.

The street offered nowhere to park, so we continued on for another two blocks. As we went, things quickly grew busier and more congested on every side. Cars and people and bikes zipped this way and that. Horns honked. Someone yelled. A bike swerved and barely missed being hit. My pulse began to race. There was so much going on here. It felt chaotic and exciting at the same time.

Ginny put on her blinker and made a right turn. "I'll loop back around."

"Don't bother. Just pull in here," Isaac told her, pointing to an empty parking spot ahead. "We can walk back."

"You sure?"

"Of course."

As we came to a stop at the curb, I looked at all the commotion on the street and hesitated, watching as Isaac handed Ginny a slip of paper with the address of where she could pick us up at six o'clock.

"You got it," Ginny said, taking it from him. "Have fun, you guys."

I grabbed my bag and jacket and climbed out of the car. Isaac had the barn book in his hand, but I took it and put it in my bag.

He stood with confidence, smiling down at me as people flowed around us like water around two rocks in a stream. I felt myself tense, waiting for people to start staring at us, but most just dashed on by. That was a relief.

"Fortunately, we're not that uncommon of a sight around here," Isaac explained, as if reading my mind. "Reading Terminal Market is just a few blocks that way."

"Oh, okay. Good." I knew a number of Amish people worked there, bringing in produce and smoked meats and homemade jams and jellies and such and selling them in the large farmer's market. I guessed that meant folks around here were used to seeing people who were dressed like Isaac and me.

"Ready?" he asked, and then we began walking back the way we'd come.

When we rounded the corner, he got a few steps ahead of me, but before I could catch up someone bumped into me, hard. I must have gasped because Isaac whirled around. "You okay?"

I nodded, but I was glad when he stayed beside me after that. In another block we reached the building.

Isaac held the door for me, but I stopped short as soon as we were both inside. Just ahead was a large contraption, one that nearly blocked the way. A woman in a navy blue police-type uniform sat in a tall chair next to it, staring at a mounted screen.

"It's okay," Isaac said softly, giving me a nudge forward. "Just put your tote on the conveyor belt and walk through."

I started to do as he said but then hesitated, clutching the bag to my chest. "Will I get it back?"

That made the woman laugh, but not in a mean-spirited way. "Sure will, honey," she responded, even though my question hadn't been directed at her. "Put down the bag and then keep on going. You'll see."

As promised, once I'd walked through a free-standing doorframe, my bag reappeared on the other side of the contraption, still moving forward on the conveyor belt. Two policemen were standing nearby, chatting with each other, and one of them gave me a nod. I assumed that meant it was okay to take my bag back, so I did.

"What is all this?" I asked Isaac once he'd come through the doorframe as well.

"Security," he replied, taking my elbow and steering me toward a hallway on the left. "It's to make sure nobody comes in with a—" he paused and lowered his voice to a whisper, "gun or a bomb or whatever." Raising his tone back to normal, he added, "This is a government building. They have to be careful."

We came to a stop in the short hallway and turned our attention to a big sign on the wall, which explained how to proceed once we were inside the department of Vital Records, which was just ahead. Take a number, fill out the correct form(s) as needed, wait until our number was called. Sounded simple enough to me.

We continued on and soon were standing at a tall counter inside the large, sunny room, staring at an *Application for Certified Copy of Birth Record*.

I filled in its blanks as best I could, first with my own information and then with what I knew about my grandmother—her name, her parents' names, her place of birth, listing the town but leaving the hospital blank.

At her date of birth, I hesitated, thinking of my conversation with *Daed*, who had calculated it based on the age she'd been when she died. Finally, I wrote, *Not sure, but somewhere around 1921*, scribbling small enough to fit it all within the line.

Once the form was as complete as it could be, we took a seat near one of the long windows to wait our turn. The place didn't seem all that crowded, with maybe fifteen people scattered among at least twice as many chairs. Though I tried not to stare, the crowd was an interesting mix. Moms with antsy toddlers. Men in jeans and T-shirts. A woman in business attire. There was one older couple, obviously wealthy, dressed all fancy as if they were headed to a ball, and a trio of teenagers with multiple piercings and tattoos.

One of those teens had bright pink hair with purple tips, and she glanced up at me just as I was looking at her. We both reacted with surprise, and then we shared an embarrassed smile. For that moment, despite our obvious differences, it was as if we were just two people, making a connection. I thought of my relationship with Kristen and was once again grateful that the Lord had given me an *Englisch* friend, opening my eyes to those outside the Amish faith.

After a while, Isaac suggested that we look at the book of Pennsylvania barns while we waited. I pulled it out, and soon we were immersed in its pages. The first barn in the book had a stone foundation and weathered wood plank walls, much like Sadie's, but the next one looked as if it might soon fall down.

"That's a lot of great boards," Isaac said. "I wonder if the building is still standing—and if the owners want to sell."

"Before I met you, I would have looked at that and seen a catastrophe. Now I see possibilities." I paused and then admitted, "Although probably not as many as you do."

He grinned and I turned the page. The next one was red and looked to be in near perfect shape. The following one was white and obviously belonged to a Plain family. There were no electrical wires coming onto the property, and a buggy was parked at the far end.

We continued through the book. There was a barn from Somerset County, but Isaac didn't recognize it, as well as the oldest barn in the state, built in Chester County in the early 1700s and made of stone.

"Thirty-seven!" a voice called, interrupting my thoughts.

That was our number. Isaac and I looked at each other, and then I quickly closed the book, slipped it into my bag, and followed him to the window. I felt suddenly nervous, but he seemed as poised and calm as ever. Obviously sensing my mood, he took charge, sliding the form through the opening in the glass.

The woman on the other side studied it for a moment and then pointed at my answer under *Intended Use of Certified Copy*. Though it offered several options, including for travel or for social security purposes, I'd checked the box marked "Other" and written *Ancestry research*.

"So you're doing a family tree or something?" she asked. "Like, tracing your genealogy?"

I nodded.

"And this is your grandmother?"

"Her paternal grandmother," Isaac said. "We couldn't fill in every single blank, but we put in as much information as we could."

"ID, please."

I passed my state-issued ID card through the opening in the window and tried not to look nervous as she compared the image on the card with the sight of me in person. Fortunately, our district was one of the few in the area that allowed us to have such cards, despite the fact that we had to be photographed for them. Considering we had no drivers licenses, it certainly made things easier sometimes.

Satisfied, the woman carried the card over to a machine, made a copy of it, and then brought back the original and handed it out through the opening.

"The birth certificate will be mailed to your house in two to three weeks," she said as she wrote something on the form and stapled the copy to it. "Twenty dollars, please."

"Wait, what?" I asked.

She let out a breath, seeming vaguely irritated, and repeated herself.

"But we were hoping to get it today," I said.

Nodding, Isaac added, "That's why we're here."

She shrugged. "Sorry. We only do expedited service for emergencies. Do you need it for travel within the next five days?"

"No. I just thought—"

"Then you're out of luck. Twenty dollars, please. Checks only."

We didn't *have* to get it today, but I felt crestfallen just the same. As I fumbled for my checkbook, Isaac must've seen my disappointment because he leaned closer to the glass and put on his most charming smile. "Can't you make an exception?" he asked sweetly. "We came all this way to get information about her grandmother. I know that's not an emergency, but until we have the birth certificate, we're kind of stuck."

"Honey, even if this were a legitimate emergency," she replied, for the first time actually making eye contact through the glass, "the fastest you could get it would be tomorrow."

And that was that. I tried not to let my disappointment show as I wrote out the check and handed it through. I was about to walk away but Isaac stayed, giving it one more shot.

"What if it's not a certified copy? We don't need the raised seal. We just want to see it."

"Then you're in the wrong place," the woman said, shaking her head. She bent forward to retrieve something from a lower shelf, adding, "At least you're in the right city. Philadelphia is a treasure trove of genealogical resources." When she found what she was looking for, she stood and slid a printed page to us through the opening. "Try one of these instead. Good luck."

An hour later, Isaac and I were settled in a cozy corner of a local historical society, one that had been included on the list of "Pennsylvania Libraries, Archives, and Repositories for Genealogical Research" the woman had given us. Now we were poring over the printouts and copies of all the relevant documents we'd managed to find thus far. The woman at Vital Records had been right. There were so many resources, and the people working at this place were especially helpful.

Apparently, it was a slow day for family trees because we seemed to have the main docent at our disposal, an older fellow who'd introduced himself as Mr. Cadwallader. He had a formal air and an old-fashioned mustache that ended in a stiff curl on each side of his mouth, and I wasn't sure what to make of him at first. But he'd turned out to be thoroughly knowledgeable of both their physical collection and their online genealogy resources, and he was a nice man besides. Thus far, with his help, Isaac and I had managed to dig up some relevant census records, a deed, several tax records, and even a draft card showing conscientious objector status for one of my great uncles. Meanwhile, Mr. Cadwallader was hard at work himself on our main goal of tracking down a birth certificate for my grandmother.

"Did you see this?" Isaac asked, leaning toward me across the table to show me the page where he was pointing. "According to the 1920 census, your great-grandmother's occupation was listed as 'Apiarist.' Any idea what that is?"

I shook my head, wondering if there was a dictionary around here so I could look it up.

"An apiarist is a beekeeper," Mr. Cadwallader said, coming around the corner. "Not an unusual occupation for a farmer's wife back then. They probably had fruit trees and needed a sufficient bee population for pollination."

Isaac and I shared a smile at this man who seemed to know everything about everything.

"May I join you?" he asked, coming to a stop at our table. "I think you're going to be very happy if I do."

My eyes widened. "You found it? The birth certificate?"

"Yes, ma'am." He beamed as he pulled up a chair at the end of the table and then laid the printout down, turned so we could see it.

Sure enough, this was, indeed, the document we'd been hoping for. *Annette Sabine Bender. November 15, 1920. Caernarvon Township.*

I ran my fingers across the name, filled with sudden wonder. This wasn't just some random person. This was my grandmother, my flesh and blood.

I gave Mr. Cadwallader a big smile. "This is so fun, and so helpful," I said. "I can't thank you enough."

"Oh, I'm not done yet," he replied, eyes twinkling. "When I was looking for that one, I ran across Georgette's as well. 'Annette Sabine' and 'Georgette Nadine.' That's clever."

My head jerked up. "What?"

"Their names."

"Whose names?"

"Annette Bender and her twin sister, Georgette Bender."

"She didn't have a twin sister," I said. But then he took a second page and set it beside the first.

Eyes wide, I looked from one to the other and back again.

Annette Sabine Bender. November 15, 1920

Georgette Nadine Bender. November 15, 1920

My eyes skimmed down the page. Same date of birth, same date filed, same place, same parents. Different times—but by just fifteen minutes.

I looked at Isaac, stunned. "My grandmother had a twin."

"Your grandmother had a twin," he echoed.

"But how?" I asked. "Why have I never heard of her?"

Isaac shrugged. "Maybe she was born but then died soon after?"

"Maybe," said Mr. Cadwallader. "Why don't I go check for a death certificate? It shouldn't take long. They're easier to track down than birth certificates."

"That would be great. Thank you."

With that, he rose and returned to his work area, leaving Isaac and me to puzzle over the matter on our own.

"I can't believe no one ever mentioned that my grandmother had a twin," I said. "I wonder if my *daed* even knows. And what about Ina Mae? She never said anything about it. Surely she would have mentioned Georgette if she'd known her, or even if she'd known about her, right?"

"I would think so," Isaac replied. "You said she was very forthcoming. There's no mention of a Georgette in your family directory?"

"No. It lists *Mammi* Nettie and her twelve siblings, but not one of them was named Georgette."

We grew quiet for a moment.

"Hey, what about the census reports?" I gestured toward the pile of pages in front of Isaac. "Is she on those?"

Quickly, he laid them out in order of year, in a row, and then we checked.

The 1920 census was dated in January of that year, and, as expected, they weren't listed on it since they weren't born until November. The 1930 census, however, had both names, Georgette and Annette, with their ages marked down as ten.

By 1940, both of their parents were deceased, and though Nettie, age 20, was shown as living with Ina Mae's family in Hopeland, there was no listing for a Georgette anywhere on the page. In 1950, Nettie was listed with Joshua Mueller as his spouse in West Lampeter, but again there was no sign of Georgette.

How bizarre.

"All right. Well, there's no death certificate," Mr. Cadwallader announced as he came our way once more.

"No death certificate?" Isaac said. "So what does that mean? That she didn't die in Pennsylvania?"

The older man shook his head. "No. I checked both the state and the national indices. There was nothing for her in either."

"You mean there's a chance this Georgette person is still alive?" I cried, incredulous. "But she'd be nearly a hundred years old by now."

He nodded, absently twisting one end of his mustache between two fingers.

"How about other kinds of records?" Isaac asked. "Such as adoption? Or marriage?"

"We know she wasn't adopted," I said, gesturing toward the census forms. "At least not prior to the age of ten."

"We also know that from the birth certificate," Mr. Cadwallader added. "When a child is adopted, their original birth certificate is sealed. But if Georgette Bender's had been sealed, I wouldn't have been able to find it. So she definitely wasn't adopted by someone else. Not legally anyway."

"And marriage?" I asked hopefully.

He sucked in a breath, looking suddenly reluctant. "I'm sorry, kids, but we'll need to stop here." Glancing at his watch, he added, "We close at eleven. That was ten minutes ago."

"I used to come here to study," Isaac said as we stepped through the library doors. Though Mr. Cadwallader had felt bad about kicking us out, he had given us a few suggestions for how to proceed. He said our marriage question could be answered online, and that we should head over to the Free Library of Philadelphia and do it ourselves. Isaac had thought that was a great idea, and so now here we were.

"You studied in art school?" I asked, looking around at the large facility and its rows and rows of bookshelves. "I thought you did art."

He smiled at me as he nodded. "We studied art history and history in general. We also had research and writing classes. I took a film class, which included a lot of research and writing as well."

I was about to tell him about my brother-in-law Zed and how he'd gone to college for filmmaking when Isaac added, "Oh, and math too."

"Really?" I used math quite a bit as a quilter, but I hadn't thought about it in drawing and painting.

He nodded. "Measuring. Lines. Ratios. Surprisingly, I turned out to be pretty good at it and ended up doing some tutoring on the side."

"Oh." I pulled another book from the shelf and pretended to be interested in it. Tabitha was right about his past. I couldn't even imagine what his time in Philadelphia had been like. The part of me that longed for him to be interested in me deflated. Why would he be? I had nothing to offer him.

When it was our turn at the computer, Isaac pulled another chair up so we could both sit down. He logged on and then typed in "Georgette Bender" and "Pennsylvania."

The name popped up on Facebook and LinkedIn, but none of the women lived in Pennsylvania. Next he Googled just "Georgette Bender." Lots of entries popped up. He clicked through the links. Some were obituaries, but none of the women were elderly, and all of them lived in Texas, California, Maine, and other places. Clearly, Georgette Bender could have left Pennsylvania, but she couldn't have changed how old she was.

Isaac clicked the mouse, hopped over to the Lancaster County government website, as Mr. Cadwallader had suggested, and found the link to the index for marriage certificates. "What year should we start with?"

"Hmm...1938? She would have been eighteen."

The entries were listed by both the bride's and groom's surname and the year, which made it easier to skim through the entries. We found

Annette Bender and Joshua Mueller listed on October 25, 1940. We kept skimming and skimming. When we reached May 21, 1946, we found Georgette Bender and Paul W. Johnson.

"Bingo," Isaac said.

I quickly jotted down the information, and then Isaac opened up a new window and Googled Georgette Johnson. Again, lots of names popped up, but none who were the right age. Next, he searched for a wedding announcement, using both Georgette Bender Johnson and Paul W. Johnson, but nothing appeared for that either. Then Isaac typed in "Paul W. Johnson, Lancaster, PA." An old newspaper article popped up. Apparently a Paul W. Johnson had been a representative to the State House from 1959–1965. In another article, the writer mentioned Paul's six children and devoted wife. Unfortunately, she was only referred to as "Paul Johnson's wife" and "Mrs. Johnson," with no first name given.

Using this information, Isaac Googled more specific entries and came up with a short article about the same Paul W. Johnson, which said he was a partner in an insurance firm and a member of the local Chamber of Commerce. Next, Isaac found the man's obituary from 1969, which said he'd died of a pulmonary embolism at the age of just fifty-one. Again, his wife's first name was not given.

"Do you think that could be her?" I asked as I dug in my bag for pen and paper.

"Maybe." Isaac hit the print button on the obituary. "I'll print all of these out," he said. "Don't worry about writing everything down."

Once he was all finished, he collected the articles, handed them to me, and then paid for the copies. I carefully added them to my file as I thanked him. I didn't know how long it would have taken me to find the information he'd discovered in just a few minutes. He was even better at this stuff than Kristen was.

"How about some lunch?" he asked, "Then we can do a little sightseeing. There's a place I'd like to show you. After that, we can go by the gallery I need to visit. Then, if our timing is right, we can have an early dinner."

"That all sounds lovely," I said. "It's been a crazy morning. It would be nice to switch gears and think about something else for a change."

We made our way back to the busier street where Ginny had dropped us off and then ate a light lunch at a little café inside one of the high-rise buildings there. Isaac seemed familiar with the place. We both ordered sandwiches and sat at a table beside the window. "How far is your college from here?" I asked.

"Not far at all."

"Could we walk by it?"

"Sure," he said. "We can do that before we head to the gallery. We can even go inside if you want. I haven't been by there in a while."

"What made you decide to go to art school?"

When he didn't answer right away, I felt as if I shouldn't have asked. But then I realized he was just organizing his thoughts.

"It's a pretty complicated answer. I have loved to draw and paint for as long as I can remember. When I was in school, we had a teacher who encouraged it, which thrilled me but not my *daed*. The older I got, the more he was bothered by my artwork. He felt it was a waste of time."

"What about your *mamm*?"

"She really liked my art, so it wasn't as if she discouraged me, but she didn't see how it could be part of my future, at least not much." He took a bite of his sandwich. After he swallowed, he continued. "After school, when I was sixteen, I entered a painting in the county fair without telling my parents. I won first prize, and the next week one of the judges came out to the farm to talk with me about my 'gift.' Of course neither my *daed* nor my *mamm* was thrilled with that. Both felt I'd been prideful to enter and feared I'd grow even more so with the positive feedback."

I nodded. That was how any Plain parent would feel. I ate my sandwich as he talked.

"When I was seventeen, I got a job working with a gardening crew one spring and moved out. I was frugal and saved everything I could. By winter I had a job in a restaurant, making tips and continuing to save money. From there, I moved to Philly with an *Englisch* friend and got a job waiting tables again and making even more money. I found out about art school, so I got my GED and then applied. My financial aid was good because I was on my own, and I worked full-time. I started selling my paintings too, so that helped."

"So basically you were *Englisch* from the time you were eighteen until—"

He nodded. "Last year. For nine years."

Which made him twenty-eight. Nine years older than me. No wonder he seemed so mature compared to other young men I knew.

"What made you decide to come back?"

"Community. Family. But, ultimately, my relationship with God. It was harder for me to keep my commitment to Him in the *Englisch* world than in the Plain."

I tipped my head. "How did your parents react when you returned?"

"They were skeptical."

"But they got over it?"

He shook his head and finished his sandwich.

"They're still not over it?"

"They were supportive of me taking the membership classes and joining the church. I just think having me around was a painful reminder of what I had put them through. And I think they're fearful I'll leave again."

"Will you?" I asked, a lurch in my stomach.

He met my eyes, looking surprised that I would ask. "No. Never. I made a commitment."

I believed him. My heart filled with empathy for Isaac. That would be a difficult position to be in, to have come to the place of doing the right thing only to have his parents doubt him.

"So where exactly are you taking me for this little sightseeing adventure?" I asked as we exited the restaurant and began making our way down the busy street. I knew that Philadelphia held a number of important historical sights, and judging by the signs we passed at the corner, we were headed into the heart of that. "Are we going to see the Liberty Bell?"

Isaac flashed me a smile. "That's not our final destination, but we will pass it on the way." He didn't elaborate, so I didn't press him for more. Instead, I just kept walking at his side, taking in the sights and sounds and smells of this beautiful sunny day in the city.

At the next block, we reached what looked like a park of sorts, with a wide expanse of grass stretching out on both sides. People were milling about here and there, making their way between the various buildings that lined the green.

"Let's cut through here," Isaac said, "just so I can kind of orient you to where we are." He glanced around and then took me by the elbow to lead me out of the throng and over to one of several red brick walkways. He told me about our surroundings as we went, saying that we were in the heart of America's Most Historic Square Mile. "We're surrounded by so much history here, it's unbelievable. Of course, the most important place of all is that one."

He stopped walking, turned, and gestured behind us, pointing toward a stately old red brick structure that sat at the far end of the grassy area. "That's Independence Hall, where both the Declaration of Independence and the Constitution were signed."

"Wow." I took in the building with its pleasing symmetry and beautiful tower and steeple.

Turning back, we began walking again, and as we went, he pointed out the Liberty Bell, visible through a large plate-glass window, and then a couple of other significant historical structures, including the National Constitution Center and the US Mint. At the next block, we turned right and began moving along a less busy street this time, passing a historic Quaker Meeting House on the corner and then the grave of Benjamin Franklin, easily visible through a brick-and-wrought-iron fence.

"Where are we headed?" I asked, eager to reach our destination.

"A historical attraction I think you'll really enjoy. There are so many in this city, it was hard to decide which one to take you to. But then it finally dawned on me...the perfect site for a quilter."

With that, he paused and gestured toward a modest building just ahead, one with a shady courtyard and a giant flag hanging outside. In front was a sign: *The Betsy Ross House.*

"Welcome to the home of the seamstress who's thought to have sewn America's first flag," he said.

For the next hour, Isaac and I explored the place, learning all about Betsy Ross. The whole house was fascinating but especially the center point of the tour, which featured a recreation of her 1700's upholstery shop. There we listened to a historic interpreter pretending to be the woman herself, telling us all about the night George Washington showed up at her door with a request to make a flag for what would become the United States of America.

As it turned out, she hadn't been a quilter after all but rather an upholsterer, a fact that we learned early on in the tour. Throughout the house, in fact, we spotted exactly one quilt, a simple patchwork draped over a chair in the corner of a bedroom.

"I'm so happy you brought me to the perfect attraction for a *quilter*," I teased Isaac as we finally emerged from the house into the afternoon sunshine.

"Who knew?" He was grinning, but I could tell he was a little embarrassed.

"Hey, seriously," I said, pointing toward a pair of chairs across the courtyard under a broad sycamore tree. "I hope you know I loved that. She may not have quilted, but she did work with needle and thread and fabric. So it really was the perfect choice for me."

We walked over to the chairs and sat, not even noticing until we did that we were facing a circular fountain that held a trio of sculptured metal cats.

"Look. It's Whisper!" I cried, gesturing to the black one on top. Made of iron, he was adorable, perched on a stone cylinder with his tail hanging down behind.

"Yes it is," Isaac replied, acting as if he'd known all about it. "And that's the real reason I brought you here, Linda, not for any quilts but to surprise you with the sculpture of Whisper in Betsy Ross's courtyard."

The only college I knew anything about was Goshen College in Indiana where Zed went to school. Izzy had once described it as a bunch of brick buildings on acres of green lawns with concrete pathways meandering around the grounds. As it turned out, however, Isaac's college couldn't have been more different from that. For starters, it was on the fifth and sixth floors of a high rise, and it was in the busiest part of the city. We took the elevator up, and when we stepped off, the first thing that was visible was a sign that read "Philadelphia College of Art." The woman at the front desk looked at us for just a moment before breaking into a broad smile.

"Isaac!" She stood and rushed to give him a hug. "How are you?"

"Good." Then he added, "Better."

She stepped back. "What has it been? A year?"

He nodded.

"So you really did it."

"I did."

"And you're happy?"

"I am. Honestly."

"That's so good to hear."

"Margie, I'd like you to meet Linda." Isaac smiled down at me. "I'm living in Lancaster County now, close to her family. We've come into the city for the day."

The woman shook my hand. "It's nice to meet you." Her voice was warm and kind.

"Linda quilts. Beautifully," he added. "She really has a gift."

My face grew warm.

"Oh, I love quilts." The woman clasped her hands together. "Especially Amish quilts. I get out to Lancaster every once in a while."

I told her about the Arts & Crafts House and said she should stop by sometime.

"I'd like that." She turned to Isaac. "Are you still painting?"

He nodded. "I don't have as much time, but I'm doing what I can. I'm going to go check in at the gallery later to see what new things I can send them."

"I'm very glad to hear that." She inhaled, deeply. "I was so afraid you would quit."

Isaac shook his head and then said, "I'm just going to show Linda around. I know classes are in session. We'll be quiet."

She smiled. "Take your time. It's so good to see you." She patted him on the shoulder.

As we walked down the hall, a man came out to shake Isaac's hand, and the scene was repeated. Isaac introduced him as one of his professors. On the sixth floor, a student in the hall greeted Isaac. Again he introduced me. Isaac had tutored the young man in math. It was obvious Isaac had been well known and well liked.

After telling Margie goodbye, we took the elevator back to the street.

As we exited the building, Isaac said, "We should take a taxi to the gallery so we have time to eat before Ginny picks us up."

Before I could answer, he stepped to the curb and raised his arm. A second later a taxi stopped, and Isaac opened the back door. "Scoot all the way over."

Even with the traffic, it didn't take long to get to New Vision Gallery. It was much bigger than I'd expected—two-stories high—and classier. Its artwork included paintings, sculptures, and mixed media. All were well placed with plenty of space between each item.

"My paintings are on the second floor." Isaac led the way to the staircase, which was wide and open and provided a view of the first level of the shop as we ascended.

When we reached the top, I saw that this floor had paintings and sculptures too, along with fabric art. Before I had time to examine any of it, I noticed what had to be Isaac's paintings along the far wall.

A woman dressed in pants, a flowing top, and high heels walked toward us, carrying a brief case. "I was afraid you wouldn't get here in time. I have a meeting in ten minutes." She wore her blond hair long and parted on the side. I guessed she was probably in her midthirties.

After Isaac greeted the woman, whom he introduced as Cheri Bethune, she welcomed me and then turned to him and said, "I have your paperwork right here. And a check." She pulled a large envelope from her briefcase. "We've sold three of your paintings, and I've been talking with a fourth buyer. We'd definitely like more."

Isaac asked if she wanted similar paintings or something completely different.

"I want whatever you can bring me," she said. "Or, if you'd rather, I can send someone out to pick them up."

As they talked more, an exhibit of quilts caught my attention, and I wandered off toward them, looking at a collection of cobalt-blue glass vases first. By the time I reached the appliqué quilts, Cheri and Isaac had joined me.

"This is gorgeous." I examined one that was quite complicated—a flower garden of blues and purples with oversized green petals and leaves. All of the elements worked perfectly, but I knew how much could have gone wrong. I couldn't imagine ever making anything like this. The appliqué quilts I'd tried so far were simple and geometric and symmetrical. Just the thought of doing something this wildly creative made me feel out of control.

Isaac turned toward Cheri. "You know, Linda's an incredibly gifted quilter. You should consider taking on one of her pieces."

My face grew warm at his words, but I couldn't help but be pleased at what seemed to be a very sincere comment.

Cheri turned to the shelf behind the quilts and retrieved a catalog. "Well, these are the latest listings. See how yours compare, and then if you still think we might be interested, e-mail me some images and we'll go from there."

My face grew warm as I took the catalogue from her. I knew mine wouldn't be good enough, but I was curious about what the gallery had chosen to represent.

Cheri was all business as she quickly turned back to Isaac and they began discussing how many paintings he currently had available to send in. As they talked, I flipped through the pages of the catalogue.

There were patchwork and appliqué quilts, both traditional and modern designs, all beautiful. I landed on a full-page spread. Perhaps I gasped because Cheri stopped what she was doing to lean my way and take a look.

"Oh, yes," she said. "Those are made by a woman in Lancaster. They're hand-appliquéd, stitched, and quilted."

Isaac looked over as well and did double take.

"What is it?" Cheri asked.

"What's the name of the quilter?" I asked her.

"I don't know. Her listings aren't done by name. She sells under 'Twinkle Star Quilts.' I assume that means she's Amish because we've worked with other Amish artisans before who asked to keep their names out of it. Can't imagine why, but we're happy to accommodate them."

I thought about explaining why. Leaving off their own names helped keep them from getting prideful about their work, but I doubted she would understand the concept, so I held my tongue. Instead, I returned my attention to the page, glancing at Isaac as I did. "Are you thinking what I'm thinking?"

He nodded.

"What is it?" Cheri asked again.

I pointed toward a swirl of red that swooped down from the sun into the horizon and became the path upon which an Amish man was walking. "See how the sun becomes the path?" I pointed to the quilt beside it. "And here it is again."

"Yes, that is one of her signature elements," Cheri commented. "She's used it before in other pieces."

"It's not just that." Isaac took the catalog from me and studied it more closely. "The whole *style* of this quilt…It's almost identical to the style of your grandmother's painting."

He and I gaped at each other, both of us certain there had to be some sort of connection between this unnamed quilter, whoever she was, and my *Mammi* Nettie. For all we knew, she could be the mysterious twin sister.

Ten

Isaac explained the situation to Cheri, telling her how my grandmother had been an artist and how she'd done the exact same thing with the sunset in one of her paintings. He also described the similarities between her artistic style and that of the quilter, though the terms he used—things like "line work" and "color pallet" and "juxtaposition"—were mostly over my head. As an art dealer, however, Cheri understood exactly what he was saying, and she seemed to grow more intrigued by the minute.

In response, she offered to make a call or two and try to find out the name of the quilter, which she could then pass along to Isaac. That reminded him that he needed to update his contact information now that he'd moved to Ruth's and had a new address and a new phone number.

As they took care of that, I continued to stare at the full-page spread. The appliqué was beautiful, no matter that it was just a photograph. I'd never seen anything like it, not even online when looking with Kristen. It was almost as if the pieces of fabric, in all different shapes and sizes, had been painted rather than sewn.

Finished with Cheri, Isaac appeared at my shoulder. "The sunset is incredible, but look at the hillside too, how she used all sorts of different greens." He pointed to the darker green. "That's an alfalfa field." He pointed to the lime green. "And that's a pasture." It *was* incredible, all of it.

He practically had to pull the catalogue from my hands, saying we could study the image further over supper. I was about to ask how he could even think about eating at a time like this when he added, "I want to take you to a restaurant where I used to work." From the tone of his voice, I could tell it was important to him, so I gave in, tucking the catalog inside my bag.

Cheri bid us both farewell, and we left.

There were lots of pedestrians on the sidewalk weaving around each other. I was tired and hungry and a little overwhelmed. Isaac must have sensed that because he grabbed my hand. I relaxed as he gently led me through the mass of people. His hand was warm against mine, and I couldn't help but wonder if his intent was to keep track of me or if there was more behind the gesture.

My heart raced. I hoped there was more. I was so glad he'd brought me to Philadelphia and showed me his former world. He'd lived *Englisch, ya,* but I didn't see any evidence that he'd been wild. He had a gift and had wanted to learn how to use it. That seemed to be it. How much happier would my grandmother have been if she'd been able to do the same thing?

A few minutes later we reached a café in what Isaac called a brownstone. He let go of my hand and opened the door for me. It took a moment for my eyes to adjust and by then he had stepped in beside me.

"Hey! Isaac? Is that you?" A man with a full beard and mustache approached with his hand extended. "I figured I'd never see you again."

It's me." Isaac had a grin on his face. He quickly introduced me to Guy. The man grabbed two menus, showed us to a table under a window, and then excused himself, saying he'd be back in just a minute.

I looked around at the walls, which were covered with little sayings and paintings and plaques and old rusty antiques, such as a washboard and eggbeater. The style of one painting looked very familiar—it was of an owl on a split rail fence.

I turned back to Isaac. "Is that yours?"

"It is. Like I said, I used to work here way back when. I gave it to Guy as a thank-you when I left."

I kept looking around and found a plaque that read, *Life Is Not a Fairy Tale*. I sighed. Today had been.

When I glanced at Isaac, he was smiling at me. But then he opened the menu. "Everything they serve here is locally grown and homemade. They work with farmers, some Amish, and only buy organic."

"Hey." It was Guy again, ready to take our orders, but really it seemed he wanted to talk. While I glanced at the menu, he asked about Isaac's artwork, and the two launched into a lengthy discussion.

Finally, Guy asked what we wanted to eat. I decided on the handmade pasta with roasted chicken, beets, and herbs. I couldn't decide if it sounded fancy or just delicious. Isaac ordered lamb with garlic-mashed potatoes and an in-season vegetable medley. After Guy left, Isaac met my gaze and asked if I'd had a good day.

"It's been a perfect day. Seeing the Betsy Ross House and your art school and the gallery—all of that was so fun."

Isaac's eyes shone as I talked.

"Plus, we found so much information on *Mammi* Nettie—and learned she had a twin! And then to happen upon the catalogue and the photo of that quilt." I patted my bag. "It's all so unbelievable." I had the urge to give him a hug but restrained myself.

He must have been feeling the need to connect with me as well because he discreetly reached for one of my hands under the table and took it in his. "Unbelievable is right."

We shared a smile, and when he squeezed my hand, I squeezed back, feeling a warmth spread through my body, all the way down to my toes. So this was what it was like to be in love, I thought dreamily. How had I denied the possibility of this happening for so long? I'd been dumb enough to buy my own lie that I would always be alone because I would never find anyone I could truly love. But I could. I *had*. And he was right here with me now, gazing into my eyes, reflecting that feeling back to me even if he hadn't yet said the words.

Isaac's expression grew more serious.

"What is it?" I whispered, my pulse beginning to race. Perhaps he was going to say it now, out loud—and then I could tell him that I loved him too.

"I just hope you know that you can ask me anything." He leaned forward and lowered his voice. "You haven't yet, but I spoke with Sadie, and she said you're aware of my story. You've been so kind and understanding even though we haven't talked about it..."

I inhaled. His story? Tabitha had told me a few things about Isaac's past, but not much. And Sadie had never said a word to me about it at all.

"I don't want to assume too much or be too forward, but I'm ready to move on, and there's no one else I'd like to do that with than—"

"Isaac?"

I turned.

A woman with short gray hair stared at us.

"Phyllis." He let go of my hand and stood. "What are you doing here?"

She grinned. "Tracking you down. I got a call from Margie, who said you were in town today and that you'd been over at the school."

"Oh boy." Isaac smiled, shaking his head. "You know what they say. Telephone, telegraph, or tell Margie."

Phyllis chuckled. "I was so eager to see you that I thought I'd give it a shot. You were gone by the time I could get there, so I tried Cheri's gallery instead, on the off chance that's where you'd gone next. I missed you there too, but then she said she thought she'd heard you mention something about having dinner 'at the restaurant where you used to work.' So I rushed over. And sure enough, here you are."

She seemed so proud of herself, but then her eyes traveled to me, and her smile faded. "I'm sorry. Maybe I shouldn't have been so persistent. I didn't mean to interrupt anything."

"No, it's fine," I said.

She smiled again, but it seemed as if a pained expression passed over her face.

"Of course it's fine," Isaac said. "Phyllis, this is Linda. The girl I mentioned in my letter. Linda, Phyllis."

I stood, shook her hand, and told her I was pleased to meet her. I expected Isaac to explain who she was, but he didn't. Perhaps she'd been a past teacher of his too.

"Everything is going well?" the woman asked.

Isaac glanced at me and then nodded.

"I'm so glad," she said. "Did you get my last letter?"

"I did," Isaac answered. "I started a response but just haven't finished yet. I'd love to have you come visit in Lancaster. My grandmother would too."

"Splendid. Just let me know when would work best. Give me a call."

Isaac nodded.

She smiled again, the sadness in her expression now gone. "It was very nice to meet you, Linda." She took my hand. "And I really do mean that. Truly, I do."

Taken aback, I said it was nice to meet her too. Her sincerity seemed genuine, but her emphatic tone was rather disconcerting.

"I'll let you two be."

"I'm happy you tracked me down," Isaac said. "Sorry you had to go through all that. I'll talk with my grandmother and give you a call soon."

Phyllis hugged Isaac and then left, walking past Guy just as he was bringing our food.

We sat as we were served, and then once Guy was gone Isaac led us in a silent prayer. I felt a bit unsettled about the encounter with Phyllis, but I prayed I would have an open mind as he explained to me who she was.

After the prayer, I came right out and asked. Nodding toward the door, I whispered, "*Vi vou sell?*" Who is that?

Isaac's face fell. "I'm so sorry. I thought it was obvious. That's Bailey's mom." Leaning toward me, he added, "My mother-in-law."

I certainly couldn't eat and I could hardly listen, but still Isaac kept talking. "Sadie said you and your sisters were discussing me and my situation the night you stayed over. Not long after Robert's funeral, when Izzy and Becky were still in town."

I shook my head. "Believe me, I would remember that." I scooted my plate forward an inch. "We had no such conversation, and I haven't a clue why she said we did."

"I'm so sorry." He glanced down at his untouched food and then back up at me. "I guess I'd better start at the beginning."

"I guess you'd better." I clamped my lips shut, startled at the sharpness in my tone.

He ran a hand through his hair and blew out a breath. "I met Bailey my last year of art school, at a church I visited with a friend. She'd just graduated from college and was teaching first grade. She moved back in with her mom because her father had died the year before." His eyes grew serious. "Soon after we met, Bailey and I started dating."

I wasn't even sure what that meant. Did he have a car and drive to her house? And take her to dinner and a movie? They certainly weren't going to singings together.

"Then after I graduated, we married the next September. We kept things very traditional," he said. "As far as dating and marriage. We shared the same values."

I nodded. I understood what he was saying. He was *Englisch*, but he wasn't wild.

"Bailey kept teaching and I opened, with her mother's financial help, a studio where I taught art classes, mostly for kids in the community, and did my own work too. After we'd been married for a couple of years, Bailey started feeling unwell. Tired. Run down. Short of breath." He paused as if not sure what to say. "Anyway, after several doctor's visits and lots of tests we found out she had dilated cardiomyopathy."

I'd never heard of it but knew it must've had something to do with her heart.

"She'd been active her whole life, playing soccer, hiking, swimming. But by the time they did the tests, her heart function was only at ten percent—the disease affects the muscle and eventually causes heart failure. She quit her job, started drug therapy, and got on a heart transplant registry, but she died a year later." He folded his hands together. "I stayed in our apartment for a while and kept running my business. But nothing felt right. So after a lot of prayer and a number of conversations with Phyllis, I ended up selling our car, most of our belongings, and my business and going back home to Somerset County."

I didn't know what to do or say. How could everyone be aware of this but me? And how could I have been so stupid not to guess that Isaac's past was this complicated? I'd feared he might have had an *Englisch* girlfriend, but I never guessed he'd had an *Englisch* wife!

"I'm sorry," Isaac said. "I was waiting for you to bring it up—and when you didn't, I thought you had no problem with it."

I exhaled slowly.

"Do you?" he asked.

"Do I what?"

"Have a problem with the fact that I was married before?"

I opened my mouth to say something but nothing came out. I felt sympathetic toward Isaac. He'd gone through a horrible tragedy. But I felt so tricked. Would I have let myself fall for him if I'd known?

The truth was, I wanted to marry someone who hadn't been married before. I could never compete with the memory of a late wife, much less one who'd died such a young and tragic death.

"Linda," he said.

I couldn't help the tears that flooded my eyes. I felt horrible. Why couldn't I just have empathy for him and leave it at that?

"I need some time," I managed to say. "To think."

"That's understandable." Isaac stared at me for a moment, his eyes kind, and then picked up his fork and started eating his food. I picked at mine. After a while Guy brought the check and a box for me.

After Isaac paid, he said, "We should get going. It's almost time to meet Ginny."

I nodded, stood, and grabbed my bag. Isaac picked up my box of food. Our eyes met. "I'm really sorry," he said.

"I know," I managed to reply. "It's not your fault." I felt awful about the misunderstanding. My whole life, I'd never measured up to Sadie, Becky, Izzy, and Tabitha. And now I'd never measure up to Bailey either. She graduated from college. Taught school. Was a committed Christian. And she loved Isaac. More than that, he loved her.

It was obvious in every gesture, every word.

Ginny dropped me off first. I thanked her and dug in my purse to help pay.

"I've got it," Isaac said.

"No." I kept digging. "I should help."

He just shook his head and said, "See you in the morning."

I closed my purse, grabbed my box of food, and told them both good night.

Dusk was falling as I walked toward the house. The scent of the daphne nearby wafted up toward me. *Mamm's* red geraniums, planted in the barrels along the sidewalk, seemed to have grown since morning.

I loved our farm, our house, our home. The setting had always been so comforting to me. But tonight I didn't feel that comfort. I felt restless. Frustrated. Heartbroken.

I opened the back door and stepped into the kitchen. Stephen and Thomas both sat at the kitchen table, eating bowls of ice cream.

"You're in trouble," Stephen teased.

I raised my eyebrows as I put my box of food in the refrigerator.

Thomas yelled. "*Mamm,* she's home!"

Mamm stepped around the corner from the living room, holding a book in her hand. I expected her to be upset with me, but she didn't appear to be. "Hmm," she said. "A whole day with Isaac. You could have told me. I had to find out from Ruth." She smiled. She wasn't upset. Quite the opposite.

Even though she was teasing, I didn't appreciate her attitude. Since when did parents insinuate themselves in their adult children's love lives? Every one of my siblings had dated without intrusion. So why was I being treated differently? Because I'd never dated before? Or because the man I was dating was a widower, with a world of experience I could never understand?

"I don't see that it's any of your business," I replied, trying to keep my tone from sounding rude or disrespectful. I must've pulled it off because her smile didn't fade for a second.

"You're right. It's not," she replied, eyes twinkling. "But may I at least inquire as to whether you had a good time?"

I murmured something that may have sounded affirmative and said, "I'm really tired. I'm going to go on up to bed."

"What's the matter?" *Mamm* put the book on the corner of the table.

"Nothing. It's just been a long day." I blinked back my tears as I turned toward the staircase.

I couldn't sleep. I felt an utter loneliness, one that wouldn't have been helped by Tabitha in the room with me, or any of my sisters. My heart ached in a way I didn't know possible. I lay awake, staring at the dark ceiling as I heard Stephen and Thomas get ready for bed. I heard *Mamm* and *Daed* too and then the house was silent. My stomach began to growl. I thought of my box of leftovers in the fridge below. I traipsed down the stairs, careful to skip the third from the bottom that always squeaked.

I was sitting at the table in the dark, eating my cold food, when I heard *Mamm* and *Daed*'s bedroom door open. Maybe one of them had to go to the bathroom. I took another bite. The footsteps came toward me.

Light from the moon shone through the kitchen window, just enough so that I could make out a figure emerging from the hall. *Mamm.*

I whispered, "Don't let me scare you. I'm at the table."

She came closer, her slippers scraping over the wood floor, cinching her robe as she walked. "*Ya*, I heard you come down but not go back up." She sat in the chair next to me. "What happened today?"

I shrugged my shoulders.

"Linda," she said. "You need to talk with someone. Either tell me now or talk with Sadie in the morning, but don't keep it inside."

I took a bite of beet. I felt too humiliated to talk about it.

"Did Isaac say something? Or do something? Did he hurt you in some way?"

"Not on purpose," I said.

"Did he talk too much about Bailey? About their life together in Philadelphia? Instead of focusing on you?"

I shook my head. My *mother* even knew Isaac's wife's name. So why hadn't she thought to mention the woman to me before? Wasn't that what mothers were supposed to do? Help prepare their daughters for their futures?

"No, he didn't talk too much about her. In fact, that's the problem."

Even in the near darkness I could make out the puzzled look on *Mamm*'s face. "You wanted him to talk about her more?"

"No, I—he." I grunted, trying to rein in my emotions. "He should have mentioned her to me sooner. Or you should have. Or my sisters."

Mamm shook her head. "Sadie and Tabitha both assured me you knew all about his past."

"No. Sadie told Isaac the same thing, but it's not true. I knew nothing except for a couple of vague references that Tabitha made about him having a 'complicated backstory.' No one has ever said that backstory included him having been married before."

"But how could you not know? The entire district knew."

I put down my fork in the box of pasta, but it fell over the side and clattered to the floor. When I reached down to pick it up, I couldn't find it in the dark. I got down on my hands and knees to look.

In the meantime, *Mamm* lit the lamp. I grabbed the fork and took it to the sink, and then, as I stood there, I burst into tears.

Mamm stepped to my side and put her arm around me.

"I thought I loved him," I blubbered.

"Loved? As in, past tense?"

I nodded, wiping at my eyes with the sleeve of my robe.

"So in one day you changed your mind? Because you found out he's a widower?"

Ya, I knew how heartless I sounded, but I couldn't help the way I felt.

I remembered the saying on the plaque in the restaurant earlier in the evening. *Life Is Not a Fairy Tale.* I knew it wasn't. I'd just wanted to start out my relationship with Isaac with a fresh slate. But now I knew that could never be.

"Goodness, Linda. This is no time to be idealistic." *Mamm* let go of my shoulder, reached for a box of tissues, and handed it to me. "His wife died. It's not like he's divorced or something."

"Obviously not." I dried my tears, blew my nose, and threw the tissue in the trash. If that were the case he'd never be allowed to marry again in the church, at least not while his wife was alive. "But I never intended to fall in love with a widower."

"What difference does it makes?"

I stammered, "I-I don't want to spend my entire life being compared to someone else. Especially not a dead woman. It's obvious that he really loved her."

"And that's a good thing," *Mamm* said. "He was a good husband once. He'll be a good husband again."

"Unless I—or whomever he marries—never measures up."

"Stop being ridiculous," *Mamm* said. "Go back to bed and get some sleep. All of this will look different in the morning."

I groaned.

"What is it now?"

"The morning. I'll have to do the milking with him."

Mamm stifled a yawn. "So?"

I stepped to the table and began closing up the box of food. "So he's going to want to talk about it. What do I say?"

Mamm thought for a moment. "Look, I know you're disappointed. The reality of the situation goes against your expectations. But Isaac hasn't changed."

I carried the box to the fridge and slid it inside. *Disappointed* didn't begin to cover it.

"If I were you," *Mamm* continued, "I wouldn't discuss it with him, not yet anyway. Pray about it first. Listen to the Lord's leading."

"Why?" I closed the door and turned to face her. "It's not like the Lord can make the late wife disappear, make it that she never happened."

"No," *Mamm* said thoughtfully, "but He can make your reservations disappear. God can transform anything, including the hardest of hearts."

My eyes filled with fresh tears. "My heart isn't hard, *Mamm*. It's breaking—for myself, *ya*, but for Isaac too. I can't image what he went through." Speaking of hearts, I winced at the thought of how horrible dying must have been for Bailey. I swiped again at my eyes and tried to get control of myself.

"But that's the thing, Linda. Isaac did get through it. And now he's ready to start again with someone new. With you."

I looked away, toward the window. What I saw in my reflection was the dumbest, most uninformed, most naïve girl who had ever been born. Why hadn't someone just told me?

Suddenly I was overwhelmed with exhaustion. All I wanted was to be in bed—and not have to get up and face all of this tomorrow.

"*Ya*, I'll pray about it," I said softly, hoping that would be enough to convince my mother to let the matter drop for now.

Satisfied, she gave me a final hug, extinguished the lamp, and bid me a soft good night before padding off to her room.

Back upstairs, I knelt on the worn wood floor beside the bed, bowed my head, and tried to do as I'd promised, but no words came.

"Dear Lord, please fix this somehow. Amen," I whispered.

Then I climbed into the bed, slid under the covers, and tried not to think about how much I was dreading seeing Isaac again so soon.

ELEVEN

The next morning Stephen and I rode our scooters over to Sadie's long before the sun came up, the way we did every morning now. I yawned several times. I'd hardly slept at all. I felt as if my heart were shriveling, which physically hurt.

Isaac was already in the barn with the lights on, heading toward the far door to let in the first of the cows. He turned and waved at us before continuing on his way. We all worked in silence, including Stephen. I wondered if he sensed something was wrong.

When we'd finished, I told Isaac goodbye. He stood for a moment looking at me.

"What?" I asked.

"Could we talk?"

"I need to go check on Sadie," I said, not meeting his eyes.

Stephen waved and headed toward home, most likely hungry for his breakfast. As Isaac and I left the barn and then turned in different directions, Whisper rubbed up against my leg. I bent down and scooped him up, holding him for just a moment, but then he squirmed and jumped down, running after Isaac.

When I reached Sadie's house, Bobby was in the highchair and the girls were still in their nightgowns. Sadie wore her robe, and she had dark bags under her eyes. Bobby began to fuss, and I stepped toward him. He put his arms up, and I lifted him out of his chair.

"How are you?" I asked Sadie.

"Sick again today," she said.

"Have you been to the doctor yet?"

She shook her head.

"When do you plan to go?"

"Soon." She turned toward the table and the box of crackers. "Could you serve the girls' their oatmeal?"

I did that as I held Bobby and then dished up a bowl for him too while Sadie sat at the table, nibbling on a cracker. The girls ate their breakfast without saying anything as I fed their baby brother. "Have you told *Mamm*?" I asked Sadie.

She shook her head.

"Have you told anyone but me?"

She nodded, glancing at the girls. They were both staring straight ahead as they ate, not paying us any attention.

"I told Jedediah," she said in a low voice.

That surprised me. "What did he say?"

"He's worried."

"About?"

"Me. My health. He's afraid grief will affect…" Her voice trailed off, and I didn't press the matter.

I stayed while Sadie and the girls got dressed. Then I changed Bobby and played with him for a bit. A little while later I handed him over to his mother and said, "I have to go. I start work at ten." I headed toward the door, and she followed me out onto the porch, into the bright sunshine.

"Oh, wait," she said. "Tell me about your trip to Philadelphia. I had no idea you were going until *Mamm* told me."

"It was fine," I said, feeling humiliated again.

Sadie's eyes narrowed. "What's wrong?"

I sighed. I didn't want to go through the whole thing, but I did have one question for her. "Why did you tell Isaac I knew he'd been married before?"

"Because you did."

I shook my head. "Well, I do now. But I didn't. Not until it was obvious that I didn't yesterday, and he had to spell it all out for me, rather painfully I might add."

"Oh no."

I could feel a frown growing on my face. "Why did you think I knew?"

"We talked about it that night, when Izzy and Becky were here. After Robert died."

I shook my head. "No, we didn't."

"We did."

"Maybe before I arrived?"

"No, you were here. I'm positive." She shifted Bobby to her other hip.

"I would remember if I'd heard Isaac had a wife, believe me." I sighed, trying to recall that night. I'd left the room during a conversation about Ezra to go and deal with the girls. When I returned, they were still talking about someone, but I had come in on the tail end of it and hadn't been sure what they were saying or even whom they were talking about. I explained that to Sadie now.

"That was probably when," she replied. "I'm so sorry. I really thought you were a part of the conversation."

Tears stung my eyes, and the familiar feeling of being unseen and unheard swept over me. I was so invisible, my sisters didn't even notice whether I was there or not!

"I can see it'll take a while to get used to, but he didn't intend to deceive you, not at all. He asked me weeks ago if you knew because he was worried about it. You're so innocent and have such high expectations."

I exhaled. That was how they all saw me. Maybe they were right.

"He thought it might be a problem, and then he was so relieved when it wasn't. It was sweet. He really cares about you."

My heart lurched.

"I can see that you wanted to marry someone who hadn't been married before. I get that," Sadie said. "But do you still feel that way, now that you know Isaac?"

"That's the problem," I said. "I'm not sure how I feel."

Sadie twisted her mouth. "Well, I hope someone is willing to marry me someday."

Taken aback, I said, "It's not the same. You'll find a widower whose children need a mother—and yours will get a father."

She wrinkled her nose. "Perhaps. Or perhaps I'll find someone who's never been married."

I thought of Jedediah. Sadie had already confided in him about the baby, before telling *Mamm* and *Daed* even. I tried not to think what that said about her relationship with him.

But now she was asking me to compare Isaac's situation with me to her situation with Jedediah or someone like him, some young man who was as innocent to the world as I was.

I didn't answer her. I had no idea how to respond. Didn't I have a right to my own feelings? The truth was, I wouldn't have fallen in love with Isaac if I'd known he'd been married before. It was enough of an issue for me that he'd lived as an *Englischer*, and it had taken all the grace I possessed to try and get past that. But now that I knew he'd had an *Englisch* wife? No. That I could not live with. The only choice I had was to fall out of love with him—though it wouldn't be easy.

"I'm sorry," Sadie said. "Being a perfectionist about a quilt is one thing. Being a perfectionist about relationships is something entirely different. It's not Isaac's fault his wife died."

"It is his fault he went off to Philadelphia to college and didn't join the church when he should have."

Sadie wrinkled her nose again. "I hate to be frank, but you're not ready to get married. Let Isaac go. He deserves someone else—someone who loves him regardless of his past. Someone who's not so hopelessly idealistic."

She turned around, the baby still in her arms, and started back into the house.

"Sadie…" I stepped toward the door, but it shut. My sweet, loving, pregnant, grieving oldest sister had just slammed her front door in my face.

I fumed as I rode my scooter back home, showered, dressed, and then harnessed Blue. It was another gorgeous day, and traffic was congested as I drove to the Arts & Crafts House. Several tourists snapped photos of me with their phones as they sped past.

The season was definitely ramping up, and Kristen had been right, Saturdays were busier than weekdays. From the moment I got to the store, I never stopped. It seemed hordes of visitors had landed in Lancaster County, and most of the women, and many of the men, found their way to the Arts & Crafts House. We were swamped. In between assisting customers, my thoughts drifted to the other things that had happened yesterday, especially learning that *Mammi* Nettie had a twin sister. The fact that I'd forgotten to tell *Mamm* and *Daed* about that last night showed just how upset I'd been over the whole Isaac thing.

As I directed customers to certain sections, measured fabric, and cut cloth, my mind went to the quilt in the catalogue. Seeing it had almost made me want to try the same technique with the one I was making of the barn, but I knew I never would. Just the thought of it overwhelmed me.

Still, it was amazing to learn that fabric could be used that way. It wasn't just a new level of appliqué work. It was pure art. It was painting with cloth.

Kristen and I both worked hard all day. Ten minutes before closing, I was looking forward to turning the sign, putting everything away, and going home when Isaac walked through the front door, still in his work clothes. When he saw me, he said, "I'm not stalking you, honestly. I needed some supplies, and this is the best place to get them."

My face grew warm. I avoided looking at Kristen as Isaac stepped toward the art section, his long legs moving quickly. A few minutes later he returned with tubes of ultramarine and sienna, two paint brushes, and a can of gesso.

I longed to ask him what he was working on but couldn't seem to find my voice.

As I rang up his purchases, he asked, his voice low, "How has your day been?"

I shrugged. "All right. Yours?"

His eyes grew heavy. "Honestly?"

I nodded.

"Painful."

When I didn't answer, he said, "I'm sorry. I shouldn't have said that." He gave me his card, and I ran it.

As I handed it back to him along with the receipt, he asked what my parents had to say about what we'd learned of my grandmother.

"I haven't told them yet." I slipped his supplies into a bag.

"Oh?"

I didn't want to explain that I'd been so upset I'd totally forgotten about all of that. "I will tonight," I added.

"Well, Cheri doesn't work on Saturdays, so I doubt she got back to me about the quilter yet, but I'll check the messages on *Mammi's* phone just in case." He slipped his card back into his wallet.

"*Danke*." I handed him the bag.

"See you at church tomorrow."

I forced myself not to watch him leave the shop.

"What was that all about?" Kristen asked.

I struggled not to cry.

She patted my back. "Tell me once we're closed. Ten more minutes."

I checked out the last of the customers, and Kristen switched the sign at six o'clock sharp.

I returned bolts of fabric, arranged thread, straightened out the books, and tidied up the art section while Kristen took care of the money. Once we were both done, she said, "Tell me what happened."

I explained the whole thing to her, what a wonderful day Isaac and I had, and then about what everyone thought I knew—that I didn't.

Kristen's eyes grew wide.

Then I told her how I reacted. "Or overreacted," I said. "That's what my *mamm* and oldest sister seem to think anyway."

Kristen gave me a sympathetic smile. "I'm so sorry."

"What do you think? Am I overreacting?"

"No," she said. "Of course you're shocked. It wasn't what you expected or what you would have chosen."

"But am I being foolish?"

"Because he's such a great guy? Because he's perfect for you?"

I nodded.

"No. I'd be in a state of shock too, believe me. You need some time to figure it out. Stop being so hard on yourself."

I looked away. "But I feel like such a *dummkup*."

Kristen smiled. "A what?"

I laughed. "An idiot."

"You rarely slip into Pennsylvania Dutch," she said.

"Usually when I'm stressed."

She pointed toward the display against the wall. "How would you say thread in your language?"

"*Naitz.*"

"Paint?"

"*Faub.*"

"Fabric?"

I laughed. "Material."

"That's interesting," she said.

I shrugged. "Pennsylvania Dutch is a mix of a German dialect and English. There's not really a written form, so it probably changes more quickly than a lot of languages."

"Fascinating." Kristen reached out and patted my hand. "I'm so thankful for you."

"Ditto," I responded. That was definitely not a Pennsylvania Dutch word. "Thank you for listening. Now you'd better get home to your family."

She nodded. "And you should do something for yourself tonight— like work on your quilt."

"About that…" As we walked out back, I told her of the appliqué quilt I'd seen in the catalogue, though it was hard to convey just how amazing it was. "I've never seen anything like it." I explained to her about finding out my grandmother had a twin and then discovering the similarities between her painting and the quilt in the photograph.

"I hope you can figure it out," Kristen said. "This is all so fascinating, not to mention inspiring."

"*Ya.* Though I'd have a hard time trying anything that daring myself."

"Why?"

I wrinkled my nose, trying to figure out how to explain. "It's all so imprecise. So creative. There's so much room for error."

Kristen shook her head at me. "Sometimes you just have to take a risk. Sure, your first try might not be perfect. Or even your second. Or third. But that's what practice is for, right?"

I nodded, but I wasn't so sure. I liked being successful with my quilting. It truly was something I could control. If I tried to produce something like Twinkle Star Quilts had, I'd be venturing into completely unknown territory, the very opposite of control.

We said our goodbyes, and then Kristen unlocked her car and put her things inside as I opened the buggy and took out Blue's harness along with a couple of sugar cubes. Heading for the fence, I glanced Kristen's way and was surprised to see her hesitate before closing her car door again and walking over to join me.

"One question," she said. "About the whole Isaac situation."

"*Ya?*" I whistled for Blue and saw him look up and then slowly start walking my way.

"What is it that's bothering you about the English element of this equation?"

I turned to meet her gaze. "What do you mean?"

"You keep stressing the English part, saying he had an *English* wife. What's that about? Just because she wasn't Amish doesn't necessarily mean she was a bad influence on him."

I gasped, realizing she'd completely misunderstood. "No," I said quickly, "I know that. It's something else." This was hard to admit, but I probably needed to say it all the same, just to get everything out on the table.

"Which is?"

Blue reached the gate, and I gave him the sugar cubes and a few pats on the neck before slipping on the harness.

"Bailey was *Englisch*." I led my horse through the gate and over to the front of the buggy. "Which means she would've been fancy. I'm sure she wore makeup and cute clothes and styled her hair. She was more highly educated, more worldly wise. More sophisticated. Put that all together, and there's no question that she totally dazzled her Amish-raised husband. I could never compete with that. I'm Plain. *And* I'm plain. You know?"

I looked to Kristen, who was shaking her head at me. "You're kidding, right? Linda, you're not plain, you're adorable."

I shook my head in return. "No, I'm not, but either way, it doesn't matter. Physical beauty passes. It isn't important. Amish men know that too, and they are taught to find the beauty in a woman's heart. But if Isaac has been of the world and married to a woman of the world, then maybe he's forgotten. Maybe a part of him has learned to expect beauty on the outside too."

"I don't understand." Linda crossed her arms over her chest. "He's made it clear that he's attracted to you. And why not? Any guy would be."

My cheeks growing warm, I busied myself with positioning the harness on Blue. She was just being kind. "But what if the man in him still yearns for the rouged cheeks and the tinkly little bracelets and the painted fingernails? That's not ever going to be who I am. And I can't bear the thought of living with a man who'll look over at me someday and—" I stopped, unable to say the words.

"And what?" Kristen gently prodded.

I took a deep breath, blew it out, and met her eyes. "And find me wanting."

TWELVE

I drove Blue home slowly, although I couldn't enjoy the beauty of the day or the setting before me. Traffic was heavy with tourists, most heading to restaurants or to the outlets for some final shopping before calling it a day. I couldn't believe things were this crowded and it wasn't even June yet. It was only going to get worse from here.

I stayed as far to the right on the road as I could, and I tried to ignore the whizzing of cars as they passed by and the impatient glares of those who'd had to lose precious seconds because of me. Why were the *Englisch* always in such a hurry?

Ignoring all that as much as I could, I found my mind wandering back to the events of the last two days yet again. I wondered if Isaac was home now, painting away in his studio in the barn. Probably so. Several of Ruth's daughters had been taking turns with the cooking and cleaning around the house while she was ill, which gave him more time to paint. And obviously Cheri wanted more of his work to sell.

I could only imagine what the bishop of our district would think once he found out what Isaac was doing. Surely he didn't know or he would have said something. Perhaps he was even more obtuse than I was. Not only was Isaac painting and selling his work, but he was selling it in

Philadelphia and had a website too. My heart fell. Perhaps that was the real reason Isaac left Somerset County. Maybe his bishop wouldn't put up with it.

I was a little surprised our bishop hadn't been notified by the one from there. Even when there was no formal connection between different Amish districts, the bishops often communicated.

I turned into our driveway and then continued on toward the barn, where I found Sadie's buggy parked along the side and another buggy as well. I stared at it for a moment, realizing it was Jedediah King's. I recognized it from the day Isaac and I saw him at Sadie's. Considering that both horses were untethered and out in the pasture, Jedediah and Sadie had been here a while—either that or they'd recently arrived but were planning to stick around.

I unharnessed Blue and led him into his stall. Then I fed and watered him and brushed him down. When he'd finished eating, I took him out to the field, slowly, reluctant to go inside where I knew Sadie and *Mamm* would gang up on me. Or maybe they wouldn't with Jedediah here.

As I closed the gate, someone called out my name.

I turned. Sadie was strolling toward me. I so seldom saw her without children that she looked odd alone. She waved, and I waved back. I smiled but braced myself. I didn't want to be chastised again.

I started toward her as well.

The first thing she said as we came face-to-face was, "I'm sorry about this morning."

Caught off guard, I responded, "That's okay."

"No, it wasn't. I was too harsh with you. I'm afraid I was identifying more with Isaac than with your concerns."

"Really, it's fine." I started toward the house.

"Could you wait a minute? There's more I want to say."

I stopped.

She took a deep breath. "I know you're young, and I get that—but I think there are some things you need to consider in this situation."

I turned toward her. "Such as?"

"Me."

"What do you mean?"

"My life. *Mamm. Daed. Mamm* before *Daed.* Now *that* was a complicated backstory. But if *Daed* could get past him, surely you can get over Bailey."

I tilted my head, confused.

She stepped toward me. "Don't tell me you don't know what I'm talking about."

I laughed. "I don't. Honestly."

"That *Daed* isn't my biological father."

"What?"

"That *Mamm* had me before they married."

"Sadie," I said. "*Daed* is your father. It's as clear as anything. You're as close, or closer, to him than any of us are."

"*Ya*, he's my father. That is true. But he did not father me." She sighed. "How could you not know this either? Do you not listen to anything that's said around you?"

I gaped at her in astonishment for a long moment before finding my voice. "You're saying *Mamm* was already pregnant—and by another man, no less—when she married *Daed*?"

"No."

My heart surged with relief—until she added, "She gave birth to me first, then they got married a couple of months later."

I turned away, an odd sort of pounding in my head. How could this be? My beloved sister was only my half sister? My *mamm* had had…premarital relations? She'd gotten *pregnant*—and by someone other than *Daed*?

I spun back around to face Sadie, my heart pounding. "Tell me the whole story."

"Sure." She launched in, her tone almost matter-of-fact despite the enormity of her words. "*Mamm* had a Plain boyfriend who left the church and wanted her to leave too. She wouldn't, but it wasn't until after he'd moved away and was living and working in Philadelphia that she realized she was pregnant. A church elder went and talked to him, but he refused to return."

"No way."

"Yep. His local Amish family members weren't much better and basically turned their backs on the situation too. But then *Mamm* met *Daed*, and they courted and got married when I was about three months old."

"Have you ever met him? Your biological father, I mean."

She shook her head. "And I don't want to. Nor do I have any desire to meet those other relatives or to have them tell me about him. Like you said, *Daed* is my father. He's all I need."

"I can't believe I never knew this. I had no idea." I shook my head in astonishment. But then Sadie gave a soft *tsk*, as if my ignorance on this matter was somehow my fault. I threw up my hands. "How was I supposed to find out? Did I miss another big conversation at a different sleepover?"

"Don't ask me," she said, and then she began to count off on her fingers. "Becky knew, as did Matthew, Mark, Melvin, Izzy, Tabitha..."

"But probably not Stephen or Thomas."

She exhaled. "That could be."

"Or me." I shook my head in wonder. "Shouldn't *Mamm* have told me herself, or at least made sure I knew?"

"It probably never occurred to her. It all happened more than thirty years ago."

"But she was *pregnant*," I hissed. "Outside of *marriage*."

Sadie didn't respond. Instead, she just stood there, lips pursed, allowing my words to hang between us. Instantly, I felt ashamed. This was our mother I was talking about after all.

Looking away, I took a deep breath and tried to pull my thoughts together. Finally, I turned again toward my sister and said softly, "*Ach*, I'm sorry. It's just that I keep getting blindsided. First Isaac and now this. What else should I know about that I don't?"

"Nothing, I'm sure. Well, except..." Sadie gestured toward the pasture. "You are aware of Blue's addiction to cigarettes, wild mares, and whiskey, right?"

We both laughed, and then we stood there together in silence for a long moment.

"So now that you know about *Mamm*," Sadie asked, "are you going to think less of her?"

I blew out a breath. "To be honest, I'm not sure. It's just so weird to find this out now."

"Well, don't judge her. Please."

"I won't," I said, hoping I wasn't lying. I knew I wouldn't intentionally.

"Obviously *Daed* didn't judge her. He completely embraced her—and me too. He never held her mistake against either one of us."

"I get it, Sadie." *Daed* was one of the most loving, forgiving people in the world. Obviously I didn't take after him.

"It's actually fairly common, you know. For one man to raise another man's child. For a husband to forgive a wife. For a wife to forgive a husband."

"Why are you telling me all of this?" I asked.

"Because you're an idealist. You have such high expectations of yourself, and of others too. It's time you accept the fact that nobody's perfect. Life isn't like one of your precisely cut, pieced, and stitched quilts. Everybody has a history. Everybody comes into a marriage with *something*."

I set my jaw, anger rising in me yet again. "They don't have to, not if they follow the *Ordnung*. We're given those rules for a reason—so we'll live the right way, do the right things."

"*Ya*," she said. "But absolutely no one does, not every single time."

"I've certainly done my best to follow the rules."

Her eyes flashed. "Well, if you think you've never faltered, then you're lying to yourself."

"Hey, I—"

"That's why we need Christ, Linda. That's why He gave His life for us."

"So we could sin?"

She shook her head as if disgusted with me. "So we could be forgiven. And forgive."

I frowned. "I'm not stupid. I know that. But we're also supposed to do the right thing in the first place."

"*Ya*, but we will fall short at times. Each and every one of us. Including you. 'For *all* have sinned,' Little Sister."

She must have seen the look on my face because now her hands were on her hips and her brown eyes bore into mine. "Relationships are messy. Love is hard. The power to hurt others is much stronger than you think—and it goes both ways."

I chewed my lip for a moment, forming my response.

"I get that you all see me as naïve and inexperienced," I replied evenly. "I am. But I'm not ashamed of it, and I can only make decisions based on what I've been through and what I know."

Sadie rolled her eyes. "You could try to learn from those who love you. It might save you some grief in the long run."

A buggy turned down the drive, interrupting our argument. "Are *Mamm* and *Daed* expecting anyone else?"

Sadie turned. "Not that I know of."

My eyes went to the extra buggy that was already parked beside Sadie's. "Is Jedediah staying for supper?" I knew my voice sounded harsh.

Sadie either didn't notice or simply chose not to acknowledge it. "*Ya.*"

I harrumphed. "I don't understand this. Your husband has only been gone for..." I counted in my head, wanting to be exact for emphasis.

"Forty days," Sadie said, beating me to the punch. "What are you implying? That Jedediah and I are courting?"

My face grew warm.

"Well, we're not. *Mamm* invited him. I didn't even know he was coming."

Feeling as if I'd overstepped, I said, "Okay, I'm sorry."

She nodded. "Jedediah was a good friend to Robert. And he's been a tremendous support through all of this to me. For now, our relationship is nothing more than that."

My eyes narrowed. " 'For now.' "

"Linda, I don't know what—or whom—God has in store for me," Sadie said, sounding weary. "But I do know two things. One, at this point I'm still in mourning for my husband. And two, when the time does come to consider courting again, I could do a lot worse than Jedediah King."

I didn't reply. From the tone of her voice, I knew the subject was closed.

Silent, we started toward the house together, both of us watching as the buggy stopped at our hitching post and the driver opened the door and jumped down.

Isaac.

"What is he doing here?" I groaned. "Please tell me *Mamm* didn't invite him for supper too?"

"I don't know," Sadie muttered under her breath. "But you'd better be nice to him."

"Oh, I will be," I replied. "As for *Mamm*…" I couldn't remember ever being as angry as I felt at the moment. Why in the world would she go behind my back like this and invite him over? She knew how upset and confused I was right now.

I waited until Isaac had secured his horse and gone in through the front before making a beeline for the back door, with Sadie right behind.

When we reached the kitchen, the table was set, and I didn't even have to count the plates to know my hunch had been right. *Mamm* was at the stove, and Isaac and Jedediah were in the living room talking with *Daed* and the children.

"Get washed up," she said to me cheerily. "We're ready to eat."

I stepped toward her and spoke in a tight whisper. "How could you do this to me?"

"Do what?"

Scowling, I gestured toward the table and then the living room.

"Ah. Our guest. Sorry about that. I stopped by Ruth's today, and she was leaving to go to her oldest daughter's house for the rest of the afternoon and evening. I felt bad for poor Isaac home alone without a meal, so I left a note inviting him to join us for supper. It didn't dawn on me till I was halfway home that it probably wasn't the best idea I'd ever had."

"No. It wasn't. Besides, he knows perfectly well how to cook for himself."

"He does?"

"*Ya*. He does."

"Well, like I said, sorry about that. But it is what it is. Nothing you can do about it now."

With a heavy sigh, I turned and went to my bedroom. When I summoned the courage to come back down and join the gathering at the table, everyone was already seated except for Jedediah, who was putting Bobby in the high chair.

I sat across from Isaac, between the girls, and Jedediah took the empty spot next to Sadie. After the prayer *Daed* asked Jedediah about his crops, and the conversation stayed on farming. After a while, *Mamm* asked Isaac about his business.

"The current job will end next week," he told her, "but I have a couple more lined up after that, and some new bids out too."

"Sounds like you're doing quite well for yourself," *Daed* said, probably for my benefit.

"The Lord does provide," Isaac replied humbly. Then his eyes went to me. "Speaking of yesterday, though, that reminds me, I had a message from Cheri when I got home today." He grinned widely. "She found the name of the quilter."

My pulse surged. "Already? I thought she didn't work on Saturdays."

"She doesn't, but she was really curious about the quilter and couldn't get your story out of her head. Did you get a chance to tell your parents yet?"

"I only just got here before you did."

"Oh. Sorry."

"Tell us what?" *Daed* and *Mamm* asked in unison.

Together, Isaac and I filled them in on the story—starting with the fact that *Mammi* Nettie had had a twin sister.

"No, she didn't," *Daed* said calmly, dabbing at his mouth with a napkin. "You must be mistaken."

"Yes, she did," I replied. "We saw a copy of her birth certificate. Her twin's name was Georgette. Georgette Nadine Bender."

Daed's eyes widened. "I doubt that. I would've known about a twin." He thought for a moment and then added, "Unless maybe she died as a baby. I suppose that's possible."

"Actually," Isaac said, "it's pretty clear that she didn't die as a baby. Not only is there no death certificate on record, but there are also records showing that Georgette got married twenty-six years later. To a man named Paul W. Johnson."

He let *Daed* take that in and then added, "Which means one of two things. Either there *was* a death certificate, but it got misplaced somehow, or…" He let his voice trail off, looking to me to finish.

"Or she's still alive," I said with just a hint of drama.

We paused a beat, looking around the table to see the various reactions. *Daed* still looked confused. *Mamm* seemed to be thinking. The younger ones weren't even listening, and Jedediah and Sadie appeared mildly interested at best.

"She couldn't still be alive," *Mamm* said finally. "She'd be too old."

"She'd be ninety-eight," I replied. "So it's not likely but certainly possible."

Isaac nodded, glancing from my *daed* to my *mamm* and back again. They seemed to need a moment to process all this, so he looked to me instead.

"Have you thought about talking again with Ina Mae? Maybe she knew about Georgette and just didn't tell you."

"I could try," I answered. "Though it sure didn't seem like she was holding anything back the first time."

Isaac shrugged. "There could be lots of layers to this story. Perhaps the family was ashamed that Georgette left, so they never spoke of her again. That's pretty much what happened with me while I was gone." He said that last part without self-consciousness or embarrassment, which impressed me. These were the facts of his life.

"Even so," I said, "don't you think the Amish grapevine would have kept that information alive—at least to the point where *Daed* would've heard about it? Surely someone would've thought to tell him that his mother had a twin."

Even as I said the words, I felt my face color.

Surely someone would have told Linda that Isaac had been married before.

Surely someone would have told Linda that her oldest sister had been conceived by a man other than her father.

"Anyway," Isaac said, his tone light as he brushed past the moment. "Here's the big news. According to Cheri, the name of the person who made that quilt was listed as 'N. Johnson.'"

I slowly repeated what he said. "'N. Johnson'? No first name?"

"No. Sorry."

"And you're sure it's 'N' and not 'G'?"

He nodded.

"Okay, so what's the next step?"

Isaac grinned, pulling from his pocket a folded strip of paper, which he set on the table, and then with one finger he slid it across the shiny wood surface to me. "I'd say we try this."

With a gasp, I grabbed the paper and opened it up to see in his familiar scrawl the name *N. Johnson* followed by a telephone number.

My smile wide, I glanced at the clock, pleased to see that it wasn't too late to call her if I did it right after supper. But then my eyes went back to Isaac and my excitement diminished. If I headed to the barn, he would expect to come out there with me—and I did not want that. *Ya*, in the excitement of this whole matter tonight, I had let down my guard a bit, but the bottom line remained. I had to get over Isaac, which meant the last thing I needed was to be together with him in a dark, intimate space, all alone.

My smile fading, I refolded the paper, slipped it into my pocket, and avoided his eyes as I said flatly, "Thanks for this. I'll be sure to let you know how it turns out."

Everyone was so silent I knew they'd all picked up on my brush off of Isaac. Quickly, cheeks burning, I rose from the table and began clearing away the dishes. We still had to get through dessert, but at least the conversation started up again after a beat, and eventually the awkward moment passed.

As we dug into our bowls of shortcake, the topic came around to this year's garden, especially the strawberries. These were early berries, *Mamm* said, but the fact that they were sweeter and redder than early berries usually were bode well for the rest of the season.

As soon as dessert was done, I once again busied myself, first by clearing the table and then starting in on the dishes. Jedediah thanked everyone and left, saying he needed to finish a chore before it got dark. Stephen and Thomas followed to play on the lawn, and Sadie sent the girls out with them. A few minutes later, she asked *Mamm* to walk with her to the buggy.

Once they were all gone, *Daed* vanished into the living room suspiciously fast, which left Isaac and me alone in the kitchen. And he clearly had no intention of leaving, not yet anyway. Instead, after a moment, he simply appeared at my side, clean towel in hand, and began to dry. We worked together silently for a few minutes, my mind spinning and my heart aching the whole time. What was there to say to him? *I'm sorry, but you're no longer husband material for me?* I'd never put it that way, but it was true.

Finally, he cleared his throat and then spoke. "Linda, you know—"

"Isaac, please. It's too soon. I'm sorry I was rude earlier, but I just can't talk about this yet."

He took the glass from my hand and slowly wiped it as he tried again. "I was going to say, Linda, you know how I come into the shop now and then to buy tubes of oil paint?"

Okay, safer ground. I let out a breath. "*Ya?*"

"Well, ready-made tubes are my preference nowadays, but back when I was in art school, I also learned how to make paint from scratch. The simplest version consisted of just two things, dry pigment and linseed oil."

As he described the measuring and mixing, I thought of *Mammi* Nettie and how she used to make her own paints.

"Done right," he added, "the freshly mixed paint goes onto the canvas beautifully—smooth and vivid and perfectly textured."

"Interesting." I handed him a wet glass and then started in on the plates.

"The thing is, there are other uses for pigments," he continued. "There are other uses for oils. But when you put them together, pigment plus oil, to make paint? That's when they're at their very best. As a pair."

My actions slowed. So much for safer ground.

"You and I are at our best when we're together, Linda." From the corner of my eye I could see that he'd turned to face me, the towel set aside on the counter. He continued. "I know you know that. We're a great team. I understand why you're upset about Bailey, I really do, but I'm hoping you can get past this—and sooner rather than later. Maybe if you knew more about her, maybe if I told you some of the details, like how we met and why I fell in love with her—"

"No!" I dropped the dish into the sink with a splash and slapped my soapy wet hands against my ears, squeezing my eyes shut. "Stop! I don't want to hear this! I don't want to know anything about Bailey! Ever!"

Heart pounding, I just stood there like that, trying to calm down, trying to get a handle on myself. I didn't know where my outburst had come from, but I felt sure it had been building inside of me since that terrible moment yesterday when I first learned the truth about Isaac's former life.

I took a deep breath, lowered my arms, and opened my eyes. I knew I owed the man beside me an apology. But when I turned, ready to try, I realized he was gone.

Mortified, I ran to the door and opened it just as he was starting down the porch steps.

"Isaac, wait. Please. I'm so sorry."

He paused, the set of his shoulders heavy and defeated. When he turned back, I saw that there were tears in his eyes. He blinked them away.

"I never should have said that," I added softly, glancing toward the barn. I could hear Sadie and *Mamm* in conversation around the corner, near Sadie's buggy, and I was glad they were too far away and too immersed in their own discussion to have heard. The boys and the twins were a lot closer, but they were busy playing tag on the grass and paying us no attention. Again, I met Isaac's eyes. "Please forgive me."

He sighed, his shoulders sinking even lower. "Of course I forgive you, Linda. I understand why this is so hard for you…"

I knew what he wanted me to say. That I'd try. That I just needed more time. That I'd pray about it and think on it and find some way to get past it.

But any of those things would've been a lie. And I think in my silence, and in my eyes, that's exactly what he came to understand.

When I went back in the kitchen, *Daed* had taken over with the dishes. I would rather have finished alone and then gone up to bed, but it seemed I had no choice. Instead, I handed him the towel and told him I'd wash.

"Wanna talk about it?" he asked after a moment.

"No. But thanks." I knew he must've heard my outburst from the next room, and he probably had all sorts of questions.

"All right. I'm not going to give you any advice, then. I'll just say this. Whom you court and marry is no one's business but your own. You'll know what the right thing to do is, sooner or later. God will lead the way."

I blinked hard as I thanked my father for his wise words, grateful that at least one member of this family didn't see me as naive and sheltered and judgmental.

Daed and I were quiet for a while after that as we worked. That was one of the things I really loved about him, that we could be together without needing to fill the silence and feel as close as if we were sharing our deepest thoughts.

Finally, as he put a stack of dried plates away, he spoke. "Your *mamm* and Sadie sure are having a long conversation out there."

"*Ya.* I'm afraid it might have to do with me."

"Oh?"

I took a deep breath and explained about my discussion with Sadie earlier and what she'd told me, about her biological father. "She was surprised I didn't know."

Daed didn't respond for a long moment but then said, "I guess I am too. I thought everyone knew."

"I'm pretty sure Stephen and Thomas don't."

Daed chuckled. "I'm pretty sure they wouldn't care."

"Why?"

"Oh, I don't know. Men—boys—don't seem to bother too much about that sort of thing. They know I love their oldest sister and that I've always considered her my daughter. That would be enough for them."

I glanced at him as I rinsed a serving bowl and put it in the rack.

"Did it bother you? When you met *Mamm*?"

Daed picked up the bowl and then froze for a moment. "I'm trying to remember…That was so long ago."

I kept quiet and washed another bowl.

He shot me a glance. "I'm going to be frank—and honest. At the time I wished your *mamm* hadn't been with another man. But I couldn't change that she had been. And we wouldn't have had Sadie." His voice trembled a little. "And you know how much I care for Sadie, how much I care for all of you."

I nodded. I did.

"So, did it bother me that the woman I fell in love with had a baby? No. It didn't. Not at all."

"Did it bother other people?"

He nodded. "My mother, for one. She felt as if Peggy was—" He hesitated. "I can't say what term my *mamm* used. She was a bitter old woman by then. Looking back, once Peggy and I were married, we never should have stayed here. I thought I was honoring my parents, but in fact I wasn't caring for my new family—my wife and child—the way I should have. That's my one regret."

I was dumbfounded.

Daed dried the bowl and put it in the cupboard. "People are complicated, Linda. So are relationships. Never forget that. The good and the bad—it's all woven together. Or mixed, like paints. Or quilted, like what you do. I saw the good in my *mamm*, but she only showed Peggy the bad, I'm afraid. Still, Peggy nursed her to the end. I know it was hard on her, but she did it anyway, and she extended my mother great comfort in her final days."

He dried a plate and put it away. "I remembered something tonight when you said my mother had a twin."

"Oh?"

"You recall what I told you about the woman who came that day my mother stopped painting? The big scene out in the driveway?"

"*Ya.*"

"At the time I thought she was younger, but maybe that's just because my *mamm*'s hair was gray by then, and this woman's was a deep auburn color. Now I'm thinking maybe they were the same age, and her hair might have been dyed. She was dressed fancy, with a wide skirt and high heels and red lipstick. At the time I remember noting a similarity and, like I said before, thinking maybe she was a younger cousin or some other relation. But now I wonder if she was a sister instead. A twin sister. Georgette. Maybe she left the Amish and was shunned. Maybe that's why my *mamm* and no one else ever talked about her."

The next day church was held at Jedediah's parents' place. I'd always gotten irritated at Tabitha whenever she let herself be distracted from the worship service by some current behind-the-scenes drama related to a boy. But today, for the first time ever, Tabitha was six hundred miles away, and the only boy drama going on here was mine.

The truth was, I absolutely dreaded seeing Isaac.

He was there, of course, looking handsome but somber in his place among the men. I had lingered at the buggy so I could slip in at the last moment, so at least we hadn't had to talk before things got started. But once church was over, I knew that awkward moment would come. And because the service was always followed by a shared meal, the two of us would be stuck here for even longer.

Ruth was with him, and she sat beside me at the long table as we ate our bean soup, bread, and peanut butter spread. I asked her if she'd ever heard anything about my grandmother having a twin sister. "Never," she answered. "Isaac already asked the same thing."

Although Ruth was doing much better, she mostly picked at her food, and when the meal was done, she seemed more than ready to go home. As I told her goodbye, she said, "Come have a cup of tea soon. And a chat."

I promised I would, although I had a feeling she just wanted to tell me the same things *Mamm* and Sadie already had, albeit in a nicer way.

I was surprised to see Ezra at our church, considering that Tabitha was still off with Izzy in Indiana. Then again, maybe he was just here to see Jedediah. They were good friends.

As I was getting ready to leave, Ezra approached. "Are you coming back for the volleyball game and the singing tonight?" he asked.

I glanced around, just to make sure he was talking to me. "No. I don't go to those anymore."

"Why not?"

I glanced over at Jedediah, who was alternately pushing Hazel and then Hattie on the Kings' swing set. At seven, they were certainly big enough to push themselves, but it was always more fun when an adult did it. "Don't tell me that you and Jedediah are going?"

Ezra grinned. "We're thinking about it."

I dropped my voice to a whisper. "Aren't you guys a little old?"

"Technically, no." His grin widened. "Though, yeah. Probably. But how else are two bachelors supposed to find good Amish wives if not at a singing?"

Startled, my eyes went again to Jedediah. If his intentions were set on Sadie, then why would he bother to go wife-hunting at a singing? I figured it had to be one of two things. Either I'd been wrong all along, and his interest in Sadie really was just as a friend and helpful neighbor, or I'd been right, and his interest in Sadie had been with an eye toward marriage—but then the fact that she was pregnant had scared him away. Though I didn't approve of a courtship for my sister any time soon, for a moment I actually felt sorry for her.

"Linda?"

My eyes returned to Ezra, who was waiting for an answer to his question. I hesitated, considering. I'd given up going to singings the year before, after Tabitha started courting Mark Wittmer again. It wasn't fun knowing she'd be going off with him while I drove home alone. So that part of me really didn't want to go. On the other hand, I was curious how the reformed Ezra Gundy and the best neighbor ever, Jedediah King, would act around a bunch of eligible and eager young women.

"Sure," I said.

"May I pick you up?"

Again, I was startled, but this time for a different reason. Was Ezra offering as a friend? Or was he asking me for a date? Because Amish young men often gave Amish young women rides home from a singing—but they rarely picked them up and took them. Just the thought of riding either way with Ezra overwhelmed me as yet one more thing to deal with right now.

After a moment's hesitation, I simply shook my head and told him no thanks. "I'll meet you there. But just for the singing, not the volleyball game." Tabitha was great at sports. Me? Not so much.

He grinned again. "Got it. See you then." He traipsed off and joined Jedediah in pushing Sadie's twins ever higher, their renewed shrieks and laughter making them seem, for the moment, like the happiest little girls in the world.

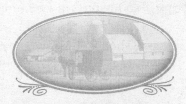

Thirteen

Once we were back home and everyone had dispersed to their various Sunday-afternoon leisure activities—the boys playing outside and *Mamm* and *Daed* relaxing and reading on the porch—I finally had a chance to call "N. Johnson."

The whole walk out to the barn I focused on building up my nerve and practicing what I was going to say, and by the time I got there, I was as ready as I could be. Unfortunately, the call went to voice mail, one of the few times in my life I was disappointed not to reach an actual person on the phone.

I was also disappointed by the voice on the greeting, which definitely did not sound like someone in their late nineties. It was a woman, but she was middle-aged at most. Then again, she never actually said her name. She just said thank you for calling "Twinkle Star Quilts" and invited me to leave a message.

I wasn't sure what to say, so I hung up. I sat there and thought about it for a few minutes. When I called back, I waited for the beep and then launched right in. I said that my name was Linda Mueller, and I was trying to locate the artist named "N. Johnson" whose beautiful quilts I'd seen in the New Vision Gallery. "I got this number from Cheri Bethune," I added, hoping that connection might give me credibility. "I can explain what this is about once we talk. It's kind of a long story." I gave my number and then hung up.

I was disappointed to have reached a place and not a specific person, but as I tucked the paper into my pocket, I told myself that at least we were one step closer.

Before heading back to the house, I dug out the number for Ina Mae and left a message for her as well. I didn't know if another visit with her would tell me anything new or not, but it might now that I knew of my grandmother's twin. I figured it was worth a shot. And at the very least I'd get to enjoy some more of her delicious cookies.

The singing was at the same place where church had been held that morning, out in the shed at Jedediah's parents' farm, and I realized that could be the reason Jedediah was attending. So much for my theory about him shying away from Sadie's pregnancy. Perhaps he was simply being a good son.

Several of the girls I'd gone to school with were there, chatting after the volleyball game. They all seemed surprised—but pleased—to see me. I'd been so busy in the last couple of months that I hadn't spent any time with them except at church.

We all sat around tables for the singing, the girls on one side and the boys, along with the two who were definitely men, on the other. Ezra caught my eye and grinned. I smiled back, though minus the flirty glint he'd just given me. My life was complicated enough already, thank you. The last thing I needed was one of my older sister's hand-me-downs inserting himself into the mix—especially considering he came with almost as complicated history as the man I was already dealing with.

I began to grow weary after the first hour. Where the others were still belting out the songs at the top of their lungs, my voice had fallen to a whisper. After the second hour of singing, including old favorites such as "Amazing Grace" and "How Great Thou Art," it was snack time. The Kings had set out trays of chocolate chip and oatmeal cookies and bowls of popcorn and potato chips, as well as tea and coffee. They even had hot cocoa, though the evening was warm.

I chatted with my friends for a little while until Jedediah's mother, Naomi, asked me to help her bring out more snacks from the kitchen. It felt as if she wanted to talk with me about something, probably Sadie. As we stepped outside, we saw Ezra and Jedediah, who were hovering near the door, and Ezra gave me a little wave. I barely smiled in return this time. Couldn't he tell I wasn't interested? Or was he always so successful with women that he couldn't even grasp the concept?

When we reached the kitchen, Naomi handed me a bowl of popcorn while she picked up another tray of cookies.

"I was wondering…" she said. Here it came. "How is Sadie doing?"

"All right." I feared Naomi had noticed that Jedediah was spending time over there and didn't approve, but if she expected me to gossip about my own sister, she'd misjudged me.

"She's seemed so tired lately. I know she's grieving, but I worry about her. I'm just thankful she has so much support, including all of you, and Jedediah too."

"Yes, he's been a huge help." My face warmed at my earlier thoughts. The woman wasn't being critical of Sadie. She was concerned for my sister, that was all—and grateful her son was being a good neighbor. And I got the impression that if Jedediah and Sadie did end up courting, Naomi wouldn't object. She seemed to genuinely care about my sister's well-being.

"We should get back with these goodies," I said. "The others snacks are probably all gone by now."

As we approached the shed, Ezra stepped out and took the bowl from me. "Wait here," he said. I did as instructed, standing near the doorway and peering inside. Nearby, Jedediah was talking with my group of friends, and though they were all smiles, he looked miserable. I couldn't help but think of how comfortable he seemed when he was with Sadie, holding Bobby.

Ezra returned and nudged me. "Let's go for a walk."

Let's go for a walk. The five words so many young women yearned to hear from him. Looking up at him now with this twinkly eyes and bad-boy half smile, I had to admit that he *was* incredibly…sexy. There was no other way to put it. But he wasn't my type.

I hesitated. Was he? He had baggage, *ya*, but that baggage did not include a late wife. And Tabitha had said she was no longer interested in him. What if God's will was for me to be with Ezra? What if He'd used what happened with Isaac as a way to open my eyes and make me more receptive to the one He truly wanted for me?

"Okay," I said finally, feeling suddenly shy. I followed along, around the shed and toward the pond. The moon was high in the clear sky and stars twinkled about. We fell into step together, side by side.

Ezra sighed. "Beautiful, isn't it?"

I agreed, but all I could think of was Tabitha, about how she would know exactly what to say to Ezra. That she'd be teasing him, flirting with him, and having a great time by now. I clearly wasn't doing any of those things.

Ezra talked about how beautiful the night sky was in Alaska, which led him to describing the Northern Lights. I imagined what it would be like to quilt something like that, using the appliqué techniques I'd seen at the gallery.

"You seem a million miles away," Ezra said. "What are you thinking?"

I could have told Isaac I was thinking about quilting, but not Ezra. He wouldn't understand. His feelings would probably even be hurt, not realizing there was a connection between what he was saying and what I was envisioning in my mind's eye.

"How amazing all of that sounds," I said instead. "Have you seen the Northern Lights anywhere besides Alaska?"

"No. Although they are visible, at times, in the lower forty-eight."

There was a long pause and then I felt his hand brush against mine, as if teasing at the chance to hold it in his. Feeling a sudden rush of something I couldn't quite understand, I folded my arms across my chest and turned to face him.

"Excuse me, but weren't you interested in my sister a couple of weeks ago?"

Even in the dim light, his smile was radiant. "Your sister isn't here. Besides, you're the one who makes the best lemon sponge pudding on the planet."

I laughed. "*Ya*, well, that's my specialty. Otherwise my cooking's pretty average."

"I'm not looking for a cook," he said, a twinkle in his eye. "I learned how to feed myself when I was on my own. But I don't make dessert."

There was something in the way he said it, something in the curve of his lips on the word *desserts*, that implied so much more. My face flushed with heat as I tried to think of the right response. The truth was, Ezra wasn't just handsome and appealing, he was a nice guy—and a lot of fun. And Tabitha had said she wasn't interested in him anymore. A quick prayer flashed through my mind. *God, is this the one You have in mind for me?*

I forced myself to meet Ezra's eyes. To my surprise, however, his smile faded, he immediately broke our gaze, and then he took a small step back away from me. Had I done something wrong? Before I could ask, there was a rustling behind us and then Jedediah called out Ezra's name.

"Over here," he called back.

Jedediah emerged from around the shed and walked toward us. "Let's get going. I can't—" He finally saw me. "Oh, hello, Linda. I didn't realize you were here too."

"No problem, I should be leaving now anyway." I turned toward Ezra, still confused about his odd change of demeanor but relieved I would have time to pray and think more about all of this before seeing him again.

"We'll talk later," Ezra said, though this time there was no lilt to his words, no subtle flirting that I could detect.

"*Ya*," I replied. "Sounds good."

Jedediah apologized as we all turned and started back toward the shed.

"No worries, buddy," Ezra replied lightly, giving his friend a little punch on the arm. Was it my imagination or did he actually sound just a tiny bit relieved? Whatever that had been about, I wasn't sure I wanted to know.

Then again, maybe I'd just misjudged the situation. Misjudging situations—and people—did seem to be my specialty lately.

The next morning over at Sadie's, Isaac and Stephen and I worked quickly and quietly as we handled the milking. After we finished, I was heading for the house just as a driver picked up Isaac to take him to his painting job in Lancaster. I watched from the porch as the car turned onto the highway. It was hard to tell in the morning light, but I thought he glanced over his shoulder. I couldn't help but wonder if he was looking for me.

The first thing Sadie said when I walked inside was that she'd told *Mamm* about the pregnancy.

"*Gut.*" I was so relieved to have the weight of that particular secret lifted from my shoulders.

She nodded. "The truth is I'm still feeling awful, and I need more help."

I agreed. Between *Mamm* and me, we'd be able to get her through this. If not, we could always ask others from the community, who'd be happy to pitch in as well.

Fortunately, it was my day off, so I could stick around and help for as long as I wanted.

Halfway through the morning, Jedediah stopped by with some questions for Sadie about her herd. To my surprise, Ezra was with him. Jedediah and Sadie wandered off to the barn while Ezra and I stayed behind with the children. The girls were playing house on the porch, and Bobby was practicing his crawling, making his way up and down the planks.

Ezra grinned. "Looks like you've got your hands full."

I smiled back. "They're not too bad." I nodded toward Jedediah. "How come you're hanging out with him today?"

He squinted. "Right? That's a good question. Why would I be with such a bad influence?"

I couldn't help but laugh. No one ever thought of Jedediah as a bad boy. If they did, Tabitha would have managed to court him long ago.

"Seriously," Ezra said. "I'll be working for him over the summer."

"Oh. Why?" I hoped Jedediah wasn't getting behind in his own chores because of the time he spent over here, helping with the milking.

Ezra shrugged. "It just ended up that way. He needed a hand, and I was interested." Then he smiled again. "At least I'll be closer."

"That's great," I replied. "Tabitha's coming home in a couple of weeks. She'll be happy to know that."

I was trying to be funny and expected him to respond by teasing me somehow, maybe even bringing up my lemon sponge pudding again. Instead, he just turned his attention to Bobby, who was beginning to fuss. Ezra scooped the toddler into in his arms, but then Bobby began to cry, so I took him. By the time Sadie and Jedediah returned, he was screaming. Sadie reached for him, but he lunged toward Jedediah instead.

"Look," Ezra teased. "Now Jedediah's a bad influence on Bobby. You'd better watch this guy."

We all laughed. Once the baby grew quiet, Sadie told me I could go on home. "*Mamm* can probably use your help before she comes over this afternoon."

"Are you sure?"

She nodded. "We'll be fine."

Back at the house, the first thing I did was head to the barn and check for messages. There was nothing from Twinkle Star Quilts or N. Johnson, nor from Ina Mae.

After helping *Mamm* with the household chores and weeding in the garden, I headed to my sewing room. Thanks to N. Johnson and her incredible appliqué work, I still hadn't shaken the idea of trying her method for myself on my quilt of the barn. In my mind, I could see how I wanted it to be, a beautiful fabric painting of brown, gold, blue, and green. But once I sat down, I couldn't bear to risk trying it, fearing I might ruin the quilt.

Instead, I pulled out a different quilt, the partially finished one I'd tucked away a month ago, when I decided not to make it for Tabitha. I studied it now, thinking about what to do with it instead. I would turn it into a crib quilt for Izzy and Zed's baby.

I prayed for Izzy as I worked, and for her baby too. Then for Sadie and her children. That made me think of Jedediah and Ezra. And then of Isaac.

Not a good idea. I'd gone back to praying for Izzy when I heard Stephen call my name. "Hey, Linda," he yelled, probably from the back door. "Tabitha's on the phone."

I stood up so fast my chair fell over. I ran out to the barn as quickly as I could. For some reason I just knew what this was about. *Mamm* was over at Sadie's and I doubted if Tabitha would have told Stephen, so if I was right, it seemed I was going to get the information first. It was practically a miracle, considering I usually found out things last—if at all.

I grabbed the phone. "Tabitha! It's me, Linda."

"Big news." She sounded out of breath. She also sounded close, as if she were right across town and not two states away. "Izzy had her baby! A little girl."

"I knew it!" I cried, joy filling my heart. A baby for my big sister. Just the thought brought tears to my eyes. "Where are you now?" I asked, dabbing them away.

"At the hospital at Goshen."

"How's Izzy? And our new niece?"

"Both are doing great. Izzy had a pretty easy time of it, actually. Zed was with her through the whole thing. And the baby was seven pounds, so a perfect size, and she looks like Izzy. Dark eyes. That quizzical look." Tabitha sounded so happy. "She's even got curly red hair, just like Izzy did when she was little, before it turned brown. It's so cute."

I tried to picture it, but the Izzy I knew had always been a brunette.

Tabitha gave more details, saying they'd come to the hospital late the night before and that she had spent time with Izzy but had gone to the waiting room this morning when things started ramping up.

"She's so lucky to have you out there," I said. "How much longer do you think you'll stay?"

"Just another week or two. Zed's mom is going to come the middle of June."

Mamm hadn't said anything about going to help, and perhaps no one expected it. She hadn't gone when Becky had her babies either.

Tabitha's voice grew shaky. "I'll have fun with the baby and everything, but otherwise I can't wait to come home. I really miss everyone."

"We all miss you too," I said, though I feared it came out sounding less emphatic than it should have. We did miss Tabitha, just maybe not as much as she missed home.

"How is everybody?" Tabitha asked. "Have you seen Ezra?"

Startled at the question, I answered slowly. "*Ya*, he came over to Sadie's this morning with Jedediah, something about the cows."

"Oh?"

I felt so guilty, I couldn't help but add, "*Ya*, and I saw him…last night."

"Where?"

"The singing."

"You went to the singing?"

"*Ya.*"

"Why?"

"I've been thinking I should be more social."

"That's good." Tabitha sounded supportive. "Wait," she said. "Ezra went to the singing?"

"*Ya.*"

"Why?"

"I don't know," I answered. "You'll have to ask him." My face grew warm at my lack of honesty, remembering his comment about bachelors going to singings to find good Amish wives.

"Oh, I will," Tabitha responded. "As soon as I get back."

I hesitated, startled at the possessiveness of her tone. "Wait a minute. You said you weren't interested in him anymore, remember? You said you were going to look for someone in Indiana."

"I wasn't serious."

I froze, stunned at her denial. Of course she'd been serious. I remembered our conversation quite vividly, how she said she was hoping to find someone in Goshen, how she wanted to see what was available in Indiana.

Inside I was fuming, but before I could decide how to respond, Tabitha gasped. "Linda! You didn't go to the singing with Ezra, did you?"

"No." It was true. After all, I had driven myself.

"How about at Sadie's today? Did he go there to see you, in particular?"

"No," I said again. "I told you, he was there with Jedediah."

"Linda, what's going on?"

"Nothing," I answered. It wasn't the whole truth, but I refused to tell her about the invitation to the singing. The walk to the pond. The hand brushing against mine. If she'd wanted me to stay away from him, she should've been more honest about her feelings for him.

She didn't say anything for a long moment. "So how are you and Isaac doing?" she finally asked.

"We're not."

"What happened?"

I gave her the short version.

"Linda," she said when I'd finished. "How can you be so clueless? We've all known that Isaac had been married before."

"I didn't. And apparently that wasn't the only thing I didn't know around here." I told her what I'd learned about Sadie's origins.

"I'm sorry," Tabitha replied. "That one's mostly my fault."

"What?"

"I never told you on purpose."

"Why?"

"Because you've always been so naive. So innocent. I thought it would make you think differently of *Mamm*. You know, getting pregnant outside of marriage and everything."

"Are you calling me judgmental?"

She huffed. "If the shoe fits."

"What else have you held back so I couldn't judge?"

"Well, things about my courting life, for starters."

"Tabitha."

"It's true. There's all this stuff you don't know anything about, but you act like you do. I feel sorry for Isaac."

I exhaled into the receiver with enough force that the strands of hair that had escaped my *kapp* danced against the side of my face. "Could we talk about Izzy? And the baby?"

"Fine."

Pausing for a moment, I tucked the loose strands away where they belonged. "So what did they name her?"

"Margaret Mary."

"After *Mamm*. That's really nice. Will her nickname be Peggy too?"

"Probably not, though Izzy said they might go with Maggie. She does kind of look like a Maggie."

"That's cute."

I assumed Mary was after *Mammi* Nettie's mother. Izzy must have remembered that.

"Anyway, I'd better go," Tabitha said. "I'll be home in a couple of weeks." She cleared her throat. "But could you do me a favor in the meantime and not court Ezra while I'm gone? I really do think I'm interested in him—seriously."

I was still irritated about her odd reversal on Ezra. She had a lot of nerve claiming to be over him before leaving town and then acting now like he was her one true love. I thought about saying as much, but I didn't. After all, I'd just been praying for her a few minutes before. And the truth was, as much as I enjoyed Ezra, he wasn't my type. I wasn't even sure if I had a type. "Fine," I said. "You know I'd do anything for you."

"*Danke.* I owe you."

"Just come home as soon as you can." I realized I actually meant it. Difficult or not, Tabitha was my sister.

"Oh, I will," she said. "And when I do, I'm going to talk some sense into you about Isaac. I've protected you for far too long. It's time you grow up and stop being so idealistic. Ezra is definitely not your type—but believe me, Isaac is. I'll set you straight."

I couldn't help but smile. That was the Tabitha I knew and loved, at least most of the time.

FOURTEEN

The next morning it struck me that I hadn't thought to check for phone messages after talking with Tabitha yesterday, nor for the rest of the evening. I decided I would do so once we got back from milking at Sadie's. But before we even headed over there, Stephen noticed that the front tire on his scooter was low, so while he fiddled with the pump, I ran into the barn and checked. Sure enough, I had a new message, though only one. From Ina Mae.

"*Georgette*. I haven't heard that name in seventy years," she said in her shaky voice. "Maybe you should come up again for another visit. Any time works for me. Just give me a call back and let me know when you'll be here."

I listened twice more, hoping to pick up something from the tone of her voice. But it was no use. I would just have to wait and see what she had to tell me.

As soon as Stephen and I got to Sadie's, I relayed Ina Mae's message to Isaac.

"That's great," he said. "When do you plan to go?"

"I'm not sure yet." I turned away, wishing he could join me but knowing that wouldn't be a good idea. *Ya*, he and I had been in on this thing

213

together since the beginning, but that had all come to an end on Friday in Philadelphia, when everything changed. No, I would visit Ina Mae without him—though I wouldn't go alone. I had someone else in mind.

For the next while, the three of us worked quietly together in the barn. Isaac finally broke the silence when Stephen led some of the cows outside, leaving the two of us alone.

"Heard you went to the singing on Sunday," he said, trying to sound nonchalant. "Did you have fun?"

My face grew warm. How had Isaac learned about that?

"Naomi King brought some leftover cookies to my grandmother," he added as if I'd asked the question out loud. "You know how that goes."

I nodded. There was nothing older women in the community loved more than to chatter about the younger women—especially when one of those younger women was being courted by one man on a Friday and somehow ended up strolling in the dark with a different man by Sunday. I might as well have hung out a sign that said, "Another Tabitha in the making."

Isaac must have seen my mortified expression because he immediately apologized. "Hey, I'm sorry. I didn't mean to embarrass you. It's none of my business."

I took a step backward, nearly tripping over Whisper. I scooped up the cat and held him close.

"Are we still friends?" I asked Isaac.

His face fell. "Of course, Linda," he said. "I shouldn't have brought it up. I'm sorry."

I wasn't sure how to respond.

"So Izzy had her baby, *ya*?" he asked, filling the silence.

"*Ya*," I answered. "A girl."

"I guess that means Tabitha will be coming home soon."

I nodded. "In two weeks." I hugged Whisper until he began to squirm and then opened my arms for him to jump down.

"Well, I'm sure you'll be glad to have her back." He pulled out a wrench and leaned forward to adjust a valve fitting on the milk vat. "She still interested in Ezra?"

"Apparently," I said.

Stephen returned and we got busy after that, but I just kept thinking about Isaac's last question. Had he simply been making conversation? Or was he wanting to know about Tabitha for his own sake?

Isaac didn't seem the kind to switch affections so quickly and easily. Then again, neither did I. Yet just two nights ago I'd let Ezra talk me into a moonlight stroll—one that had now surely made the full rounds of the grapevine by now.

What had I been thinking?

That evening I walked across the lawn, around the horseshoe pit, and down the driveway to meet up with *Daed*. He'd worked extra late, and we'd gone ahead and eaten without him an hour and a half before.

I walked along the field where the corn reached mid-calf, hoping it would be a good year for the crop. *Daed* had worked construction since he was a young man. Early on, his father had helped with the farming and then my older brothers had, but *Daed* only farmed after work and on Saturdays. *Mamm* always said *Daed* was the hardest worker she knew. On Sundays he did just the basics with the chores and then took the rest of the day off, like all of us.

Now Stephen had a lot of the responsibility of our farm, besides helping with Sadie's milking too. He was a hard worker like *Daed* and did well, which was a relief because I could tell our father was slowing down some. He seemed more exhausted after a day of construction work, and he didn't do as many farm chores in the evenings as he used to. It wasn't unusual for him to fall asleep in his chair after supper.

He'd turned sixty-one in February, and although he still looked as strong as an ox, and in many ways still was, he wasn't a young man anymore. He had used his body—his sheer strength along with his skills—to provide for us all of these years. I had no idea what my parents' finances were like, and when or if *Daed* would be able to retire.

I was thinking about that when an oversized pickup pulled to a stop at the end of the driveway. *Daed* opened the passenger door, jumped down, and then gave a hearty goodbye to the driver.

"See you tomorrow morning," the unseen *Englisch* man boomed.

"Yep," *Daed* responded. "See you then."

For a moment he sounded as *Englisch* as anyone.

I called out to him.

"Linda." He seemed surprised to see me. "What are you doing?"

"I wanted to talk with you," I said. "Right away."

"Sounds serious." He stepped to my side. "What's going on?"

I told him about Ina Mae's phone call. "I'm going to go back and talk with her on Sunday. Would you go with me?"

He chuckled. "Ah. Whew."

"What?"

"I'm just relieved that your topic isn't as serious as I feared."

"*Daed*," I said. "It is serious to me."

"*Ya*," he replied. "But it's not nearly as bad as some things we've had to deal with."

I nodded. The truth was I probably didn't know all of the serious things my parents had dealt with, although I had an idea of some of the stressful times they'd gone through. Izzy not joining the church and not marrying an Amish man. And my older brothers' *rumspringa*, I surmised, though I'd pretty much ignored all of that. I was young enough that it didn't affect me, but mostly I didn't want to know and be disappointed in them.

Finally *Daed* said, "This matters to you?"

"*Ya*, it does. I'd like to find out what I can about your mother and her twin."

He sighed. "Do you need someone to go with you?"

I smiled as beguilingly as I could. "Need? No. Want? Yes."

"What about Isaac?"

"*Daed*," I said. "We're not exactly spending time together."

"Well, maybe you should."

I shook my head.

He sounded puzzled. "Honestly, you're hard to figure out."

I felt almost betrayed. I couldn't believe he was now on the bandwagon with everyone else. He must have sensed my pain because he patted my shoulder and returned to the topic at hand.

"My *mamm* didn't have a relationship with her side of the family, so I didn't either. I've never felt a need to get to know any of them."

"Aren't you curious about your mother's twin sister, though? We don't even know if they were identical or not. If they were super close like Hattie and Hazel, or if they didn't get along. And what if Ina Mae has information about Georgette—not just from then, but now too? What if she's still alive? Wouldn't you want to meet her?"

Daed frowned. "Not necessarily."

My heart sank until he added, "But if it's important to you, I'll go along."

"*Danke, Daed.* It would mean a lot for you to come with me. And I promise, you'll really like Ina Mae. I'll call Ginny to see if she can drive us."

We walked along in silence until Thomas came dashing out of the barn, followed by Stephen. I wondered what Thomas had done to get himself chased like that until I realized they were both laughing. Stephen tackled Thomas, and they rolled on the grass. Stephen was so mature these days, it was nice to see him acting like a kid again, being all rough-and-tumble for his little brother.

That was the first thought that came to mind. But then I realized the more important factor here, and I was so surprised, I came to a complete stop.

"Look at Thomas," I whispered to *Daed*. "I haven't seen him playing around like that in a long time."

Daed nodded. "He does seem to be showing signs of improvement. What was it, just a month ago when you first suggested he might be depressed?"

"I guess."

"Amazing. God is *gut*."

I didn't understand his attitude and considered reminding him that Thomas had gone through happy phases before. The point was that they never lasted long and then he'd be back where he was. Truly, the child needed some outside help, whether it seemed like it at the moment or not.

Still, I would save those thoughts for a better time. For now, as the boys wrestled on the ground nearby, I thanked *Daed* again for agreeing to go with me to Ina Mae's and veered off toward the barn to call and make the arrangements.

As I walked, Stephen popped up and ran alongside me. "Thomas can take over with the milking in the morning so you don't have to."

I stopped. "Really?"

"*Ya*," Thomas said, joining us. "I've been doing it in the afternoons with Jedediah. I'm happy to help Isaac and Stephen in the mornings too."

"That way you won't have to get up so early," Stephen added. "And, you know, see Isaac."

Why wouldn't she want to see Isaac?" Thomas asked.

"They had a falling out," Stephen said. "Everything's all stiff and awkward between them now."

My face grew hot.

Thomas turned toward me. "What happened?"

"It's not a big deal. We're still friends."

"You weren't friends before?" Thomas asked.

"No, we were."

"I'm confused," Thomas said.

So was I, but it wouldn't make any sense to my brother to say so. "*Danke* for doing the milking," I said instead. "I appreciate it."

He shrugged and then started off toward the fence. Stephen followed him. I was happy Thomas was doing more of the work and that Stephen was thinking about me, but I would miss seeing Isaac every morning.

Daed was right. I was hard to figure out. I couldn't even do it.

Ginny picked us up the next Sunday at eleven a.m., after her church service. It was our Sunday off, which was the reason we could make the trip. *Mamm* didn't seem happy about us going, and I couldn't blame her. She didn't get much time with *Daed*, considering how hard he worked during the week and on Saturdays too. Sunday was their only day together, and when we had church, that took up over half the day. *Ya*, I could see why *Mamm* wasn't pleased.

I'd taken my parents' relationship for granted all of these years. They never showed any affection in front of us children, but they never argued in front of us either. I'm sure there were times they disagreed, and *Mamm* could have a bit of sass to her. She could also be pretty independent. But I knew they loved each other and valued the time they could spend together.

As Ginny sped north, she and *Daed* chatted, and I thought more about how hard both of my parents worked. I'd taken that for granted too. Along with the actual physical labor they did, they'd raised a family of ten kids, kept a farm running, made house repairs, paid their taxes, and taken care of the horses and the couple of steers we raised every year to help feed ourselves. Maybe they hadn't done everything perfectly, but they worked well together. I wondered why it had taken me so long to notice.

Ina Mae's district didn't have church that day either, and when we arrived, kids of various ages were sitting in the grass, playing a board game. Ina Mae's great-great-nephews and nieces, no doubt. It was overcast but warm enough to be outside without jackets. A woman sat in a lawn chair nearby with a book and stood as soon as we climbed out of the car.

"Hi, I'm Sandra. I'm married to Ina Mae's great-nephew," she explained. "She's expecting you."

We thanked the woman and headed on toward the *daadi haus*.

When I knocked, Ina Mae called out, "Come in." I opened the door. She sat at her little table, a plate of cookies in the middle.

As she turned toward us, her face lit up. "Eli?"

"*Ya*," he answered. "I'm surprised you remembered."

"More of a lucky guess," she admitted with a grin, leaning on her walker to stand. "Linda, would you grab the other chair from the living room? And then pour the hot water into the teapot?"

I followed her instructions. As I placed the teapot on the table, I noticed that Ina Mae had *Daed*'s hand in hers. He was telling her about his life now and listing off all of us kids, adding our ages and what we were doing. Then he started on the grandkids.

When he finished, Ina Mae said, "I really must update that directory." She turned toward me again. "Linda, would you get my notebook and pen off the coffee table? And then write down what your father just said. I don't want to miss this opportunity."

I did as asked and started jotting down names and birthdates while *Daed* told her about our farm and then about the end of his mother's life. "She wasn't exactly an easy person to be around," he said. "But my Peggy cared for her well."

"I'm sorry I didn't come for the funeral. I didn't hear about her passing until after."

"Then I'm sorry," *Daed* said, "for not notifying you. It wasn't intentional. I just didn't think about it."

Ina Mae nodded. "I understand."

I was anxious to hear about Georgette but continued writing while Ina Mae and *Daed* chatted for a while longer. Either *Daed* was quite the actor or he was actually enjoying spending time with his cousin.

I'd finished my list and put it down on top of the notebook. Then I poured tea for all of us, handed out the mugs, and passed around the cookies. Key lime again. I imagined that Ina Mae's little freezer was probably full of them. Perhaps she actually had a lot of visitors. I wouldn't be surprised if that were true.

Ina Mae then directed her attention to me. "Well, this young lady has come for specific information, and I promised to provide what I know."

I nodded. "I'm grateful you allowed me to return."

"I don't have much to tell you, I'm afraid," she said. "And I have no physical evidence. Just a few vague family stories through the years. I'm so sorry I didn't think of any of this when you were here before. It took hearing that name to remind me."

Daed and I shared a glance as Ina Mae continued.

"I remember when I was young hearing about the twin sister that Nettie 'lost.' Georgette. Georgie for short. I assumed she had died, so that's what I always thought—until Nettie came and lived with us and I learned otherwise."

"She told you she had a twin?"

Ina Mae shook her head. "No. I overheard it during an argument. My father had forbidden Nettie from painting, but one day he caught her at it anyway. He was furious, and at one point I heard him yell something like, 'The wrong sister left. It should have been you, not her.'"

"Left?" I gasped. "Like ran away?"

She shook her head and smiled a little. "No. I don't know any of the details, but it involved their parents too. It seemed they'd let Georgie go off and live with a different family. It all felt very hush-hush and embarrassing somehow, and nobody wanted to talk about it. I did get the idea that that family wasn't Amish, which may have been part of what made it so shameful, but that's the most I was ever able to figure out. Eventually

I stopped asking, and I didn't include the twin in the family genealogy because I couldn't find the information I needed. So although the Benders actually had fourteen children, I only listed thirteen."

"Makes sense," *Daed* said.

Ina Mae didn't seem pacified, however, and I understood why she felt that way. As the family historian, she was clearly a detail-oriented person who took great care to keep accurate records. It must've rankled her to omit someone just because the other relatives refused to discuss the matter. Kind of like the time I accidentally sewed a single block at the center of a quilt upside down and didn't realize it until the quilt was completely finished. That one "off" block wasn't too noticeable, and everyone told me not to worry, especially because it was for a gift and not to sell, but I couldn't stand it. People like me, and like Ina Mae, didn't tolerate much in the way of errors or omissions. And just as I'd had to undo the row and fix my mistake, a tedious process that took hours, this woman was clearly still itching to adjust her records, even after all these years.

"Don't feel bad," I said. "It wasn't your fault that no one would talk to you about it."

"I don't know," she replied pensively. "I probably should've tried harder before giving up." Turning, she added, "That's one thing I like about you, Linda. You have questions too, but you just keep on asking them. Something tells me you won't stop until you've turned every stone."

Daed chuckled. "Linda is definitely persistent, you're right about that. Whatever task she takes on, she's always very precise, detailed, and thorough."

Ina Mae nodded approvingly. "Solid character traits indeed."

"*Ya*, when they're not taken to the extreme." *Daed* shot me a glance, and I knew what he was implying, that striving to do one's best was commendable—but striving for absolute perfection in all things to the point of overkill was not.

I cleared my throat, eager to get back to the topic at hand. "Why would Georgette have gone to live with another family?" I asked. "Especially one that wasn't Amish?"

Ina Mae shrugged. "Remember, this was during the Depression. Among poorer families, it wasn't at all unusual for children to be shifted around. Sometimes just one less mouth to feed could make all the difference. It happened more than you might think. These things weren't formalized like they would be nowadays, with legal adoptions and such. There was usually just an understanding between families. That's how it was done.

"And too," Ina Mae added, "I'm not sure what age Georgette was when she left, but if she'd been old enough, she could have been taken in as a mother's helper or for household work or the like. Again, that sort of thing was fairly common at the time. Back then, children and teens weren't viewed in the same way as they are now."

I couldn't imagine one of my siblings—or me—being sent away to live with a different family. How heartbreaking. "Where was the community in all of this? If the Benders were struggling, wouldn't their district have helped them out?"

Ina Mae and *Daed* shared a glance, and I realized how naïve I sounded.

"The Depression was a terrible thing." Ina Mae returned her gaze to me. "And it wasn't selective. Most folks were barely keeping their heads above water. Some were better off than others, *ya*, and they gave their widow's mite and then some. But when a family had no money and no home and no assets, even the most generous community help could only go so far, especially when the members of that community weren't much better off themselves."

I considered her words for a moment, recognizing yet one more thing I'd taken for granted in my life, the relative prosperity of our modern-day communities. *Ya*, many of us may have been "land rich and cash poor," as *Mamm* liked to say, but when a member fell on hard times, there were always enough resources, once pooled, to help them set things right.

"So you never heard anything about Georgette again?" *Daed* asked, interrupting my thoughts.

Ina Mae took a sip of tea. "Actually, I did. Much later than that, sometime in the '60s, one of my older relatives mentioned that we were related to a politician. I asked how, and she whispered, 'The politician's wife is your aunt, the youngest of all the siblings, although no one talks about her anymore.'"

The politician's wife. I shot *Daed* a glance. "That fits in with the information we have on Georgette Johnson." I went on to describe the articles

Isaac and I had found, including Paul W. Johnson's obituary. Georgette and Paul had had six children, and some might still be in the Lancaster area, so that would mean even more relatives around here that we had no acquaintance with. How sad.

Then I told her about the quilt I'd seen that had been made by N. Johnson and how the style resembled *Mammi* Nettie's paintings. "I tried to contact the quilter," I added, "but I haven't heard back yet."

"How fascinating," Ina Mae said, shaking her head. "One might think the similarities mere coincidence if not for the name attached. 'N. Johnson,' eh? I wonder if the quilter could be one of Georgette's daughters—though why her creation would so closely resemble Nettie's artwork, I can't imagine."

"My thoughts exactly, and I can't either."

We all grew quiet for a moment until *Daed* asked Ina Mae, "Do you know if twins run in our family?"

"Not as far as I know," she replied. "Except for Nettie and Georgie, I'm not aware of any others."

I started to mention Hattie and Hazel, but then I remembered that there was no actual blood relation between them and *Daed*. I wondered if there were any twins on *Mamm's* side, or maybe in the family of Sadie's birth father.

"Did you know that Plain folks tend to have more natural sets of multiples than *Englischers* do?" Ina Mae asked. "And it's not always genetic either. Part of it is statistical. Older women are more likely to have multiples, and Amish women tend to keep having babies later in life. So it just works out that way."

"Interesting," *Daed* said. "I didn't realize that."

Ina Mae nodded. "Back in the day I did a fair amount of research on twins."

"Because of your missing aunt and the questions you still had?" I asked.

"No. I was studying about twins who'd been separated because of a problem I was having with one of my students. What I found was that losing a twin can cause a deep wound that never fully heals."

I thought of Georgette—Georgie—and Nettie and how hard their separation must have been for them. Then my mind went again to Hattie and Hazel, and I couldn't imagine how one would ever survive without the other.

"Even if they have no memory of their twin, they may feel as if something is missing their entire lives," she continued. "And if they weren't separated until school age or older, as I have a feeling happened with Nettie and Georgie, it could be even more devastating."

It could also explain a lot, I thought, about the sad, lonely, resentful woman Nettie had become.

Ina Mae brushed away cookie crumbs as she went on. "When I was teaching, a boy in my class died from cancer, at just ten years old. His twin brother was devastated. He became withdrawn—except, occasionally, when he would lash out. Through my research into twins, I learned a few techniques to help him with his grief. I made time to encourage him to talk about his brother and then to listen, and I forced myself to accept wherever he was in his grieving process, even if anger was part of that process. It didn't come naturally to me, but I learned to do it. I also encouraged him to write about how he felt. It took years for him to recover and he always carried the loss with him, but he did get better."

"How sad," I said, thinking devastated was probably an apt description for Nettie as well, from what I'd been told.

Daed wrapped his hand around his mug. "Do you think losing her twin may have affected my mother that deeply too?"

Ina Mae nodded. "Oh, yes. *Aenti* Nettie was such a sad person, so melancholy."

"As you mentioned to Linda when she was here before," *Daed* replied, "she may also have been clinically depressed. I sure wish I'd realized that back when she was still alive." After a beat, he added, "Our youngest son has problems with depression too. I just thought he was lazy, but once Linda suggested there might be more to it than that, Peggy and I took him to a clinic, where, sure enough, he was diagnosed."

My jaw dropped as *Daed* continued.

"That was last month. Since then he's started seeing a counselor, and though he's only gone twice so far, it already seems to be helping. The doctor says he might end up needing medication in the long run, but for now he's making good progress just from the therapy."

I was flabbergasted. Over the years *Daed* had often had to be an absentee parent because of his work schedule, but he'd always been attentive and involved in his own way. That's why I had talked to him about Thomas that night in the kitchen, because I knew he'd do what was best for his son even if he did find the subject uncomfortable. Since then, however, no one had said anything about it, so I had assumed nothing had changed. Instead, here I was finding out that not only had *Daed* discussed my suspicions with *Mamm*, but they'd had Thomas evaluated and taken him to get counseling—and he'd already been to two sessions! I couldn't believe it.

The subject moved along and Ina Mae and *Daed* continued to chat easily, but I was too distracted to contribute much. When I heard Ginny's car outside, I was almost relieved it was time to go.

Standing, *Daed* and I thanked our hostess, and I told her I'd let her know how everything worked out. She squeezed my hand, and then with tears in her eyes she turned toward *Daed*. "I hope I'll see you again."

"I'll make sure of it," he said. "I'll bring Peggy with me. Perhaps in a few weeks?"

She nodded. "I'd like that."

When we stepped outside, Ina Mae's great-nephew was waiting for us. He shook *Daed*'s hand, and they both seemed pleased to have met. We chatted for several minutes and then joined Ginny in her car.

None of us spoke much on the long drive home, but after she dropped us off, as *Daed* and I were walking to the house, I asked him how they'd found a counselor for Thomas and when exactly they had managed to do all of this without me even knowing about it.

"You didn't know?" He looked genuinely surprised. "Considering it was your idea in the first place, I just assumed your mother would've told you."

I shook my head, resisting the urge to make a snarky comment. I'd been completely in the dark, as usual, but this seemed more *Mamm*'s fault than *Daed*'s. "Where'd you get the counselor?"

"The Mennonite place in Mount Gretna," he said, referring to a much-beloved mental health care facility in our region that had a large Amish clientele. "I called for an appointment the day after we talked. Thomas goes on Wednesday mornings at eleven."

At least that explained how this had happened under my nose. On Wednesdays, I was always at work by nine.

"I wanted to be at the first session," *Daed* continued, "so I arranged for an hour off and met Thomas and your mother there. Ginny had driven them, and one of my workmates brought me."

"Wait, you told people you work with about this?"

He nodded. "They're my friends. They're supportive of our family."

I was surprised. Kristen was like that with me—I just didn't know *Daed* had the same kind of relationship with the *Englischers* he worked with.

He continued, "Anyway, all three of us went the first time, your *mamm*, Thomas, and me, but last week it was just the two of them. It went fine, so they'll probably do it that way from here on out."

As we reached the back door, I wondered what other information I might not have about our family. It made *Daed* never knowing about Georgette seem more likely. We definitely seemed to be on a need-to-know basis. And there was a lot it seemed I didn't need to know.

FIFTEEN

Thomas did help with the milking the next day. And the next.

Work was slow on Tuesday, and Kristen and I had more of a chance to talk than usual. There were times when I felt that some Plain people had an arrogant attitude toward *Englischers*, as if they were helpless folk who could barely take care of themselves. That they didn't know how to garden, preserve, cook, build barns and houses, fix plumbing, and tend to animals. They had little common sense. They indulged their children. They went into debt for things they didn't need. They didn't care for their parents the way they should. I knew *Daed* didn't feel this way about *Englischers*, especially the men he worked with. Sure, a couple had gotten divorces through the years or made a habit of frequenting bars and that sort of thing, but the way *Daed* spoke of them they mostly loved their families, worked hard, and tried their best to be good people. I could tell *Daed* believed he had a lot in common with them, although of course not everything. And now I knew that some of those men had *Daed*'s back, as the *Englisch* would say—and our family's too.

That was how I felt about Kristen. *Ya*, we lived completely different lifestyles, but we had a lot in common, and more than just quilting—though that's what our conversation was about at the moment.

After that, because her phone was in her hand, Kristen began showing me pictures of her boy, Logan. They'd just bought a little pool for him, and on warm days he was having a lot of fun splashing in the water.

Then she showed me a photo taken the day before at a barbecue at her house with her parents and an older woman who sat on a lawn chair, her feet dangling in the wading pool with Logan. "Is that your grandmother?"

She nodded. "She's sixty-nine but acts like she's forty."

A pang of envy startled me. The next photo was of her grandmother reading a children's Bible to her little boy. I thought of Ruth with Hattie, Hazel, and Bobby, and my jealousy was replaced with longing. To see Ruth. And Isaac.

I exhaled. "These photos are all so sweet."

Kristen nodded. "It was such a fun day."

There was a photo of her aunt, whom I recognized because she owned the shop. And then a photo of Kristen with three cousins. She had a lot of support. I knew her mother and a cousin both helped with childcare. And that she and some of her women relatives sometimes quilted together.

"Oh, I have a gardening question." She went on to tell me something that was eating her tomato plants.

"Sounds like cutworms," I replied. "You can make a paper collar or just cut the bottom out of a plastic cup. Put the collar around the plant so the cutworms can't get to it."

Talking with Kristen was just like talking with an Amish woman. She had all the same interests, and it seemed as if others in her family did too. In fact, several times she'd attempted to share recipes with me, but the truth was, I just wasn't that interested in cooking and was happy enough with the recipes I'd already learned from *Mamm*. We talked about gardening until a customer stepped through the door.

After she left, Kristen asked me how my quilt of the barn was coming along. I admitted I'd stopped working on it. "Once I saw the photo of N. Johnson's quilts, I felt a little defeated."

"We talked about this, Linda, remember? How you just have to practice until you get it right?"

I shrugged, not even trying to explain.

"What about Tabitha's quilt?" she asked.

"The one I started after her latest breakup? When I should have known she'd be back in another relationship before I was halfway done? I decided not to make it for her after all."

Kristen laughed. I told her about Ezra and meeting him at the singing.

"But isn't your sister interested in him?"

I nodded. "Well, she told me she wasn't—then that she was. Who knows? When she first met Isaac, she seemed attracted to him too. She's just that kind of person. I guess we'll find out how she really feels about Ezra when she gets back."

"Which is when?"

"Next week, probably."

"If it all works out for her and Ezra, you could always make the quilt as a wedding gift."

"Actually, I decided to make it a baby gift for Izzy."

"Good thinking." Kristen was quiet for a moment, as if lost in thought, and then she met my eyes and spoke. "Good thing Tabitha didn't choose Isaac, though. He's right for you—not her."

I shook my head. "He's not right for me."

Kristen's face grew sad. "Then what about Ezra?"

I wrinkled my nose. "I don't think so."

"Opposites attract, right?"

"I wouldn't know."

Kristen cocked her head, so I added, "Honestly, Isaac is the only guy I've ever really been interested in. And I don't think we're opposites—except for our pasts, which couldn't more opposite if we tried."

After I finished the dishes that evening, I sat on the front porch and watched Thomas and Stephen playing horseshoes. Stephen had just mowed the lawn that afternoon and the day had been hot, so the smell of the freshly cut grass tickled my nose. I couldn't fathom how the boys still had this much energy after working so hard since before dawn.

I heard a buggy coming up our drive. I hadn't seen Sadie and the kids for a couple of days and expected it to be them, but then I realized it was too late in the evening. The kids would be in the bath and getting ready for bed by now.

I stood and walked to the railing of the porch, where I could see the driveway. It was Isaac. Stephen and Thomas both went running toward his buggy as it pulled to a stop at the hitching post. I sat back down.

The boys yelled, trying to get Isaac to join their game, but he begged off for now. Instead, he came around the corner and up the stairs, removing his hat as he did. "Mind if I join you?"

"No," I answered, though really I did. Yet I didn't. Both, actually. My stomach fluttered, confusing me even more. How could I love someone yet not bear to be with him?

"Big news," he said as he sat beside me. "I had a message today from Cheri Bethune. Turns out, she gave us the wrong phone number for N. Johnson."

My eyes widened, both in dismay and relief. At least this explained why I'd never gotten a call back.

"Well," he amended, "the first number was correct. It just wasn't the best one to use right now. Apparently, N. Johnson always goes to California this time of year."

"Oh." I blinked, my image of the quilter shifting from that of a Plain old woman quietly sewing away to a jet-setting young artist rubbing elbows with movie stars. "So did Cheri give you that number instead?"

He shook his head. "No, it's not a business line like the first one. She can't just give it out without permission. So I gave her your number and asked her to pass it along on our behalf. Hopefully you'll get a call from the mystery quilter soon."

"That would be great," I said. "*Danke.*"

I guessed he'd leave then, but when he didn't a part of me was glad. I offered him some lemonade.

"Please."

I excused myself and headed for the kitchen. When I returned with a glass for each of us, I asked how he was doing.

"All right." He sighed. "Though Bishop Yoder stopped by yesterday afternoon to talk about my artwork. He asked to see it."

I winced even though I'd expected it would be a problem sooner or later. "Did you show him?"

"*Ya.* It wasn't like I had a choice." He took a long drink of lemonade.

"What did he say?"

"Nothing. He just made noises. Like a combination between clearing his throat and grunting. When he was finished looking, he said he needed to do some thinking and praying and then he'd be back in touch."

I didn't know how to respond. I couldn't tell him everything would be all right when it might not.

Isaac took another drink. "I knew this was a possibility, that a bishop might not be understanding of my art. I was willing to give it up to join the church—and I still am, in theory. But, to be honest, now that it may actually be starting to happen, I'm having a hard time with it."

When I still didn't answer, he said, "I'm sorry. You probably didn't want to hear me whine about this."

"No," I blurted. "I do—not that you're whining. I'm just not sure what to say except that I'm sorry."

"*Danke.*" He drained the rest of his lemonade and then held up the glass. "And thank you for this too."

"You're welcome." It seemed he was ready to go, but I wanted him to stay longer. "How is Ruth doing?"

"Good. She said to tell you hello."

"I'll stop by and see her soon."

He asked me about my quilting, but I replied that I'd been pretty busy. For some reason I just couldn't admit to him that N. Johnson's beautiful quilts had totally discouraged me.

I told him more about visiting Ina Mae with *Daed* and what she'd said about Georgette.

"That sounds like good information," he stated.

"*Ya*, it's a start."

He nodded. "I hope we can get to the bottom of all of this soon." He hesitated, one hand going to the back of his neck. "Sorry."

"Whatever for?"

"Saying 'we.' This is your pursuit, not mine."

"But you've helped me so much. Of course you want to know what happens."

His eyes met mine, making my stomach flutter even more. *We.* He leaned toward me, a tender expression on his face. Was he thinking what I was? That *we* sounded so beautiful. *We* had such possibilities until—

"Want to play?" Stephen and Thomas stood at the bottom of the steps with horseshoes in their hands.

As my face burned with sudden heat, all I could think to do was tease them. "You're asking *me*?" I knew they'd meant Isaac. No one ever asked me to join in a game of anything unless they were desperate.

"You can play too," Thomas offered quickly.

I shrugged and glanced at Isaac. "Why not?"

After we'd gone a few rounds, *Daed* came out and joined us and then *Mamm* followed. A slight evening breeze blew through the field of corn, but the evening was warm. Thomas and I were on Isaac's team, while *Mamm* and Stephen were on *Daed*'s team. We grew quite competitive but laughed a lot too. I was the worst at pitching a shoe, but Isaac made up for my lack of skill. And Thomas did so well that I guessed he and Stephen had been practicing during their work breaks. In the end, our team won the final game, twenty-six to twenty-four.

Isaac didn't leave until after the sun was starting to set. As he did, both of my parents looked at me as though I were pathetic.

"What?" I asked.

"Nothing." *Mamm* slipped her arm through *Daed*'s and headed toward the house. No matter how clear their message was, they couldn't shame me into changing my mind about Isaac. But I could see their point. I enjoyed being around him. And obviously they did too.

I checked the answering machine that night and again the next morning, but there were no messages. Once work was done that afternoon, I was eager to check again, but I stopped by Ruth's first on the way home. Isaac wasn't there, which I'd expected.

She was happy to see me and put on a pot of hot water. I asked how she was doing. "I'm happy to be back to normal, whatever that is," she joked. She had a stew simmering on the burner and bread in the oven. "I'm so thankful Isaac's here with me. Cooking for two is so much better than cooking for one, don't you think?"

I chuckled. I'd only ever cooked for a whole family, though these days we were down to just five.

Ruth and I had tea and a nice chat, and then I left. When I turned onto the highway, a car—with Isaac in the passenger seat—turned toward Ruth's house. He waved and I waved back. I wasn't sure if I was disappointed or relieved that I'd departed before he arrived.

After I unharnessed Blue, and brushed, fed, and watered him, I stepped into the shed and then into the little phone room and closed the door firmly behind me. *Daed* had constructed the room out of sheetrock, and it was no bigger than one of those old-fashioned phone booths. It was also unfinished on the inside. A pencil hung from a string that was tacked to the wall and sometimes a notebook hung there too, but often we wrote messages and numbers directly on the sheetrock. Someday *Daed* would have to finish the room to get rid of all of the writing.

There were two messages on the machine. I tried not to get my hopes up, though I held my breath while I listened to the first. It was only Tabitha, telling me to call her back. As the second one started, I gasped. Sure enough, it was the call I'd been waiting for.

"Hello, I'm trying to reach Linda Mueller. I was given this number by Cheri Bethune. She said you had some questions about one of the quilts you saw in the catalogue. I'd be happy to help if I can. Call me back whenever. This is my cell so you should be able to reach me."

She gave her number and I jumped into action, grabbing the pencil and scribbling it onto the wall. When I hung up the phone, I looked at the digits for a long moment, knowing I was one step closer to finding out whatever had happened to my grandmother's missing twin sister.

Summoning my nerve, I dialed the number and again held my breath until she answered. She sounded friendly, as if she'd been hoping to hear from me, and curious about why I'd been trying to get in touch.

"Cheri wouldn't tell me much. She just said that there was a young woman who'd been into the gallery, seen one of the quilts, and had some very interesting questions about it and about the quilter. So how can I help you?"

"It's complicated, but before I get into it, I just have to ask. Do you know a Georgette Johnson? That's not your name, or maybe your mother's or grandmother's name, is it?"

"No, sorry. Our last name is Johnson, but I don't know of any Georgettes in the family. Why?"

"How about Georgie?" I asked, ignoring her question.

"No," the woman said.

My voice grew softer. "Nettie Mueller? Ever heard of her?"

"Again, sorry, no. What's this about?"

I took a deep breath and blew it out. "It's kind of a long story, but I'll keep it as simple as I can."

"It has something to do with the quilt you saw?"

"It does."

"Okay, go ahead," she replied. "This is good timing, actually. I have about ten minutes while the roast finishes. Until then, I'm all yours."

I smiled, picturing this friendly woman settling down at her kitchen counter, ready to hear me out.

"Thanks." I thought for a moment and then launched in. "My late grandmother's name was Nettie Mueller, and she was an artist for much of her life. A painter. I've only seen one of her works, but it's really something. She was obviously quite gifted, with a very unique style."

"How nice."

"The one painting we still have shows an image of two little Amish girls out in a field at sunset." I went on to describe it as best I could, remembering the vivid colors, the emotion in the girls' postures, the feeling evoked by the whole scene. When I got to the most important part, though, I hesitated, wanting to say it in the right way. "The weird thing is," I told her, "she did something unique with the sunset. It would be hard to explain except that it's not—because your quilt was done the same way, with the rays of the sun kind of swirling down and creating the path the girls were walking on. In fact, that whole quilt looked almost exactly like a fabric version of something my grandmother would have painted. That's why I needed to talk to you. I just couldn't imagine such similarities were purely coincidental."

She didn't respond, so I kept going.

"Though it could be coincidence, if not for another connection. And here's where it gets more complicated. It wasn't just the strong resemblance between the painting and the quilt that caught my eye. My grandmother had a twin sister named Georgette, although she went by Georgie. Her married name was Johnson. Georgette Johnson. So when I learned the quilter was a Johnson, I knew there was something going on here. That's why I've been trying to reach you. I want to figure this out. I know it sounds odd, but between the common style and the common name, I have to believe there's some connection between my grandmother's painting and your quilt. More specifically, between my grandmother and you."

I forced myself to stop babbling and waited for her to speak. It struck me that my little speech might have come across as accusatory somehow, as if I were saying she'd stolen my grandmother's ideas and techniques and used them as her own.

When she spoke, however, she mostly just sounded confused. "Okay," she said, drawing out the word. "First things first, I'm sorry, I guess I didn't make this clear. I'm not the quilter. My mother is. I just handle her affairs when she's out of town. My name is Jan, by the way. Not sure if I said that before."

I sat up, chills tingling my forearms. "Jan, what age is your mother, if you don't mind me asking?"

"Oh, she's quite up there. I'm her youngest and I'm fifty-three, so you can imagine."

My heart began to pound as I did the math. If Jan was fifty-three and her mother had been, say, forty-five when she had her last child, then if she were still alive now, she'd be...ninety-eight.

I swallowed hard. "What's her first name? You're sure it's not Georgette?"

She laughed. "I'm sure. My mother's name is Natasha."

Sixteen

Natasha.

My mind reeled.

It seemed I'd found one more piece of the puzzle—perhaps a very big piece. If this woman was the same Natasha who had inscribed that old art book to my grandmother, then here was yet another link, one that might end up answering an ever-growing list of questions.

I explained as much to Jan now, telling her about the book and the inscription, *To Nettie, With love, Natasha.*

"So that's three connections," I added. "Your mother's first name is the same as the one in there, your mother's quilt looks just like my grandmother's painting, and your mother's married name is the same as my grandmother's twin's married name."

"I do have to admit," Jan replied, "it is starting to sound like there might be something to this. As I said, I don't know of any Georgies in the family, but my mom might."

"So how can I speak directly with her?" I didn't mean to sound pushy, but now that I'd come this far, I was more eager than ever to keep going. "I'd prefer talking face-to-face, but I can do this by phone if need be. Is there a number out in California where I could reach her?"

"Actually," she replied, "she might be willing to meet with you in person. She goes to San Diego every summer to spend a few weeks with my sister. But she's flying home tomorrow."

"Oh." My pulse surged. "Do you think she would let me come see her? I'm free on Sunday after church, or Monday, any time. Doesn't matter where. If it's too far for the buggy, I can hire a driver."

Jan was quiet for a moment. "Buggy," she said finally. "Are you Amish?"

"*Ya,*" I answered. "Did I not mention that?"

She chuckled. "No, although now that you say it, I'm hearing the accent. I probably should've guessed."

"Does your mother have any connection with the Amish community?"

"Not that I know of."

"Amish friends?"

"Not close friends. I mean, she's lived in Lancaster most of her life, so she's certainly had her share of friendly Amish acquaintances, like at her favorite produce stand or the men who put the addition on our old house. But being in the city itself, it's not as though she had Amish neighbors or anything."

"And you're sure there's no one named Georgie on the Johnson side of the family?"

"No, but just because the name doesn't ring a bell for me doesn't mean it won't for her."

I started to reply when she added, "Speaking of bells, there's my timer. I need to go."

I realized she was about to hang up so I spoke quickly. "How should I proceed? I'd really like to meet with your mother as soon as possible."

"Yep, I know. Let me get the roast out, and then I'll give her a call and get back to you."

"Thank you. I'll wait here by the phone."

"Okay."

I could hear an incessant beeping in the background and then a *click* and she was gone. Returning the phone to its cradle, I sat there in the little room in silence for a long moment.

My mind and heart were such a jumbled mess that I closed my eyes, breathed in deep, and began to pray. *I ask Your blessing on this endeavor and that You would bring clarity to the forefront. Please open the hearts and minds of those involved. And show me the whole truth of this matter—if it be Your will.* I had to believe this little search of mine that had taken me so far was a good thing, a right thing to do. But I knew I must temper my enthusiasm with respect for God's plan in this, not my own.

When my prayer was over, the phone still hadn't rung, so I sat there for a while thinking about all the blessings that had come from this search thus far. It had brought my *daed* and me even closer, which was a lovely thing. It had opened my mind to the realization of what might be wrong with Thomas, and he'd ended up getting a diagnosis and treatment for it at last. It had introduced me to my sweet cousin Ina Mae, who'd told me all sorts of interesting things about our family. And it had shown me a whole new method of quilting—and my artistic limits.

There was one other result, though I hesitated to call it a blessing. Isaac. This search had given me not just extra time with him but also something for the two of us to focus on. It had allowed me to grow close to him. To fall in love with him. And even though I knew we could never be together, maybe that was a good thing anyway. At least it showed I was capable of such feelings. At least it showed the truth to my lie that I would never marry. Surely God had a mate in mind for me, somewhere. Somehow.

I just had to fall out of love with Isaac first.

When the phone rang, I nearly sprang to the ceiling. Quickly, I grabbed the receiver and then almost dropped it in my startled enthusiasm.

"*Hallo?*"

"Linda? It's Jan. Okay, we're all set. Monday it is, though it'll have to be later in the afternoon. How's four thirty?"

"Four thirty Monday is perfect," I said, grabbing for the pencil and then scribbling down the address as she dictated it to me. "Did she explain anything to you about all of this? Does she know a Georgie Johnson?"

"She didn't go into it," Jan replied, "but it definitely seemed like she knows something. She sounded really surprised—but also like she wasn't surprised at all, you know? It's hard to explain. It was weird."

It didn't seem weird to me. Natasha Johnson did have some connection to Georgie.

"The weirdest part?" Jan continued. "As soon as I told her someone was asking about a Georgie Johnson, she goes, 'Is this someone Amish?' I hadn't even said anything about that."

My heart began to pound. So she really did know who Georgie was. *Thank You, Lord.*

"And that was about it for our call. I told her yes, you were Amish, and she said to set something up for Monday. Then she had to go."

I smiled to myself, a deep satisfaction surging through me. Finally I would have some answers.

Relaxing back against the chair, I asked Jan to tell me a bit about her mother, just so I'd know something about of this woman I was going to meet. Other than our odd connections, the only facts I had at this point were that Natasha Johnson was a gifted quilter, she had at least two daughters, one who lived out west, and she was healthy enough despite her advanced age to fly back and forth each year to see her.

"Oh, sure," Jan replied. "Though I only have a minute, then I need to finish getting supper on."

"Of course."

"Let's see, well, as you can imagine, she's very healthy for her age, very active. She's in a sewing club, and a book club too. She used to be in a garden club as well, but she gave that up when she moved into the place where she lives now. She still volunteers twice a month at a thrift store, one that supports low-income families. And there are her quilts."

"Which are amazing."

"Yes, so many people love her work—it's incredible the accolades she's received." She went on to tell me of different shows and exhibits and even museums where her mother's quilts had been displayed. "She's always done other kinds of handiwork, like embroidery and sewing and stuff, but she didn't find her true artistic calling until she started quilting."

I nodded, even though Jan couldn't see me. That had been the case for me as well.

"Believe it or not," she continued, "she didn't even start quilting until she was in her seventies. Can you imagine? By that point, she'd already lived a long, full life, raising us kids, helping my dad with his career, and then being a single mom after he died, plus doing all of her activities and charity work. Who could've guessed she was about to enter an entirely new chapter, completely different from anything that had come before?"

"Interesting," I murmured. I couldn't help but compare Natasha Johnson's life with my grandmother's. They were around the same age. But while Natasha had been embarking on phase two of what sounded like a very fulfilling and happy existence, *Mammi* Nettie was winding down toward death, miserable to the end.

"Hold on a sec," Jan said, and before I could reply the phone clunked and then I could hear the rattle of a pot and lid in the background. When she came back on the line, she said, "Sorry. Had to stir the potatoes. I really do need to go."

"Sure."

"One quick question for you first, though. What is it you hope to find out from all of this, Linda? I mean, obviously this is about more than just seeing a beautiful quilt that reminded you of your late grandmother's artwork. What's the story?"

I hesitated and then said I was happy to explain but that my answer wouldn't be quick.

"Streamline it for me. Like, the condensed version."

"All right..." My voice trailed off as I formed my thoughts. *Englischers* were always in such a hurry. Either she needed to go or she didn't, but why put that pressure on me?

I launched in, starting with the day back in April when I learned my late grandmother had been an artist. "Once I saw the picture she'd painted, I *had* to find out more about her. I'm a quilter myself, and something in her work connected with that artistic part of me, you know? It's hard to explain. I just kept wondering about her, and several questions in particular kept nagging at me."

"Oh, I get that," Linda said. "As my mother likes to say, 'Sometimes a notion sticks like gum on a shoe.'"

"Exactly. So, anyway, a friend and I decided to do a little research into my grandmother, and that's when we uncovered an even bigger surprise. Turns out, she had a twin, a sister named Georgie. The thing is, none of us knew about her, not even my father. His mother never once mentioned having had a twin sister."

"She died young?"

"No. Actually, we did some more digging and found that at some point she broke off from her family and went to live elsewhere. I don't know exactly how old she was then, or where she went, but it had to have happened when she was a child or maybe a young teen, so the assumption is that a different family took her in, one that wasn't Amish. After that, I think her own family just sort of cut her out of their lives."

"They shunned her?"

I blinked, visions of questioning tourists with misguided assumptions filling my head. "No. She probably left at too young of an age to have joined the church yet. Only church members can be shunned for something like that."

"So they cut her off, but more in an unofficial capacity."

"I suppose you could put it that way."

"Interesting. Okay, one last thing, and then I really, really have to go. You said there were several questions that kept nagging at you. What are those questions, if you don't mind me asking?"

"I don't mind." I smiled, thinking of the initial curiosities that had set me on this journey. "I just kept wondering, why did my grandmother start painting, even though it was frowned upon in our community? And more importantly, why did she stop?"

"She stopped?"

"*Ya*. According to my father, one day when she was in her forties, she put down her brush and never picked it up again." I didn't add that she also threw that brush—and her paints and other supplies—around the room in some bizarre fit of rage. The important point was that she quit painting, for good.

"How unusual," Jan said. "Maybe she just felt like she'd peaked, you know? Like she wanted to go out on top."

I didn't reply. My guess was that Jan was no artist herself. If she were, she would understand that creativity wasn't something a person could just turn off and on at will. I'd read about volcanoes in *National Geographic*, and to my experience, it was more like that. For some, creativity was always bubbling under the surface, always needing to release its heat one way or the other. Whether that release came through the slow and steady expulsion of steam or in one giant explosion of lava, the need was there. It would always come out somehow.

I was trying to decide what to say when another round of beeping kicked in on Jan's end and she ended our call.

As I hung up the phone, I acknowledged she wasn't the only one who needed to get supper on the table. I hurried back to the house to help *Mamm*, and it wasn't until halfway through our meal that I realized I'd been so distracted by my conversation with Jan that I hadn't called Tabitha back.

Laughter interrupted my thoughts. Stephen was describing a calf who'd started bucking when it had gotten spooked by the shadow of a crow, and Thomas, of all people, was cracking up. Two months ago he wouldn't have reacted to a story like that at all. Professional help was already clearly making a difference for him.

My mind went to the twins, and suddenly I wondered if they might benefit from some professional help as well. They didn't suffer from depression, but ASD presented its own unique challenges. Maybe they could be helped too. For several years, ever since their diagnosis, we'd all been assuming there was nothing that could change or be improved for them. But if a single little barn cat could break through their isolated shells, then maybe other things could too. At the very least, it wouldn't hurt to look into it. And who was in a better position to do that right now, I realized, than Tabitha, their teacher, who had access not only to a computer but also research guidance from Zed and Izzy, the two smartest and most educated members of the family?

Right after supper I slipped out of the house, telling *Mamm* I'd be right back to wash the dishes, and hurried to the shed to call Izzy's number. It took her a while to pick up, and when I said hello, she responded with, "Linda! It's you. Hold on a second." I could hear her talking to someone and then saying, "Could you take her?"

When she came back on, she said, "I wish you were here. You'd love our little Maggie! We're not getting much sleep, but that's okay." She laughed and then continued, going on and on about the baby. I could hear Zed's voice in the background cooing to the little one.

"I like that Maggie's middle name is after our great-grandmother," I said when I had a chance to get a word in edgewise.

That brought Izzy up short. "What?"

"*Mammi* Nettie's mother was a Mary. Mary Bender."

"Seriously? I didn't know that. I learned all about *Mamm*'s side of the family, but not too much about *Daed*'s. I feel terrible. *Mammi* Nettie and I were so close when I was young, and she talked about her mother sometimes. I can't believe I didn't remember the woman's name."

She sounded so guilty. I told her not to feel bad, that that entire branch of the family tree was pretty much "out of sight, out of mind." "With *Daed* being an only child, it's not like we've got tons of Mueller aunts and uncles and cousins running around. Look at all the trouble I'm having to go to just to find information about *Mammi* Nettie's mysterious twin."

"True. Well, I think it's great what you're doing. Keep me updated, would you?"

"Will do. Listen, is Tabitha around? I had a message to call her."

"*Ya*, I'll get her for you. At the moment she's outside talking to one of Zed's students."

"What?" I cried. "Don't tell me Tabitha is seeing someone."

Izzy laughed. "I doubt it. The particular student she's talking with is thirtysomething. And married. And a *she*. She brought over a bag of hand-me-downs from her own babies, the cutest little nighties and T-shirts and things. Tabitha was just walking her out."

I heard the sound of a door opening and then Izzy called, "Tabitha, Little Sister is on the phone."

I winced.

There were goodbyes in the background, and then after a moment Tabitha came on the line. "Hey, Linda, thanks for calling me back. Big news. I'm coming home on Monday. On the bus. I get in at five p.m. It's your day off, so I figured you could get Ginny to drive you and meet me at the bus station in Lancaster. I can't wait!"

"All right." I wrote it on the drywall. *Monday 5pm—Lancaster bus station.* Then I hesitated. "Hold on," I said. "That won't work. I already have something important scheduled for then."

"So change it. What could be more important than me?"

I smiled, though I knew she was only half kidding. "I can't. I'm going to see...a quilter."

"Can't you reschedule it? I've been gone almost a month, for goodness' sake."

"No, I can't. Sorry."

I could sense Tabitha was pouting. "I'm so sad."

We both knew she was perfectly capable of hiring a driver to meet her and bring her home by herself. But I understood her desire not to do things that way. After being gone for so long, she wanted to be welcomed by a loved one, not just somebody who was paid to be there.

"Maybe Ezra can go."

"Nope. I already asked him," she said.

"Ouch. Good to know I wasn't your first choice."

Tabitha just laughed, not even acknowledging the insult. "Ezra's working with Jedediah, and he doesn't feel like he should take the time off." Her voice brightened a little. "But he is going to come over to the house that night." Quickly her tone fell again. "I guess I'll call Ginny and ask if she can come without you."

I hesitated. "Actually, I've already arranged for Ginny to drive me to my meeting at that time."

"Well, ouch to you too then. Where is this big meeting? Couldn't you work it out for her to do both?"

I chewed my lip, thinking. I didn't mind sharing our driver. I just didn't want Tabitha coming to Natasha's apartment. This was my quest, my meeting, my appointment. "I suppose Ginny and I can figure it out," I said. "Maybe she can drop me off first and then go pick you up. And then come back and get me, and then take us both home."

"Okay, whatever. You'll set it up?"

"Sure."

"Great." It sounded like Tabitha was walking, and then I could hear Zed cooing to the baby in the background. "I've got to run for now," she added. "I'll see you Monday."

"No, wait. I had one more thing first. It's important."

"Fine. Hold on a minute." It sounded like she was making her way to some other room. As I waited, I tried to think of how best to present my thoughts. Absently, I reached again for the pencil and wrote on the wall, *Hattie and Hazel.*

"Okay, what's up?" Tabitha said at last.

Quickly I shared with her about Thomas and the help *Mamm* and *Daed* were getting for him. I told her about that day at Sadie's in the garden with the cat and how alive and engaged the girls had seemed. Then I went into Ina Mae and the research she'd done on twins back when she was a teacher and how she'd found information about things she'd been able to do herself that had helped her student.

"Maybe you need to do that too for Hattie and Hazel," I said. "Being on the spectrum, they face certain issues that other children don't. Maybe you need to learn more about autism."

In a cool tone she asked, "What are you getting at?"

"I'm not implying that you aren't a good teacher. You are. I'm just saying that it might help you figure out a better way to handle Hattie and Hazel if you did some research. And being at Izzy's might give you more opportunities for that than you'll have once you're back home."

"Linda, you know as well as I do that if the girls required a special needs teacher, the board would've gotten them one. Hattie and Hazel aren't a problem."

"To you," I responded. "But their behavior will be a problem to them in the long run. You say they don't interact with the other students. They get upset with any changes to the routine. All those things. Maybe there's information out there that could help you help them."

She was silent for a long moment. "I see what you're getting at," she said. "I'll give it some thought."

I told her I really was looking forward to seeing her, even if I couldn't rearrange my schedule. I'm not sure she believed me. "See you on Monday," I said. "Give the baby a kiss for me."

After we hung up, I said a prayer for Tabitha and *der bose Gheist*. Her prideful spirit. That was one of the things we guarded against—but I knew how easily it could sneak up, seemingly out of nowhere. It dawned on me that maybe Tabitha was in over her head when it came to teaching. Maybe she felt inadequate, and that was why she'd acted defensively.

If so, then maybe me telling her she needed to learn more about how to handle the twins made her feel as if she'd failed somehow. Worse was all that info about Thomas, which also had to make her feel bad. Here she'd been frustrated with him all year and kept demanding he change his behavior when it turned out there was a reason for that behavior. In the light of our new knowledge, it was obvious that her nagging and griping had been pointless—and even a bit cruel.

I stared at the names Hattie and Hazel again. *Sisters.* I hadn't meant to hurt mine. I quickly redialed Izzy's number. Thankfully, Tabitha was the one to answer. "I'm sorry," I said. "I didn't mean to make you feel bad."

"No, I'm sorry I was gruff," she replied. "I know you were just trying to help. I really will think about what you said."

I started to say goodbye again, but she interrupted me. "And I'm glad Thomas is doing better. Depression, huh? Poor kid. That makes sense, actually."

I agreed. We hung up, and I counted the days until Monday. *Five.*

Five days until Tabitha would be home.

Five days until I would meet Natasha Johnson face-to-face.

Five days, Lord willing, until I would finally get some answers to my questions.

Church on Sunday was at Bishop Yoder's house. Isaac sat a row ahead of me on the other side of the shed, looking so handsome that more than once I had to force myself to turn away. I couldn't deny that I yearned for him. What could I do to make it stop? As the service came to a close, I wondered if the solution was to focus on our friendship rather than our failed romance.

Inspired by my new plan, I sought Isaac out after the meal and told him all about my phone call with Jan and my plans to visit Natasha the next day, and he seemed as excited as I was. With a roll of my eyes, I added the whole part about my sister, how Ginny was going to have to take me to Natasha's house and then pick up Tabitha at the bus station and then come back to get me again.

"So then Tabitha will join you?" he asked.

I shook my head. "I'm hoping Ginny can stall for a bit, and then they can just wait in the car. It's kind of hard to explain, but I don't want her there."

He smiled a little. "Do you want anyone there?"

I want you there, I thought with regret, looking into his loving eyes.

Then again, why shouldn't he be there? He'd been such a big part of all this from the beginning, it seemed only right that he get to share in what could be a really big breakthrough. I decided to invite him along—though I didn't want him to get the wrong idea.

"I do, actually," I said. "Can you come?"

He reacted with such delight that I quickly added, "You know, as a friend. You've been such a big help throughout this whole thing. I think it's only fair. And it should be really interesting."

His smile evaporated, and for a moment I caught a flash of that same hurt I'd seen on his face that night on my porch two weeks ago, after I'd had such a fit when he tried to talk to me about Bailey.

"It's at four thirty, so I guess you'd have to meet me there," I added, sounding as awkward as I suddenly felt.

"*Ya*," he replied, eyes averted, all business. "Sounds good."

"I don't have the address with me, but it's in Lancaster, a place called Waverly Village."

He nodded. "I'll have my driver drop me off there after work. We should be able to find it."

"*Gut*. Then whichever one of us gets there first can just wait outside for the other?"

I so badly wanted him to look at me, but his eyes stayed trained to one side.

"All right. See you there." He turned and walked away.

A knot tightened in my gut like a fist as I watched him go. Maybe this friendship stuff was going to be harder than I'd expected.

I wanted to go after him, to ask him if Bishop Yoder had given him a decision yet about his art. But his pace was brisk as he headed toward the pasture gate, and Sadie was already helping the kids into her buggy. Reluctantly, I went and joined her.

As we were driving away, I turned back for one last look and saw Bishop Yoder approaching Isaac, as if he wanted to talk. I hoped the news wasn't bad. I couldn't imagine Isaac not being able to do his art.

Sadie shot me a sly look. "I saw you talking with Isaac. Any change in your feelings toward him?"

"No." I couldn't explain to her that I still found him as fascinating as ever and wanted to be his friend—I just couldn't see him romantically. Changing the subject, I asked how she'd been feeling.

She shrugged. "About the same."

"How are things going with Jedediah?"

"He's still helping with the milking."

"That's not exactly what I meant."

She glanced at me. "Thankfully you're not one to start rumors."

Once back at her house, Sadie rested in her room while I put Bobby down for a nap and then sat with Hattie and Hazel at the table. I read to them from *Little House in the Big Woods* until they asked if we could do a puzzle. They chose one of kittens. No big surprise there. But I was surprised—and pleased—that they chatted a bit as we worked, mostly about cats and the different kinds there were and Whisper's soft black fur, which they both felt was by far the very best color for a cat. They still didn't make much eye contact with me, but they included me in the conversation, which was a huge advance. Many a time I'd sat with them in silence for an hour or more as they rotely performed the task at hand, communicating only occasionally and only with each other.

A half hour later I heard a buggy out front. I stood to go see who it was, but Sadie emerged from her room and was already heading toward the door. To my surprise her hair was perfectly neat under her *kapp* and her apron hadn't a wrinkle on it. She certainly didn't look as if she'd been lying down.

"I'll be back soon," she said. "You're good?"

I gave her a nod, and she headed outside. I could hear muffled voices and then nothing. I stepped to the window and moved the curtain just enough to see out. Sadie was walking with Jedediah toward the pathway around the field.

"*Aenti* Linda, come back and help us," Hattie said. Neither twin was interested in what was going on with their mother at all.

I returned to the table and worked on the puzzle with them some more until Bobby woke. I changed his diaper and then fixed a snack for the kids. When we heard steps on the porch, Hattie and Hazel went to the door together and opened it.

Jedediah gave them a hardy hello and they ventured forward, although tentatively. Bobby began squirming in his chair, so I pulled him out and carried him to the porch too. Soon he was in Jedediah's arms.

I felt awkward and wondered if I should go ahead and walk home. But then Sadie excused herself, leaving us there on the porch without her, and I knew it would be rude to leave now. After a moment I could hear her clanking around in the kitchen, and I realized she was probably in there pulling together some tea or lemonade and maybe a snack for the adults. I was about to head in and tell her I could do that for her when Jedediah spoke.

"I hear your sister's coming home tomorrow." He bounced a contented Bobby on his hip.

"Tabitha? *Ya*, on the bus. It'll be nice to have her back." And it was good timing. She could help Sadie now.

Jedediah nodded. "Poor Ezra's counting the minutes until he sees her tomorrow night."

I looked at him, eyebrows raised.

He smiled and then shrugged. "I think he's been lost without her—especially considering how things were between them when she left."

I nodded, though in truth she'd given me such mixed messages about the situation I no longer knew what to think.

"Poor guy. He really did believe they were courting," Jedediah continued, shaking his head. "Then she decided to go to Indiana without even discussing it first. He was really hurt, especially because she wouldn't even talk about it, and he didn't push the matter. I think that's their biggest problem, you know? It's all well and good to be able to have fun together and make each other laugh, but you gotta be able to get serious once in a while too."

I was starting to feel uncomfortable with our conversation, which was drifting precariously close to gossip. But then he added, "Of course I wouldn't say all this to just anyone, but you and Tabitha are so close. I'm sure you have an even better perspective than I do."

"We are close," I replied, my cheeks growing warm. I knew I should admit to Jedediah how blind on this issue I really was, but it was a little late for that. He would probably be mortified if he knew he'd been sharing secrets I hadn't been privy to.

The baby was getting squirmy, so Jedediah lowered him to the porch floor and then sat down himself so that his body blocked the steps—a good idea since Bobby seemed intent on pulling himself up and toddling around the narrow railed space. Once more feeling awkward, I stepped to the nearest chair and sat.

"The good news," Jedediah said, "is that Ezra has made a decision. And I'm sure he wouldn't mind my telling you that. This time he's going to insist that they talk things out. He's not taking no for an answer."

"No to what?"

"To having a serious discussion, like he tried to before. He's ready to make a commitment, but he needs to know that she's ready too. If she won't even talk about it, well…" He shook his head as his voice trailed off.

I thought about that for a moment. If Ezra was so ready to make a commitment, why had he gone to the singing just the week before? I said as much to Jedediah now.

"In fact," I added, "why was he flirting with me that night? What was I, some sort of consolation prize? He couldn't get the Mueller sister he wanted, so he went for the next one down the line? The Little Sister."

Jedediah shook his head, one eye on Bobby, who was now toddling back and forth between him and the girls, who were perched on the rail facing the barn. "Actually, I think he was just trying to move on, like she said he should. But you know how it is. Sometimes you have to be with one person to realize how you really feel about another."

I looked away, remembering that night myself and how I'd wished Ezra had been Isaac.

"Here we are," Sadie said, emerging from the house with a tray bearing three mugs of coffee and a plate of sliced banana bread. We helped ourselves and then sat there enjoying the food and drink. The girls moved to the opposite end of the porch, and Bobby crawled after them. They all sat and watched the traffic, mostly tourists creeping by slowly on the road, some peering back at them in delight as they passed.

As Sadie, Jedediah, and I chatted, I felt very much like a third wheel, and again I considered leaving. But in the end I stayed, mostly because I knew it wouldn't look right for the newly widowed Sadie to be out here alone with a man, sipping coffee and nibbling treats and quietly talking and laughing, within full view of anyone who happened to pass by.

Then again, whether their behavior was appropriate or not didn't seem to matter all that much to the two of them. As far as I was concerned, they shared way too many lingering glances, not to mention several private jokes, little turns of phrase that made them both chuckle in some shared humor I couldn't grasp. I was about to excuse myself and leave when Jedediah stood and said he needed to be going.

Sadie gave him such a doe-eyed look that I had to glance the other way as they said their goodbyes.

She and I stayed there on the porch, watching as Jedediah turned his buggy around. He gave a big wave as he drove past. The girls went back in the house, and Bobby began to fuss on the floor of the porch, where they'd left him. I picked him up and turned to Sadie.

"So what is going on between you two?"

She shrugged. "We went for a little walk, is all."

"Well, there's that," I said. "But it's more the way you look at each other, and act with each other."

She stood and started toward the door. "Why would I tell you?"

"Why wouldn't you?"

"Because there's a lot you don't understand. And I don't expect you to." Sadie sighed as she reached for the doorknob. "You're young. You've never been married. You haven't even been courted."

I winced.

"Robert would be pleased that Jedediah is interested, believe me." She let go of the doorknob.

"So you admit it? That this really is more than just a little neighborly friendship?"

Sadie sighed. "It's not like we're going to marry anytime soon—after all, I have a new baby coming in September." She put her hand on her belly. "But our talking and spending a little time together isn't hurting anyone. In fact, we have Bishop Yoder's blessing."

"What?"

"*Ya*. Jedediah spoke with him. The only concern he raised was for the children, saying that it might be hurtful to them to see me with someone else so soon."

"Other children, maybe," I replied. "Not yours. Bobby clearly adores Jedediah, and the twins would be oblivious no matter what you did."

"Which is what Jedediah told the bishop, which is why he gave his blessing."

I couldn't believe it. Did no one else see how wrong this was? Robert had been gone less than two months!

"You know," Sadie said, "no one has a problem with this but you."

I whispered, "What about Ruth? Wouldn't she be hurt if she knew her late son's wife was already getting serious with another man?"

Sadie exhaled. "I don't believe she would. I'm sure she expects I'll remarry. Who better than someone she knows? Someone who was a friend of Robert's. Someone who is good and kind to his children."

I didn't answer. I knew what she was saying made sense. I did seem to be the only person having a hard time with Robert being replaced so soon. Tears stung my eyes.

She crossed her arms. "If you think you miss him more than I do, stop it. I miss him every single day. But he told me to go on living, and that's what I plan to do."

I nodded and then handed Bobby to her. "I'm going to walk home," I said.

"I can give you a ride."

I shook my head. "I'd rather walk."

By the time I reached our driveway, what pained me the most was Sadie saying that she'd chosen to go on living.

The question was, when was *I* going to start living? I'd been content with my life before meeting Isaac. But somehow quilting, working, and weeding the garden didn't feel like nearly enough anymore.

SEVENTEEN

On Monday, when we got to Natasha's address, I told Ginny to take her time with Tabitha. "Maybe talk her into getting something to eat," I added. "She's bound to be hungry after such a long trip."

Ginny laughed. "All right," she said. "I hear you. I'll keep her out of your hair as long as I can."

I gave her a grateful smile and climbed from the car, Nettie's old art book under my arm. Isaac was waiting for me at the main entrance, under a sign that read *Waverly Village Senior Living*. He'd changed out of his work coveralls and looked like any Amish man. When I approached, he met my eyes and gave me a warm smile, the awkwardness of our last encounter apparently forgotten. Thank goodness.

Once we entered the building, it was clear to see that it was a place for old folks, albeit an elegant one. There was a dining hall off to the side, full of elderly people being served their supper. The lobby was well furnished with clusters of wingback chairs and sofas. The walls were covered with textured wallpaper, and a chandelier hung from the ceiling.

"Wow," I said. "This is one fancy nursing home."

"Actually," Isaac replied, "it's not a nursing home. It's an assisted living facility. The residents have their own apartments, so in that way they're completely independent, but meals, housekeeping, and activities are provided." He motioned toward a counter. "We probably need to sign in." Sure enough, there was a piece of paper on a clipboard where we wrote our names and the name of the person we were visiting.

"She's in 307," I told Isaac, and we moved toward the elevator. Up on the third floor, he took the lead and I followed. When we got to her unit, he paused to give me an encouraging smile and then knocked. A moment later the door swung open, and we were greeted by a woman who looked to be in her early fifties. Thanks to her warm yet efficient demeanor, I knew right away this had to be Jan.

"Linda?" she asked.

"Jan?" I replied.

"Yes. Hi. It's great to meet you in person."

"*Ya*, you too," I said. "This is my friend Isaac. I hope it's all right that I brought him along."

"Of course. Hi, Isaac, nice to meet you. Come on in." She shook both of our hands and gestured us inside. "Mother's expecting you."

We stepped into a small living room to see an elderly woman walking toward us. Though slightly stooped, she didn't use a walker or cane and seemed steady on her feet. Her silver hair was pulled back in a bun at the nape of her neck, and she was about my height. She wore white pants and a pink cardigan sweater over a pink top.

She smiled as she came our way. "Hello," she said. "I'm so happy to meet you."

She reached out her hand to me, and I squeezed hers in return. As she moved on to Isaac, I glanced around and saw that there were framed photos everywhere, propped on various surfaces and adorning one entire wall. Some of the pictures were obviously old, but others seemed quite new, and they featured people of all ages, from infants to the elderly.

After she shook Isaac's hand, Natasha asked us to sit down. There was a couch, a comfortable chair, and a coffee table holding a platter of cheese, crackers, and pear slices, along with four plates and a stack of napkins. "I'm guessing you don't drink wine," she said.

"No, I don't. But thank you." In our district, drinking alcohol wasn't forbidden as long as it was done in moderation, but neither was it encouraged, and I didn't know a single person in our church who drank. Either way, I had no interest. I looked to Isaac for his own answer. Maybe he did—or used to.

"How about some sparkling water?" she suggested.

"Please," Isaac said as I nodded my head.

"I'll get it." Jan walked the few steps to a small kitchen.

"Is this your family?" I motioned toward the photo wall.

"It is," she said. "Six children, twenty-five grandchildren, and three great-grandchildren. There was nothing more that I wanted to be than a mother and then a grandmother, and the good Lord saw fit to bless me in abundance."

She pointed to a photo of herself holding a newborn. "That's me with the latest, not long after his birth in February." She picked up a smart phone from the coffee table. "Here's a current one. My granddaughter just texted it to me this morning."

The picture was of a little boy on his back on a blanket on the floor, grinning and drooling.

"He's precious," I said.

"Yes." Natasha held the phone to her bosom. "I love getting texts like this. It makes my day."

Her enthusiasm for her photos surprised me. In our church we'd always been taught that photography encouraged vanity. But seeing the joy Natasha obviously took from these pictures, I realized that maybe there was another side to it. For her, as for Kristen at work, pictures seemed to be about connection more than anything else.

Jan brought us the water and motioned to the platter of snacks. "Help yourself," she said.

Isaac picked up a plate, handed it to me, and then took one for himself. "Do any other family members live in Lancaster besides Jan?"

"Yes, two of my sons and several grandchildren, but goodness, the rest are scattered all over. San Diego. Chicago. A little town in Wyoming. They've gone far and wide. I don't complain, though. Each one of us must find our way in this life. As long as they keep in touch and occasionally come to visit, I'm happy." She smiled sweetly. "Thankfully, Jan is a huge help to me, always has been, but especially since she retired earlier this year."

Jan had just pulled over a chair from the small table, and she sat down to join us.

"Oh? What did you do?" Isaac asked her.

"I was a hospital administrator," she answered.

I wasn't exactly sure what that meant, but Isaac seemed to. I placed a cracker and piece of cheese on my plate as Isaac asked her how she was enjoying retirement.

"Love it," she said. "I'm still busy as ever, just in a different way, and with a lot more flexibility. I've joined a twice-weekly Zumba class, and I volunteer at several different organizations. I also come by and help Mother a couple of days a week with whatever she needs."

Natasha gave her daughter a warm smile. They seemed to get along well, and even though I'd just met the older woman and still didn't know how we were connected, I was happy she had such a good family looking after her.

Once there was a lull in the conversation, Natasha put her hand on my arm and spoke earnestly. "Jan relayed why you asked to visit with me, dear, but I want to hear in your own words, if you don't mind."

With a nod, I launched in, telling Natasha about seeing her quilts in the catalog and how they reminded both Isaac and me of my grandmother's painting. I added that my grandmother had a twin sister named Georgie, who later married a man named Johnson. So there was that connection too. Then I held up the book in my lap. "We discovered this among my grandmother's things, with a note from a 'Natasha.' So when I found out that was your name, I hoped perhaps it had come from you."

She took the book but then said, "Oh my. I need my glasses."

I stood, eager to keep things rolling. "I'll get them. Where are they?"

Eyes twinkling, seeming amused by my enthusiasm, she replied, "In the hall, on the table."

"Okay. Be right back."

I moved quickly in the direction she indicated. The hallway was dark, but I could make out a table and found the glasses. I was so focused on my task that I didn't look up until they were in my hand. That's when I saw the two paintings on the wall. One was of Amish garments on a clothesline, but it wasn't exactly realistic looking. The shapes were blocky, the colors super bright, and the sunlight behind the objects spread through the entire painting. The other featured a boy sitting on a fence, seen from the back, his head tipped upward to the sky, where a hawk soared overhead. That style, without a doubt, was *Mammi* Nettie's. Even the other one, although more abstract, definitely felt like it could be hers too.

I returned to the living room, my mouth still agape as I handed over the glasses. Natasha took one look at me and said, "Yes, dear, your grandmother Nettie painted those."

I swallowed hard. "May I show them to Isaac?"

"Of course. But turn on the light so you two can see better."

Isaac joined me back in the hall, and together we studied the images. They were magnificent. So alive, so balanced, so full of feeling.

"She really had a way with composition," he murmured, and then he went on to point out how she'd used light and color to lead the eye in such a way that the viewer got the feeling of actually being *in* the painting. Once he said it, I knew exactly what he meant—and he was right.

"Why are the two so different?" I gestured toward the more abstract piece.

He shrugged. "Artists grow and change. Sometimes they'll have phases where they use a particular technique or subject matter or even color. Have you ever heard of Picasso's Blue Period? For several years he worked almost exclusively in blues and blue greens. My guess is that your grandmother went through an abstract period, which would explain this lovely piece here."

"Amazing."

Reluctantly, we returned to the living room, and as I sat down, I told Natasha that I'd only ever seen one other of my grandmother's paintings, perhaps the last one she ever did.

Her eyes grew watery, and she removed her glasses and set them aside. I realized she'd been looking at the inscription while she waited for us, but now she closed the book and placed her hands atop it. "Do you have time for a story?"

We both nodded.

"Good," she said. "Because I have one to tell you. About two little Plain girls, Nettie and Georgie."

Natasha began with what we'd already learned at the vital records office, when and where the twins were born. "They were the thirteenth and fourteenth children in their family. They lived on a farm in the township of Caernarvon. Their father was older, but he worked hard. Times were difficult—first there was the Farm Depression in the early twenties, and the price paid for crops barely covered the seed. The family lived off the produce they raised in their garden and their large flock of chickens. Then the Depression hit. The girls were nine when the market crashed." She went on to say that some Plain people got along well enough through the Depression, but not Nettie and Georgie's family. They really struggled. Apparently their father had taken out a second mortgage on their land to help one of his older sons buy property back in 1919. When a big balloon payment came due in 1929, they barely covered it. When another payment came due in 1934, they couldn't.

"No one helped them?" Isaac blurted. I glanced his way, realizing I must not have told him about this part of the story, which I'd already learned from Ina Mae.

Natasha shook her head. "There were some hard feelings about the problem and discussion about who should be responsible. Perhaps the son that the father had mortgaged his property for? Or the other ones he'd made loans to over the years? Honestly, I'm not sure what all happened. I just know that the bank took possession of the property and they were forced to move into small house, closer to Lancaster. The girls were fourteen at that point."

She continued, explaining that during that time a distant relation of the Benders, a Mennonite couple by the last name of Vogt, helped when they could. "The wife, Lois, was a second or third cousin of their mother's. And her husband, Heinrich, who was a Russian Mennonite, was a kind man. They were both good people who'd never had children of their own, so I think their hearts went out to the twins. They were timid but determined. And I should add that they weren't Old Order by any means. They lived in Lancaster and attended a church there that was open to new ideas."

I actually wasn't surprised that a Russian Mennonite family showed up in the narrative, given what Ina Mae had suggested about the name

Natasha possibly being of Russian Mennonite origin. Maybe Natasha had some connection with the Vogts and she'd met the twins through them and learned the details of their stories.

"The Mennonite cousins didn't have enough money to help with the mortgage," she continued, "but they bought food and clothes for the girls. Nettie and Georgie were slightly different in their personalities. Nettie was quiet and shy and withdrawn. Her painting was really the only way she expressed herself.

"Georgie wasn't exactly gregarious, but she was more outgoing than her sister and more interested in others. Nettie's artistic gift wasn't appreciated by her parents, which is, of course, no surprise to you two. When they lived on the farm, she did everything she could to paint. She'd squirrel away any paper she got her hands on, and she'd make her own paints too."

Natasha glanced back down at the book and then up at me. "She was driven, even though back then any kind of artwork was forbidden. Well, quilting was fine, as long as it wasn't fancy—time was in short supply, so a patchwork quilt was all that was needed—and woodwork, as far as making furniture and such, was allowed, but no elaborate carving. Bottom line, Nettie was definitely being disobedient, both to her church and her family, every time she went back to her painting. Georgie didn't have the same gifts or drive, so she didn't have the same struggles.

"Back when they'd been living on the farm," Natasha continued, "Nettie had been able to hide what she was doing fairly well and stash away all of her drawings and paintings. But once the family was in that little house near Lancaster, it was a lot harder to get away with. It was there that her parents realized the full extent of what she'd been up to, and they grew quite alarmed. Their father was not a nice man, and he did what he could to convince Nettie that painting was a sin. He wasn't one to use physical discipline, but he did spend hours lecturing and yelling and bullying her, which was damaging in its own way. Yet still she persisted. Eventually their new bishop found out, and he declared that she was never to do any sort of art again—which set her father into another round of 'convincing.' It was all so awful.

"That's when Nettie's mother confided in her Mennonite cousins about the situation. In their church, expressing oneself through art wasn't just allowed but encouraged, as long as it was done for the glory of God and not out of personal vanity. They wanted to help."

She continued, her voice steady as she spoke, saying the Vogts took the girls for a couple of days at first. Then for a week in the summer. The parents agreed to it because they were still so poor and they knew at least their two daughters would be well fed and cared for. The twins were shy around the couple and had trouble adapting to their environment, though Georgie eventually settled in and grew to like it there. Nettie, however, didn't fare so well, despite the fact that the Vogts encouraged her to paint and even provided her with a few art supplies.

As miserable as Nettie's home life was, it was as if she couldn't break free of it. The whole time she was at the Vogts' she wanted to go back to her own house. She had trouble eating, even though they always had plenty of food. She would spend her days painting to her heart's content, but then she would cry herself to sleep each night, so conflicted about what she was doing and whether it really was right or wrong in the eyes of God.

A few months later the twins' family was evicted from their house. The only option left at that point was for them to move into what was essentially a shack on the property of the oldest son—and they were lucky to get that. He was the only one who had any extra room at all. The other children were struggling themselves or already had relatives living with them or were living on their in-laws' farms.

Natasha paused for a sip of water. Isaac placed more crackers and cheese on his plate, and I nibbled at a pear slice, both of us waiting in silence for her to go on, not wanting to interrupt the flow.

"It was after they'd moved into that shack," Natasha continued, "that the girls' mother first fell ill. They cared for her as best they could and took on her duties, but Nettie continued to paint in secret whenever she had a chance. Once she was inevitably found out, she had to contend not just with her father and bishop this time, but also with her oldest brother, who was appalled that she would bring such shame on his household. Furious, he threatened to throw all four of them out if he ever caught her painting again.

"That's when the Vogts came up with a new plan, to take Nettie into their home and raise her themselves. She would be able to paint, get enough to eat, go to school, and be clothed. They would take her to their Mennonite church, though she would be able to see her family whenever she wanted. Sadly, they could only afford to take in one child, not both, so that meant that for the first time in their lives, the twins were to be separated.

"Initially, their parents refused to consider the Vogts' proposal—and Georgie was relieved. She couldn't imagine life without her sister. But the mother got sicker and the father had a hard time finding any work at all. Nettie didn't dare paint lest she get them kicked out, and she grew more and more miserable without her art, more and more despondent. Eventually Georgie got so concerned for Nettie's health and well-being that she decided, separation or not, she only wanted what was best for her sister. She began to plead with her parents on Nettie's behalf, and eventually they gave in and contacted the Vogts.

"It was January, and a cold front had settled in. All of the family was tired, cold, and hungry. The night before Nettie was to leave, as she and Georgie huddled under the quilts on their bed, she cried and cried and said she couldn't do it. Georgie begged Nettie to go, saying she would be able to paint and even study art, and she would always have enough to eat. If she remained here, her amazing, God-given talent would be like a light smothered under a bushel. Nettie said she was fine with that. She could continue to stay away from painting—as long as she wasn't taken from her family.

"The next morning when the Vogts came to pick up Nettie, she stayed in bed, refusing even to speak with them. Georgie went out to tell them that her sister had changed her mind. But Georgie didn't come back. Nettie got up and went outside, only to find that the Vogts and her sister were gone. Nettie ran in the house and told her mother that her sister was nowhere to be found.

" 'I know,' she replied. 'You didn't want to go to the Vogts' so she took your place. Wasn't that kind of her?'

"Georgie flourished. The Vogts—"

I interrupted, unable to hold in my question. "Wait. Didn't the Vogts care that it was Georgie and not Nettie?"

"Oh goodness, did I fail to mention the girls were identical twins? Their parents could tell them apart, but few others could," Natasha said. "The Vogts couldn't. And Georgie didn't tell them."

"So they thought Nettie was the one who went home with them?"

"Yes. Though Georgie had always seemed a bit more comfortable there, both girls had been so quiet that the Vogts hadn't learned their distinct personalities—and Georgie knew her sister well enough to pull off an accurate imitation."

"But how could Georgie do that to Nettie?" I asked. "Didn't she feel horrible?"

Natasha nodded, her expression solemn. "Yes. She did. On the one hand, she felt safe and cared for at the Vogts, but she longed for Nettie and feared her sister would never forgive her for what she'd done. Gradually, she justified the decision she'd made and hoped in the long run she'd be able to help Nettie, just as the Vogts were helping her."

I still couldn't wrap my head around the twins being separated—and the Vogts being tricked. "But didn't the couple grow suspicious that the wrong twin had moved in with them?"

"I'll get to that." Natasha folded her hands in her lap and then continued with her tale. "Georgie kept up the guise for as long as she could, which was quite a while. She avoided doing any artwork. And even though the Vogts had promised frequent visitations, Nettie and her parents soon moved from the shack on the oldest son's farm to a sister's home more than an hour away, which made potential visits less likely."

Natasha paused for a moment to sip some more water and catch her breath, and I realized she was looking a bit weary. Suddenly I felt guilty for imposing on her like this. But then she continued, and I didn't stop her. Surely Jan would intervene if she sensed her mother was getting too taxed.

"Georgie began to bloom," Natasha went on. "She consistently had enough to eat for the first time in her life. She had new clothes. Modest, to be sure, but with a hint of style. She worked hard to help around the house and received affirmation for that. And best of all, she continued on with her education, which she loved. She finished out the eighth grade in a public school, where she sailed through classes in literature and arithmetic and worked hard to soak up what she'd missed in science, a subject that hadn't really been covered at her Amish school. Each day she grew more accustomed to her new life and connected more with the Vogts. They did become suspicious that she was Georgie instead of Nettie after she avoided doing any artwork over and over, but they were becoming attached to her, regardless.

"Now and then the Vogts would ask Georgie if she wanted to visit her parents, but each time she declined for some sort of reason. She had a cold and didn't want to expose her mother. She had an assignment due the next day. That sort of thing. She never admitted that she dreaded seeing them again. She hadn't received any letters from her parents or her sister, and she feared if she saw Nettie, she would be overcome with grief and want to give up her new life.

"Georgie started high school, found a job on Saturdays at a drugstore, and attended church with the Vogts every Sunday. She gained confidence and made friends. She saved her money except for the few dresses she bought for herself and the paints and paper she got for Nettie and tucked away in her closet. Someday she would see her again and try to make up for what she'd done.

"Eventually she stopped wearing the Mennonite *kapp* and began styling her hair. The Vogts didn't exactly approve, but there were other girls in their congregation who were doing that too so they didn't say anything. Georgie knew the Vogts had surmised long ago that she wasn't Nettie, but they kept calling her that anyway. They were timid people in many ways and may have felt awkward about having taken the wrong daughter. When Georgie suspected they knew, she sat them down and admitted that she wasn't Nettie."

Jan cleared her throat, interrupting the flow. "Which sounds like a good place to take a break," she said. Turning to her mother, she added. "How about you rest a bit while I show these kids around the facility? They might enjoy seeing the pool or the theater."

Natasha was quiet for a moment. "Actually, I am rather fatigued." Looking from me to Isaac, she added, "Could the two of you come back tomorrow instead?"

Of course we were more than willing to do whatever was needed to make Natasha more comfortable. It was good timing to end this meeting anyway, because Tabitha and Ginny were probably waiting for us down on the street by now.

But oh, how I hated to go! We arranged to return the next evening at six, which meant I'd need to get off work a half hour early. I thought Kristen would be all right with that because Tuesdays were usually slow days at the shop anyway.

Natasha squeezed my hand and then Isaac's as we left. "It's so good to spend time with a young couple like you," she said earnestly. Ignoring the part about us being a couple, I was about to reply that it was good to spend time with an old woman like her too, which I meant sincerely, but I wasn't sure if she'd take it as a compliment or not, so I didn't say anything.

In the elevator Isaac and I barely spoke, but there was no need. Somehow I felt closer to him than ever, and I knew our minds were in exactly the same place, lost in a fascinating story and wondering where it might take us next.

Eighteen

When we reached the street, Tabitha climbed out and greeted us, giving me a long, sisterly hug. "You sit in the front, Isaac. I'll get in the back with Linda."

He held the door for me while Tabitha stepped around to the other side. My mind was still deeply immersed in thoughts of our visit with Natasha, and I would've preferred to keep quiet for a while longer, but silence and Tabitha didn't exactly go hand in hand—especially not in the excitement of her homecoming.

She started talking immediately, before Ginny had even pulled away from the curb, saying how wonderful it had been to be there but that she was really glad to get back. She went on to tell us all about Izzy and Zed and the baby. Just when I thought she was winding down, she launched into a big explanation of the research she'd been able to do on twins using Zed's computer. Part of the problem, she said, was that all of us tended to treat the twins as a single unit, but that was a mistake.

"What I learned," she said, "is that I need to start seeing Hattie and Hazel as individuals instead of as a one 'person,'" she said, making the quote marks gesture with her hands. "I need to acknowledge their unique gifts. For example, I think Hattie is more outgoing and might interact better with other scholars if she's in a group without Hazel. Of course, I'd need to hang out with Hazel for her to feel comfortable without Hattie. And I'll need to reinforce each of them when they step out of their comfort zone. And I need to encourage Sadie to spend time alone with each of the girls too, so I'll go over there consistently this summer. I know she needs the help anyway."

She leaned back against the seat, appearing quite pleased. My mind went to all Natasha had told us about Nettie, who'd been inseparable from her twin for fourteen years and then that twin simply went away—by her own choice, no less. I couldn't imagine what that might do to a person. No wonder Nettie had been so depressed.

I realized Tabitha was waiting expectantly for a reply, so I said, "Good work."

"*Danke.*" She reached over and patted my leg. "And thank you for talking with me about it. That was the push I needed to educate myself." She glanced over her shoulder, toward the trunk. "I have more information in my suitcase. Zed let me print out a whole bunch of stuff."

I gave her an encouraging smile, pleased she'd taken a suggestion of mine seriously. It was perhaps the first time she ever had.

Ginny dropped off Tabitha and me first. Isaac hopped out, pulled my sister's bag from the trunk, and then headed for the house with it. I stayed at the car, paying the driver and then asking about tomorrow, if she could take me to work in the morning and then pick me up after to take me to Natasha's by six. She was available, though as we arranged all of the details, Tabitha stood nearby and listened to every word.

"I left your bag on the porch," Isaac told her once he rejoined us. Then he looked to me, a sudden reluctance filling his eyes. "Guess I'll see you tomorrow."

I swallowed hard, an unexpected pang of agony catching in my chest. Obviously he wasn't any more ready to part than I was. We'd gone through such an emotional journey together at Natasha's, one that we were still mulling over and hadn't even discussed yet. Somehow ending things here and now felt so...premature, but what choice did we have? "*Ya.* See you."

He got back in the car and they drove away.

Of course Tabitha hadn't missed a thing. As she started peppering me with questions about Isaac and why he'd gone with me to visit a quilter of all things and why he and I needed to go back again tomorrow, it struck me that maybe one reason I was the last to learn things around here was because I didn't hover and listen and then pester for details. Perhaps cluelessness had an upside after all.

Fortunately, I was rescued by *Mamm* and *Daed*, who came out to welcome Tabitha home. They wanted to hear all about her trip and about the baby, so I was able to fade into the background and keep my own business to myself—for now at least.

I was up in our room a short while later, fiddling with my *kapp*, trying to tuck in an errant lock of hair, when Tabitha appeared in the doorway with her suitcase and immediately started in again on the questions. Rather than evade them, I decided to try a different tactic, one that was almost guaranteed to work.

"Before I go into things with Isaac," I said, putting down my comb and helping her lift the suitcase onto the bed and open it up, "I want to know about you. Were there some nice guys out there? Did you go to singings or on long drives with anyone?"

Sure enough, that did the trick. Tabitha started telling me all about her various adventures in Indiana and the several young men who'd tried—and failed—to get her to go out with them.

"You mean you never dated once the whole time?" I asked, genuinely surprised. "Why? What happened?"

She shot me a glare. "I am capable of living without a man, you know."

"*Ya*, but you told me you were hoping to find someone in Goshen."

"Oh. Right. I guess I did say that." She paused in her unpacking and lowered herself onto the bed, her expression growing somber. "It was the weirdest thing, Linda. One morning, maybe three or four days after the baby was born, I was just sitting in the living room, rocking her, when I found myself crying—like, seriously crying. Sweet little Maggie was looking up at me with the most precious expression on her face, and I think all of a sudden it just hit me—this is what *I* want. This is what I've been wishing and hoping and praying for, for so long. My own baby. My own home. My own husband."

Seeming almost embarrassed by her admission, she broke our gaze and returned to her unpacking as she continued. "But it wasn't just *any* husband I wanted. It was *Ezra*. I don't know how he feels about me in return—and that's part of the problem. We never seem to get serious. We don't ever talk about real things. Important things. Like the two of us sharing a future." Her cheeks flushing a faint pink, she added, "Well, I say 'we,' but mostly me. I think he tried to talk before I left, but I wouldn't really go there. I just laughed it off so he let it drop."

"And that's what happened before you left town?" I asked, thinking of my conversation with Jedediah and how he'd accidentally spilled the beans on the whole Ezra-Tabitha relationship. "You two didn't sit down and talk, and so you left thinking he didn't care and he saw you leaving and thought you didn't care, when the real truth was that you both cared? A lot?"

She nodded, tears filling her eyes. "I hope so. At least that's how it went on my end. I cared so much—and I still do. I love him, Linda. I really think he's the man God wants for me."

Blinking the tears away, Tabitha paused in her unpacking, turned, and met my eyes, looking as vulnerable as I'd ever seen her. "So what do you think? Do Ezra and I have a chance? Or did I totally blow it?"

I considered telling her what I knew. I thought about sharing my conversation with Jedediah and putting every one of her fears to rest. But I didn't think it was my place to meddle; plus, she'd find all that out soon enough anyway. Instead, I simply stepped closer and put an arm around her, giving her shoulders a squeeze. "There might still be a slight chance," I said somberly. Then, stifling a smile, I added, "But I'll definitely keep you in my prayers just in case."

Ezra came over after supper, and as soon as he walked in the door, it was obvious that his feelings for Tabitha had only deepened in her absence. Like two magnets, they were drawn to each other, and though they didn't embrace, it was easy to see they wanted to. I was relieved. I hadn't seen Ezra since that night at the singing, so I'd been afraid things might be a little awkward between us once we saw each other again. But he was too captivated by my sister to think of anything or anyone else, least of all me.

"Walk us out?" Tabitha asked as they were leaving. She slid an arm through mine and tugged me forward. Before I could squeak out a protest, she whispered in my ear, "Ezra said he needs to talk to you for a minute. Alone."

Once outside with the door closed behind us, she let my arm go, and then she turned to Ezra, gave him a sweet smile, and said she'd wait in the buggy.

Then, to my astonishment, the nosiest sister on the planet simply walked away, leaving the two of us there on the porch to converse in private.

"Listen, Linda." Ezra spoke in a low voice, looking almost embarrassed. "I just wanted to apologize about…that night at the singing. I shouldn't have put the moves on you that way. I don't know what I was thinking."

I appreciated his apology, but I was still confused about his behavior. "What *were* you thinking?"

"Honestly?" He flashed me an embarrassed grin, took off his hat, and ran a hand through his hair. "I think I was hoping you and I might click the way your sister and I had. She was gone and you were here, and I really do think you're great and all, but…" His voice trailed off.

"But when it came down to it, I felt more like a sister than a girlfriend?"

"Exactly," he said, the relief evident in his voice. "I think it was when you fussed at me for flirting with you so soon after I'd been courting your sister. All of a sudden I knew who I wanted—and no offense, but that person was a certain someone out in Indiana. It had nothing to do with you. It was about me and her."

I smiled. "I get it. But thanks for the apology."

"So we're *gut*?"

"We're *gut*."

He blew out a breath. "*Gut*. Now I just have to tell Tabitha what happened."

I chuckled, assuring him she would understand—and truly hoping she wouldn't assume that I had encouraged him in some way. I started to go inside but then turned back impulsively. "Hey, Ezra? For what it's worth, I like you as a brother too." With a wink, I added, "But even better as a brother-in-law."

He broke into a broad grin, which told me everything I needed to know about his intentions for my sister.

"For now," I said, "I think you better get out there." I gestured toward the buggy where Tabitha was still waiting. "And hurry too. If she strains any harder to hear us, she's going to end up bursting an eardrum."

The next day at work, when I told Kristen I'd met Natasha Johnson, she was intrigued. "Did you see more of her quilts?"

I explained that we hadn't. Oddly there wasn't even one on display in her living room. Not on the back of the couch or chair. Not hanging from her wall.

"What did she say about her quilting? Where did she learn to appliqué like that? What inspires her designs?"

I realized I knew none of the answers to these questions, not yet anyway.

"We didn't really talk about quilting," I replied. "But I'd like to go back tonight—if you can let me off a half hour early. Hopefully we can discuss it then."

"Sure." Kristen thought for a moment and then her eyes lit up. "I don't know why I didn't think of this sooner. I bet she has a website."

"*Ya?*"

No customers were in the shop, so Kristen stepped to the computer and I came and stood beside her to watch as she Googled Natasha's name. In response, lots of Natasha Johnsons came up—on Facebook, LinkedIn, and Twitter. There were athletes named Natasha Johnson and businesswomen and a mayor and a doctor and all sorts of people.

"That was silly of me," Kristen said. She narrowed the search by adding "quilter" and "Lancaster County, PA." Lots of links appeared about quilt shows and shops and that sort of thing in Lancaster, but there was no website for Natasha as there had been for Isaac. As Kristen scrolled down, she came across a couple of articles about quilt shows where Natasha was mentioned. Her work was highly praised, but words like *reclusive* and *reserved* were used to describe her personally. Funny. She hadn't seemed that way to me at all, and I said as much to Kristen now.

"Well," she replied, "maybe she's gotten more open or something as she's aged."

Or maybe, I thought, she was just one of those people who was different in public than in private. Either way, I felt blessed that with Isaac and me she'd been the very opposite of reserved—warm and welcoming and completely forthcoming.

Isaac and I met outside of Natasha's building promptly at six and took the elevator up together. Like yesterday, he had changed out of his painting clothes, but this time there were a few lingering smudges on his forearm.

Natasha opened the door before we even knocked. Jan was there too, putting together sandwiches in the kitchen. We told her it wasn't necessary, that they didn't have to feed us, but she just smiled and said her mother had insisted.

As we sat down, in the small dining area this time, Natasha gestured toward Isaac's arm. "Is that paint?"

Glancing down he replied, "*Ya*, sorry," and began rubbing it off.

Her eyes twinkled. "Did all that talk about art yesterday inspire you to do some painting yourself?"

He laughed and said that yesterday had indeed been inspiring but that actually this was from a job, that he painted houses for a living.

"Ah." She sounded disappointed. "I hoped you were an artist."

"Oh, he is," I said, "and a very gifted one too."

"Really?" Natasha grinned. "I knew I liked you, Isaac. My favorite people in this world are artists."

"And offspring," Jan chimed in from the kitchen.

"Yes," Natasha amended with a chuckle. "My very favorite people in this world are my children and their families. *Then* artists."

We all shared a laugh.

"So are you two ready to keep going with our story?" she asked, her face growing more serious.

"I've thought of little else," I admitted breathlessly with a glance to Isaac, who nodded in agreement.

"All right then." She turned toward the kitchen just as Jan emerged with a tray of sandwiches. "I'll lead us in a prayer and then you all can eat as I talk."

Jan served the food and beverages—chicken salad sandwiches, apple slices, and sparkling water—and then sat and joined us. We all bowed our heads, and Natasha asked the Lord to bless our food and our time together.

As we dug in, she continued with her tale.

"I believe we ended right where Georgie was revealing her true identity to the Vogts?" she asked, and we both nodded.

"Well, that conversation actually went better than Georgie had expected it to. Her confession was so heartfelt that they couldn't be too angry with her, and, as I explained yesterday, they'd long suspected it anyway. Once she told them, they forgave her and said that perhaps it had been the Lord's will for her to be the one to live with them after all. She was forgiven, and life went on for Georgie even better than before.

"When the girls were seventeen, their mother died, and the Vogts took Georgie to her funeral, which was the first time she'd seen Nettie in three years. She brought along all of the art supplies she'd collected, hoping they might serve as a peace offering."

I got tears in my eyes just imagining it—the heartache, the joy, the bond between twins that had been stretched far enough to potentially break.

"Not surprisingly, Nettie had changed. She seemed even more withdrawn, not to mention that she looked gaunt and exhausted. Georgie struggled with the guilt of having left her twin behind, and she tried to speak with her sister about it, but Nettie refused to discuss the matter at all. At least she accepted the supplies."

I smiled, remembering Ina Mae's tale about catching Nettie with those supplies out behind the old shed. I could still clearly see the adorable little painting of the goat that she'd shown me when I was there.

"As for Georgie's other siblings," Natasha continued, "mostly they just criticized her, for having abandoned her family, for wearing worldly clothing, for leaving the Amish fold to become Mennonite instead. She didn't bother to clarify, but she hadn't actually joined the church yet. Truth be told, she doubted she ever would. She enjoyed her growing freedom too much.

"Over the next few months, Nettie cared for her ailing father, then when he died she was forced to go and live with one of her brothers and his family in northern Lancaster County, in Hopeland."

She was talking about the farm where Ina Mae lived. It was so interesting how Ina Mae's and Natasha's stories were woven together. Having heard both perspectives, I could just picture Nettie, orphaned at eighteen, moving in with yet another sibling, this time minus her twin *and* her parents. How lonely she must have felt! Even though Ina Mae had been enthralled with her *Aenti* Nettie, she'd been too young to have offered all that much in the way of companionship.

"As for Georgie," Natasha continued, "she graduated high school, and though there wasn't enough money for college, she was able to attend a business school in Philadelphia. The Vogts were persistent in their desire for her to join their church, but she kept putting it off. She began dating a young man, a Presbyterian, who was a student at the nearby University of Pennsylvania, and more and more she found herself attending services at his church.

"Meanwhile, Nettie was struggling with her new living situation. She'd been devastated to find that her brother and his wife were even more negative about her doing artwork than her parents had been. In defiance, she kept on painting in secret. Well, for the most part anyway. There were occasional periods where she began to feel convicted and would put it all away, determined to give it up for good. But eventually she would find her way back, brush in hand, lost in her vision for the canvas in front of her.

"Around that time, at a cousin's wedding, she met a really nice man named Joshua Mueller. He lived south of Lancaster, but soon he was coming up to the farm and visiting Nettie as often as possible. Eventually, she told him about her art, and much to her surprise, he had no problem with it. He asked her to marry him, saying if she did she could paint to her heart's content. Nettie accepted his proposal.

"After the wedding he brought her to live on his family farm, where he remained true to his word. They kept Nettie's painting a secret, and for the first time in her life, she was, if not happy, at least content. The farm was on a beautiful knoll, surrounded by lush hills, and she had plenty of privacy to paint whenever she wanted."

I shot Isaac a smile, hoping he understood that Natasha was talking about *my* house, my farm, where I'd grown up and still lived today. A shiver tingled down my spine at the thought of my very own grandparents just starting out there, settling into the family homestead as newlyweds, and carving out a life together.

"Meanwhile," Natasha continued, "her sister Georgie became engaged to her young man, though they decided not to marry until he was established in his career in Philadelphia. She was with the Vogts again, but they'd given up on the hope that she would ever join the Mennonite Church. Ashamed for not having raised her the way they'd promised her parents they would, they avoided seeing her older siblings entirely. They grew so out of touch, in fact, that they never even heard about Nettie getting married."

Natasha went on to explain that Georgie had saved money for a nice wedding and was just starting to make plans for an elaborate ceremony when the Japanese bombed Pearl Harbor. Her fiancé joined the army the next day. When it was time for him to deploy, they shared a tearful goodbye, and once he was gone, all she could do was pray that he would return.

His absence sent her into a lonely spiral, and she began to miss Nettie more than she had in years. Thinking she'd like to see her sister again, she started collecting more art supplies. Eventually, as the war dragged on, she took the money she'd saved for the wedding and bought a car instead. Then she drove to her brother's farm in Hopeland to see her twin sister— only to learn that Nettie was now married and living in West Lampeter Township.

She headed there instead, and when she arrived, Nettie was out in her little workshop in the barn, painting. Joshua was beside the buggy shed, brushing down a horse. He saw the car coming and stepped toward it, but then he froze in astonishment once it parked and his own wife climbed out, dressed as an *Englisch* woman complete with fancy clothes, makeup, and high heels.

"You see," Natasha explained, "Nettie had never told her husband she had a twin sister. You can imagine his shock when Georgie appeared there out of the blue, looking just like a fancier version of Nettie. Of course, as he got closer he could tell it wasn't his wife, but he was still utterly speechless. Georgie realized almost immediately what was going on, and so she was the one who had to tell him that his wife had a twin sister."

Natasha took a sip of water and then continued, saying they talked there beside Georgie's car for a few minutes, with Joshua still reeling from the shock. Though he didn't say as much to her, she could tell he felt deeply hurt, betrayed even, by his wife. How could Nettie have kept such a big secret from him all this time?

Eventually Nettie emerged from the barn and was shocked to find her sister there. Then she saw the look on Joshua's face and her astonishment turned to guilt for not having told him about Georgie before and for him having to find out this way instead. She also couldn't help but feel jealous. Why was Joshua looking at Georgie the way he was? There she stood with her red lipstick and nail polish and flared skirt and heels. Did he find her beautiful? Did he wish he'd met her first instead of Nettie?

Of course Joshua didn't. He was just shocked to see an *Englisch* woman who, minus all of the fancy details, looked *exactly* like his wife. He was also devastated because of Nettie's secrecy. He couldn't even bring himself to look at her once she joined them, so overcome was he with emotion.

He excused himself and left the two women there alone to converse. Their encounter was awkward and strange and brief, and though Nettie accepted the art supplies, she wasn't exactly glad that her sister had come.

Eventually, Joshua and Nettie managed to find their way through her one big deception and come back together. They both wanted a large family, but slowly it became clear that wasn't going to happen. As Nettie tried to accept the fact that she might never have children, she fell into a depression and stopped painting entirely for a while.

A year later Georgie returned with more art supplies. She knew she'd be in the area selling war bonds and had decided stop by. She'd been surprised to see Joshua there and couldn't imagine how he hadn't been drafted, or at least forced to join as a medic or sent off to fill some other conscientious-objector role. It turned out that he'd received a farm deferment instead.

In late June of 1944, Georgie learned that her fiancé had been killed on D-day. Inconsolable, she ended up reaching out to Nettie, appearing there one afternoon when Joshua happened to be gone.

Nettie seemed to sense that this was a different sort of visit, and for the first time she invited her sister inside. There, in her kitchen over coffee, with her husband safely over at the farrier's, she listened to Georgie's lament. It was the closest they'd been as sisters since Georgie left with the Vogts all those years before.

The two ended up pouring their hearts out to each other, even sharing how they'd felt through their years apart. Nettie described how devastating it had been for her when Georgie left and about her time in Hopeland. She shared that she feared now, because she'd been married for nearly five years and hadn't gotten pregnant, that she'd never be a mother. Georgie talked about the guilt that had plagued her since the day she'd left, and how she'd spent those years telling herself that someday she would help Nettie the way the Vogts had helped her.

But their new-found closeness didn't last long. As soon as Joshua got home and came inside, Nettie grew suspicious and defensive. It wasn't long before she turned on Georgie, saying that her fiancé's death had been God's judgment for deceiving her own flesh and blood, and for leaving the Amish and not joining the Mennonites.

"Georgie was deeply hurt," Natasha said, "and she left. Joshua followed her out and tried to apologize on Nettie's behalf, explaining that she was depressed, that she didn't know what she was saying, that she didn't really mean it. But the fact that the two just stood there talking at the car for a minute or two before Georgie drove away made Nettie even more furious with them both."

Natasha paused to sip some water, and Jan urged her to eat as well.

"All right, dear, but just a few bites for now."

As her mother nibbled on an apple slice, Jan looked to the three of us and said, "I don't get the whole jealousy thing. Why would an Amish man find an English version of a woman more appealing than the Amish version? From what I understand, his ideas of beauty and worth would have been connected to the women of his faith his whole life, to the radiance of peace and simplicity of an Amish countenance. He probably saw Georgie's clothes and makeup as silly and fanciful and wasteful, not attractive."

"Exactly," Natasha replied, dabbing at her mouth with a napkin. "But Nettie refused to believe it."

She took one more sip of water, and in the silence my heart began to pound and my face surely turned a vivid red. I thought of Kristen and how she and I had talked that evening in the parking lot, when I confided my fear that I could never measure up to the fancy beauty of Isaac's late wife. Now that I'd heard this part of Nettie's story, I realized how wrong that thought had been. Jan was right. Amish boys were raised to look to a woman's heart, not her exterior, for true beauty. Just because Isaac left the faith for a time didn't mean he had lost all the lessons of his youth.

Fortunately, Natasha continued her tale. "In early 1945," she said, "Georgie moved out of the Vogts' home and into an apartment of her own. She was working for an insurance company and was given more and more responsibility. After the war, a veteran was hired at the firm, and soon he and Georgie fell in love. She sent Nettie a handwritten note, apologizing for how she had deceived her when she left. 'It was unbelievably selfish of me,' she wrote. 'I'm so sorry for what I did. Please, as we were taught, forgive me.' She then invited Nettie and Joshua to her wedding in August of 1946."

Nettie didn't tell Joshua about the wedding invitation. Instead, she told him she had an errand to run in Lancaster and asked a neighbor to give her a ride. Joshua hoped she was going to buy art supplies so she could start painting again, and he even made sure she had extra money, more than what she needed to pay their neighbor for gas for the trip.

After slipping into the last pew of the downtown church, Nettie watched the world her twin had become a part of with wonder. It was an Episcopal church, and the organist played music that stirred Nettie. Considering that in her own church services no instruments were used at all, she had never heard anything like it.

A priest in a white robe stepped onto a stage, and then Georgie's fiancé and three other men, all in suits and ties, joined him. Three women, adorned in identical peach-colored dresses and carrying small matching flower bouquets, came down the aisle. Then came Georgie, wearing a white gown with a train trailing behind it. She seemed to float along on the arm of Heinrich Vogt, completely at ease, though he appeared uncomfortable in the ornate setting. Nettie only saw her twin's face for a second, through a sheer veil, but she was wearing even more makeup than usual. And Nettie couldn't imagine how much the dress cost, especially considering the horrible shortages of fabric and other supplies that still existed after the war.

There were several responsive prayers that involved the congregation and different people read Scriptures. Nettie only half listened. Soon she was distracted from the service by the stained glass windows on the exterior walls of the church. She'd never seen anything like them. The blocks of jewel-toned colors. The image of Jesus carrying a lamp. The figure of a woman in a lavender gown. She couldn't get over how the geometric shapes of the glass lent them an abstract-yet-somehow-realistic feel, which, along with the light that shone through them, combined to create an almost otherworldly effect. Her fingers tingled with the sudden urge to take brush in hand and try out a more abstract approach to her own art, wondering if she could paint in a way that would merge more geometric shapes into non-geometrical images, much as the individual pieces of glass came together to create these scenes.

That's what was on her mind when something in the sermon touched her deeply. The priest read from Exodus 31: "I have filled him with the Spirit of God, with ability and intelligence, with knowledge and all craftsmanship, to devise artistic designs." She thought it odd that the scripture was part of the service, but then the priest compared the creation of art to the work it takes to build a marriage.

She'd heard a lot in her life about what the Bible had to say about marriage, but never once about what it had to say about art. She'd just always taken her *daed*'s word for it that it was wrong. She grabbed the pew Bible and looked up the verse for herself and then read it again and again.

I have filled him with the Spirit of God...to devise artistic designs.

God didn't hate painting at all; in fact, His spirit was the very *source* of the creative drive.

Sitting there on the hard pew, Nettie began to feel the same harmony she did when she painted. As the service continued, a sense of love that she hadn't felt for years swept over her.

However, it was short lived.

After the priest declared the couple man and wife, her peace was overtaken by a surge of sadness and regret. What would her life have been like if she'd gone with the Vogts that day instead?

Everything would've been different. Because even if she had found the nerve to leave with them, she never would have stayed there permanently as Georgie had. Instead, she would've lasted a few days at most and then would've been begging to go back home again. She and her sister never would have been separated for so long—but now they were separated permanently.

Soon, Nettie guessed, her twin would be blessed with a houseful of children, something she herself yearned for so deeply. It wasn't that Nettie wanted Georgie's life—she just wanted Georgie back with her, back as her sister. Her twin.

As the bride walked up the aisle on the arm of her new husband, she beamed at Nettie. Her expression was of pure joy, with perhaps a bit of gratitude too that her sister had actually attended.

For the first time Nettie blamed herself for Georgie leaving. After all, Nettie was the one who had agreed to go with the Vogts in the first place. And Nettie was the one who'd chickened out when they came for her. If only she had been braver that day, if only she had followed through with the arrangement, then everything would have gone differently, for both of them.

As the guests rose to leave, Nettie slipped out the side aisle to the far door leading to the foyer, bypassing the bridal party. She hurried through, and though she heard Georgie call after her, she kept on going, racing down the steps and into the car of her neighbor, who'd been waiting for her.

Nettie started painting again, trying her best to recapture the sense of harmony that she'd felt for that fleeting moment in the church that day. Thanks to the Bible verse she had discovered during the wedding, she was able to paint without guilt for the first time in her life. Finally, her art was no longer this thing that had always felt so right on one level and so wrong on another. She entered a new phase, one with an abstract element, and creating was pure bliss.

A year later a car pulled into the Muellers' driveway and parked while Nettie and Joshua were weeding the garden. A man wearing a suit jumped out of the driver's seat and hurried around to open the passenger door. Georgie emerged, carrying a baby. The man stepped to the trunk, opened it, and pulled out a large bag.

Nettie and Joshua put down their tools and started toward the couple. Joshua invited them into the house, and after Nettie cleaned herself up, she served them lemonade and berry cobbler. After they ate, Joshua took

Georgie's husband for a tour of the farm while the women stayed in the house with the baby. When Georgie asked Nettie if she wanted to hold the little one, Nettie took him in her arms. Her heart swelled at the closeness of her nephew—but then it broke at the thought she might never have a child of her own. She quickly returned the boy to her sister.

Georgie told Nettie that she missed her and wanted to restore their relationship. Nettie listened but didn't say much in return, although when Georgie asked if she could visit again, Nettie didn't say no.

After they left, Joshua told Nettie that he had sent some of her paintings with Georgie's husband, explaining that they couldn't keep hiding all of them on the farm. She thought that was a good idea and even suggested that if Georgie's husband felt like trying to sell some of them, she wouldn't be averse to the idea.

Two years later Georgie returned again—with another baby and another bag of supplies. Her husband also came bearing a big roll of money, cash earned for the sale of several of Nettie's paintings. Joshua insisted that he keep at least some percentage of it for his troubles, and the two men worked things out in an amicable arrangement that suited them both.

Thus the pattern repeated every couple of years. With every get-together, Nettie opened up more about her art and life to Georgie, who hung onto every word her sister shared, grateful for the growing intimacy between them. Each visit was a reminder of Nettie's own childlessness, which she was honest about with Georgie, but she welcomed the moments with her twin and the glimpses of her nieces and nephews—not to mention the bags of art supplies. Every time Georgie's husband handed over some more cash, and Joshua gave him new paintings in return, minus the cost of the supplies, which were now covered by the profits. Nettie and Joshua had always been able to make do before, but the occasional infusions of cash came as a real blessing. With it, they were able to expand and improve some of the buildings on their small farm, and one time even bought a pair of strong young draft horses to augment the efforts of their one old aging mare.

The arrangement between the two couples went on for a good while. When Nettie was thirty-seven years old, she was astonished to realize that

God had chosen to bless her with a baby at last, after seventeen years of marriage. Once Eli was born, she was so content and all-consumed with her new role that for a time she stopped painting entirely. She didn't pick it up again for several years, in fact. But when she did, she found herself entering an entirely new artistic period, her "children" phase.

"Meanwhile, Georgie's family continued to grow," Natasha said, "but once Nettie had a child of her own, she didn't mind so much. Instead, she was able to relax even more and truly enjoy her sister's visits. Joshua really liked Georgie's husband too. The man was still in the insurance business, but he'd begun to take on more civic-minded roles as well. First he served on the Lancaster School Board. Then as a city councilman. Then he ran for—" Natasha stopped speaking midsentence, her expression oddly anxious. She glanced at Jan before finishing. "For state representative."

Natasha grew quiet after that, but I was so intent on the story that I picked it up from there just to keep things going.

"And he won that election, right?" I prodded. "Paul W. Johnson? We found their marriage certificate and articles about his life—and his death."

Something was happening at that table, though I wasn't sure what it was. Isaac seemed to be noticing too. Natasha's expression was unreadable, and Jan merely looked confused.

"Mother?" she asked, brow furrowed. "Was Father married before?" Growing more alarmed, she added, "Don't tell me you were his second wife."

I stared at her for a moment and then returned my gaze to Natasha. That was when it hit me. She wasn't Paul Johnson's second wife. She was his only wife.

"You're Georgie," I whispered in wonder.

She pushed away her plate, folded her hands atop the table, and gave a single nod. "Actually," she said, "I'm both Georgie—and Natasha."

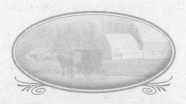

NINETEEN

"I'm so sorry, dear." Natasha reached out to Jan and took her daughter's hand. "I know this wasn't the best way to reveal my past to you."

"Ya think?" Jan snapped. After a beat, she jerked her hand back and put it in her lap. I was startled by the action and by the sarcasm in her tone, but her poor mother looked as if she'd been expecting exactly this reaction.

"At least you finally know the whole story," she offered. "I wasn't sure how I felt about your finding out, but now that it's done, it's actually a big relief."

"I'm glad one of us feels better."

"Please don't be cross. I debated telling you kids about this for years."

"Why didn't you?"

Natasha sighed. "I guess the timing never felt quite right. And I kept putting it off. But then when you called and told me about Linda's search…" She gave me a reassuring look. "I realized the moment had come. It's not like I was hiding it, exactly. It's just been easier not to talk about it over the years. Now that you've heard the whole story, though, I'm happy to answer any questions you might have."

"Fine." There was still an edge to Jan's voice, although it wasn't quite as sharp. "Maybe we should start with some technicalities. If you're Georgie, then who's Natasha?"

Natasha sighed. "I am. It's hard to explain. Once the Vogts knew I wasn't Nettie, it felt weird to be called Georgie, so we decided I should go by something new. They suggested my middle name, but 'Nadine' didn't feel quite right. I was fifteen at the time, that age when more than anything I just wanted to fit in. Like the Vogts, some of my friends were Russian Mennonites, and they had such beautiful names—like Marika and Helena and Tatiana—that I wanted a Russian-sounding name too. So, in the end, I took my middle name and just dressed it up a bit. 'Nadine' became 'Natasha,' and that's what I've gone by ever since." She smiled, embarrassed. "I was a fanciful girl."

"But was it legally changed? At fifteen? I mean, it must have been. I've seen your passport, your license, all sorts of legal documents with your name on them. You've always been listed as Natasha. I would've noticed anything different."

She nodded. "I did have it legally changed—though not until I was in my twenties, after your father and I got married. Since I already had to go through all the trouble of changing my last name to his, I decided to change my first name too. By the time I was legally a Johnson, I was also legally a Natasha. That's what I'd been going by for years, so it just seemed easier to make it official."

Jan grew quiet for a moment, considering her mother's words. Sadly, I understood all too well how she was feeling. From the shock of learning Isaac had had a wife to the surprise that my oldest sister was in fact my half sister, I'd had more than my share of revelations lately myself. There was just something so unsettling about learning a truth that others could have told you but for some reason did not. It was disconcerting, and I didn't blame her for being upset.

"So if you'd died without telling me all this," Jan said, "we would have figured it out once we went through your papers? That would have been terrible, and so wrong. You should have shared all this with me a long time ago."

Natasha nodded. "I can see that now. And I am sorry. I did tell my lawyer the story, and I wrote a detailed letter about the circumstances years ago. It's in the first file cabinet, with all of my important papers."

Jan shook her head. "I can't believe you're the girl in that story, you're Georgie—or at least you were before you turned yourself into someone else."

Natasha hesitated for a moment, as if searching for the right words. "Georgie is still inside of me, dear. She's still a part of who I am. She's who made all of you work so hard as children. She's who insisted we plant a big garden, preserve our food, create a community in our church and neighborhood. She's the one who told you to 'waste not, want not' even when your father made good money and we had plenty of resources. She's the one who wouldn't tolerate you children playing army or belittling someone who was different from you. She's the one who admonished you to love the Lord." Natasha shrugged. "I held on to what I believed was most important. I taught you all of that."

"What about family?" Jan asked. "What about the aunt and uncle we never knew? And the cousin." She gestured toward me. "Cousins."

I was startled, realizing she was right. I was related to these two women by blood. My search for extended family members, which *Daed* had been so hesitant about, had led me to this delightful older woman, who just happened to be my great-aunt, and her feisty but not unlikeable daughter, who would be my first cousin once removed. Beyond that were a whole host of Natasha's descendants, including six children, multiple grandchildren, and three great-grandchildren. Unbelievable.

"That was Nettie's doing, not mine," Natasha said to Jan. "I begged her to allow us to all spend time together, as families. I took each of you children out to meet her when you were babies, and she was receptive to that, to a point. But she was still always a bit guarded, especially when Joshua was around. Somewhere in the late forties or early fifties, however, he took a side job at a local plant, so I started timing my visits for midday in the midweek when I knew he'd be off working. That seemed to help a lot. Nettie would make lunch for the two of us, and then she and I would have long, sisterly chats while my little ones played on the floor around us. That went on for a good while. Any occasions of deep sharing were still rare, of course, but they did happen, and over time she told me her whole story and shared her feelings—and Joshua's perspective and feelings as well. That's why I'm able to explain all of this to you now in such detail. Even so, she never allowed us fully into her life because she never entirely forgave me for leaving her when we were young."

"But isn't forgiveness a huge part of Amish doctrine?" Jan asked.

All three of us nodded.

"Sadly," Natasha said, "she thought her greatest sin was painting, when in fact the painting was fine. Her greatest sin was unforgiveness. It ate her up like a cancer and eventually forced a separation between us that I was never able to repair, no matter what I did."

The room grew quiet for a long moment.

"When did you and Nettie last spend time together?" I asked Natasha, interrupting the silence. "I'm guessing it had to have been before my father was born, because he thinks he saw you briefly once when you stopped by the farm, when he was about ten. He didn't know who you were."

Natasha's eyes grew misty. "Actually, he did know me. He just couldn't remember. I saw him a few times before he started first grade. He was such a cute little thing. But once he entered school, he wasn't around for my occasional lunch visits anymore, and so we went about five years without seeing each other at all. That's time enough for a child to forget."

I blinked, trying to picture my *daed* as a kid, interacting with this woman who would've looked to him like a fancy version of his mother. "So what did he call you?" I asked. "Georgie or Natasha?"

"*Aenti* Georgie. To that side of the family, I was always Georgie."

She went on to describe my father as a little boy, saying how sweet Eli was, to the core, just like his own *daed*.

"That's how he still is," I interrupted. "A very kind, dear man."

Natasha's eyes shone. "Then you are fortunate indeed." She paused, overcome with emotion. As she collected herself, dabbing at her tears and then taking a sip of water, Jan reached out and put a comforting hand on Natasha's back, gently rubbing her shoulders. Like an ice cube left out in the sun, Jan's hurt and indignation seemed to be melting away right in front of us. Here in the face of her mother's pain, she must have understood, at least in part, why the woman had never been able to bring herself to tell this story to her children before.

"Prior to that awful day," Natasha finally continued, "things had finally begun to look up for Nettie, which makes what happened next even more heartbreaking."

I leaned forward, eager to hear the rest of the story.

"When your father was six or seven, Linda, Nettie's bishop passed away, and their new bishop was somewhat more progressive. He was also a good friend of Joshua's, so he knew a little bit about the situation. He was aware that the money from Nettie's paintings helped to support the family. He also understood that she painted out of a strong creative drive and not from some need for recognition or accolades. Pride simply wasn't a part of the equation for her at all and never had been. In light of that, to Nettie's amazement, this bishop came over one day and told her that he had no problem with her art as long as it didn't become a source of pride or cause her to ignore her other duties."

"God bless him." Isaac spoke for the first time in quite a while.

I gave him a reassuring look, hoping our bishop would say the same to him.

"Once Nettie got the go-ahead," Natasha continued, "it's like her creativity went into overdrive. She did some of her best work during the next few years, and I know it was because she was finally painting without shame or regret or fear. She blossomed as an artist, and it showed all over those canvases—or at least the ones I got to see. Sadly, at least half of them ended up being destroyed."

"Destroyed?" I cried.

Natasha nodded somberly. "In a fire. But I'll get to that in a minute."

The fire. No doubt the same fire my *daed* had already told me about, the one where the only thing that burned was an old outbuilding, yet they acted as if they had lost far more than that.

"With Nettie being so prolific," Natasha continued, "her paintings were starting to pile up. She no longer had to keep them hidden, but neither could she just leave them out for all to see—and she definitely couldn't hang them in the house. They knew I'd be coming for a visit in another month, and I'd be taking them off their hands then. In the meantime, her work space was getting so crowded that she and Joshua decided to stash some of her pictures elsewhere, just temporarily. There was an older outbuilding on the property, a former wash house, I think it was, where Joshua kept some farming supplies. It didn't have a ton of extra room, but they figured it was enough to hold at least half of the pictures, so they wrapped the finished canvases and moved them there."

"This doesn't sound good," Jan murmured, listening as intently as the rest of us.

"It wasn't. Oh, how I wish they had called and told me what was going on! I would have come down and gotten the paintings right away. With no ventilation or insulation, that structure was a terrible place to store art. But they didn't know that. They just knew they needed to get some of those canvases out of the way until my next visit.

"Sadly, a few nights after they moved the paintings, a big electrical storm rolled through. That little building wasn't grounded like the barn and the house were, so when a bolt of lightning hit, the structure caught on fire and ended up burning down, destroying the entire contents, including every single one of the paintings."

I glanced at Isaac, thinking that had to be an artist's worst nightmare.

"Fortunately," Natasha continued, "the flames didn't spread any farther, so the rest of the farm was safe. But that fire did a different sort of damage. Right away Nettie took what had happened as a sign. That old wash house had been out there for decades, but it wasn't destroyed until it was full of her paintings. By her reasoning, God Himself had been sending her a message, loud and clear. Despite the bishop's permission, painting *was* a sin and the Lord wanted her to stop."

"What?" I cried.

Natasha nodded. "Just as she'd claimed, years before, that my fiancé's death had been God's judgment on me, she saw the destruction of her paintings as His judgment on her. And that sent her into a tailspin."

Jan interrupted her mother, looking from her to Isaac and me. "Do the Amish believe that? That we get what we deserve? That bad things are God's punishment for our own misdeeds?"

I shook my head and was trying to form a response when Isaac answered instead.

"It's not part of Anabaptist teachings, no," he said, "but I do think as humans most of us struggle *not* to believe it sometimes—even knowing what we do about grace."

"Exactly," Natasha replied. Turning to Jan, she added, "Sometimes people start believing it so strongly that they'll completely ignore what the Scriptures have to say on the topic. They integrate a retribution theology into their thinking instead. That's surely what happened with my sister."

"I see. Okay. Go on."

Natasha continued with her story. "One night, I got a phone call from Joshua, desperate for my help. He told me what was going on and said that he was very worried for his wife. Not only was she completely distraught, but he feared what she might do to her remaining paintings. Finished canvases were still safely sitting in her work space in the barn, but she was getting so agitated that he feared she might run out there and destroy them. I told him to move them somewhere else temporarily, where she wouldn't find them, and that I would be there the next day to get them."

I nodded, remembering the story my father had told me in the kitchen, how a woman showed up in the midst of some crisis with his mother, and he'd watched from his bedroom window upstairs as his father loaded a bunch of wrapped packages into the trunk of that woman's car. His mother had been hysterical, yelling at the woman to leave. I couldn't believe she was the same person I was sitting here listening to now.

"When I pulled into the driveway," Natasha continued, "little Eli was the one I saw first—though he wasn't so little any more. I couldn't believe how much he'd grown since I'd last seen him. I called out to him, but just then his father emerged from the buggy shed and gave him one of the smaller, wrapped paintings to take into the house, so we never had a chance to speak."

"Were you able to save the other canvases?" Isaac asked.

She nodded. "Just barely. The night before, after we talked, Joshua had hidden them in the backseat of the buggy, which I thought was rather clever—and, as it turned out, fortunate. Because early the next morning, just as he'd feared, Nettie went out to the barn intent on destroying the rest of her paintings. When she discovered they were gone, she had flown into a fit of rage. She went crazy trying to find them, tearing through the barn and the house, but to no avail. Joshua wouldn't tell her what he'd done with them, so she went back out to her workspace and tore it up instead, throwing paints and brushes and even damaging her beloved easel. It broke poor Joshua's heart.

"By the time I arrived, Nettie's rampage was done, for the moment at least, and she'd gone back into the house. When Joshua saw me turning into the driveway, he ran to the buggy shed and retrieved the one painting he wanted to keep. He'd taken it straight from Nettie's easel the night before, wrapped it up, and set it aside for himself. She hadn't touched it in a week, not since the fire, and he must've known even then that it would end up being the last painting she'd ever do."

"And that's the picture he sent into the house with my father?" I asked, the image of the two girls at sunset filling my mind.

"Yes. Once he'd done that, he turned his attention to the rest. Together he and I managed to get all of the canvases out to my car. We were just putting in the last load when Nettie appeared, screaming at me to leave and never come back. It was a horrible scene, but as I was driving away, all I could think was that this was our father's fault, more than anything else. He had taken the words of a loving God and twisted them into something false and condemning and ugly. My poor sister would never be out from under that man's delusions because she'd been fooled into thinking that God was as wrathful as our father. She would spend the rest of her life paying the price for his ignorance. Poor Nettie. God had created her to paint, and it tormented her soul not to do so."

Natasha paused for a moment as we all took that in. I felt so sad for everyone involved—Natasha and Nettie and Joshua and Eli. *Daed* had been the same age Thomas was now when it happened. I couldn't imagine how disturbing that had been for him.

"Sadly," Natasha continued, "Nettie didn't want to see me after that. When it came to me, she'd always vacillated between grace and legalism, though somehow the harmony her painting had brought her in the past had weighed the balance toward grace. But once she stopped painting for good, she swung far in the other direction. All the old resentment bubbled to the surface, where it remained for the rest of our lives.

"At first, the separation was so hard for me, and I spent a lot of time writing to Nettie and trying to get her to come around. But she wouldn't budge. In fact, when I sent her the check for the sale of those final paintings, she sent it back to me, saying it was dirty money and she wanted nothing to do with it. I certainly wasn't going to keep it, and I highly doubted her husband felt the same way she did, so eventually I asked Paul to drive it down to Joshua's workplace and give it directly to him there. The man had seemed a mix of gratitude and embarrassment, but Paul was so good with situations like that. By the time he left, Joshua seemed fine and all was well."

"Your Paul sounds like a wonderful man," I said.

She nodded. "He was. It was such a shock when he passed, just two years later. Died of a blood clot to the lungs at forty-nine years old."

"I'm so sorry."

"Yes, well, after that, as a single mother with six children, I hardly had time to think about Nettie anymore. It was all I could do to get through each day. Paul had become a partner in the insurance business he worked in, where we'd met. So I went back to work, to keep our investments, all while raising the children, including a toddler. It was a crazy period of my life, and I could have used Nettie's help but I never asked. There were times when I've wondered if I had, if perhaps she would have given it. Perhaps I was too prideful. Or too foolish. Or too fearful of her rejection yet again."

Natasha took a sip of water. "I wrote to her on our seventieth birthday but didn't hear back. She did send a note when Joshua died. I wept—he was such a good man, and I'm sure it was his love and kindness that kept Nettie functioning all of those years. When we turned eighty, I drove out to your farm to wish her happy birthday. No one was home except for two boys. They told me she'd died two years earlier."

Those would've been my oldest brothers, Matthew and Mark, who probably hadn't thought to mention to anyone later that an *Englisch* woman had stopped by to call on their deceased grandmother.

"It nearly broke my heart," Natasha said. "I would have loved nothing more than to help care for her when she was sick, than to have spent time with her before she passed. I consoled myself with the thought that at least I still had some of her paintings. Paul had sold many of them over the years, twenty-four to be exact, but I still had fifteen in storage. Plus, I had photos of the other twenty-four."

"Photos?" I asked, my pulse surging.

"Yes," Natasha replied. "I thought it was a great idea when Joshua told us to try selling the paintings, but I found it hard to part with some of them. Paul bought me a camera so I could take pictures first, and that really did help. Once Nettie had passed away, I treasured those photos even more."

My heart raced at the possibility of seeing these images of *Mammi* Nettie's paintings. "Could I look at them?"

Natasha smiled closely. "Of course." She turned toward her daughter. "Do you mind, dear? The album is on the bottom shelf by my bed."

When Jan returned, I quickly picked up the plates from the tabletop and carried them over to the counter. As I sat back down again, Natasha placed her hands on the closed album and regarded each of us in turn. "I put the photographs in chronological order, as much as I could. I had to guess the specifics within each year's batch, but they definitely fell into three distinct periods."

She slid her fingers to the edge of the cover. "I don't have any of her earliest paintings from childhood or from the years she lived with our brother. I don't have any, actually, until she started painting on the canvases I gave her after she married and I first visited her on the Mueller farm."

I interrupted to tell her about the one Nettie had done of the goat for Ina Mae. For some reason that brought tears to Natasha's eyes, which in turn brought tears to mine. With self-conscious chuckles, we both wiped them away, and then we returned our attention to the album, which she opened.

"Her early works were of landscapes, although as she continued to paint, it seems her longing for a family began to come through too."

There were paintings of farms, houses, silos, barns, buggies, and then cows with calves and horses with foals, all set during the spring. Then a landscape with a boy and a girl sitting on a fence, far in the distance, set in the fall.

Natasha pointed to the next photo. It was of an empty swing tied to an oak tree with the back of an Amish woman working in a summer garden. Natasha continued to turn the pages of the album.

"The one of Amish garments on a clothesline is a transition piece," Natasha explained. "It's the beginning of her second period, but with themes from her first." The photo was of one of the paintings in Natasha's hallway. "Notice the woman's dress on one end and the man's pants on the other?"

I nodded. "And the little dresses, pants, and shirts in between?"

"Exactly. That shows her longing for children, but the shapes are more abstract and the colors are jewel tones—inspired, she told me later, by her experience at my church."

It seemed to me that style developed more and more with each painting. She'd transformed fields into dots and swirls of emerald and forest green. A barn and a bed of geraniums became dots and swirls of white and red. A sunset over our farm became a splash of pink, orange, violet, and purple.

Gesturing toward the photos, Natasha said, "In my midsixties I began taking quilting classes. I studied Amish patterns and folk patterns. I immediately picked up on the technical aspects of it. I'd been doing all sorts of needlework for years, so that part came easily to me. But when I started trying to create scenes using appliqué, I was hopeless at composition. I lacked an artist's eye for it.

"When I was younger, I'd fully repented for what I'd done, and I knew God had forgiven me. But Nettie never did, and that weighed on me, especially as I grew older. After she passed, I found myself yearning for some sign of transformation, some way to redeem all the hurt and pain that had come between us in her lifetime. I prayed about it a lot, asking God to lead me somehow. I loved looking at the photos of my sister's artwork and the paintings I still had. As always, I wished I could paint like her, wished I could create something so beautiful from scratch. And the more I looked at the photos, and at Nettie's actual paintings, the more inspired I became.

"Then one day I decided to try and emulate her painting style in fabric—and the rest is history. Creating that first appliqué quilt was the closest thing I'd ever found to the harmony she discovered in her art. It went so well, in fact, that I made more, pouring my grief into them, thinking always of my sister as I worked. And somehow it felt as if I were giving her designs a second life. Eventually I came to understand that God had answered my prayers. That this was the sign of transformation I'd been seeking.

"Those quilts were met with a very favorable reception. As the interest in the Amish grew, so did the popularity of my work. I owed it all to Nettie, and my quilts became an homage to her, a way to silently honor her art. And also her losses. Creating those quilts brought me a peace I'd never experienced before, even as it stirred up old emotions." She glanced at Isaac. "Which I believe may *not* be an entirely foreign combination of feelings for artists."

He nodded.

She flipped the page. "After Eli was born and Nettie started painting again, she entered her third phase, what I call her 'children' period. Many of these images included twins, of course."

My mind went to the two little girls in the painting we had at home, and I described it to Natasha. Its composition fit right in line with this third phase, which made sense given that it was her final work.

"When I first saw it," I added, "it made me think of my nieces. Did I tell you my sister has a set of twins?"

Natasha's face lit up. "Really? How lovely. Identical?"

I nodded. "You can't imagine how similar they are, not just in appearance, but in behavior too. Sometimes it's almost like they're the same person."

"Oh, yes," she said, "Identical twins can be alike in so many ways. Personality traits. Mannerisms. Preferences. The thing is, while the similarities in behaviors will likely remain consistent or even increase over time, similarities in appearance tend to lessen through the years. One will skip the sunscreen and end up with extra wrinkles. The other one will get in shape and develop a physique. They might wear their hair at different lengths and glasses rather than contacts. Features change and grow too. Sometimes older adult pairs of twins can end up looking different enough from each other that you might not even take them for siblings. It can be rather shocking, actually, how two people who start out so indistinguishable can end up so different."

I'd never thought about that, but it made sense. Already, Hattie carried a scar on her chin that Hazel did not. I supposed their differences would only increase with time.

"How about you and Nettie?" Jan asked. "Did you two still look like each other when you were older?"

"Not really," Natasha said. "We always had the added dimension of Amish versus non-Amish, of course. But even without all of that, other differences emerged as the years passed. That last time I saw her, we were in our midforties, and I don't think most people would have taken us for twins even then. Her hair had gone gray, and she'd put on a little weight. I'd kept my hair auburn and pampered my skin in ways she hadn't. But it was more than that, though it's hard to explain…" Her voice trailed off.

"If I had to guess," Isaac offered, "I'd say it probably had to do with your dispositions and how they affected your physical appearances."

We all looked at him with interest as he continued.

"She was negative and inwardly focused, you were positive and outgoing. You probably carried yourselves in completely different ways."

Natasha nodded emphatically. "That's it exactly. We did. Our dispositions were reflected in our looks, and I think that's what made us, in the end, barely identical at all."

I thought about that for a moment and my mind returned to Hattie and Hazel and how different they might look years from now. Then I thought of their quilt, the one I'd always wanted to do. My initial vision for it had been fuzzy and unclear, lacking any sort of focal point. Now, however, it struck me what I'd been missing. Just like Tabitha, I'd always thought of them as a single "person," in a sense, rather than as individuals. But they *were* individuals, separate and whole in their own right.

And then the design came to me, a quilt that was neither patchwork nor appliqué but instead a mix of both. I would start at the bottom with patchwork, very regimented and geometric, exactly the same all the way across, as tight and closed off as the twins themselves had always seemed. But then as it went upward, that geometric design would begin to deviate and evolve into appliqué instead, the geometric pieces spinning out from the center into a beautiful explosion of color—one that was slightly different on each side.

Robert always used to say that the girls' ASD was beautiful in its own way, and that in God's eyes they were perfect exactly as they were. He was so right. Now with Tabitha's new knowledge and all of our help, perhaps they could begin to see that for themselves and find a way to connect with the larger world that existed outside their own little circle of two.

"In Nettie's paintings," Natasha said, interrupting my thoughts, "the twins are always children, always young, and always identical."

We returned our attention to the photos, and I saw where *Mammi* Nettie had painted two tiny girls dressed in Amish clothes, seen from the back, identical in size and shape, with a garden in the foreground. A different one showed our farmhouse with a toddler on a blanket in front of it, and then a barn with what looked like twin boys playing to the side. Another painting was of older girls strolling down a lane. Several had her trademark sunset, and there were other twin images included, not just in people, but in nature too—calves, birds, and even bunches of double daffodils.

"My sister's work continues to inspire me," Natasha said as we reached the end of the album. She sighed. "I just hope I'll be able to quilt in heaven, perhaps while sitting with Nettie and watching her paint." She closed the book and held it in her lap, and I realized she had something else to say.

"I know you won't judge me," she began, "because it's not your way. But I want you to know I'm aware of what a tremendous debt I owe to your grandmother—quite literally. My quilts have made some money over the years, quilts based on her designs. They wouldn't have been even half as successful without Nettie's paintings for a starting point. When I first began making them, I viewed each of my creations as an homage to my beloved sister. But once they began to sell, it did present a conundrum. I—"

"Of course!" Jan interrupted, smacking a palm against her forehead. "The money. The donations. I get it."

The two women shared a smile.

"Yes, dear, and I hope it all makes more sense now." Natasha turned back to us. "After my first sale, I decided that I would donate that and all future profits from the quilts to charitable organizations, ones that helped people just like Nettie. In the end I chose two different mental health groups, one being a national association and the other a local facility that specializes in treating the Plain community."

I wondered if she was talking about the same place where Thomas was now going for counseling. If so, what a lovely full circle that would be.

I didn't go into all of that, though. Instead, I simply thanked her for coming up with such a perfect solution and assured her that my family would be thrilled to learn that Nettie's art had played some small part in such a wonderful outpouring of generosity. I didn't know all that much about psychology, but I did know that a Plain person who needed help usually did best when treated by someone who was also Plain. Mennonites were allowed higher educations, so those who became counselors were a good choice for Amish patients. Without Plain backgrounds, not only would counselors be far less likely to understand the bigger picture of their patients' lifestyles, but sometimes they would focus on the Amishness itself, treating it as if it were part of the problem. That was one reason why places like the one Natasha had been funding were so valuable to our community.

"That's where the name came from as well," Natasha added, interrupting my thoughts. "Twinkle Star Quilts."

She smiled mysteriously but didn't elaborate. We all stared at her for a moment, then Isaac and I both spoke at the same time.

"*Ya!*" I cried.

"Oh!" Isaac said.

Natasha grinned, but Jan just shook her head. "I don't get it."

"*Twin*-kle," I told her.

"As in *twin*," Isaac added.

"Wait, what?"

Natasha nodded. "When I finished that very first quilt based on one of Nettie's paintings, I knew it had truly been a joint effort. No way was I going to put just my name to something that we both had an equal part in. So I decided to file for a DBA instead."

"A DBA?" I asked.

"A 'doing business as' name. It lets me promote and sell as Twinkle Star Quilts rather than Natasha Johnson. I felt a lot better doing it that way. I even got a separate phone line for the business, just so my name would stay out of it."

I glanced at Isaac, thinking of Cheri Bethune and what she'd said that day in the gallery, about how some of their Amish artists only worked under business names and not their own names. They probably used DBAs too.

"Anyway," Natasha continued, "I spent a good week playing around with all the possibilities, combining pieces of our names, like 'Around the Bend Quilts' for Bender, or using other related words like 'Sister-hood Needleworks,' things like that. In the end I settled on doing something with 'Twin.' I liked Twinkle, and since twinkle goes with star, and star is a type of quilting pattern, it just seemed like the best fit. Twinkle Star Quilts."

Jan shook her head, a bemused expression on her face. "No wonder you wouldn't listen to me about needing a better name. This one is perfect."

"Yes, it is," I added. "I think my grandmother would've been touched."

I rose and went to Natasha, putting my arms around her for a long hug. I couldn't believe we'd only just met the day before. In a way, it felt like I'd known her my whole life.

It was time for Isaac and me to go, and I said as much now.

"Oh, wait," Natasha replied. "Your book."

She gestured toward the coffee table, where Nettie's art book sat. Isaac retrieved it and then set it in front of Natasha. She opened the cover again slowly, reverently, then ran her hand across the inscription.

" 'To Nettie, with love, Natasha,' " she read. After a long moment, she added, "I gave this to her at our mother's funeral, in with the bag of art supplies. It was the first of many art books I brought her over the years. She devoured them—and gave them all back except for this first one."

"Did you keep in touch with any of your other siblings?" I asked.

Natasha shook her head. "Only Nettie. No one contacted me—and I never reached out to any of them except for one older sister. But she wasn't happy to see me, so that was that."

"Do you regret leaving?"

She hesitated a moment and then said, "I always regretted the *way* I left. And of course I regretted losing Nettie. But, no, I didn't regret leaving. I grew so much as a person after I was gone. And I loved Paul. Plus, I wouldn't have the children I have." She glanced toward Jan. "Or any of the life I ended up with. I don't regret it at all."

With that, she closed the book and handed it over. Part of me wondered if I should offer to let her keep it, but instead I accepted it. I wanted to take it home.

As Natasha and Jan walked us to the door, Isaac said he had a question, if she didn't mind.

She turned toward him, a sweet smile on her face. "What is it?"

"May we see more of your quilts? And the rest of Nettie's paintings?"

She contemplated the question and then said, "None of my quilts are here right now, and the paintings I have left of Nettie's are in storage, but I'm having an exhibit at my church here in town in September. Now that I've told my secret, with your *daed*'s permission, I'd like to include Nettie's paintings too, the ones I have left. I'll have to check with the coordinator, of course. It's a lot to ask of her, but I'd like to do it. And I'd be thrilled if both of you could attend the opening."

My heart raced at the thought. I glanced at Isaac, and he nodded. I told Natasha that we'd like that very much.

"Could I come out and meet your *daed*?" she asked. "Do you think that would be all right?"

I swallowed and then found my voice. "I think he'd like that," I said. "I'll talk with him."

"Give me a call with his answer." Natasha reached for paper and pen on the small desk behind her and quickly jotted down her personal phone number for me. I took it from her and slipped it into my apron pocket, grateful I'd have further contact with this dear woman.

Dusk fell as Ginny drove us home. Isaac turned toward me from the passenger seat and asked if I minded if he got out at my house too. I gave him a nod, glad we didn't have to part just yet.

Once there, we paid Ginny, and then as we walked toward the house, Isaac said, "Do you want me to speak with your *daed* and *mamm* with you? Do you think it would help?"

I nodded, hoping *Daed* was still awake. "I think maybe it would."

"The whole story is incredible," Isaac said. "I'm sorry that life was so hard for your grandmother. No wonder she was so miserable, especially once she gave up her painting for good."

I couldn't imagine what my life would be like if I'd been taught that quilting was wrong. "I hope the bishop will allow you to keep painting."

Isaac wrinkled his brow. "Isn't it funny that Natasha would discredit her own quilting because she was inspired by Nettie's paintings?"

"But she didn't come up with the original ideas—I get what she's saying."

Isaac shrugged. "There are very few original ideas."

"But I understand how she feels. Although it's not that I'm worried about not being original—I just can't seem to come up with anything at all that I like."

Isaac told me I would, eventually. "Quilting like what Natasha does— and what you're learning to do—is definitely an art. And all-consuming. My advantage is that a painting takes much less time than a quilt."

I stepped through the door as he said, "Natasha isn't giving herself enough credit."

"Natasha?" *Mamm* said from the sink. "Did you find her?"

"*Ya*," I answered. "We have quite the story to tell you and *Daed*, followed by a request."

"Good timing, then, especially if we need privacy. Tabitha is still over at Sadie's, and Stephen and Thomas are spending the night there."

"Oh. Why?"

Mamm shrugged. "The boys wanted to. It'll be quicker for them in the morning when it's time to do the milking, and it's nice for the children to have them around. Plus, it's a help to Sadie."

It just showed how much better Thomas was doing, that he was considered a help to Sadie and not a hindrance.

Mamm called *Daed* in from the living room, then the four of us sat around the table with cups of coffee and strawberry pie, made from our own plants. We explained what Natasha had told us up until the time she revealed herself as Georgie.

Daed stammered, "M-My mother's twin is still alive?"

"*Ya*," I said. "She's the one you remember from when you were young. She came and rescued your *mamm*'s paintings that day, just as you thought."

I went on to explain the rest of what Natasha had said and then added that she was having a quilt show in September and wanted to include *Mammi* Nettie's artwork in it—but only with his permission.

When *Daed* didn't respond, I said, "More importantly, though, she would like to see you."

He folded his big hands together on the tabletop and said, "I'll think on that and let you know."

We were all silent for an awkward moment, and then *Mamm* asked how Ruth was doing and Isaac told her. We chatted a little longer, and then I told Isaac I'd give him a ride home.

"I can walk," he said.

"Don't be ridiculous," I answered. "I'll drive you."

Mamm gave *Daed* a sweet smile as we said our goodbyes. It was so obvious they both liked Isaac. And who could blame them?

Isaac helped me harness and hitch Blue. Then he lit the lantern, and we were soon on the road. The night was warm, and the moon was just rising over the treetops. It was amazing how much stronger smells seemed at night, Sadie's dairy in particular. But then came the sweet scent of daphne farther down the road. I was certain I could even smell a patch of strawberries as we rattled past.

As Blue trotted along, I thought of what Natasha had said about always feeling as if there was a different life for her. I asked Isaac if he'd felt that way when he left.

He smiled a little and said, "No. I wasn't that analytical about any of it. I kind of took things one day—and one decision—at a time. That's probably why it was easy, or at least possible, for me to come back."

"What do you mean?"

"It wasn't as if I'd had some transformational experience. I wanted to move to Philadelphia, but I thought I might return home. Then I wanted to go to college, which made it seem less likely I'd return home, but I wasn't opposed to it. Then I fell in love with Bailey, and I had to make a choice, but still it wasn't philosophical. It was entirely based on love. Then after she died, I realized I could return if I wanted to. So I did." He shrugged and then gave me a shy smile.

"Did you feel shame during that time? When you were gone?"

"Shame?"

"For not joining the church."

"Linda," he said. "I know in the eyes of many I should have. But I hadn't done anything wrong. I honestly trusted God each step of the way. I prayed about my decision and weighed the pros and cons. Then I went for it. I had nothing to feel ashamed about. I understand those in the church believed my leaving was shameful, but I don't think it was to God." His look was tender as he spoke.

We'd reached Ruth's place so the conversation came to an end. Isaac told me to park by the barn. "I have something to loan you, for however long you want to keep it," he said. "Wait here."

When he returned, he was carrying a large canvas in one hand and a flashlight in the other. "I painted this not long after you said how much you liked Robert's barn, and I was going to show it to you then. But once you started your quilt, I hesitated to give it to you because I didn't want to influence your own artistic vision. So, believe me, I'm not giving it to you to influence you in any way—but simply to inspire you."

My heart flooded with such emotion that I could barely squeeze out a reply. "*Ya*, you should."

With a shy grin, he turned the canvas around, raised it up, and shone the light on the painting, revealing a breathtaking image of the old barn. It was of the interior, with the light coming in from one side. A swallow flew below the rafters, which created geometric shapes along the top, and Whisper was curled up on a bale of hay in the left-hand corner. The whole thing had a rustic feel, and it was painted on canvas with a barn board frame, just as he'd first described it to me.

"It's beautiful," I said, fighting back tears as I took it from him and set it carefully on the seat beside me. And it was. "*Danke*."

"You're welcome." Isaac cleared his throat. "Thank you for being a good friend to me. I know I hurt you, but you haven't held it against me."

"You didn't hurt me," I replied. "And how could I hold it against you? You're the kindest—" I stopped, unable to continue, and looked away.

We were both quiet for a moment.

"Linda," he said, the gravity in his tone making me turn back toward him again. "There's something we need to talk about."

I swallowed hard, my heart suddenly hammering in my chest. I couldn't speak, so I simply gave him a nod.

Standing there beside the buggy, just a foot or two away, his eyes even with mine, he launched in. "You've made it clear that you only want to be my friend, and I understand that. But the thing is, I can't be just your friend. My feelings are too strong. It hurts too much."

"Oh, Isaac," I whispered, yearning to reach out and touch my fingertips to his handsome, somber face. "I'm so sorry."

"You got a big shock at first, *ya*, and I completely understand your reaction then, I truly do. But you've had time to think things over since, to get used to the idea of my past. I've tried not to give up hope, but I think we've reached that point where a decision has to be made."

"A decision?"

He nodded gravely. "I can't seem to get over you, Linda. But I also can't keep tormenting myself like this. I've given it a lot of prayer, a lot of thought. Either you need to get past this and we start courting, or…"

His voice trailed off as he broke our gaze.

"Or what?"

After a pause, he returned his eyes to mine. "Or I need to move. Like, away from here. Away from you."

"What?" I felt as if I'd been punched in the stomach. "But what about your new business? What about your grandmother?"

He shrugged. "Most of my current contracts are coming out of the Harrisburg area anyway. One of my brothers lives in Mount Joy, so if I move in with him I'll actually be closer to the jobs than I am here. As for *Mammi* Ruth, she'll be fine. I'll miss her, but she lived alone before I came. She can do it again. I just keep thinking I'm new enough in this area that moving is still an option for me. I haven't fully settled in, haven't even completely learned my way around, haven't developed any deep friendships yet—well, except with you."

Tears sprang to my eyes.

"What I'm saying," he continued, "is that I'm still portable, so to speak, as long as I go soon and don't wait until I've become fully enmeshed. I'm in a position to pick up and go, which would probably be a lot easier in the long run than staying and somehow forcing myself to get over you despite the fact that you're still in my life."

My mind reeled, astounded by this turn of events. Isaac couldn't leave. He just couldn't.

"Please don't go," I whispered.

"I don't want to," he replied. "But if I stick around here, all I'll be doing is setting myself up for disappointment. Do you know what it's like for me every time I see you? Every time I hear your voice, your laugh? My first reaction is always a moment of absolute happiness. But that's followed by the most terrible pain. I want to build a life with you, Linda. I can't just be your friend. I can't just pretend there's nothing more between us than that."

He searched my eyes, but I was speechless. What could I say? Nothing had changed on my end. I loved him, but I couldn't marry him. It was that simple.

And yet it wasn't simple at all. Just the thought of him leaving broke my heart. I couldn't imagine my life without Isaac in it. These past few months he had become one of the most important people in my world. I lived for his smile. I delighted in his mind. But I couldn't marry him, I just couldn't.

When I didn't reply, he took a deep breath and laid it out there. "I need to know, Linda, once and for all. Will you ever get past what's come between us? Could you let yourself love me?"

Tears filled my eyes. That wasn't the question. "Of course I could," I whispered. "I already do."

His eyes filled with hope, until I added, "But that's beside the point, Isaac. I can't be with you."

He froze for a long moment, searching my face, searching for the other answer, the one I couldn't give him.

"All right," he finally replied, taking a step back and slipping his hands into his pockets. "That's it, then. I'm sorry, Linda, but if courting really is off the table, I can't stick around here. I'll start making plans to relocate."

I cried all the way home. At one point I was crying so hard that I would've missed a turn if not for Blue, who instinctively slowed as we neared that particular intersection. I was just glad it was dark and traffic was light, because otherwise the whole world would've seen the most ridiculous sight, an Amish girl driving a buggy while bawling her eyes out.

Thankfully, the house was dark when I got there, which meant *Mamm* and *Daed* were already asleep. After putting away the buggy and tending to Blue, I pulled myself together enough to head inside. I tried to be quiet as I made my way upstairs and got ready for bed. By that point, I felt numb, as if I were moving through a dream—or, more likely, a nightmare. At least Tabitha hadn't gotten home from Sadie's yet, which was a relief. The last thing I felt like doing was explaining my swollen eyes and blotchy cheeks to my nosy sister.

I was so weary from all the crying, but once I got under the covers, I simply couldn't fall asleep. Every sound felt magnified—the chirping crickets out there in the dark, the gentle whinny of a horse in the barn, a distant car accelerating on the road.

Eventually I got back up and lit my lamp, then I retrieved Isaac's painting, which I'd set on the floor beside the dresser, its image turned toward the wall. I couldn't display it, but that didn't mean I couldn't look at it. Settling back on the bed, I studied it by the flickering light for a good while. I knew I could never quilt this image—it was Isaac's vision, not mine— but the longer I sat there gazing at it, the more I began to feel inspired.

Despite my sadness, the urge to create rose up inside of me, making me even more awake, not less. And so eventually, painting in hand, I tiptoed back down the stairs to my quilting room. After a little rearranging of the closet, I was able to fit Isaac's picture inside, propped on the shelf in such a way that whenever I wanted to look at it, all I had to do was open the door. I felt sure God wouldn't mind me keeping it there, carefully stored just out of sight but within easy reach for continued inspiration, as I worked on my own version of the barn. Only on a quilt instead of a canvas.

Once that was settled, I turned my attention to the task at hand, pulling out some graph paper and redrawing the pattern for my quilt. Despite my apprehension about trying a form of quilting that was new to me, where I might make mistakes and produce something less than perfect, I decided to take the plunge and make it a full-blown appliqué quilt anyway. Kristen was right. It would take some practice, but if I tried hard enough, I really could learn to do this.

Energized by my decision and my new resolve, I played with shapes, with lights and shadows. Though it took me a while, I eventually came up with something I thought would work. It wasn't anything like Isaac's painting, but it had been inspired by it. I'd opened up half the barn, showing the interior, while the other half featured the exterior, along with a few geometrically shaped cows and one lone black cat, Whisper, off to the side on a field of green. I'd need to rip out what I'd already done and purchase more fabric, but I was happy to start over.

When my eyelids began to droop, I put my things away and headed back up to my room. I'd heard Tabitha come in while I was down there, but now she was already fast asleep, sprawled across her bed, her breathing even and deep. Quietly, I slipped under my own covers and rolled to my side, staring toward the window. Enough moonlight came through that I could see the top of the willow tree out in the front yard, below our room. The leaves fluttered in the night breeze, mostly just dark shapes. But every once in a while I could make out a bit of green. I wondered if I could express willow leaves on a quilt.

Lying there, my mind again went to Isaac and how he'd decided to leave the Amish and not come back but then eventually came back anyway. Step by step. He hadn't planned everything out. He'd trusted God with it. That sounded like what it meant to live by faith, something I tried to do too—but often didn't.

Now he had made a new decision, to leave here and start again elsewhere. I wasn't sure if that had also been a step of faith or if he'd done this one on his own, a rash reaction to a temporary problem. But either way, the fact was that I would soon be losing him forever. Like extinguishing a lantern on a moonless night, that thought left me feeling disoriented and alone, plunged into utter darkness.

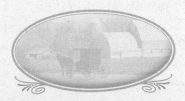

TWENTY

I didn't see Isaac at all over the next few days, especially as Thomas was now doing the morning milking in my stead. I worked at the shop and quilted and helped *Mamm* with the household chores and weeding the garden. Tabitha spent her mornings and afternoons with Sadie and her evenings with Ezra, so I didn't see her either, except sometimes at breakfast.

On Thursday morning, as Tabitha and I were neatening up the kitchen, she shared that Becky had called Sadie the day before. She dropped her voice and leaned toward me. "Our once flawless sister is having a hard time with the terrible twos." Tabitha grinned. "Believe it or not, she actually wanted some advice."

I stifled a smile. As much as I hated gossip, it did feel good to know that Becky could admit she wasn't a perfect parent with perfect kids.

I changed the subject. "How are Hattie and Hazel doing?"

"Great." Tabitha glanced at the kitchen clock. "But speaking of, I'd better get going."

On Friday, she was off with Ezra and *Mamm* seemed tired, so I was doing the dishes by myself after supper. As I worked, *Daed* stepped into the kitchen and told me he'd made a decision about Natasha.

"I'd like to see her," he said. "I think that's the right thing to do. Why

309

don't you call and invite her for a visit this Sunday afternoon? Say around two or three? Invite Ina Mae too, though she'll need to hire a driver to get here. If the weather's nice, we can sit outside and spend some time together talking and catching up."

My pulse surged. "*Ya*, I'll call both of them."

"*Gut*. Ask Isaac if he'd like to join us too. I know he'd want to be here."

"All right." As difficult as it would be to see him, I decided I would extend that invitation in person. "Ruth has been a part of my search too, at least in the beginning. May I invite her?"

"*Ya*. Of course. Ruth and Isaac."

Daed started to leave the kitchen but then stopped. He cleared his throat. "Speaking of Isaac…"

His voice trailed off, so I just waited, hiding my sudden nerves by plunging a plate into the rinse water and swishing it around.

"Just a thought," he continued. "I remember my father telling my mother once that hate in her heart would only damage her own soul. I wonder if that doesn't apply to things other than hate too."

"Like?"

"Idealism, to name one. Expecting life to follow a certain path. Putting those expectations before the realities, before actual people. Maybe idealism can also damage a soul."

I didn't know how to reply so I simply thanked him and said I'd pray on it.

"*Gut*. See that you do."

I felt stiff and self-conscious until I heard him leave the kitchen and rejoin *Mamm* in the living room. As I continued washing, I mulled over his words. Was I letting my idealism get in the way of my life? Did I value my plan for my future more than I valued an actual future? More important than that, was I not trusting the plan I knew God had for me? To give me a hope and a future, as Scripture taught?

I found myself praying as I plunged the final pot into the soapy water, asking the Lord to forgive me for being so self-oriented and for thinking I had to take things in my own hands instead of giving them fully over to Him. I told Him how much I yearned to be His servant and not be ruled by my own desires and whims and fears. I asked Him to help me in that and to stay with me no matter what, to teach me patience and trust and dependence on His ever-present love and care.

Filled with a deep sense of God's peace, I dried and put away the pot. I wiped down the counter, hung the damp towel, and headed outside.

Out in the phone room, I called Natasha. She picked up right away, and after chatting for a minute, I invited her and Jan to come at two p.m. on Sunday. She accepted, with glee. I asked if it would be all right for me to invite Ina Mae and Isaac and his grandmother as well, and she was delighted with the idea. Once our call was over, I dialed Ina Mae and left a message for her.

"Oh, and one more thing," I added before hanging up. "I know that Natasha would love to see the little painting of the goat, if you're comfortable showing it to her. If so, maybe you can bring it with you when you come."

Then I drove over to Ruth's. When I arrived, she was sitting by herself on her porch. She greeted me warmly and asked me to join her. As I sat down she added with a chuckle, "Though maybe it's not me you came to visit?"

My face grew warm. "Actually I'm here for both you and Isaac. Is he around? Out in his studio perhaps?"

Ruth shook her head. "No, he said he wouldn't be home until late tonight."

"Oh." A moment of panic seized me. Was he over at his brother's in Mount Joy? Making arrangements to move there?

"What did you need us for?" Ruth asked.

I put aside my fears for now and tried not to act as rattled as I felt. "I just came to deliver a message from my *daed*. We're having a sort of get-together on Sunday afternoon, and we were wondering if the two of you would like to join us."

"How nice. What time?"

"Around two?"

"Sounds *gut*. I'd love to come, and I'll let him know."

"Great. Thanks."

"What's the occasion?"

I smiled. "A very special guest is coming to visit. Natasha. Has Isaac told you anything about her?"

"*Ya*," she answered. "A bit."

"Well, *Daed* has decided that he wants to see her, so we've invited her over for Sunday. We're also inviting everyone else who's been a part of my search, which is our cousin Ina Mae, Isaac, and you."

"Me? I didn't do much."

"You got me started," I said. "That was more important than you might think."

"I suppose." She smiled. "Now that you've found your answers, sounds like it was worth the trouble, *ya*?"

"Oh, absolutely. Natasha's wonderful, and so forthcoming. The things she shared with us explained so much." I glanced at Ruth. "Did Isaac tell you about the day my father saw her all those years ago? He was ten at the time."

Ruth's eyes sparkled with interest. "No. What happened?"

There in the cool breeze that came down from the row of poplar trees just past the house, I shared with Ruth the whole story, starting with the old wash house catching fire and ending with *Mammi* Nettie never painting again.

Ruth considered my words, saying she well remembered the little fire over at the Muellers' and how, once all was said and done, something had seemed so odd about it. Apparently her husband had been among the neighbors who'd come running once the blaze was in full force to try and help put it out.

"They kept it from spreading to any of the other buildings, not even the chicken coop, which was pretty close by," she said. "Once the fire was out, everybody was in good spirits, thrilled that only one small outbuilding had been lost. The odd thing was, though, Joshua and Nettie seemed utterly devastated by that fire. People couldn't imagine how anyone could get so upset over losing a few tools, but there was no question that both were extremely distraught."

"I guess they didn't tell anyone about the paintings that had been inside when it burned."

"No, they didn't. Once my husband was home and the storm had passed, he sent me back over there with some extra tools we had. He'd told me how devastated they'd been, so I expected they'd be especially grateful

for what I took over. Instead, when I gave them the tools, they acted like...
I don't know, like I was offering a tiny bandage to someone who was bleeding to death. At least now I understand why. How very sad indeed."

We sat in silence for a long moment, mulling things over.

"Such a pity she gave up painting for good," Ruth said, breaking the silence. "Though I have to say that for the next few years after that fire, she raised flowers as if they were a painting. She did wonderful things with her flowerbeds. Always knew precisely what should go where for the greatest effect."

"She was gifted at composition," I replied.

"I don't doubt that. Her flowerbeds were magnificent. Though the bishop had to put an end to them eventually."

"Why? There's nothing wrong with gardening."

Ruth shrugged. "Anything done out of pride is wrong, Linda. Her heart was not in the right place with those flowerbeds, and it was obvious."

I thought about that for a moment. "Actually, knowing what I know about her now, I have a feeling it probably wasn't about pride at all. I imagine it was just the same creative urge that had compelled her to paint. Creativity has to come out somewhere, you know? And for someone like her, who was so artistically gifted, I imagined when it did come out, it manifested in a very visual—and, sadly, very noticeable—way."

"You may be right about that." Ruth shook her head sadly. "Poor Nettie. I wish I'd been a better friend to her then."

"It doesn't sound as if she would have been very receptive."

"Perhaps not." Ruth thought for a moment and then turned to me. "I'll tell you this, though, Linda. Always err on the side of kindness. Don't ever assume there's not a good reason for why people act the way they do."

I didn't hear from Isaac on Saturday or even by Sunday afternoon, so I had no idea if he was coming to our little gathering or not. I knew he hadn't moved out yet, but just the thought that he soon would caused my stomach to cramp and my heart to ache.

Ina Mae left a message that she would join us. And right before she was scheduled to arrive, Sadie and Jedediah and the children and Tabitha all showed up too.

I gave *Mamm* a surprised look.

"I asked them to come," she explained. "I thought they'd want to meet their relatives."

As they all piled out of the buggy, I searched for Isaac and Ruth, but they weren't among them. Ezra was, however.

My stomach churned. Where was Isaac?

Ina Mae arrived next. *Daed* and I both hurried to help her out of the car. Her driver pulled her walker from the trunk, and *Daed* took over from there.

We'd put out a few tables and chairs, and Stephen and Thomas were setting up more. My anxiety increased, and I realized the only thing that would make me calm down was if Isaac were here. What if Ruth forgot to tell him? Or, more likely, what if she had but he'd chosen not to come? He'd said it was too hard to be with me. Maybe he'd decided to stay away.

Another car came up the drive. I started toward it, squaring my shoulders, ready to greet Natasha. I'd have to be brave on my own, without Isaac. But when the car came to a stop, the person who climbed out wasn't Natasha but Isaac.

I stammered, "I-It's you."

He smiled, turning to help his grandmother out as well. "Were you expecting someone else?"

"To come here via car? Yes, I thought you were Natasha. What's going on?"

He held up an index finger as if to say, *Just a minute*, and then he leaned into the window and spoke with the driver. I looked to Ruth, welcoming her and thanking her for coming, but she wasn't her usual cheery self. Instead, the look she gave me in return was sad and pensive, and it struck me that perhaps since I'd seen her last, she'd learned from Isaac what was going on, that he was moving out because of me.

To my relief, *Daed* showed up at that moment, greeted Ruth, and then offered her his arm. As they headed off toward the others, I returned my attention to Isaac, who was wrapping up his conversation with the driver.

"Anyway, thanks for the lift," he said, stepping back and standing up straight.

"No problem," the man replied, a grizzled older fellow in jeans and a

Reading Fightin Phils T-shirt. With a chuckle, he added, "Anything to get out of mowing the lawn."

As he drove off, I looked to Isaac questioningly.

He shrugged. "I was running late, so while *Mammi* Ruth was waiting for me, she arranged for a neighbor to give us a ride. He's a real talker, so she knew he wouldn't mind."

"I was afraid you weren't coming." I didn't even try to hide the emotion behind my words.

"I wouldn't miss this, Linda." His tone deep and reassuring, as if he sensed my anxiety.

"Thank you," I whispered.

"Bishop Yoder came by to discuss his decision about my artwork. That's what held us up."

"What did he say?" I blurted, but as soon as the words were out of my mouth, I realized it didn't matter. Isaac was leaving. Once he was living at his brother's, he'd have a completely different bishop to deal with.

Isaac shrugged. "I told him I was sorry to have taken up his time with the whole matter but that the situation had changed. He seemed disappointed to hear that I was leaving, but he understood. We had a good conversation, actually. He's a nice man."

"Did he tell you what his decision was going to be? If you weren't… leaving, I mean," I asked, that last word sticking in my throat.

Isaac nodded. "*Ya.* He was worried about pride, for good reason. I understand that. His idea was that I'd sell my work anonymously, as some other Amish artists do."

"Just like Cheri was saying that day at the gallery. That's great. How about 'Barnwood Arts'? That could work."

"*Ya*, except it doesn't matter now anyway."

My heart sank. Of course it didn't. "Your new bishop might not be so flexible," I reminded him. "Almost sounds like a good reason to stay."

He met my eyes. "There's only one reason I'd stay."

My emotions swirling, I turned and gestured, and we started walking toward the others. After a moment, sick at heart, I couldn't help but ask if he had any idea of his timing yet for the move.

I glanced at him and saw a pained expression cross his face. "My brother's all set, and I've been working on finding transportation for my business. But I need to finish up some projects around *Mammi* Ruth's farm first. And I only told her this morning."

"Ah. That explains the less-than-happy look she just gave me."

"*Ya.* She's pretty upset about it, more than I'd expected. To be honest, I'm going to miss her. A lot. We've been real compatible, she and I."

We grew quiet for a moment, but it wasn't the kind of comfortable silence we usually shared.

"Natasha isn't here yet," I said.

"She will be," he replied.

Trying to get a handle on my emotions, I took him over to meet Ina Mae. *Daed* made the introductions, referring to Isaac simply as a family friend.

We were turning away from her as another vehicle came up the drive. It was an SUV, an expensive-looking one, with Jan at the wheel. I caught my breath, the sight of our new guests snapping me back into the moment.

My excitement growing, I waved and motioned for her to stop at the walkway. She did, and I greeted her through the open window and showed her where to park once her mother was out. Then I walked around the vehicle to see if I could assist Natasha, but she didn't need my help. She scooted down off the seat, a large wicker handbag under one arm.

She wore white slacks, a coral top, and an orange silk scarf around her neck, and she looked even more elegant than either time I'd seen her before. She gave me a hug and kissed me on the cheek.

"Come and meet the rest of the family," I said.

She slipped her arm through mine and walked beside me until she saw Isaac. Then she stepped toward him and linked her arm in his. Jan caught up to me, and we walked along together. "I've never seen her nervous before," she whispered. "She changed her outfit three times. She didn't say a word the entire drive down here."

I wondered if Natasha was remembering the last time she'd come to this place, all those years ago when she found out that her twin had passed away.

Isaac took her straight to *Daed.* He stood and stepped toward her, extending his hand.

She grasped it with both of hers and held on to it. "Eli," she said. "This is a dream come true."

Daed seemed choked up for just a moment, but then he introduced her to *Mamm*, Ina Mae, and the rest of the crowd. Natasha greeted each person with enthusiasm, but especially the twins. When *Daed* introduced them, she bent down and spoke warmly. "Well, tell me now, who is Hattie and who is Hazel?"

They hesitated, eyes on the ground. "I'm Hattie, and she's Hazel," the more outgoing of the two said at last, and Hazel nodded in agreement.

"It's so very nice to meet you." Natasha shook each of their hands. "I'm a twin too, you know."

Their eyes widened, and for a moment they actually met her gaze. "You are?" asked Hattie.

Natasha nodded. "My twin was your Great-Grandmother Nettie." For a moment I feared she might be overcome with emotion, but she pulled it together and then added softly, "Treasure each other."

After *Daed* was done introducing Natasha, he turned toward Jan and welcomed her as well, shaking her hand and calling her cousin. Then he introduced Jan to the others.

We all sat around drinking lemonade and eating the snickerdoodles and oatmeal cookies *Mamm* and I had made. Isaac and I sat away from Natasha, letting others have a chance to visit with her. But after a while she called out my name and asked if I could show her Nettie's last painting.

I glanced at *Daed* and he nodded.

I went and retrieved it from the sewing room. When I handed it to Natasha, she looked at it for a long moment, staring at the backs of the twin girls and the sunset in front of them.

"It's definitely Nettie and me when we were young. I'm the one a step ahead. It's beautiful. No wonder your father kept it." She looked at *Daed*. "I saw him send a painting into the house with you that day, and I had a feeling it must be something special. I was right."

She handed the painting back to me but then reached into her purse and pulled out her smartphone. "May I?"

"*Ya.* Of course."

Not wanting to be in the photo myself, I handed the painting over to

Jan, who seemed to know exactly how and where to stand for her mother to get the best picture, as if she'd done it a hundred times before.

When they were finished, she gave the painting back to me and I carried it into the house. As I set it down, I thought about the barn painting Isaac had loaned me and was tempted to bring it out and show it to her as well. But something about it felt private, between Isaac and me, and though I would like to share it with Natasha, I didn't feel like doing so in front of the whole crowd. Besides, I doubted that Isaac would want me to.

"There is one more thing I'd like to see, if you don't mind," Natasha was saying to *Daed* as I returned to the group. "Nettie's old work area, in the barn. She only let me go in there once, and I'm sure it's quite changed since then. But I'd love to see it just the same."

"Of course." *Daed* held out an arm for her to take.

Jedediah and Ezra had drifted over to the horseshoe pits with Stephen and Thomas. The twins played on the porch, and Tabitha held Bobby while Sadie looked as if she'd like to put her feet up. Jan, *Mamm*, and Ina Mae were deep in conversation.

Isaac touched my shoulder and then pointed toward *Daed* and Natasha as they made their way toward the shed. "I don't think they'd mind if we tagged along."

We caught up with them just as they went into the barn. They were talking easily, as if they'd been acquainted forever.

"If I'd known about you," *Daed* was saying, "I would have asked you to come out while she was still alive. She was difficult, *ya*, but she talked more in that last year about her life as a child than she ever had before."

"Yet she never mentioned me?"

Daed shook his head. "Sadly, no. She didn't talk about her paintings either. Perhaps she'd boxed all of that up and stored it away in her mind. Perhaps it was too painful for her to remember."

He opened the door to his shop and held it for Natasha and for Isaac and me too.

As we stepped inside, Natasha looked around, seeming confused.

"I don't understand," she said. "I know I only saw it once, but there's no way Nettie's work room was this big. She had a tiny little area, not much more than a closet."

Daed smiled. "You're right. It was a storage closet before, and once she stopped painting, it went back to being one. The wall used to be right here." He pointed out a faded strip on the cement floor, adding, "About four years ago I decided to expand the space and turn it into a woodworking shop."

"Oh, thank goodness," Natasha said, patting her chest. "I thought I was crazy for a minute."

We laughed. My smile lingered as I watched *Daed* moving around the original space, happily pointing out where his mother had kept her easel, where she'd stacked her finished paintings, and where she'd stored her supplies. I'd always wondered why he put the woodworking shop there when it probably would've been easier to leave the closet and convert the old tack room instead. But now I had a feeling this choice was not so much an architectural decision as an emotional one. This had been about merging his creative space with the one that had belonged to his mother.

When Natasha was satisfied, she turned her attention to my father's woodworking projects, oohing and aahing over almost every piece in sight. They were all simple, with no ornamentation. But each one showed *Daed*'s own touch, in the stain or the angle of the legs or the shape of the tabletop. I hadn't ever thought of my father as being artistic before, but for the first time I could clearly see it in his woodworking.

"That's lovely," Natasha said, pointing toward a beautiful old maple box up on a shelf.

In response, *Daed* took it down, set it on the worktable, and opened its hinged lid to reveal the contents. I stepped closer, astounded at what I saw. Inside were six or seven small, carved animals, each one a masterpiece in its own way.

"I used to carve when I was a young man, before I married," he said shyly as he held up first a sparrow, about two inches long, then a horse. And then a cat.

"Goodness," Natasha said, taking the bird from him and studying it more closely. "These are magnificent."

"They really are," Isaac added, leaning closer to get a better look. "Such detail and symmetry. Amazing."

Daed smiled a little. "I had more time back then than I do now—and more energy. These were the ones I felt were worth saving—the others I threw away."

Natasha shook her head. "What a shame."

"No," *Daed* said. "It took a lot of practice. I'd like you to have one. Take your pick."

Natasha didn't hesitate. "This sparrow," she said, clutching it to her chest. "Thank you."

Daed turned to me. "I want you to have one too, Linda. And you, Isaac."

Isaac insisted he should give his to someone in the family instead.

"No," *Daed* said. "I don't have enough for everyone. And you're an artist—sounds like you'd appreciate it more than some would."

Isaac thanked him and then told me to choose first. I took the horse, because I wanted Isaac to have the cat. "Are you sure?" he asked.

"*Ya*," I said, thinking of Whisper. Thinking of what I was just beginning to understand.

Our little gathering was a success, even better than I'd hoped. It also made for some interesting pairings over the course of the afternoon, some more surprising than others.

Not surprising was the fact that *Daed* and Natasha seemed to click so completely. At one point I was watching them interact when I realized she probably provided something he had sorely needed for a long time: a happier, more whole version of his mother. Perhaps a relationship with his aunt would heal some of the pain that had inevitably come from being the child of a woman who grappled with depression.

One connection that was a bit surprising was that between *Mamm* and Jan, who ended up chattering and laughing like a raucous pair of hens. I realized that what I'd instantly liked in Jan was what I'd always seen in my own mother, a no-nonsense, independent, tell-it-like-it-is sort of style. No wonder they'd hit it off.

Ina Mae sat with Sadie and talked about Hattie and Hazel in particular and twins in general for quite a while, but most surprising of all, however, was the strange, hilarious bond that seemed to develop between Ezra and Ina Mae.

Once she told Ezra she remembered him from the restaurant he worked at in Florida, they sat off by themselves, deep in conversation. When I went to get more lemonade, Tabitha was in the kitchen slicing lemons, one step ahead of me, and I asked her what that was about.

She gave a bemused roll of the eyes. "Alaska. Canada. Wyoming. Apparently our elderly cousin out there has spent much of her life filled with wanderlust, yearning to see the world but having to be satisfied with nothing more than annual trips to Florida after she retired. Right now she's traveling vicariously through him—and he's more than happy to oblige."

Grinning, I looked out the window and realized that he was, indeed, the one doing most of the talking while she looked on and listened, a dreamy gaze in her eyes.

"I also think she has a little crush on your boyfriend," I said.

"*Ya*, well, who doesn't?" she replied lightly.

Fearing that might be a dig at me, I gave her a sharp glance.

"Oh, Linda, no," she assured me. "Trust me, I know where you stand, and it's not with the giggly young women who follow him around like a gaggle of geese after a gander."

I washed my hands and then joined her at the counter, pressing the lemon halves onto the juicer and twisting them back and forth to squeeze out every drop. "He told you what happened?"

She nodded. "He did."

"And?" I didn't know why I was prodding her except that I suddenly felt the need to get this over with. If Tabitha was angry with me or felt like lecturing me or whatever, better she went ahead and put it out there. And I couldn't blame her. *Ya*, the whole situation between Ezra and me had come out well in the end, but I had gone to the singing at his invitation, and I had strolled with him in the moonlight, two things I probably shouldn't have done despite her having said she wasn't interested in him anymore.

"And…" She put the knife in the sink, took over the strainer, and held it above the pitcher as I poured in the last of the juice from the lemons. "It reminded me of what a good sister you are."

Startled, tears filled my eyes. I blinked them away, embarrassed.

"Come on now, none of that," she said sweetly, pouring in the sugar and then adding the water. "We need to get back out there. With all that talking Ezra's doing, I have a feeling he could use a little refreshment."

She was heading out the door, an icy glass of lemonade in hand, when I finally found my voice. "Tabitha?"

She turned back. "*Ya?*"

"You're a good sister too."

We shared a smile, and this time tears came to her eyes.

"Can I ask you a question?" I added.

She nodded.

"Does it bother you? Ezra's past, I mean. All that travel, all that experience, all that *living* he's done. Aren't you afraid you won't measure up somehow? Like, because of all he's seen and all he's been through, he's going to want more than you can give him?"

I knew how terrible, insulting even, my question sounded, but I couldn't help myself. Fortunately, Tabitha didn't look offended, merely thoughtful.

"No," she said. "I guess, well, it's kind of like a quilt. Think about it. What's a quilt made from anyway? Thread? Batting? Little scraps of fabric?"

I nodded.

"A big bunch of nothing, basically. But then in the hands of someone gifted, someone like you, all that nothing comes together to become a whole lot of something."

I considered her words. "So what you're saying is, you're both quilts. It's just that he's an appliqué quilt, and you're more like a double wedding ring pattern?"

She chuckled. "No. What I'm saying is that when all is said and done, quilts, like people, are greater than the sum of their parts. He's got his scraps and I've got mine, and they may look very different. But in the end all that really matters is what the Maker does with them."

With that, she turned and went out, the screen door slapping shut behind her. Standing there in her wake, my heart began to pound. Leave it to my silly, flirty, flighty sister to be the ultimate voice of wisdom. She was right. She was absolutely right.

How could I have been so blind?

Back outside, I was surprised, though not necessarily disappointed considering my state of mind, to see that people were standing, gathering their things, and a car was idling in the driveway. Ina Mae's driver had returned for her, precisely at five, which had probably been the cue for everyone to start wrapping things up.

I looked over at Isaac, who was folding some of the lawn chairs and propping them against a tree. He was a good man, a decent man, strong and loving, striving always to be Christlike. He was nothing at all like what I had imagined—nay, *expected*—for myself. Yet he was exactly who I needed.

Forgive me, Father, for thinking I knew better than You what Your plan for me should be.

Looking to the others, I saw that Ina Mae was saying her goodbyes, first to *Mamm* and *Daed* and then to everyone else. She had brought along the goat painting, as requested, and I could see Natasha taking one long last look before handing it back to her and giving her a warm hug. At the sight, I was reminded that Natasha was Ina Mae's aunt. One day soon I'd have to pull out that family tree I'd sketched over at her house and add a fourteenth sibling. Georgette.

When Ezra gave Ina Mae a hug and then a kiss on the cheek, Tabitha caught my eye and gave me a wink. I laughed aloud.

I joined in with my own goodbye then, and as Ina Mae and I hugged, she held on extra tight.

"You are such a blessing," she said as we pulled apart. "Thank you for including me in all of this. I've had the loveliest afternoon."

We agreed to stay in touch, and as I watched her car drive away, I found myself wishing she lived closer. We might never reconnect with that whole branch of the family, but at least that door had been opened, and we'd always have Ina Mae.

Sadie and her crew left next, minus Ezra but plus Ruth, whom they were giving a ride home. She knew Isaac would want to stick around as long as Natasha was still here, but she was feeling tired and ready to call it a day.

Though Ruth had been sad when she first arrived, she had seemed to cheer up as the afternoon wore on. When we said our farewells, however, the sadness seemed to return.

"Oh, Linda," she told me softly as I walked her to the buggy. "Don't do this. You shouldn't throw away something wonderful just because it's not exactly as you'd pictured."

"You know what, Ruth?" I confided. "I think you're right about that."

She looked at me, confused, then understanding—and a great big smile—lit up her face. I held one finger to my lips, and she nodded, eyes sparkling with secret delight as she headed out.

Tabitha and Ezra were the next to go, clip-clopping away in her buggy with Ezra at the reins, off for a Sunday-evening drive.

That left Natasha and Jan, *Mamm* and *Daed*, Stephen and Thomas, and Isaac and me.

Isaac and me.

Why did that suddenly sound like the most perfect combination in the world?

It wasn't hard to tell Natasha farewell, because I had no doubt she was going to become a regular part of our lives. Jan too, for that matter, who seemed to have had a most enjoyable time. As mother and daughter drove away in their fancy SUV, my *daed* and *mamm* stood in the drive, waving and watching until they were out of sight. Then, almost as one, they turned and headed for the house, discreetly clasping hands as they went.

The boys nagged Isaac into tossing around the ball, and I turned my attention to the cleanup. I did it gladly, thoughtfully, scooping together the last of the trash, wiping the tables, folding up the remaining chairs. Eventually Isaac called a halt to their play and joined in helping me wrap things up as well. Stephen and Thomas followed suit, and I was surprised and pleased to see how comfortably Isaac and Thomas interacted as they worked, almost like brothers. I realized that was probably because they'd been spending so many mornings together, doing the milking over at Sadie's.

Within minutes, the chairs and tables had all been put away, the last of the dishes carried into the kitchen, and all the trash picked up. Back outside, I stood on the porch, surveying the scene to make sure we hadn't missed anything as the boys tried to talk Isaac into a game of horseshoes.

"Just one," he said. "But then I really need to get on home."

As soon as the words came out of his mouth, I could almost see the sink of his shoulders, the weight of his pain, and I was filled with remorse for all I had put him through. Once again, I realized, naive little Linda was the last to know—this time the last to know exactly who God wanted for me.

Standing there watching the three of them, I thought of Ruth's words from yesterday, when we'd been talking about *Mammi* Nettie. *Always err on the side of kindness. Don't ever assume there's not a good reason for why a person acts the way they do.*

I thought of Sadie. I didn't have any idea what her life was like. Not really, even though I'd been an eyewitness to it. I didn't know what it was like to have a husband fight cancer, go into remission, have the cancer return, and then die in such a short time.

My breath caught. I didn't have an understanding of what Isaac had gone through either. No one's life, except for perhaps mine, would fit onto a piece of graph paper. Not my siblings'. Not my *mamm*'s. Not my *daed*'s either. Life was messy. It had curves and dips, hills and valleys. Straight lines were meant for nine patch quilts. Real life was more like Natasha's quilts—and *Mammi* Nettie's paintings. Bright colors, dark shadows, and unexpected twists at every turn.

Bottom line, just as Tabitha had said, we were all basically just a bunch of scraps and thread and batting, and in the end what really mattered was what the Maker did with us. With His handiwork, we were all, indeed, far greater than the sum of our parts.

Unable to hold back my smile any longer, I was about to interrupt the rousing game of horseshoes still taking place on the lawn in front of me when Isaac scored the final winning point and it was done. He was grinning widely from his victory until he turned my way, and then his smile faded fast. "Time to go," he muttered.

"I'll give you a ride," I said, trying not to speak too soon, trying not to blurt everything out right there in the middle of the driveway. With a nod, he joined me as we walked around the barn and out to the pasture gate. I could see Blue in the field, happily munching away on the rich green grass, but I didn't call to him. Instead, I turned to the man beside me and prayed for the right words.

"I have something for you," I told him, feeling suddenly shy.

I expected him to look intrigued, but instead his features were almost pained.

"What is it?" he asked flatly. "A goodbye gift?"

I paused. Smiled. Reached out and placed a hand on his arm. Beneath the fabric of his sleeve, I could feel the strength of his forearm, the muscle and sinew and lifeblood of a man who worked hard and loved fully, one who had been a good husband once and would be a good husband again—this time, Lord willing, to me.

"Nope," I replied. "More like the opposite of that."

He looked down at me quizzically, something inside of him beginning to catch on.

"A hello gift?" he ventured.

I shook my head. "Not quite. I guess you could call it a don't-say-goodbye-at-all gift?" There were so many things I needed to say. To ask his forgiveness. To explain what had taken me so long. To tell him how very much I loved him. Instead, I met his gaze and simply stated, "What I have for you is…a reason."

Either he still didn't get it, or he didn't quite trust what he was hearing. "A reason?"

"You said it earlier, when you first got here, when we were talking about your moving away. You told me there was only one reason you'd stay."

He nodded warily. "And?"

"And, well, I assume that reason was me. If it is, then you've got it. You've got *me*, Isaac, if you still want me after all I've put you through."

I watched him take in my words, watched him go from doubt to understanding to something like joy. Then, as if he'd been opening a door inside, he suddenly closed it again, his features growing still. "I can't change my past, Linda, and I won't apologize for it either. I am who I am."

I nodded, stepping closer. "I see that now. And I'm willing to embrace all of it. I even want to hear more about Bailey—and your life before. Not now, necessarily, but if and when you're willing to tell me."

He paused for a long moment, studying my face, as slowly that door opened again.

"I love you, Isaac. I want to share my life with you. I'm sorry it's taken me so long to get to this point, but I'm here now, and I'm—"

He didn't even let me finish my thought. Instead, with a mighty yelp, he wrapped me up in his arms and lifted me off the ground. As he held on tight and spun me around, the strings of my *kapp* flying wildly behind me, I tilted my head back and laughed out loud.

We must have made quite a noise, because before Isaac had even set me on my feet, Stephen and Thomas came running around the side of the barn, wide-eyed and breathless.

"Are you okay?" Stephen asked.

"What's wrong?" Thomas cried.

They ground to a halt several feet away, gaping at us both.

"Nothing's wrong, boys," Isaac said with a broad grin, putting me down but leaving one arm around my shoulders. He shot me a tender glance, adding, "In fact, things couldn't be more right."

I n late September, Sadie had a little girl. She gave birth at home with Marta Bayer, Izzy's mother-in-law, serving as her midwife, and she had an easy time of it, or so I was told. I doubted any birth could actually be easy—it just wasn't as hard as some. God willing I'd find out myself in the future.

Of course, it was bittersweet. She missed Robert, but she welcomed the new baby with joy. Later that day *Mamm*, Tabitha, and I were all at the house, and mother and child were on the couch. Sadie's feet were up, and she was eating a peanut butter and jelly sandwich while holding the little one on her lap. Sadie had named her Nettie Mae, after our *mammi* and Ina Mae, whom Sadie had bonded with over the twins. Ina Mae had been sending her all sorts of information to help with her parenting, which reinforced what Tabitha had told her too.

Just as Sadie finished her sandwich, Jedediah stopped by. He sat down next to her, and she slipped the baby into his arms. He seemed as comfortable with the infant as he'd always been with Bobby and the girls, holding her easily, gazing down at her in wonder. Tears stung my eyes. *Ya*, life was complicated, that was for sure.

Five days later, on a gorgeous autumn afternoon, Ginny drove Isaac and me to the opening of Natasha's quilt show, featuring *Mammi* Nettie's artwork, at the St. James Episcopal Church in Lancaster. *Daed* would have come with us, but he and *Mamm* were watching the kids while Tabitha took Sadie and the baby to their first postnatal checkup with the midwife. I was sorry he hadn't come, but he did say he'd try to get into town and see the show before it closed.

Not sure where the display was, we stepped into the sanctuary of the church first. It was as beautiful as Natasha had described it to us, through Nettie's point of view. Sunlight came through the stained glass windows on the west side and bathed the wooden pews in jewel tones. I spotted the organ up front, to the left, and then glanced at the vaulted ceiling. No wonder Nettie had been so taken by this place. I could see how it would inspire her to paint again.

We heard voices to the left and followed the sound to the hall where the show was. The sign read *Natasha "Georgie" Bender Johnson and Nettie Bender Mueller: A Twin Retrospective.*

Ahead were the quilts, hung on dividers where *Mammi* Nettie's paintings were displayed. I wanted to take Isaac's hand and squeeze it. I'd never been so excited about anything in my entire life. The paintings were affixed to the walls of the hall, alongside the quilts. There were several partitions in the middle of the room where more paintings were displayed. Those partitions blocked the view, and we didn't see Natasha at that moment, so we started making our way through the exhibit on our own. A good turnout of people had already gathered, and I was glad for her.

The show was separated into three categories: landscapes, Amish scenes influenced by stained glass, and children. The first group was a lot of fields, streams, and hillsides in spring, summer, fall, and winter. Then came the Amish scenes of houses, barns, silos, clotheslines, buggies, and sunsets, all depicted in Nettie's unique stained glass window–type style and some accompanied by matching versions done in Natasha's quilts. The last group were the paintings of children—always Amish, always from the back, varying in age from a toddler on a blanket to a group of teenage girls strolling down a lane. The last two were of *Daed* as a boy, and then, at the very end, we came to the painting we had loaned to the exhibit, the one of Nettie and Natasha with the sunset behind them.

To my astonishment, hanging next to that painting was the same exact image, only recreated in an appliqué quilt. Natasha's version of her sister Nettie's final work. Though we'd been in touch with Natasha frequently over the past few months, she'd never said a word about this. She must have been working on it ever since that day of the gathering on the lawn, when we showed her the painting and she'd snapped a few pictures of it with her phone. But she'd kept it a complete secret—until now.

Just the sight of the quilt filled my eyes with tears. Somehow, in Natasha's hands, the image that had been so forlorn and heartbreaking in *Mammi* Nettie's painting had been transformed into one filled with warmth and hope in Natasha's quilt.

"Well? What do you think? Is it a good surprise?"

We turned to see Natasha standing behind us, looking radiant and as elegant as ever in a plum-colored dress and black velvet jacket. Beaming, she hugged us both and kissed our cheeks. I swiped away tears and told her it was the most wonderful surprise I'd ever seen. The whole show, I said, was simply magnificent.

"I'm so pleased," she said. "Thank you for coming."

I started to explain why *Daed* wasn't with us, but she waved away my concern. "He left me a message this morning and said his thoughts were with me and he'd stop by in the next few weeks, before the exhibit closes."

I nodded, knowing how difficult—and yet also how wonderful—it was going to be for *Daed* to see his mother's paintings. I had a feeling he'd used the babysitting as an excuse and that the main reason he'd begged off today was because he wanted to be able to take it all in by himself, in peace and quiet and solitude, rather than while surrounded by others, especially ones who'd be watching for his reaction.

When Ginny returned to pick us up, it was obvious she'd been doing some shopping in town because bags crowded the passenger seat and floor.

"Sorry, Isaac," she said, leaning forward to look at him through the open window. "Can you stick those in the trunk?"

Before she could even pop it open, he stopped her, saying it was fine, that he'd sit in the back instead. I was glad. The exhibit had brought up so many feelings and emotions that I needed him there next to me, grounding me, his very presence helping me to process it all.

He seemed glad as well, taking my hand and holding it for most of the drive. We were both quiet, lost in thought, but utterly connected just the same.

Isaac and I had been courting for three months now, and every time we were together we seemed to grow even closer—emotionally, *ya*, but physically too. He was a naturally affectionate person, but, as was the Amish way, he'd been good at tempering any urges to hug me or take my hand or put an arm around me in public. In private, he'd been a bit freer to do those things, but he'd had to be patient about waiting for our first kiss. I wasn't necessarily holding off till our wedding day, but thus far it just hadn't seemed quite right. I'd gotten so much better at handling the facts of Isaac's past, but I still struggled now and then. I guess I just needed to be sure that when that first kiss happened, the only woman on his mind was me.

When we reached the house, I asked Isaac if he could stay for a while, explaining that I had something to show him. He raised one eyebrow, intrigued. We climbed out, he paid Ginny, and we headed to the porch. I served him a glass of iced tea and a bowl of peach cobbler and then said I'd be right back.

I returned with the barn quilt inspired by his painting, which I'd finished the night before. I held it up, letting the fabric fall to the floor of the porch. It wasn't as perfect as Natasha's quilts, but it was definitely a big step forward for me. In the past few months I had forced myself to go with a more fluid, relaxed style that appliqué quilting required, and in return I'd discovered a whole new side to my creativity, one that wasn't afraid to take risks with colors and shapes and composition.

"It's beautiful." Isaac stood and ran his hands over the appliqué. The barn—half exterior and half interior. The field. The cat.

"It's for you," I said.

He shot me a teasing glance. "Which means, ultimately, for us, *ya*?"

I grinned, heat flushing my face as I couldn't help but picture our marriage bed. "*Ya*," I replied shyly. "For us."

Stepping back he whispered, "*Danke*." Then he put his hand to his chest and added, "With all my heart, thank you."

I studied his face, taking him in, knowing how ready he was to move on with our life. Maybe it was today's exhibit, that strange combination of past and present that had been framed and hung and presented together as one. But suddenly all of my lingering concerns and fears simply fell away and I realized that I was ready too.

"Thank *you*, Isaac," I said softly. "For teaching me how to—be. To accept life. To embrace it in all its messy, jumbled, unpredictable beauty."

Stepping forward, he wrapped his arms around me and pulled me close. With the quilt between us, he kissed the top of my head. Then my forehead. Then my lips—but not quite. Almost there, he froze, his mouth achingly close to mine. He didn't pull away, didn't move at all, but neither did he continue. I waited, my heart pounding, my lips yearning for his.

I realized he needed some sort of sign. So I placed a hand on the back of his head and pulled him toward me, answering that question loud and clear.

He responded with an intensity that took my breath away. And though I'd been trying hard these days to let go of my old tendencies, I had to admit that his kiss was just about as perfect—and perfectly wonderful—as anything I'd ever imagined.

Discussion Questions

1. Linda's older sisters call her "Little Sister." At the beginning of the story she realizes it started as a term of endearment but that now she sees it as an insult. Why does she? Do you agree with Linda? Why or not?

2. What drives Linda to discover the story of *Mammi* Nettie's artwork? What does she have in common with her grandmother? In what ways is her life very different from her grandmother's?

3. Linda doesn't understand Sadie's willingness to get on with her life so quickly after Robert dies. Did you sympathize with Sadie? Why or why not? What do you think is the next chapter of her life, after the end of this story?

4. Every time Linda learns some important fact about her family that she should have known but didn't she feels hurt and betrayed—not because people were keeping secrets from her, but because no one ever thought to tell her. Which would upset you more, important secrets that were intentionally hidden from you or important secrets that no one cared if you knew or not?

5. Isaac explains to Linda that he made the decision *not* to join the Amish one step at a time. And then, a few years later, he did the same in deciding *to* join the Amish. How does this contradict Linda's preconceptions? What does she ultimately learn from Isaac?

6. How does quilting fit into Linda's idealistic worldview? What challenges her idealism? How do her thinking and her quilting change in the course of the story?

7. Tabitha and Ezra both like to have fun but ultimately end up having a difficult time communicating. Have you ever had a relationship built on fun, only to realize it wasn't enough? Were you surprised that Tabitha and Ezra worked things out? Do you think they make a good couple? Why or why not?

8. Natasha is a complex character. What decision did she make as a child that changed the course of her life? If you were in her shoes, would you have made the same decision? Why or why not?

9. Later in life, Natasha's quilting changes because she's inspired by Nettie's paintings. Do you think she had the right to emulate her twin's art? What did the process do for Natasha? Have you ever "copied" someone else's work? What were the results?

10. The Muellers establish relationships with several important relatives in the story. Have you ever reconnected with long-lost kin? Or developed a closer relationship with a relative as you've grown older? What was the impact on your life? To what extent would you go to find a long-lost relative or establish a relationship?

About the Authors

Mindy Starns Clark is the bestselling author of nearly 30 books, both fiction and nonfiction (over 1 million copies sold) including coauthoring the Christy Award-winning *The Amish Midwife* with Leslie Gould. Mindy and her husband, John, have two adult children and live in Pennsylvania.

Leslie Gould is the bestselling and award-winning author of 26 novels. She received her master of fine arts degree from Portland State University and lives in Oregon. She and her husband, Peter, are the parents of four children.

To connect with the authors,
visit Mindy's and Leslie's websites at

www.mindystarnsclark.com

and

www.lesliegould.com

A deathbed confession...
a dusty carved box containing
two locks of hair...
a century-old letter about
property in Switzerland...

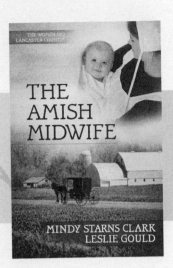

THE
AMISH
MIDWIFE

MINDY STARNS CLARK
LESLIE GOULD

Nurse-midwife Lexie Jaeger's encounter with all three rekindles a burning desire to meet her biological family. Propelled on a personal journey of discovery, Lexie's search for the truth takes her from her home in Oregon to the heart of Pennsylvania's Amish country.

There she finds Marta Bayer, a mysterious lay-midwife who may hold the key to Lexie's past. But Marta isn't talking, especially now that she has troubles of her own following the death of an Amish patient during childbirth. As Lexie steps in to assume Marta's patient load and continues the search for her birth family, a handsome local doctor proves to be a welcome distraction. But will he also distract her from James, the man back home who lovingly awaits her return?

From her Amish patients, Lexie learns the true meaning of the Pennsylvania Dutch word *demut*, which means "to let be." Will this woman who wants to control everything ever learn to let be herself and depend totally on God? Or will her stubborn determination to unearth the secrets of the past at all costs only serve to tear her newfound family apart?

A compelling story about a search for identity and the ability to trust that God securely holds our whole life—past, present, and future.

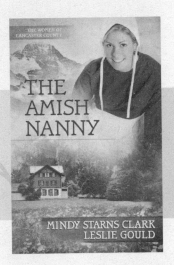

A cave behind a waterfall...
a dying confession...
a secret agreement hidden
for a century...

Amish-raised Ada Rupp knows nothing of these elements of her family's past. Instead, her eyes are fixed firmly on the future—for the first time in her life. Now that a serious medical issue is behind her, Ada is eager to pursue her God-given gifts of teaching at the local Amish school and her dream of marrying Will Gundy, a handsome widower she's loved since she was a child. But when both desires meet with unexpected obstacles, Ada's fragile heart grows heavy with sorrow.

Then she meets Daniel, an attractive Mennonite scholar with a surprising request. He needs her help—along with the help of Will's family—to save an important historic site from being destroyed. Now Ada, a family friend, and a young child must head to Switzerland to mend an old family rift and help preserve her religious heritage.

In order to succeed in saving the site, Ada and Daniel must unlock secrets from the past. But do they also have a future together—or will Ada's heart forever belong to Will, the only man she's ever really wanted?

A fascinating tale of a young woman's journey—to Switzerland, to faith, and finally to love.

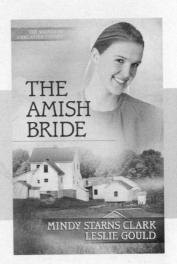

A long-lost painting...
a journal with a secret code...
a father's mysterious return...

Mennonite-raised Ella Bayer has two big dreams: to operate her own bakery and to marry her Amish boyfriend, Ezra Gundy. Ezra adores Ella as well, but his family wants him to marry within the faith.

Hoping some distance will cool the romance, Ezra's parents send him to work on an Amish dairy farm in Indiana. But when Ella's estranged father returns to Lancaster, she heads to Indiana as well—and ends up at a farm linked to her great-grandmother's coded journal. There, her attempts to break that code are aided by Luke Kline, a handsome Amish farmhand.

As Ella makes her way in this new place, she's forced to grapple with the past and question the future. Will she become Ezra's Amish bride? Or does God have something else in mind for the proud and feisty young woman who is used to doing things her way?

A captivating journey of hidden secrets, old love and new love, and discovery of how a life guided by God can be a life of incredible hope and adventure.

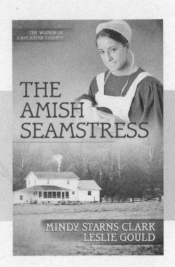

A beautiful misfit...
A handsome young filmmaker...
A shocking family secret,
hidden for 200 years...

A loner and a daydreamer, Amish-raised Izzy Mueller doesn't fit in with her family or her community. About the only person who really gets Izzy is her best friend, Mennonite-raised Zed Bayer, but soon he'll be leaving for college, hundreds of miles away. Worse, he's completely unaware she's in love with him.

Izzy works as a caregiver, a job which suits her gentle ways and kind spirit. She's also a talented seamstress and often sits with her patients, quietly sewing, as they talk and reminisce about the past. Izzy has always enjoyed hearing what they have to say—until the day one of them shares unsavory news about her own ancestors.

As Izzy searches for the truth behind that lore, she begins to question her life—her creative longings, her relationships, and her heritage. Caught in the swirling dynamics of Zed's family once she becomes the caregiver for his grandmother, can Izzy learn from the past and from others' mistakes? Or must she step out in faith and forge a future all her own?

To learn more about Harvest House books and
to read sample chapters, log on to our website:

www.harvesthousepublishers.com

HARVEST HOUSE PUBLISHERS
EUGENE, OREGON